RIVER OF DUST

RIVER OF DUST

ALEXANDER JABLOKOV

An AvoNova Book

William Morrow and Company, Inc.
New York

RIVER OF DUST is an original publication of Avon Books. This work has never before appeared in book form. This work is a novel. Any similarity to actual persons or events is purely coincidental.

AVON BOOKS
A division of
The Hearst Corporation
1350 Avenue of the Americas
New York, New York 10019

Copyright © 1996 by Alexander Jablokow
Published by arrangement with the author
Library of Congress Catalog Card Number: 95-34872
ISBN: 0-688-14605-8

Library of Congress Cataloging in Publication Data:
Jablokov, Alexander.
    River of dust / Alexander Jablokov.
        p.   cm.
"An AvoNova book."
I. Title.
PS3560.A116R58   1996   95-34872
813'.54—dc20   CIP

First Morrow/AvoNova Printing: February 1996

AVONOVA TRADEMARK REG. U.S. PAT. OFF. AND IN OTHER COUNTRIES, MARCA REGISTRADA, HECHO EN U.S.A.

Printed in the U.S.A.

QP   10   9   8   7   6   5   4   3   2   1

Prolog

"There," Brenda Marr whispered, then examined the sheer cliff of the mesa again to make sure she wasn't deluding herself. The dark oval of the air lock high above her, just a bit of human regularity against Martian rock, marked her destination, the Pure Land School.

She had been five days hiking from the nearest train station into the fretted terrain of Nilosyrtis. The recent solstice dust storms had obscured any rough trails among the crumbled, looming mesas. She had moved slowly through the sinuous, dust-choked channels, remembering her long-ago sojourn here, and the landmarks that had once been so distinctive. Nights she had spent in a fragile air cocoon barely larger than her own body, checking and rechecking her air supply and feeling the growing dryness in her throat. Her air would have run out before the rise of Phobos tonight, but she didn't think about that now. She had made it. She was back. She hoped that this was where she was meant to go.

Sunset glared above the long cliff of Shadrach's Mesa to the west. A flicker of movement caught her eye and she looked up past the tiny dot of the air lock. A group of figures stood on a spire cleaved from the edge of Pure Land Mesa and stared off at the setting sun. Some held their hands out to the sun, though it gave no heat. They wore school robes, and their air masks were completely reflective, turning their faces into roiled orange

1

flares. It had been a long effort to climb that high just to watch the sun set, and they would have to descend in darkness and feel slippery rime ice condense in already-treacherous finger and toe holds. Brenda remembered the joy of it. A few cairns in the piled talus at the base of the mesa marked the graves of those whose joy had grown too great.

Above the talus, stairs chopped into the face of the cliff zig-zagged up, taking advantage of its irregularities. They had probably been cut when Rudolf Hounslow moved out here to his self-imposed exile, a decade before, but there were those who said they were much, much older. Just by appearance, given the absence of weathering on the Martian surface and the human race's eyeblink habitation on the planet, the stairs could have been there for three hundred years or been carved the day before yesterday. Brenda knelt, pulled off her gauntlet, and felt the sharp stone through the inner glove of her skintite. Her left pinkie finger throbbed its emergency message: her air was running out. Dammit, she knew that already.

She started up. Now that she was almost at her destination, tiredness filled her bones. She hadn't felt tired since . . . when? Since stumbling out onto the rim of Coprates Chasma to open up her tracheal valves and foam blood out into the indifferent Martian air. She remembered herself standing and looking out over the canyon to the sharp opposite wall one-hundred-fifty kilometers away. A single bright light halfway up that seven-kilometer-high wall opposite had marked some still-functioning industrial operation. It flared there in the darkness, leaving a network of crisp shadows across the cliff.

That steady, indifferent light saved her life. She dropped her hands from her throat valves and stared across the vast width of Coprates in sudden fury. Her last, pathetic attempt at normal existence had just been peremptorily ended, and those bastards worked all night? She imagined that she could see the endless stream of rock spoil spilling out and cascading to the canyon bottom, a glittering sight at sunrise. Her side of Coprates was as dark and silent as it had been before human beings came to Mars.

When she stepped into the elevator for the long ride down to the now-silent quarters of Iqbal-in-Coprates Mining, her anger was vague, nothing more than a desire to hurt those who still had work left to define them. By the time she got off at the deserted dormitory, now inhabited only by a few last laggard dispossessed Iqbal employees, she knew where she had to go: the Pure Land School. Her memories of the place suddenly seemed much more significant than her actual experience there had been.

She had searched amid the foul dunes of clothing left after the worker exodus and extracted items that could be useful to her. A few scratched and dented personal weapons had been abandoned, as had a container of brutally overspiced emergency rations. Brenda had taken one last look across the ranks of sleeping alcoves, carefully not noting which one had been hers, then turned and left. Once she stepped through the security door, she was committed. It was programmed not to let any former employee back in, acting as a social Maxwell's Demon.

She had been a good week traveling northeast from Coprates to the crumbled mesas and deep channels of Nilosyrtis. Brenda had sat in a corner of a common car, tumbled promiscuously with all those other travelers too poor or too indifferent to comfort to obtain a private compartment, as she switched from magtrack to magtrack, working her way along the edge of the Vastitas Borealis, the great plain of dunes that stretched north to the polar cap. The weight of her dagger heavy on the back of her neck, she had sat on her survival pack waiting tensely for some affront, some attempted assault, her hat pulled down low over her mass of red-brown hair, but her neck open so that she could reach her weapon easily. No one had paid the slightest attention to her. Everyone seemed sunk deep in some private concern. The normally ebullient social life of the common cars had been subdued. It seemed that it was not only the former employees of Iqbal-in-Coprates who had worries. She felt a vague disappointment that no one had made a move at her. A response to that would have been easy. She would have known instantly what to do, and the flashing rush of anger would have taken care of her future. Instead, after an uneventful journey, she had gotten off at Garmashtown, on the edge of Utopia Planita, slung her pack, and started her long walk toward something she wanted to remember.

She stopped now and looked at the oval of the air-lock door. It had slid back, expecting her. She stepped in. She had time for one last glimpse of the landscape over which she had just so arduously traveled, the indigo bars of the mesas disappearing into encompassing darkness; then the door slid shut and the air lock cycled. The inside door opened and she found herself in the rock-cut antechamber she remembered.

Brenda disconnected her tracheal valves, peeled off her air mask, and sucked air gently between her lips, surprised at the sweetness of its taste. If the Pure Land School had been a few kilometers farther, she would have died. She listened to her breathing. It sounded calm to her. The Pure Land School was right here. She was breathing its air. Any other possibility was foolish.

"Brenda Marr," the fair-haired novice on duty said, with an air of having expected her. Bemused, Brenda examined the snarling cat face on her mask, the standard design of Iqbal-in-Coprates Mining, then tossed it into a disposal-sorting bin. She would be given another. The life marked by that mask was now over.

Brenda had once been a novice and worked this duty. She too had memorized the names of all those who had left before her so that she could greet them appropriately when they returned. The novice's eager face implied that she should be fooled, and find his knowledge in some way miraculous.

He helped her strip off her pack, her dusty exterior clothing, and her skintite, hanging everything on a rack where it could be taken away by someone else and cleaned. He was smaller and slenderer than she was, and when she finally stood before him completely naked he looked a little surprised, as if he had not expected the result. Her long red-brown hair was tangled and matted from being shoved under her exterior hood. She winced as she felt the tangled knots. She'd lost weight in the past two weeks of frantic travel, but she was still thick and queenly. Her heavy breasts hung ripely down on her rib cage. Her belly was round. Five days straight in a skintite had given her a strong, sour odor.

"Do you—" Her voice came out a croak. She cleared her throat. It had been weeks since she had spoken. In that time she had come close to dying twice. She was surprised she could talk at all. "Give me a robe. I should see him now."

Rudolf Hounslow, Master of the Pure Land School, always talked to returnees as soon as possible. He didn't want them cleaned up and rested. By that point, they had lost most of what made them important. He regarded them as newborn infants who might still retain some knowledge of their previous life. Aching joints and dried sweat were signs of their closeness to their memory. She remembered his intent, somehow-never-satisfied curiosity. Perhaps she could show him something that would satisfy him.

Silently, the novice, whose name was Marder, held out a tall ceramic container of water. She drank it slowly, but without stopping, until it was empty.

He was still staring at her. His blue eyes were large in his face. She stretched, feeling her ribs move under her skin. The attention, sexual or not, infuriated her. It smacked too closely of the life she had led in the Iqbal dormitories for four years. She tensed her arm to push him away—he was light, it wouldn't have been hard—but then she relaxed. That attention, intent though it was, would keep him from noticing other, more important things. Like the knife she still had strapped to the back of her neck.

She met his gaze. He stood easily, and she suddenly suspected attacking him would not have been as easy as it had first appeared. He held out a robe. "Here. Let's find him."

The Pure Land School had a sort of rectilinear logic rare on Mars. Even rows of cubicles, straight balconies opening out onto the cubical central space, light sources like beads on a taut wire: this center of Martian spirit looked like nowhere on Mars since the first era of technical settlement, during the twenty-first century. Brenda looked at the familiar hallways, hoping they would somehow be illuminated and their hidden message made clear, but they were still nothing but elemental stone.

Rudolf Hounslow squatted against a featureless wall like a corridor shoe mender. He had never had any place within the Pure Land School that he defined as exclusively his own. As free from confining definition as any corridor nomad, he made his bed where he was, on the smoothed rock, and ate with chopsticks from a bowl he held in his hands.

Now he stared thoughtfully at the floor, crossed arms resting on his knees. His dark silk robe, no different from any student's, fell around him and concealed his legs, leaving his blocky head balanced like a boulder on an outcrop. The novice, Marder, floated away along the balcony, his fine gold hair a halo around his head.

Hounslow turned his head slowly to look at her. She almost stepped back from the intensity of his gaze. There was too much need in it. There was something he wanted from her, and she was suddenly afraid she would be unable to give it to him.

"When did you realize you should come back?" he said.

"I—" She wanted to tell him all the details, her life in the workers' dormitories, her succession of indifferent lovers, the demands of her work, the humiliation of losing a job without warning or explanation. "When I found myself standing on the rim of Coprates Chasma opening my throat valves to Mars."

"Now," he said. "Now you understand. Thoughts rot in the head if they are not turned into action."

She stared at him. Four years ago, she had heard him use the same words, here in this same place. And still he sat here, calm, measured, creating the philosophy that would transform Mars.

Hounslow, after a troubled early life, had made his fortune growing silk in the caves of Charitum. His followers now wore robes made out of that silk—he could still get it at a discount. He had also had success with a couple of romantic-adventure novels, under a pen name. Brenda had read them as a girl and enjoyed them, and now wondered if they had held some concealed message that had finally brought her to the Pure Land School. Then, for his own private reasons, Hounslow had left his successful place in Martian society and started his philosophical school out here in Nilosyrtis, far from any settlement.

Here he preached the necessity for action against the increas-

ing corruption of the Martian political system. She had heard
him denounce a session of the Chamber of Delegates bill by bill,
citing the corrupt compromises that made up each one. Brenda
still remembered that particular talk with exhilaration. His words
had been as real as blows. Hounslow had become so taken with
his own impassioned rhetoric that he had attacked the wall of
the lecture room with a wooden sword he had carved himself.
He had been proud of its elegant balance, the result of much
careful work, but when he was done, it was nothing but splinters,
and his hands were bleeding. He turned back to the class, which
had not uttered a sound, and continued with his detailed denun-
ciation of routine Chamber water bills, letting the blood fall in
drops from the tips of his fingers.

But Hounslow was still here. The School was silent in the
early evening. Why had she thought the Truth was here? This
serene place had nothing to do with her own life. She remembered the corridors of Scamander, choked with anxious crowds
smelling of frying peppers, arrack, and sweat. She remembered
the society of the mining dormitories, and the frenzy of work.

In the days after the closing of the Coprates mines, she had
found herself unable to sleep, missing the endless thrum of the
slurry pipes. The pipes could have been designed and built to
be silent all along, of course, but a physical connection to the
work was always necessary. Nothing on Mars worked as
smoothly as it could have in theory, so that human beings could
feel themselves defined against the resistance of the physical.

But Hounslow had not moved. He still squatted in his corridor.

Brenda's skin flushed, and she trembled.

Hounslow nodded at her, seeing the revelation, misinterpret-
ing it.

"Teach and teach and teach," he said. "The lesson doesn't
reach its goal. Release, disregard, and illumination comes. A
phrase repeated a thousand times until it isn't anything but a
gabble of syllables suddenly pierces the heart. You are ready to
go on."

She reached up and felt the back of her neck. It was a habit
among the prostitutes of Scamander to carry a knife concealed
in the thick hair at the nape of the neck, for self-defense. Brenda

had recently seen society ladies aping it, as idle fashion, leaving a stiletto point protruding at an angle from their hair, where it could draw blood from the hand of an incautious lover. That missed the whole point. You should cut only on purpose, and then cut deep.

This blade, one she had retrieved from the discards before leaving Iqbal, was a little too heavy for the purpose. Every time she turned her head it clouted her behind the ear. The most drunken client would have felt it right away. But it had been years since she'd descended to men like that. Her last client had been as high as they came, and she'd quit after him. It would have made no sense to take such a knife in to him. His bodyguards would have caught it immediately. Her fingertips slid across the friction-taped handle of the dagger.

"Not all actions are equal," Hounslow said. He rocked forward slightly on his feet, moving his back from the wall, but didn't try to stand up. His tone was mild. He looked up at her as she tensed to pull out the knife. His eyes were pale disks in the half-light of the hallway.

She froze. He had shifted position only fractionally, but it had changed everything. He was a compact mass, ready to roll in any direction or spring up at her. She, meanwhile, would have to stab downward, like a hysterical husband in a street play, and leave herself exposed for a counterstroke. Any attempt to shift to a more efficient attack position, and he would be on her. He was combat-trained. She'd seen him spar.

She should do it anyway. At least it would remove them both from this stupid realm of words. She might still be able to wound him and give him a lesson to feel late at night when he couldn't sleep.

"Who sent you?" She could see how excited he was at the thought of assassination. His skin had flushed, just like hers. "Was it Passman?"

She had no idea what he was talking about. "*You* sent me." Her voice was loud in the corridor, so she dropped it to a whisper. "Action. That's what you said."

It no longer made any sense at all. She hadn't come here to kill Rudolf Hounslow. Nothing like that had been on her mind.

She had come to hear him and to feel his certainties.

"You're from the Vigil," he said. "A special operations unit—"

"*No.*" She reached back up behind her head, ripped the knife out. The torn hair brought tears to her eyes. She flipped the knife once, almost catching it by the blade by accident, then threw it to the floor. It skittered across the stone and came to rest against his foot.

"Check whatever you want," she said. "My life is completely out in the open. I've spent the last four years digging ore out of the rim of Coprates. That's it. You know who I am. I'm yours. You are the only person I'm *from*. So what do you want to do with me?"

His bodyguards could be on her in a second. He always pretended he didn't have any, and perhaps he even believed it himself. They selected themselves and came to crouch next to him. And he let them, because he liked the sound of their purring. Marder was still somewhere near, she was sure of it. She'd noticed the cultivated calluses on his hands, marks of intensive hand-to-hand combat training. And he'd seen the knife; of course he had. He'd let her through as some sort of test. Life at the Pure Land School was full of tests.

She would be "invited to meditate": taken up to the flat top of Pure Land Mesa to view the vast broken lands of Nilosyrtis Mensae, there to suffocate. That was always the fate of those suspected of being Vigil agents. Everyone at the Pure Land School knew that the Martian political police force was desperate to break open Hounslow's organization, though no one had ever bothered to confirm whether the dead students had actually been acting under Vigil instructions. They left that sort of tedious administrivia to the servants of the corrupt political class. The whole school always turned out for the funeral, to mourn another brave fighter for the purity of Mars.

Sometimes, of course, the funeral was for someone who had really died in pursuit of duty. Such a ceremony was, in outward appearance, no different from one for someone considered a traitor. If she died here, Brenda would receive such a funeral ceremony too.

"You should stay here," Hounslow said. "You should learn more, try to understand. . . ."

"No."

He looked up at her, expecting some further argument or justification. He was hungry for words. But she didn't give him any. The silence was long. "All right. I want you to do something for me, Brenda Marr."

Marr stared at him and waited.

"I knew a man, years ago." Hounslow picked the knife up and began to scratch its tip against the stone. "His name is Lon Passman. Right now he is Justice of Tharsis."

Despite herself, Brenda felt a response. "Justice of Tharsis" was a high title, being one of the five Judicial Lords who represented the apogee of justice on Mars. Despite his withdrawal from it, Hounslow enjoyed showing how high his contacts in Martian society had once been. The entirely voluntary nature of that withdrawal always had to be emphasized.

He looked up at Brenda. "We had a bond then. That bond was broken. Now he has presumed on it, as if it still exists, to contact me, plead with me." His brow furrowed in anger. Brenda's attempt to kill him had not called up this much emotion. "I need to send him a message. I need him, and everyone, to understand what is coming. Do you understand?"

"You want me to take the Justice of Tharsis a message." Brenda's voice was dull. Hounslow had called her back from the edge of destruction yet again in order to use her for some stupid errand.

"Not just a message!" He extended himself slowly and finally stood. At the last moment he shook a little from the lack of blood circulation in his knees, and steadied himself against the wall with a hand. Brenda was taller than he was. "It's the first shot in the war. And I want you to fire it. Will you do it?"

In the inspirational plays she'd seen as a girl, this was how it always was. A powerful older figure, normal channels of power disrupted, turns to the previously ignored child and gives the child a mission, a mission only the child can accomplish. Carry a message, let the lord know I love him, tell the commander where the Technic invasion force is concealed, recite the rhyme that contains the secret to the buried treasure. Be quick, clever, and invisible. You will get your reward.

Brenda was tired of being invisible. Carrying a message, no matter how important, was not an action.

She would have to find a way to turn it into action. That would be her reward.

"I'll do it," she said.

1

From "Invisible Buildings," in *Getting Around Scamander*, by Basil Krummorn, New York, 2330:

...but you won't see it. It will be completely invisible. Martians find the Terran inability to perceive internal structures endlessly amusing, so be prepared to be directed to a stretch of blank wall and told that it is the Old Director comfort lounge. It is likely to be no such thing. But, then again, it might be. Don't rush your conclusions.

Imagine that you take a time traveler from the twenty-first century to see the Esopus Palace, spread out on its green hills in the Adirondacks. You expect him to be impressed by the Gensek's palace, the spiritual center of Union government, but all he sees is a pile of glacial till, a few trees, a fox's den. He demands glass walls, gantries, vast fractal structures, and refuses to perceive the place as inhabitable, or even existing. Won't you feel like tossing him in Esopus Creek to cool off?

The Martians react the same way to you, save they have no creek. Take a slow walk, following, *exactly*, the instructions at the end of the chapter. The Old Director and its area have fallen on hard times, and you should try to avoid Scamander's rather-too-colorful criminals.

Look up as you walk through Garline Corridor. See that brutally corrugated black rock surface that cuts the corridor at an angle? That is the outside surface of the Old Director's wine cellar. The sun-face-topped pilasters on the high side of Dempster Hollow (the noodle shops on the low side are covered in another chapter) are the side of the Old Director's Grand Ballroom. You can just see the mirrors through the windows. The huge pangolin plates that thrust inconveniently up amid the fruit stands in Saba Square are the Old Director's roof. If you climb up on them, as children sometimes do, and peer in through the thick glass, you can see people lounging at their ease in the top-floor bar.

Are you starting to see the place, hanging in the midst of Scamander's tangled corridors like a buried jewel? If you have succeeded with the Old Director, you are ready to try something like Xui House (pronounced, for no discernible reason, "Shway"). Everyone in Scamander can see Xui House from its main gates, its wall of interview cubicles in Koprolu Passage, its ornate gable thrust out into the dry atmosphere from the bastion in which Xui House hides, its cellar an inverted pyramid. To the Scamander mind, Xui House is as real and distinct a place as a Renaissance palazzo in Florence, looming above the crowded street on its rusticated base. You have to imagine it silhouetted against a sky made entirely of stone.

It's there, I swear it is. But it is entirely possible that you may never succeed in seeing it, and be unable to perceive its hallways as different from public corridors. If you can't, and you must be honest with yourself about it, you must take my strictures in the following chapter, "Private, Semiprivate, and Public Spaces," very seriously. You may find yourself in a private drawing room, think you are in a place of public refreshment, and commit a social gaffe. Confusion, consternation, and grim, unfortunate duel may result. It is always best to err on the side of formality.

"You fell off that thing once," Hektor observed. "I thought you were dead for sure." He squinted over his arm, then switched his gesture to another, more distant rock outcrop, as if the narrow focus of his pointing finger brought the past back more clearly.

"I didn't fall." Hektor's brother Breyten pressed his chest against the rock wall and stretched his arms along it, embracing it. "I jumped."

"Just as dead, either way."

"I'm not dead."

"Pure luck, that."

"Without luck, you're nothing on Mars." Breyten jumped up lightly, hooked his fingertips over a narrow ledge invisible to Hektor, and pulled himself up with one smooth movement.

It had been a long time since the two Passman brothers had been out together in the grabens of the Labyrinth, their favorite area of exploration since they were old enough to take the train out here from Scamander.

Breyten jammed his toes into a narrow vertical crack and inched his way upward. Though his younger brother could now challenge him physically, he still retained his dominance through a sheer recklessness that Hektor had never been able to match. Breyten leaned out past an overhang, silhouetted against the dusty pink sky, and looked down at Hektor. He was thinner than Hektor, fine-boned, his pale hair now hidden by his hood. In honor of Hektor's return, he'd exhumed an old air mask decorated with childish attempts at Maori stripes.

"How does it feel to be back?" Breyten asked. "Do you worry about breathing?" Behind the scrawled tattoo marks, his face was mockingly concerned.

Hektor had at that moment been concentrating on the suddenly unfamiliar feel of air sliding in through his throat valves. On Earth the external tracheal attachments had been matters of curiosity. He'd decorated them, as Martians visiting the home planet did. But now that he was back on the Martian surface and his life once again depended on them, they felt like two thumbs pressing hard on his throat.

"No," Hektor said, not quite lying. "I worry about falling. I still think the gravity's three times what it actually is. It's all hard-wired, you know. Being back on Earth reactivated everything."

He said this as a distracting tactic, then realized that this fear was real too. He hooked his arm around a rock spike and it dug through the skintite into the soft skin on the inside of his elbow. The overhang Breyten dangled from wasn't technically difficult, but it suddenly frightened Hektor. The depths of the canyon tugged at his feet.

"You'll get over it. Fall off something, get used to the gravity. Just don't forget to breathe." Breyten disappeared, his directionally transmitted voice fading.

"Thanks," Hektor muttered. He reached up, felt a solid handhold, and pulled himself up the overhang. He was floating, damn it, the gravity was nothing. He could do a swan dive into the canyon, tuck and roll, come up smiling. That sort of overconfidence killed more Martians returning from extended visits to Earth than any breathing problems.

Hektor climbed up onto the wide, rubble-strewn ledge. He looked around himself quickly, dropping automatically into a defensive crouch. Breyten was nowhere in sight, and Hektor knew that meant—

It was a clean tackle. Hektor went right down and Breyten was on top of him, laughing. But Hektor had been two years on Earth. He was already stockier than Breyten, and heavy gravity had hardened his muscles. He rolled and Breyten went with him.

"Hey!" Breyten said. "No fair."

"No fair?" Breyten was squirming, but Hektor headed for a pin. "Who jumped who?"

"That's what I mean." With a fluid maneuver, Breyten evaded Hektor's final grasp. "You should respect the advantages I've been given. It's part of the natural order—"

"Sure," Hektor puffed. "I understand that. Really." Breyten was slippery, but if he could just get his shoulder blades down on the rock . . .

"Say," Breyten said in a relaxed tone, as if they were sitting somewhere sipping tea, "you haven't told me anything about Earth. We've spent the whole time talking about me."

"Have we?" Hektor had listened to all of Breyten's observations about the past two years on Mars. Breyten had talked of life with their father, Lon Passman; developments in the Tharsis court where Lon was Justice; events in the corridors of Scamander—all in statements so eager that they stepped on each other's conclusions and contradicted one another. Hektor hadn't really learned anything, except that Breyten was as dizzily involved with a dozen things as he always had been. And that there was one topic Breyten was avoiding.

Hektor relented, and Breyten slid out from under him. Breyten sat up, leaned his back against a convenient rock, and regarded his brother with dancing eyes. "We have. I let you get as far as Cuzco. In fact, I think you were still waiting for your luggage."

The wrestling match was over, and Hektor half wished he'd waited to pin Breyten before restarting the discussion. But that was absurd. It was childish to be wrestling out here on the rocks like a couple of boys anyway. Breyten wasn't about to give up on being a boy, and while with him Hektor found himself back in their shared youth too. If the solemn staff members at the Esopus Palace could have seen him now, all their suspicions about rustic Martians would have been confirmed. At least, Hektor thought they had those suspicions. No one had ever voiced one.

"Councillor Borg was waiting for *her* luggage," Hektor said. "At least one of her bags always gets lost." The train's locomotive had puffed gentle swirls of steam into the cold air while the staff searched the baggage car. Hektor, his help not needed, had stood on the platform marveling at the ice-covered mountains. "They eventually found it under her seat. She'd put it there so she wouldn't lose it." An improbably tiny and graceful External Security captain named Westerkamp had found it and pulled it out like a conjuror with a bouquet of flowers. Hektor had been quite taken with the man, for all that he was over forty, but after his one service, he had disappeared.

Hektor had just spent two years on Earth as a member of Councillor Tsina Borg's personal staff. That first year the Council of Nationalities, which moved its formal meeting place every year, though never to Mars, had taken over the quarters of the Andes Highlands Assembly at Cuzco, Peru. Most of the Terrans had bitched about the thin air, but the altiplano was at about the pressure of a normal Martian interior. That had helped Hektor, since everyone else was gasping for breath while he was struggling with the gravity.

"Remember Tsina at Mother's parties?" Breyten said. "She was always like that, losing things. Always confused. Drove Mother crazy. Whoever would have thought she'd make Councillor? And whoever thought that you, little brother, would start your famous political career on her staff?"

Tsina Borg was a keenly intelligent woman who had trouble holding on to things: pocketbook, gloves, at least three husbands Hektor knew about. She spent sixteen hours a day at her work, and losing things was one of her few recreations. The art of losing, she said, wasn't hard to master. She said.

Breyten, tired of lolling on the rough ground, stood and balanced himself on a rock, arms held out to the canyon as if calming an unruly mob. Hektor watched him. It was easy to watch Breyten. That position on Councillor Borg's staff, minor though it was, had originally been intended for Breyten. Tsina Borg had been old friends with their mother, Sara, and after Sara's death she had remained in contact with Lon Passman, and willing to do him favors. If Lon and Sara's older son wanted to see Earth, well, she could arrange it. For a while it had seemed that Breyten actually wanted the position, even though he described it, more or less accurately, as "making sandwiches for Tsina's lunch."

Then he had arbitrarily turned it down and Hektor, full of desperate longing to see Earth, to see how things worked, to start doing something, was able to maneuver himself into it. Without making the depths of his desire known, he hoped. He didn't appreciate that crack about a "famous political career." He wanted to have one. He was going to have one. Already the contact with Tsina Borg, and the job he had done on her staff, had led to a substitute appointment to a Delegate post in the Chamber. The most junior of junior Delegates, of course, but it was another step upward. He wondered if Breyten now regretted not having taken the opportunity and resented Hektor for it.

Breyten scooped up a loose stone. "The Trellis. Up there, Milady's Head."

"Milady's—" Hektor rolled to his feet. "What's that?"

"I'll hit it, you'll see it."

Breyten curved his body gracefully and let the stone fly. It arched across the narrow canyon side on which they stood and hit a round rock that might have been Milady's Head, though Hektor suspected Breyten had made up the name even as he picked up the stone. He'd still managed to hit the target. As boys they had dubbed that cracked wall the Trellis and imagined it an artifact of the Acherusians, the mythical ancient inhabitants of the Solar System.

Hektor was darker and wider than Breyten, but he had none of his brother's delicate grace. Breyten could fly up the canyon sides. Hektor would have to content himself with plodding slowly after, carrying the supplies.

"Who is she, Breyten?"

"Ah?" Breyten turned and almost fell from his perch. He circled his arms frantically.

It was hard to get the drop on Breyten. Hektor felt pleased with himself. "Come on, now," Hektor said. "Do you think I'm dumb? In your letters, when you bothered to write one, you were always going to corridor plays, restaurants, art shows, everything you don't usually do—and all completely alone. Big hole there. Could drop Phobos into it. You're seeing someone. *Sexually.*" He whispered the last word as if it was something really foul.

That had always been Hektor's advantage over his older brother. Breyten had never been much interested in women, and Hektor had been interested since he could remember. He'd tried to use his early sexual success as a weapon against Breyten, but Breyten had never really seemed affected, and once had told Hektor, with languid unconcern, that his sibling rivalry was getting unhealthy. That was the last time in their lives they'd come close to hitting each other.

"Right?" Hektor said. "Pierre Sanserif has a girlfriend." The nickname came from an old childhood game.

"Yes!" Breyten said, as if he'd been waiting the whole time for the proper moment to bring it up. "Come on, let's get climbing. I'll tell you all about it." The cliff ahead bulked dark against the glowing pink sky, and Hektor realized he'd have to pay dearly for any information he obtained.

There turned out to be more climbing than information. Breyten was involved with a woman named Miriam Kostal, from an important family up in the Chasma Boreale, the vast, dune-filled valley that cut up into the North Polar Cap. He had met her while up there visiting. They'd climbed the Cap together, a dangerous enterprise. A month or so after he returned to Scamander, she came too—she was an officer in the Vigil. Hektor gathered that becoming a political policeman had not been part of the Kostal family's plans for her. Or Breyten's either. He spoke of the Vigil as if it was a chronic illness Miriam suffered from, something that could have been romantic in a play, but was ugly and unpleasant in real life.

The Kostal and Passman families had an ancient bond that dated back nearly a century, to the Seven Planets War, when the outer satellites had revolted against Terran rule, though no one was clear on how that bond had been formed. As far as Hektor remembered, a Passman and a Kostal had served together off Ganymede. Nothing like participating in a losing war for building personal bonds you didn't like talking about.

He even remembered Miriam. If he shook his memories hard enough, one fell out that contained a party and a dark, gawky girl with a too-short dress that revealed her knobby knees, taking the hand of Zoë, Hektor and Breyten's younger sister, to show her how to dance some elaborate step, confusing poor Zoë completely.

Poor Zoë. . . . Could Breyten be reading his mind? The timing was perfect. Hektor had gotten turned around, and not realized where Breyten was leading him. As they climbed up over the edge of the cliff, a wide view opened up over the Noctis Labyrinthus. The Labyrinth was a tangle of steep-sided faults opened by the rise of Tharsis Bulge to the west, where the great volcanoes stood high above Mars. On the east it connected to the vast canyons of Valles Marineris, where the city Scamander lay. From where Hektor and Breyten stood, the world was an archipelago of red rock platforms surrounded by shadow-filled canyons. The sun was dissolving in the haze of pink dust that always hung above the Martian horizon. Overhead, the sky grew darker.

Just below them they could see the huge slab of rock under which their little sister was entombed.

Breyten was already sliding recklessly down the scree slope toward her. Hektor paused a moment and examined the cliff face that curved around on this side. That rough spot there—was that where the rock slab had slid from, having waited millennia for just the right opportunity? Too many rocks had fallen over hundreds of thousands of years for the place to declare itself. If Hektor traversed a little and looked closely, he might find the marks of his own clawed fingers in the compacted dust, where he'd turned his head and seen the rock sliding serenely down on Zoë. But no. Too many dust storms had come and gone. He followed Breyten down.

"I just thought the three of us should be together for a couple of minutes, that's all," Breyten said. "You've been away a long time."

"Good idea." Hektor sat down on the edge of the slab and patted it gently.

He and Breyten had taken Zoë climbing with them. She'd been delighted at this unusual invitation from her older brothers. Intensely excited, she ran around and asked dozens of questions, most of which Breyten answered. They climbed from this side. There was a trail at the bottom of the graben that led directly down to a magtrack station. She made it up to this ledge, then refused to go any farther, content to watch them. Hektor and Breyten ascended the cliff above, partially to impress her with their skill. As far as Hektor could tell, it had been the vibration of their movement that had dislodged the delicately balanced rock slab. Intent on something down the graben, she had never even seen it coming. For a couple of years, Hektor had seen it every night.

They sat there for a long time, each lost in his own thoughts.

Hektor finally bestirred himself. "You know, Breyten, it's getting dark." Hektor had an emergency air cocoon in his pack, but had no desire to use it.

"Come on, then!" Breyten shouted, suddenly energized. "I'll

race you down to the station by way of Leadbutt Col.'' He jumped off the slab, slid perilously down a steep rock face, scattering fragments below him, leaped across a ten-foot fracture, and was off.

''Dammit—'' Hektor gave it up, rolled across Zoë's slab, and was after his brother, leaping the dark fractures that filled with approaching night. He wouldn't catch Breyten, he knew that. Breyten had always been able to navigate the jagged twists and turns of the Noctis Labyrinthus better than anyone, and his utter lack of concern for bodily integrity gave him an advantage. But both of them would recognize pure cowardice if, after visiting their dead sister, who had never aged, Hektor claimed to be beyond such childish games.

''Gustavus,'' Lon Passman said. ''Have they come back yet?''

The heavyset man sitting on the folding campstool, elbows on his knees as if watching troops set up an emergency shelter, straightened and shrugged his shoulders. ''There was a report of them coming in the back lock a few minutes ago. Late, in a hurry. Conspiracy, if you ask me, Lon.''

''They haven't seen each other in a long time,'' Lon said, as if defending his sons from an accusation.

Colonel Gustavus Trep stood up with a grunt, folded up his stool, and slung the resulting small package on his hip. Carrying it, as if always on maneuvers, was half affectation, half necessity. An old soldier, Trep had fought in the small wars on Earth, and as a consequence had a lower spine and sacrum that were mostly foamed steel. Battlefield medicine being what it was, his lower back had never functioned quite properly since. Sitting in the massive chairs of Xui House's dining room made him even more irritable than usual.

''Sure,'' Trep said. ''They have a lot to talk about. Breyten's carrying on a romance with one of my staff members and you're polishing up Hektor as a Passman family sacrifice in the Chamber of Delegates.'' He leaned against the side table, making the bottles rock precariously, and poured himself a glass of wine.

Lon Passman and Gustavus Trep had been friends for decades, but Lon could still be astonished by the speed of Trep's attacks.

Lon tried to ignore the fact that what he perceived as attacks usually came after an endless period in which Lon refused to get around to the subject that was most on his mind.

"I didn't know that Vigils were supposed to be celibate," Lon said, dealing with the easier problem first. Trep had to be just spouting off about Breyten. Strain was obvious in his voice. He was Commander of the Vigil, and the recent anticorruption drive had extended the Martian political police to the breaking point. Prominent politicians and businessmen were being detained daily, some under regulations of dubious legality. The Vigil was used to performing its tasks in decent silence.

"Justice and law enforcement in bed together," Trep said. "A poor image, at a time like this. What happens when some political fixer Ms. Kostal has arrested ends up in Tharsis court? 'Vigil and Court Collude!' Great, just great."

"Perhaps you shouldn't even stick around for dinner," Lon said. "You'll be seeing your gloomy mug in a newssheet tomorrow."

"This isn't funny, Lon. Is the Passman family trying to cover every eventuality? A nice strategy. No matter what happens after this shake-up, one or another of you will be in a safe position. It might even be Hektor, though I doubt it. This is the worst time since Earth established the Governor-Resident to be a junior Delegate."

"Stop worrying so much about Hektor," Lon snapped. "He knows the risks."

Lon wasn't sure Hektor really did, but then, why should Hektor care what the risks were? A slot had opened up due to an accidental cave-in that buried the Delegate from the Inner Frostwall district of Scamander, and Hektor had taken his opportunity. If he was out six months from now because of some anticorruption hearings, well, he had taken the best chance he could. Lon found himself unexpectedly impressed by his younger son. He had always been the safe one, walking after Breyten, picking up the pieces Breyten casually dropped behind him.

Trep stuck his thick lips out like a pouting child. "Sorry, Lon. It's been a rough few months." Long days of work had left his eyes red-rimmed, and the only reason his gray hair wasn't wild was that it was only a couple of millimeters long.

"I know it has," Lon said. He hadn't seen Trep and Trep's wife Melisande for all that time. He now lived essentially alone, since Breyten passed through Xui House as if it was just another stretch of his corridor territory, and Hektor had been away on Earth. Sara, his wife, had been dead for years. Lon had been reduced to begging Melisande to persuade her husband to visit. She had, as usual, come through with the goods.

Lon sipped his wine and stared gloomily at the slowly clotting artificial sunlight that came from behind the lacquer shields on the wall. Nonphysiological white lights appeared at the corners of the room with the coming of night.

Lon Passman was a slender man, and taller than either of his sons. His white hair, though receding, was long and thick, with a prominent widow's peak. Hektor had inherited the widow's peak, while Breyten had ended up with his mother's sharp V. Lon had a lean and thoughtful face, which was perfectly set off by the dark of his judicial robes, a fact that stimulated his vanity when he noted it in a mirror.

"Just as I predicted!" Melisande came through the kitchen door, followed by aromatic smoke.

"What?" Trep said to his wife. "Fabian's destroyed dinner with some new sauce?"

"Not at all." Melisande's round face was flushed with the heat of the kitchen. "I mean I predicted that if I left you two alone, you'd start talking about politics, get upset, and stare at the walls."

Lon and Trep exchanged glances. "We're sorry, Melisande," Lon said.

"Don't apologize to me. Apologize to each other."

"We already have," Trep said. "That just depressed us even more."

"Oh, really." Melisande said. "I should just have stayed in the kitchen. Fabian and Egypt are much more entertaining."

"No, no. Please." Lon pulled out a chair for her. They were heavy things, part of the original furnishings of Xui House, and had small faces carved on the backs, each of a distinct individual. "Gustavus and I need you to entertain us."

She bent her head in acknowledgment of Lon's gesture and sat down. "I think just sitting alone in this dining room is depressing, Lon. How do you stand it?"

"I don't come in here unless I have guests."

"It's not good to be afraid of parts of your own house."

"Leave him alone, Meli," Trep said.

"It's all right," Lon said. "It's true."

The three of them were huddled against one of the massive rock-cut piers that held up the vaulted ceiling thirty meters overhead. The far wall was at least fifty meters away and almost invisible in the evening gloom. The room had once been a public square, an open place for public meetings, in the days when Scamander was nothing but a precarious settlement dug into the almost-virgin rock of Mars. Vastly larger public spaces had since replaced it, and it was now part of the private space of Xui House.

"Didn't Hektor and Breyten used to play ball in here?" Trep said.

"Yes," said Lon. "It was some elaborate game, involving bouncing balls off the right number of piers, columns, and walls. They talked about printing up the rules, starting a league of some sort, turning this room into a sports stadium. Cheering crowds, all that. Breyten made a presentation one night at dinner. He was very convincing."

Melisande looked up into the shadows. "Might have been a better use for the space."

"Maybe," Lon said. "Sara told them to forget it, and they did, and got interested in something else."

"Where's that dinner?" Trep said, pulling his stool off his belt and unfolding it again. "I'm hungry." He sat down.

Melisande kissed the top of his head. "Fabian said it would be just a couple of minutes. Try to cheer up."

"Sure," Trep said. "I'll do my best." He managed to smile up at his wife.

*   *   *

Fabian Xui and his wife Egypt had set up a portable stove on the floor despite the fact that huge green-and-red enameled ovens rose around them like distant massifs. A glow light on a stand threw a beam on their work area. It was as if the kitchen was an abandoned ruin, rather than somewhere fully functional. Hektor came down the back stairs, not yet ready to confront the dining room.

"Hey, Hektor." Fabian poured thick black soy into a heated pan and tilted his head to listen to the sizzle. He was a gangly man with a long, serious face, and lay sprawled on the floor like a porter who had finally managed to dump his load. "I'd get up, but the sauce . . ."

"Oh, for heaven's sake, Fabian." Egypt jumped to her feet and hugged Hektor. She was a tiny woman with piled black hair and the well-proportioned face of an earnestly painted Madonna. Hektor picked her up off her feet and kissed her.

"Gravity!" she said. "You've been on Earth too long."

"Didn't help in the Labyrinth," Hektor said. "Breyten still kicked my butt on the rocks."

"Butt kicking." Fabian pipetted a few drops of hot oil into the pan. "The Passman family exercise. My resulting leather cheeks have served me well in the outside world."

"Fabian!" Egypt nudged her husband with her toe. "What are you so sour about?"

He raised an eyebrow, surprised at the question. "I'm just my normal languidly hostile self, dear. Nothing out of the ordinary." Fabian turned down the heat, rolled onto his back on the floor, and contemplated the ceiling with his hands behind his head. "You know, you could cook for an army in here."

"They used to," Hektor said. "Armies were quartered here during the Tumults. A century and a half ago."

Fabian was not really a Passman: he was a cousin from Sara's side, the Xuis. A few years older than Breyten, he had helped, in his distractedly precise way, to raise Hektor and Breyten.

"At least I didn't have to feed them," Fabian said.

Egypt plopped back down on the floor. She watched the tiny multibladed device chop cubes of onion, tomato, and garlic. She was from Earth, and found rational Martian vegetables endlessly fascinating.

"Everyone was here," she said. "So Fabian offered to make dinner. Now he's all resentful that he has to do all this work." Egypt tossed chopped pieces of vegetables into the pan a few pieces at a time, as if she was feeding a pet. She looked at her husband with concern. "He's just been working too hard."

"Ah, no," Fabian said. "Not work. Not at all. None of it. There's just a lot going on out there, all the time. I couldn't cover it if I stayed awake twenty-four hours a day."

"Maybe that's the problem," Egypt said. "The Martian day is half an hour longer than the Terran day. Instead of taking that extra time and spreading it around so that you can have free coffee breaks, you just made the hours longer. No wonder everything's so tiring."

Fabian pulled the pan off the stove, using two hands. He and Egypt had rented it from a streetfood vendor, allowing him to retire to a bar for the evening. Fabian had gotten used to the nomadic style of the Scamander corridors and suddenly felt uncomfortable using the built-in equipment in the Xui House kitchen. The place was intimidatingly massive. The walls were viridian stone, veined with hints of precious metals. The self-maintaining herb garden had gone wild and dry seeds lay on the countertops.

"I feel like a Goth cooking over a fire in the ruins of the Forum," Egypt said, looking up at the high shadows cast toward the ceiling by the glow lamp.

"Doesn't look like it's been used much while I was away," Hektor said. During his childhood the place had always been busy, serving visiting political figures, and often as a general catering service for the Fossic Party feeds thrown in the corridors. "Neither Breyten nor Father is much for cooking."

Fabian tasted his sauce, smacked his lips. "Tell Egypt about Earth, Hektor. She doesn't want to ask, but I know she wants to hear."

Egypt had come as a visitor to Mars many years ago to collect plots and scenery for her theatrical work, but had met Fabian Xui and ended up staying. Though she never mentioned it, both

Fabian and Hektor were convinced that she always pined for the open air of Earth. Now that Hektor had seen the place, he was even surer of it.

Hektor started loading food onto the rolling serving cart. "All right. I saw the Small Receiving Hall at the Esopus Palace. The whole place is open to the sky, with the Adirondack gardens spilling down to the river. You could see the ceremonial barges flickering their oars in the sun. They have some sort of silver coating on the blades. The clouds hung above us. Thick lumps, not like the kind we have here. They were more like white dust storms that had floated up off the ground. The air was hot, thick, sweet, like a woman's love sweat."

"Whoa," Fabian said. "Control that subtext, Hektor."

"Quit interrupting him," Egypt said.

"We were all dressed up. I was ready to faint in the heat. Meanwhile, the Gensekretarial Guards—you've seen them? Big black men and women from East Africa. Masai, they're called. We don't have anyone that purebred here. Tall. They stared at all of us as if they wanted to herd us right off the edge of the balcony into the river so that they could get to their lunch.

"Then two heads moved apart and I saw her. Twenty meters away, three-quarter view—doesn't matter. The Genseka Vasilisa. This was only a couple of months before she died and she looked really old. I almost thought she was a statue, like a Gabriel figure, but then she leaned forward to sniff a flower. Once she'd smelled it, it went into a pile that could have filled Pyramid Square. The other side of the Hall was stacked with melons, brought for her delectation, all different colors. They smelled even better than the flowers, but then, I hadn't had my lunch either." He'd practiced the description over and over in his head, trying to fix the experience before it faded.

"That sounds like a cue," Fabian said. "We're ready to serve."

"Yes!" Egypt said. "Dress me, Fabian."

Egypt held up her slender arms and Fabian dropped an embroidered robe over her. She tied the sash. She now had elaborately wide shoulders and long, swooping sleeves. It was like nothing Hektor had ever seen.

"What is that?" he asked. "Are you indicating your claim to the lost throne of England?"

She looked down at herself. "It's supposed to be the gown of the Great Logothete in the play *The Fall of Constantinople: or, A Spurned Mistress's Revenge*. Do you suppose it's historically accurate?" She held out a sleeve and dubiously examined the pattern of grinning mouse heads with huge round ears.

It was good to see his friends again. Hektor chuckled. "And who wrote this play?"

"Oh, I haven't written it *yet*. This is more in the nature of *research*, if you know what I mean. Xui House would make a great Palace of Bucoleon. Come on, let's move this food before they riot out there." They pushed through the heavy door into the dining room.

"Pure spite!" Breyten was saying. "Shooting them down just as they were entering the atmosphere. And so few of them were left as it was. . . ."

"The risks of a filibustering expedition," Fabian said, immediately. "They knew what they were up against. The asteroid Hermione was well armed." He pushed the cart up to the table.

"But they sat behind Phobos and waited! InSec vessels. Didn't even give the survivors a chance to surrender."

Fabian glanced at Trep. Filibusters were a serious sore point with the head of the Vigil, and Fabian knew for a fact that the InSec intervention against those who had unsuccessfully assaulted Hermione had caused Trep to throw an awesome temper tantrum.

"The Hermione expedition was stupid to begin with," he said. "They deserved what happened to them."

Filibusters were Mars's chief contribution to continued political tension between the Technic Alliance, on its moons around the gas giants, and the Union of States and Nationalities, on the inner planets. The treaty separating the two entities seventy-five years before had created a buffer zone in the Asteroid Belt, inviolable by military forces. Bellicose Martians constantly sent pinprick military expeditions into the Neutral Zone, ostensibly to "liberate" various asteroids from their idiosyncratic rulers, more often to loot or establish their own petty dictatorships. It was one of the Vigil's unrewarding responsibilities to restrain these freebooters, who were overwhelmingly popular among the mass of Martians.

"How can you say that?" Breyten protested. "Filibusters are part of what it is to be a Martian, aren't they, Fabian? A tradition."

"Preposterous." Trep was irritated. "Lon, you let your sons natter on like this?" Lon shrugged, waiting out the discussion until the most effective time to intervene. "Filibusters are irritating pests, Breyten, not heroes," Trep said. "If you knew how much time the Vigil had to waste tracking them down . . ."

"Filibusters," Egypt said musingly. "Those are those space pirates, right?"

"Right," Trep said.

"Wrong," Fabian and Breyten chorused. They looked at each other, unexpectedly on the same side, and laughed.

"Noble savages!" Fabian said. "Expressions of the irrepressible Martian id."

"Authentic Martian heroes." Breyten grew serious again.

"Oh, they really are quite tiresome," Melisande said to Egypt. "They come up with all sorts of elaborate political justifications for raiding innocent asteroid dwellers. Space pirates is close enough, Egypt."

"I saw a play about some of them recently," Egypt said, playing her innocent-on-Mars role. "The leader, a woman, died during the counterattack by the asteroid dwellers, along with most of her soldiers. It was a little too romantic for my taste. Martian romantic—blood poured out of her nostrils when she died, and you could smell the stink of the corpse from ten rows back." Egypt shook her head. "I'm starting to despair of understanding Martian theatrical conventions. There *was* some stuff about thumbing our noble Martian noses at the arrogant Technics of Ganymede and Titan, but it seemed extraneous to the plot. Maybe it was stuck in to satisfy the Internal Security Censorate. I think the filibuster commander was pregnant by someone on the asteroid they were attacking, but I was never quite sure. . . ."

"*Edge of the Wedge*," Breyten said. "I saw it twice." His

look challenged anyone else to find that amusing.

"Romantic heroes," Lon mused, finally drawn into the discussion. "Maybe that's why the new decrees don't say anything about them. Leave us Martians something to hold on to. Something that doesn't mean too much, of course. But maybe we're easier than we thought."

"Just a matter of resources." Trep, tired of waiting for everyone else, sat down at the table and, without ceremony, started eating his soup with a soldier's hunger. "Rodomar wants us to concentrate on political corruption in its pure form, without distractions." He shook his head. "She's a bit of a monomaniac on that score, from what I can tell. She's got some sort of Platonic ideal in mind. Filibusters just don't fit it. InSec, of course, has its own opinions—they'd rather chase filibusters than people who are more dangerous." Internal Security, the main Union political police, operated independently of the Governor-Resident's office, often at cross-purposes.

The wide yellow plates were reflected in the surface of the sirenwood dining table. Even with seven for dinner, they filled only one end of the huge table.

"I met Sylvia Rodomar on Earth," Hektor said. "Before she was named Under Governor-Resident of Mars."

He'd placed it just right. He had everyone's immediate attention. That wasn't easy, not with this bunch.

So he took a moment adjusting his chair, letting the moment pull itself tight. He tasted the soup. Good.

"This was in Cuzco, almost two years ago, not too long after I got there. It was right after her removal from Palawan, and she was there to testify to the Direct Rule Committee of the Council of Nationalities. There were calls that she be sent off to the Dry Tortugas with the other high state prisoners. Tsina Borg told me that calls like that are traditional. Rodomar had just caused a big ruckus, and they wanted her safely out of the way in Fort Jefferson, walking the old wall and looking across the Gulf of Mexico for the water-supply ship. Then everyone else could keep on with business as usual."

Sylvia Rodomar had originally been sent to Palawan to keep her out of trouble. That was in the wake of her brutal and elegant handling of the incipient Mato Grosso revolt, in southwest Brasil, where she was Regional Governor. From what Hektor had been able to gather, powerful social pressures stemming from the endless reforestation projects in the former Amazon had led to an open insurrection, led from the city but fed from the country. As usual, many of the details were still awaiting approval from the Division of Internal Security for public release. And, as usual, it was generally suspected that part of the reason the details were still restrained was because they demonstrated InSec incompetence on a wide scale.

Whatever the specifics, it was known that Rodomar had acted quickly against the leaders and ordered arrests and executions. Then, unexpectedly, she had proclaimed general amnesties for the followers. As a result, the revolt dissolved without involving the use of massive military force.

That had resulted in her first round of hearings before the Council of Nationalities. It never became clear whether the Council's objection was her initial ruthlessness or her subsequent clemency. As a result of this ambiguity, the hearings were finally continued without a clear verdict. Rodomar's career as a regional administrator survived, but suffered a serious check.

So she was sent to Palawan, an island in the Philippine archipelago. No popular revolt was likely there. The full name of the government that ruled Venus, Mars, and the various fractious nations of Earth was the Union of States and Nationalities Under the Treaty of Jakarta, and the inhabitants of the Southeast Asian archipelagos had been mainstays of Union government since that time. It was felt that Rodomar could do little harm there.

"When I met her, she was sitting huddled up in a deck chair on the edge of an observation platform. No one would talk to her. She was poison. She was just sitting there, snow swirling around her, staring off at those ice-covered mountains, all wrapped up in blankets. She had a pair of binoculars in her lap. She didn't even notice me when I came up to her. Just kept looking. It turned out that she actually was watching something. One of her consorts, Carter, was climbing some ice cliff out there, probably just to entertain her. He ended up breaking his leg in a fall. She's not easy to entertain."

"So why did *you* talk to her?" Lon asked.

Hektor suspected his father already knew the answer to that one, but he was grateful for the question. He'd been wondering how to explain himself without claiming greater prescience than he had. When he'd talked with Rodomar, he had absolutely no idea she would end up as Under Governor-Resident of Mars within the year.

"While we were en route from Mars to Earth, I made a list of people. Tsina helped a lot. I wanted people who, for one reason or another, were out of power but still close to it. Many were just young, like me, but Tsina knew who seemed promising. Some were in disgrace, like Sylvia Rodomar. Some had simply lost positions, but were angling for others. People in power barely had time to talk to someone like me. But people out . . . sometimes they had more time than they knew what to do with."

"And ten or twenty years from now, some of these contacts will be useful indeed," Trep said. "Must have been hard work. But Rodomar's an unexpected bonus! Luck, Hektor. It's an essential ingredient of a successful career. Hey, Fabian, I've been smelling that dish for a long while now. Isn't it about time you served it?"

"I didn't want to interrupt the story," Fabian said, pulling the lid off the serving dish. Egypt reached in with the serving spoons.

"It proves a story's essential interest if it can survive interruption. But no story can compete with my growling belly. Come on, now."

Hektor looked at his family. Everyone seemed attentive, or at least as attentive as a dinner-table story deserved, although Breyten was fading. Breyten had refused the position on Borg's staff, and it was natural for him to find stories about the position to be tedious. Still, Hektor wanted to hold him, to show him the sorts of things he'd been doing. It was, however, clear that no one would give him any undeserved credit for prescience. It was foolish to have thought it. Everyone was smart enough to recognize luck when he saw it. Hektor felt disappointed. Someday, he hoped, he would receive credit he did not deserve, just because his family felt like giving it to him.

"Even depressed and immobile in her chair, she was an impressive woman. She's big, but you've probably seen her here, in Scamander. She didn't want to talk about what happened on Palawan, but I finally convinced her to. Nothing much I hadn't already heard, but she sharpened some of the details for me."

"Well, Hektor," Lon said, smiling at being put in the position of a child demanding a story, "sharpen them for us."

On Palawan, Rodomar had turned her attentions to investigating local corruption. As she got deeper, she began to realize that the local Internal Security office, far from battling corruption, was deeply involved in it, and resentful of any interference. Rodomar, dangerously, turned to local forces, which had been indignant for years over how their high-level police were behaving. She went down as far as the village level, negotiating agreements directly with headmen. She protected local investigators, permitting them to reach court with their accusations.

The combination of pressures, investigations, and vigorous enforcement of local laws finally brought down a key InSec official in Manila who had been operating with impunity for decades. Unfortunately for Rodomar, the rot was found to extend all the way up into administrative departments at the Esopus Palace itself, affecting people near the Genseka Vasilisa. The Gensek was supposedly a purely ceremonial office, the genial monarch of Earth, but over the years a lot of power and influence had accreted under the ceremony. The Manila Internal Security office underwent a shake-up, and there were several transfers, but the investigation was stopped there. Rodomar left Palawan, and went to face another inquiry in the Council of Nationalities.

"She wasn't even high on my list of people to contact," Hektor said. "But she was right there. And I got interested in her." His two years on Earth had been filled with contacts with bitter and occasionally deranged office seekers. That had taken up every spare hour he was not working directly with Councillor Tsina Borg. He hoped Trep was right, and that some of them would eventually be useful.

"And a month later, Vasilisa's dead!" Breyten, silent up to

this point, sounded enthusiastic. Hektor hoped the enthusiasm was genuine.

Hektor nodded. "New elections with the elevation of Paramon. A new administration. You should have seen everyone running around. Vasilisa had reigned for thirty years. That started to seem like forever."

"And Rodomar gets Mars." Trep shook his head. "I'm glad I'm not in politics. It doesn't make a damn bit of sense. I'll leave that sort of nonsense up to you Passmans."

"She doesn't 'get' Mars," Lon said carefully. "She's subject to Governor-Resident DeCoven's authority."

"Sure." Trep snorted. "If DeCoven had his way, the Vigil would stick to licensing newssheets and monitoring public assemblies of more than five citizens, and stay away from politics. She's got us tearing the place apart."

He glowered across the table at Fabian. Fabian's sheet, the *Moebius Daily*, often had trouble getting permission to be publicly distributed, and that was partially Fabian's fault. His accounts of ritualized gang warfare were sometimes considered inflammatory. Fabian underwent the scrutiny blandly. "More chicken?" he said.

Melisande rubbed Trep's shoulder. "Of course, Fabian."

He passed some sauce to her. "DeCoven's too busy with his latest mistress to worry about what Rodomar's up to. That and his pigeons."

Hektor watched with interest, glad that this time he wasn't involved in the discussion. One of the Vigil's less happy jobs was suppressing information about their Governor-Resident's ardent sex life. It was an effort doomed to failure. As for DeCoven's hobby of breeding ornamental pigeons, jokes about that were so common that they were never funny.

But Trep surprised Hektor. Instead of exploding, he just sighed heavily. "Pigeons. Have you seen any of them? Quite beautiful, some of them. Lots of colored feathers. DeCoven's hobby, and he seems to be good at it. Leastwise, he always shows them off after Liaison Group meetings. Not a big thing, eh? People are getting arrested, detained, investigated. The entire mine Iqbal ran in Coprates has been closed as a result of the deals they made with the Coprates delegates. We've already arrested one former employee who decided to take up amateur corridor banditry. He wasn't good at it. And what are people upset about?''

''Pigeons,'' Breyten said, with an odd satisfaction.

''Damn right, pigeons. No one can agree if the corrupt dealers should be punished or not, or how severely. No one knows if guilty delegates should be impeached. No one can tell if Rodomar's orders have gone too far. No one knows if they're next on the list. But everyone knows they hate DeCoven and his goddamn pigeons.''

''And what does that tell you?'' Hektor asked. He'd been away, and not caught this piece of popular emotion. Such silly symbolic stands revealed more than reasoned dialogue.

''That people are even stupider than thirty years in police work taught me.'' Trep shook his head. ''Well, Fabian, the meal was excellent, as always. But I'm afraid Melisande and I must be going. I have more problems to face in the morning.''

''We all do,'' Breyten said, pushing his chair back. He'd been squirming in his seat like a small child, waiting for a gap in the conversation so that he could excuse himself. Hektor had been wondering about the tension in his brother. It did not seem that of a man newly and joyously in love.

''Good night,'' Breyten said, and strode off across the expanse of the dining room. Hektor looked after him, wondering.

''Do you want anything to eat?'' Egypt asked Brenda Marr, as she randomly slid open an inlaid wood panel in the anteroom wall. It was something she always did when no one who lived in the house was looking. This opening revealed a long line of polished shoes, arranged by some subtle taxonomy of toe shape.

Brenda sat in a chair, knees together under her loose skirt, carefully wrapped birdcage at her feet. She wondered what significance the shoes had, and why the woman was showing them to her. ''No,'' she said. ''Thank you.''

Egypt slid the panel shut with a bang, as if dismayed at her discovery. She looked bemusedly at Brenda. ''Those shoes are old. Antiques. Xui House is way too big, don't you think? You could lose things in here for centuries. The place is a damn city.''

Brenda didn't say anything. She had more important things to do than chat with house servants. She was waiting for Lon Passman.

"But really," Egypt said. "There's plenty of food left over from dinner. We made too much. Fabian always makes too much. . . ."

Brenda examined Egypt's elaborate gown, totally inappropriate for household service. Things had changed in Scamander, Brenda thought. There had been a time when she had been at many wealthy houses, and servants had never behaved like this. But that time had been chewed up and spit out. No need to think of it.

"When will he see me?"

Egypt shrugged. "I don't know. Fabian's up there right now with your note. Shouldn't be too long. Do you have other appointments tonight?" She eyed the wrapped cage at Brenda's feet.

"Never mind my other appointments," Brenda said, more sharply than she had intended. The dark-paneled anteroom with its countless closets, drawers, and sliding panels made her nervous.

As if by accident, Egypt nudged the cage with her foot. The bird inside burbled and shifted back and forth on its perch.

"A present for Lon Passman?" Egypt said.

"A message." Brenda spoke through gritted teeth. Everything had seemed clear as she made her way through the corridors of Scamander on her way to Xui House. She walked in on Lon Passman, conveyed her message, and went on her way to more important events. Her plans had not included this chattering woman, this impossible house.

Brenda's hair was now washed and combed to lustrous red-brown beauty. She wore a dark green silk suit, like a woman intent on some socially respected business. Her own severance money from Iqbal-in-Coprates had purchased it. She didn't know that her face reflected a barely suppressed rage, though if she'd thought about it she would have felt the tightness of her skin, the hot spots on her cheekbones, the fact that her eyes peered out through slits.

"A message? I'm curious. May I?" Without waiting for an answer, Egypt knelt and pulled the cloth aside.

The decorative pigeon poked its brightly feathered head out, blinked at the light, then withdrew again into the darkness of its cage.

"A message." Egypt peered at Marr, her wide eyes disturbingly penetrating. "A decorative pigeon, just like DeCoven likes to breed. An insult, I suppose. A political statement. For Lon Passman? Whatever for? He doesn't have anything to do with politics anymore."

Brenda just stared down at her, feeling the pressure building behind her forehead.

"And the poor thing's lost feathers. Too close in confinement. Birds are vicious things. Pack them in and they'll peck each other to death. Have you given it water?"

"No," Brenda said. It was nothing she had thought of. Hounslow had told her to pick up the bird and take it to Lon Passman when she conveyed her message, and that was all.

"Oh, for heaven's sake. A dead bird's not insult, it's just stupid. If you want to insult Lon Passman, you should at least do it with some grace. Right? There's a little water room behind that door there. There should be a cup."

The pigeon seller Hounslow had sent Brenda to contact had been grim. A man with some vague sympathy for the Pure Land School, he had nothing to do, no way to act, just filling out his life by selling birds he hated, that he would rather see roasted and served to beggars. His eyes had been buttons, rubbed to dullness by seeing the same thing every day. There had to be a way to bring life to those eyes, to the rest of the eyes in that crowded corridor.

Brenda half opened the door, saw the polished black stone sink, the crystal mirrors that repeated her furious face, then slammed it shut.

"Let it die then," Brenda said.

Egypt looked up, and for the first time perceived the threat she had let into the anteroom of Xui House. Her quick response evaporated on her lips. Brenda loomed, hair cascading down over her shoulders. She radiated heat in the narrow space.

"Well, quite a surprise," Fabian said as he entered the anteroom from the stairs. "He'll see you."

Both women turned to him as if he had interrupted a private conversation. He took in Brenda's blankly enraged glare, Egypt's dark frightened eyes, the cage on the floor, and involuntarily took a step back.

"Egypt, why are you messing with that bird?"

Egypt pulled the cloth back around it, folding it neatly into place. Her fingers were shaking. "It's for Lon. Part of the message."

"Oh." He examined Brenda more carefully. "Do you want to wash before you go up?"

"No!"

"Fine, fine." Fabian quickly regained his equanimity. "Let's go, then."

"Take up your cage, Brenda Marr," Egypt said.

They passed up into the private areas of the house. That was an honor. Lon Passman and Rudolf Hounslow had some old, strong connection that Hounslow had not seen fit to explain to Brenda. She didn't wonder about it. Old things like that didn't matter anymore.

They turned the corner to Lon's rooms. A man with pale hair stood tensely at the closed door. She didn't meet his eyes. Too many people were becoming interested in her here. She was beginning to think the whole thing was a mistake on her part. But she couldn't have disregarded Hounslow's orders.

"My name is Breyten Passman," he said. "Could you pause for a moment?" Fabian had mentioned the visitor, and he had come here to be on guard, over his father's objections that it was unnecessary.

Brenda stopped, still looking ahead, and underwent his intent scrutiny.

"Egypt," Breyten said. "Could you reach into Ms. Marr's hair and remove the knife she has hanging there?"

Egypt looked at him, frightened, then moved slowly, as if reaching to pick up a white-hot bar of iron. Brenda inclined her head to make the job easier.

"You may search me if you like," Brenda said to Breyten, her voice flat. "I don't mind."

Breyten did so, quickly and efficiently, but found nothing else. He looked at the blade in Egypt's hand and grimaced. It was made of decorative metal and could only have injured someone who lay still enough for it to bite soft skin. But no reason to be complacent.

Breyten opened the door, ushered her in, then closed it behind her.

Lon Passman blinked slowly at his visitor, and at what she carried in her hand. He had been preparing for bed, for the dreams that visited him there, and the alteration in his routine disturbed him. And the fact that he had gotten so attached to a routine disturbed him even more. But Rudolf Hounslow had finally replied to his message. He couldn't keep that waiting.

"I take it that Rudolf Hounslow has refused to speak to me," he said to the grim-faced woman. She did not look around at the decades of mementos and honors that crowded the shelves and covered the green silk walls, and didn't even notice that her suit matched the color of the walls.

"He *is* speaking with you," she said.

Lon shook his head emphatically. "No, he is not. Allow me to distinguish between a legal fiction and a reality. I tend to do that, outside of the courtroom. But forgive me, please be seated. I forget my courtesies. It's the hour." He sat down at the round table that held the center of the room. A crystal decanter, lit dramatically by an overhead light, cast prismatic sparkles across the white tablecloth.

She regarded the proffered curve-backed chair with its red cushion distastefully. "No need for courtesies."

"There is always a need for courtesies." He sat and stared at her until she set her cage on the table and sat. Already disturbed by Egypt's earlier scrutiny, the pigeon squawked in alarm.

Against the white of the tablecloth, the cage looked tawdry and cheap. Lon regarded it with distaste. "Petty thing. So what is Hounslow afraid of?"

"Nothing," she said, startled by the question. "He has a message for you. That's all."

Lon was surprised at the anger that surged up inside him. After all these years, Hounslow responded to him by sending a cheaply insulting gift whose import Hounslow probably didn't even understand. How could he, when he did not venture to walk the corridors of Scamander and listen to what was going on there? But Lon understood why Hounslow had not wanted to respond to his communication in kind. Hounslow was afraid.

"That's all? Did Hounslow tell you why he should be mindful of me? Do you understand anything of what's been between us?"

"That's not relevant," she said.

"Oh, of course not. Very well. Give me his message."

" 'Greetings, Lon Passman, from the Pure Land School.' " She spoke like a parrot, not caring about the words. " 'Thank you for your communication. But only if you come out here to join me will you understand.' " Hounslow's message was long, involving a history of the Pure Land School and an account of how Hounslow had come to found it, all common knowledge, all words that had been spoken many times before.

When she was done, he stared at her. "That's it?"

"That's what he wanted to tell you."

"And this." Lon gestured disgustedly at the cage.

"Rudolf Hounslow wants—"

"He wants a lot. But he won't get any of it if he squats on his hams out in Nilosyrtis, keeping his sphincter pure and undefiled." It was like a jolt of ice-cold laurel vodka to remember those treasured insults of the Chamber of Delegates, so long forgotten on the stony judicial bench of Tharsis! Damn the dignity of the judiciary. And God damn Rudolf Hounslow. "When you get back to Nilosyrtis, tell him this. He wants to forget it. He wants to take away what happened and replace it with something else. He can't. Even if he dies, and I die, and all who have ever known us or heard of us die, his act and its responsibilities will still exist. I'm sure this is as clear to you as it is to him. And if the responsibilities are not satisfied, he will not have done his duty. Do you understand me? Rudolf Hounslow will not have done his duty. And he will end his life so, owing."

Lon pulled the cloth away from the cage. The bird burbled in startlement. He opened the cage door and pounded furiously on the top. Beating its wings in terror, scattering feathers, the bird scraped through the tiny opening, through which it had been shoved as a much younger and smaller creature, and flew frenziedly around the room.

Brenda knocked her chair over as she stood and jumped back from Lon's fury. She stared at the suddenly strong man who confronted her in the overdecorated room, his breath chuffing. He was nothing like what Hounslow had described to her. A tired, half-dead old man, he'd said, despised by his sons, rejected and forgotten by his Party, a mere hollow Gabriel figure that had mistakenly survived past its proper time of destruction.

Hounslow did not have the true understanding. She would show him what had to be done. Taking a few strides, Lon jerked open a wall panel, revealing the upper reaches of some vast Scamander corridor. Seeing escape, the bird flew out through it.

"You'll see!" she said. "You'll all see. I'll make it clear to you." And she could see the future clear in her sight, as if it was cut into the flesh of her eyes so that she could never look away from it again. She could see the action Rudolf Hounslow needed her to take.

She took two steps toward Lon. She had no weapons. She had brought none, and the knife in her hair had been an attempt to blend into the style of the place. But she was stronger than he was. Despite his clean rage, he was old.

The door slammed open behind her. Someone leaped, and she felt a hand clamped on her arm. She was whirled around. Another man, another Passman, this one wider and darker than the previous one. That one, Breyten, was in the doorway. She was getting tired of this family.

"Father, are you—"

"That's all right, Hektor," Lon said. "Please let her go. She was just . . . trying to communicate something."

"Have you finished your conversation?" Hektor's voice was high and strained.

"I think so. Ms. Marr?"

Marr turned and walked to the door, her thoughts no longer on him, on any of them. She had things to do.

"Aren't you forgetting something?" She looked back. Lon

handed her the empty birdcage, its door dangling.

"I don't—" It was his last insult to her. Without thought, she cocked her arm to throw it back at him, and found her elbow held in a painful grip by Hektor. She felt his gaze on her. It felt sexual. She knew his kind, from before.

"Didn't you pay a deposit to the seller?" Lon said. "Return it to him." He turned away, dismissing her.

For the first time since entering Xui House, Marr manifested a facial expression. She smiled. It was a sign. The cage was a sign. It made perfect sense.

"All right," she said. "I'll do that."

2

From *Statement of Vigil Jurisdiction in the Case of Louise umm-Haqar*, presented to the Upper Moebius Police by Miriam Kostal, 3 June 2332:

> ... if, as your investigation currently indicates, umm-Haqar was killed in a brawl outside the Scilicet doss-house, as either participant or innocent bystander, then your jurisdiction holds.
>
> However, we have evidence of nonrandom contact [see attached documents]. Umm-Haqar's school was just around the corner, and she often came to Scilicet to lecture and distribute alms. Umm-Haqar was a dissident Sunni Muslim cleric of the New Teaching confession. Her position was controversial and well known. If she was killed by an Old Teaching Sunni who did not accept the reopening of the gates of *ijtihad* [attached summary of theological issues relating to the legal inquiry into the Koran, dating back to the closing of the gates of inquiry in the ninth century], then it is a matter for the Grand Mufti of Scamander and his *ulama*. A Muslim Vigil officer [list of possibilities] will coordinate.
>
> But we have indications that the killing was interethnic and interconfessional, and thus Vigil jurisdiction. Her killer, I believe, was most likely Fra Carduto, a Chaldean pilgrim just back from the Land of Israel, in North Mars, where he apparently suffered a vision. This vision involved the "purifi-

cation'' of Lastregon Corridor, where Louise umm-Haqar had her school. Fra Carduto is still at large. . . .

It was the first time she had visited the house and she found herself unexpectedly nervous. Miriam Kostal looked up at the old arch that marked the side entrance to Xui House. If, as it appeared, it had once been a passageway for vehicles from the lower house into this large, roughly carved space, it was no longer. Thick vertical panes of fused crystal now filled the arch, marked only by one tiny door at one side.

Miriam was a tall woman with typical North Martian Afro-Asian ancestry, though the relative lightness of her skin showed the inevitable admixture of other bloods through the centuries. Her eyes were green-brown, the color of moss agate.

It was brutally early in the morning. The overhead lights were just switching over to physiologically active brightness. She had gotten off night duty, changed in her office, and was here without sleep, just a quick spray in her eyes to get the grit out. Breyten, she knew, would be up early, waiting. Sometimes it seemed that he didn't sleep at all. It would be better if he slept more.

This large, vaulted space had once been an excavation vehicle yard. A no-longer-functioning air lock loomed opposite the Xui House gate, flanked by two obsolete, thick-wheeled excavation vehicles, now enameled bright yellow.

The floor and the walls were blank rock. What had once been the ceiling dome, however, was now covered by the dangling shapes of adhesion dwelling units. As the overhead lights among them grew brighter, they started to disappear from blinded view. Miriam could see mining spoil piled up by a wall. Someone was, illegally, digging through the ceiling overhead, hoping to get access to a more convenient corridor somewhere above, and was too lazy to truck the spoil somewhere else. He'd be in serious trouble soon. Meanwhile, the overhead dwellers had to rely on the spiral stairway that dangled from filament lines bolted into the dome and walls for access to their dwellings. Somewhere up there a child wailed, then was comforted.

City bats were returning to their own dangling perches for the day. One swept by Miriam, its silver helmet gleaming, streamers fluttering out behind it. Bat decorating was a popular corridor hobby, and it looked like the inhabitants of Xui House encouraged it, as one element in a complex of community relations. Bat guano served as a valuable fertilizer for hanging gardens.

She turned and knocked on the resonant panel again, hearing her knuckles echoed somewhere inside the huge house. Two young men in loose overjackets trotted past. They slowed.

"Hey," one of them said. "Want to go to a party?"

"There's no party," she said.

"We'll make one."

The two men's ancestors had clearly come from two widely separated parts of Earth. The talkative one was round-faced and pale, his friend, who automatically squatted down to rest once he had stopped trotting, was dark, with a sharp, beaky nose. Still, they were both, with their relaxed joints, their sagging multi-layered clothes, their cleverly gesturing hands, clearly natives of the Scamander corridors. Miriam, who had grown up on the surface in North Mars, was still getting used to the type.

"No, thanks," she said. "I have another appointment."

The man shrugged elaborately, taking a shuffle and turning it into a dance step. "Well, if you get tired of the legals, climb on up and ask for Sulze."

"I'll do that."

"Come on, Pruf. No luck here." The friend had fallen asleep in his squatting position, with his head on his knees. "Come *on!*"

The friend jumped to his feet. They raced up the hanging spiral stairs, making them rock perilously. With a last wave to Miriam below, they jumped into a dangling entranceway and pulled themselves up into the ovoid of their dwelling. The opening sucked shut and the place hung there in the growing daylight like a dark, sleeping egg.

If she hadn't already had things to do, she might have gone with them. It had been a long time since she'd accepted a chance invitation just to see what would happen.

She felt the door open behind her. She waited a moment, then turned to Breyten and kissed him.

"Come on, come on," he said, pulling her in through the door. The space beyond was crowded with piled black cases larger than transport coffins.

"What is this stuff?" she asked.

He looked around as if only just noticing what was there. "Oh, ancient equipment. Stuff not worth recycling, and left here for lack of anywhere else to put it." He grabbed a hold-point on a hexagonal drive unit for an automatic tunnel drill and swung himself up on it. As Miriam walked along below, he jumped from equipment pile to equipment pile. Once, his weight caused some minute shift in the stack, making it creak, and he grinned down at her, challenging her. She didn't move away.

"Once Hektor and I managed to get around the programming seals on an old air plant and got it started. We thought that maybe the old oxygen would do something for us. Make us see things, the past, I don't know. It made this terrible sound, a wail like it was dying, scared the bejeezus out of Hektor."

"Probably someone in every generation discovers that thing," Miriam said.

"Maybe." The idea didn't please Breyten. He wanted to be the first one to dig through the past of Xui House. An odd ambition, Miriam thought, to be the first one to reexperience the past.

Breyten leaped lightly down from the last stack of obsolete equipment. "Strange doings last night," he said. "Someone tried to kill Father. Hey, do you want some food? Fabian and Egypt put leftovers away in the kitchen."

"Someone tried to kill Lon?"

Breyten thought about the point as if he hadn't been the one to bring it up.

"No, not kill, I think. But it might have come to that. It was tense. Hektor jumped into the room ahead of me, grabbed the woman. He always wants to prove his devotion. I'd disarmed her beforehand, she wasn't a big danger."

"Who was she?"

Breyten carefully did not look at her. "It wasn't political, Miriam."

"Oh, for God's sake!" She really was tired. The night had

been taken up with the preliminary investigation of a possibly ethnically motivated killing in Upper Moebius. She'd just gotten the determination in before heading for Xui House. "I didn't think it was political. I was just curious."

"Police are never just curious." And he put his arm around her. His hand slid up her side. His thumb pressed just under her breast, and she felt excited despite herself. "Right?"

"Oh, we are, always. That's why we become police in the first place."

"I wondered why."

They had first made love without intending to. It was the fault of the view. They had taken a crawler out from Kostalgrad and climbed the parfait slopes of the polar cap. The corrugated dunes of Chasma Boreale opened out below them. The domes and towers of Kostalgrad vanished like a charm a child had lost in the sand. The crumbling, pitted ice was pink with the dust trapped in it. At Breyten's urging they left the crawler and climbed the higher slopes. The ice was safer in the summer, when the cardox had sublimed out of it, but it was never safe. Members of the Kostal family knew better than to climb it. With Breyten, Miriam clambered up past crumbling cornices and through eerie, twisted cracks. They pitched a shelter on a high ridge, stood looking out over Mars, got inside it. The sun didn't set at that season, but spread itself through the layer of horizon dust, making the cap glow beneath them like heated metal. After a while, the mist on the inside of the shelter had obscured the view.

They both paused and looked at each other as a low boom echoed amid the dark equipment. It was a heavy sound, and seemed to roll down the curving ramp from upstairs. It was soon followed by others in rhythmic succession.

"This is outrageous," Breyten muttered.

"What is it?"

"Hektor," he said. "Got to be. Back only a week, and—"

"I don't understand."

"Let's go." He ran and she followed.

As the ramp curved upward, the boom grew louder, and was joined by the sound of other drums. Someone was having a tremendous rhythmic jam session upstairs, quite out of place in the solemnity of Xui House.

Miriam froze at the door to the dining room, stunned. The scene in the vast space was partially concealed by the precariously balanced vortices of colored smoke popular in Scamander festivals. A giant bird, ten meters high, stalked ominously amid a cascade of colored spheres, and the half-naked, sweating drummers swung their mallets with fierce energy as they hung from their complex scaffolding. The gigantic drums lay on their sides, piled up to the balcony.

Breyten, his face distended with rage, was shouting something. At whom? Why did he think anyone could hear him? The giant bird tilted its beaky head to the side as if to examine Breyten with its huge painted eye, feathered eyelashes flopping extravagantly above it. The sunlight from the vaulted ceiling was noonday bright and hot on Miriam's head. The colored balls were being juggled by people lying on their backs and using their bare feet. The balls bounced off one another in elaborate patterns.

Breyten had found someone specific to yell at. She could see him standing over a group of people who sat at a corner of the dining table, charts and diagrams spilled out in front of them. They stared up at Breyten openmouthed, as if he was a sight fully as bizarre as a giant stalking bird or—Miriam blinked—a long-haired goat with spiraling gilded horns a meter long, peacefully chewing its cud as it balanced on a giant ball.

One by one, the drummers stopped pounding on their wall of percussion and turned to pay attention to the conflict below them. Silence spread over the huge room. Balls fell from the jugglers' feet and went rolling under the endless sirenwood dining table. The goat baaed once and jumped lightly from its ball. Miriam tried to entice it over to her, but it stood staring solemnly at her, chewing. Its hooves were gilded too.

"This is private space!" Breyten shouted. "How can you—"

"We were invited. Please—" The speaker was a young woman in a form-fitting dress that exposed her round belly. She didn't get up from her seat.

"I don't remember inviting you. Damn it, stop that!" With a

great leap, Breyten was at the feet of the nervously stalking giant bird. Before anyone could stop him, he jammed his shoulder into the thing's leg. With a strangled yelp, the man inside the mound of feathers fell off his stilts and came crashing to the floor. The bird's head came off and rolled into a corner.

The five people at the table moved closer together. The dark-haired young woman was clearly their spokesman. She attempted a smile.

"Hektor probably didn't tell you. We only talked to him yesterday."

"Oh, of course not." Breyten ignored the man who climbed dazedly out of the ruins of the bird. "Of course not. This isn't even his district, you know that? Not even his district. There's no reason for it, just a lot of excess goddam charm. A man wants to have a peaceful breakfast in his own dining room—"

"We're sorry. We didn't know." The young woman really was quite beautiful. Miriam found herself watching her. She spread her long fingers in apology. "But we needed a place to rehearse our team for the Feast of Gabriel, and Hektor Passman told us we—"

It was Breyten's fierce blue-eyed glare that silenced her. Miriam could see the fury in the rise of his shoulders, in his strangled way of breathing. The V of his pale, almost-white hair gave him the aspect of a predator.

"Oh, of course." Breyten's voice dropped, and he deformed his face to leer at the woman. Leering wasn't one of his skills. "Good old Hektor. He'll do anything for some of that—"

"Breyten, please," Miriam said.

Breyten stood silent and thoughtful among the hissing vortices of smoke, the corridor imitation of the eternal dust devils of the exterior Martian wilderness. The black disks that produced them lay almost invisible on the floor. Everyone stared at him, trying to predict what he was going to do. A man and woman in the top rank of drums seemed to be making a bet.

"Excuse me." Breyten inclined his head to the woman with sudden cordiality. She watched him calmly.

Breyten plunged his hands into several containers that stood near the table, and trailed the piezoelectric particles into the dust vortices, filling them with coruscating lights.

"My brother's smarter than I am," Breyten said. "How did that happen?" He smiled around at everyone.

Breyten then leaped lightly up on the drum scaffold. At a brusque gesture from him, a drummer gave up his mallets. Breyten glared at the drummer and danced lightly with the mallets, moving them as if they were blunt weapons, not part of a musical instrument.

His perch on the scaffold was precarious, but Breyten moved as easily as if he was on solid ground. The drummer looked around for support, but the others moved away, more interested in what was going to happen next than in protecting their friend.

With a sudden frenzied gesture, Breyten struck the largest drum, a gigantic cylinder wider than he was tall. He swung both mallets together with all his strength, holding nothing back. The translucent drumhead flexed in, then back out with a resounding boom, almost knocking Breyten from his perch. He laughed, a hysterical sound, and started beating on a set of smaller drums with rhythmic insistence.

Slowly, reluctantly, a couple of the other drummers began to elaborate on his simple cadence. Breyten matched them, adding a few swings at dangling ceramic bells.

The dark woman at the table shrugged, waved an arm, and the jugglers started tossing their balls again. One by one, the other drummers joined in. Breyten looked around himself, grinning with manic energy. Miriam could see his chest heaving with the effort. The man from the giant bird, however, just stared gloomily down at the ruins of his figure, holding the head in his hands.

The sound was painful. Miriam moved into the partial sound shadow of one of the giant piers. Breyten should tire of this soon enough. . . . The goat trotted after her, but did not come any closer.

"Here," a woman's voice said. "Give him this. Scented storax. It's his favorite. Good, because his breath used to be foul." Miriam looked down at the chunk of transparent golden resin in her hand, then at the dark-haired young woman who had followed her. She was even more beautiful close up, with wide slanting eyes and full lips. ''My name's Pamaot. So that's Hektor's brother.''

''Yes.'' Miriam held out the storax. The goat walked up slowly. Its horns really were triumphs of irrational selective breeding. It reached its head out carefully, and finally nipped the resin out of her hand. Then it darted back and resumed chewing. The smell of the resin permeated the air.

The woman peeked out from around the pier, hands on her narrow hips, and shook her head. ''Different. Really different.''

''Are they? I've never met Hektor.'' Miriam found herself curious. Hektor had been away on Earth, and Breyten's descriptions of him, while always affectionate, had been somewhat distant, as if Breyten didn't remember his brother all that well.

''Well, I have.'' Pamaot smiled slowly, and Miriam suddenly realized that Breyten's unworthy suspicion about Hektor's motivation might have some truth in it. Still, if Hektor had dragged this mob in here to increase his chances of making love to this woman, it made perfect sense.

''Can you get him out of here?'' the woman said. ''He can't drum to save his life. We have an important rehearsal to get on with. Plus, we have to start fixing the bird. Dexter's pretty upset. I can calm him down, but . . . I don't want any trouble. Not with the Passman family.''

''Sorry about that,'' Miriam said. ''I'll get him. We have work to do anyway.'' Work. That was right. She had, ostensibly, come to Xui House to help catalog the Xui House arms collection.

Old weapons had always been her hobby, and her family had hoped that they would be her profession too. It was a genteel, respectable occupation, the examination of points and edges so old that the blood had evaporated off them. Famous duels were commemorated. Families traced their history. And Miriam had a natural connoisseur's eye.

Instead, she had joined the Vigil, and involved herself in gambling, organized crime, and politics.

Miriam climbed up and physically dragged Breyten off the scaffold. He affected to struggle. She could feel the muscles sliding under his skin as they wrestled. It was embarrassing, in front of this many people. A chill went down her spine as she felt a hard shape dangling down under his arm, something she'd missed while hugging him at the gate. She didn't run a corridor beat, and it wasn't the sort of thing one encountered much at Kostalgrad, but she recognized what it was. It was bad she hadn't noticed it before, even though one did not normally embrace a lover to search him for concealed weapons. She pulled him along with greater force after that, and Breyten, feeling the real strength she was using, almost resisted.

As soon as they were out of the dining room, he kissed her and she grabbed onto him. He was lean and hard, the way she liked it, and she liked the bitter taste of his lips and his tongue that was almost sharp. He was still clumsy at times, squeezed too hard, pushed too hard, but he wasn't used to women. He'd told her that, but he hadn't had to. It was all right, and they could spend the day looking at edged weapons together, like a good couple.

But she couldn't ignore what he had under his jacket. She pulled back. "What are you playing at, Breyten?"

"What are you talking about?" he said, like a small boy denying the obvious.

"Come on. I've searched enough corridor punks to—"

"To understand? I don't think so."

Breyten reached into his jacket and pulled it out—a short bowel-smasher of the sort popular among small-time enforcers. Painful, nonfatal, no marks. Black and fashionable, with silver trim. Breyten held it loosely in his hand, and Miriam imagined him swinging it in a short, cruel arc, his victim doubled over, retching. He met her eyes, then slid the club back into his jacket. If he'd been someone she was observing in a corridor, she would have noticed it immediately. He wasn't adept at concealing it.

"It's hot down there in the lower corridors," he said. "People fight sweating naked there every day."

A few weeks ago, he'd been in pain from a cracked rib and hadn't let her hug him. A fall while climbing, he'd told her. The bruise, when she saw it, didn't look at all like anything caused by a fall. She'd seen plenty of bruises like that during police training. She just hadn't been paying the right sort of attention.

"What are you doing, Breyten?" It could have been a hell of a fight out there in the dining room, she realized. The corridors, brought right into Xui House. Lon Passman would have loved it.

"Trying to find a way to live. You found a way to live, didn't you? Why shouldn't I?"

He hated the way she had found to live. She could see that in his eyes, and see the bulge of the club in his elegant silk jacket.

It was an effort of will for her to reach out and take his hand. "You should. Yes."

"All right. Let's go on, then."

With a secret gesture, Breyten opened a hatch concealed in the floor. Below was a low, narrow tunnel that had once been a water-supply pipe, now dry and sifted with forgetfulness. He grabbed a flashlight from the supply locker on the wall and jumped in. After a moment of hesitation, she climbed down after him and, hunched over, followed past an endless line of access ports. She realized that they had moved far out from the outer edges of the house.

"They dug a trench and dropped the statues down here in the spoil zone under the cliff edge," Breyten said. "All lined up neatly, like bodies."

A vast face appeared in the wall. Miriam met its heavy-lidded gaze. The ceramic face had no individuality at all.

"Ecumenical Patriarchs," Breyten said. "They used to be all over Scamander during the Orthodox Empire. Then, when it was all done with and the Empire was over, they were just removed. I used to imagine screaming mobs pulling the statues down, hauling them through the corridors on crude carts, flinging them from the top of the cliff. . . ."

"But they didn't," Miriam said.

"No. I found out later that it was just a contract. Some private agency. The kind of thing Hektor likes to fuss with. I guess that even during the Tumults there were private agencies, contracts, dealings . . . they just sprayed sealant inside them, put valves in the bases, and used them as ancillary water storage for Xui House. Tried to get some use out of them, anyway.''

Miriam felt the blood pounding in her ears. This water pipe was constricting, but not constricting enough. She still had room to move. She slithered her way in through the base of a Patriarch's robe. Endings and beginnings should happen in places that imprinted themselves on the memory. The beginning was in a misted shelter on top of the crumbling ice of the polar cap. The end . . .

Encrustations, secret growths. Odd struts like the spongy interior of cancellous bone. An enclosed smell, something forgotten but alive—rare on Mars, where death was dry and ionized. Overall, a polymeric slickness, forbidding contact.

''The coating eventually cracked,'' Breyten said, spraying the light forward through the thin neck into the further chamber, seeing the reflection of an Orthodox cross set behind the statue's forehead. ''The water started to leak.''

Her skin was hot under his fingers and her body shook with her breathing. He clicked the light beam off but left the residual glow.

''Come on,'' he said. ''Come on.''

It was difficult, maneuvering in the tight space, just the way she wanted it to be. He slid down and, like a gentleman, lay down on the hard surface and let her kneel on top of him.

Usually she moved slowly, but this time she moved as fast as a man. She had to bend her head down to keep from hitting it against the low ceiling that was the Patriarch's belly. Anger flowed out of the heat of her groin, and she knew she was hurting herself, but couldn't stop. Damn him. Her knees pounded on the floor. He reached, slid her shirt up, and held the sides of her rib cage. She didn't take his hands, as she usually did. And she didn't look at him. Breyten didn't moan, as he usually did to please her, but she heard his breath come faster and faster.

After, she climbed off him, and out of the toppled statue. She tugged up the one trouser leg she had removed. She was crying. She didn't know it until she found it out with her fingers, the same way you'd unexpectedly find blood welling out of an unfelt cut. He climbed out after her. Her hair was too short to hide her face, so she didn't turn to look at him.

"Let's go," she said. "I have work to do in the Armory."

Once, when Breyten, Hektor, and Zoë were children, there was a sandstorm. They were common around the solstice when the atmospheric pressure was highest. It came up fast and dark and held down all surface transportation. Scamander ignored it, for Scamander had burrowed under the rock and the hissing anger of the dust concerned it not at all.

The three of them played in the hall near the Armory. It had been long centuries since such storms had threatened the surface camps of the first settlers. But somehow, through some atavistic need to hide in a cave, the three children had come here, to the rocky center of Xui House, far from their usual arenas of play.

Breyten hauled his wooden blocks on a wheeled cart, and commenced the construction of a series of bastions and ravelings, a structure of ebony, satinwood, and carmine. Hektor was permitted to assist, as long as he understood his subordinate position. He tried to comprehend the plan, asked endless questions, but was told just to put each block in its designated place. Irritated, Hektor distracted himself by putting Breyten's toy soldiers in amusingly compromising positions with some of Zoë's dolls.

This made Breyten angry, and made Zoë cry. Hektor apologized frantically to both of them. Finally, Zoë smoothed everything over by inviting everyone—soldiers, dolls, Hektor, and Breyten—to tea.

Zoë paused halfway through pouring an imaginary cup of tea, and listened, head cocked.

"It's in here," she said.

"What is?" Breyten asked.

"The storm. In the sand room. Can't you hear it?"

"The sand—" They all held their breath, trying to be as silent as possible, and suddenly they did indeed hear it, a gentle, distant hissing.

"Is the sand room behind here?" Hektor pressed his hand against the wall.

"Yes! It's where Momma and Poppa keep it. They must have let it outside. It has to be let out sometimes, just to play."

Hektor and Breyten both looked at her. She was old enough to know better, of course, but Zoë always had an oddly romantic turn of mind, and her faith in the power of their parents was absolute. It was part of the ventilation system in there, no more. Still, as they sat in the half-dark room together, it began to seem that it was the eternal sifting of sand and dust deep within the wall, as if the external world of Mars was just a coincidental manifestation of Xui House itself. Thereafter, all three children called whatever lay behind the wall "the sand room." At times, all Mars was the sand room.

Sara Passman was an operations chief with North Tharsis Rescue. A single vehicle had tried to make it from Tharsis Tholus to Hebes before this storm hit. It had failed. Once the wind died down, Sara Passman went out to the wrecked vehicle. This time she took her children with her.

The crawler had tried to hunker and pull itself into the sand. A futile action. It lay overturned and twisted, having been tossed for kilometers across the rocky plain that extended north of Tithonium. Its coordinates had been entered into Sara's computer directly from the surveillance satellite. Still, it was Zoë who first saw the glint of sunlight off the stripped metal of the destroyed crawler.

Before their mother could stop them, the children climbed up and stared through the windows of the shattered crawler. Two figures were huddled against each other, obscured by dust.

"Please get down now," Sara said distractedly. A larger recovery vehicle was lumbering down their crawler tracks toward them. Its rear precipitator was malfunctioning, and it sent a huge rooster-tail of dust into the now-clear air.

Zoë settled down to play, digging in the infinite sand and dust with a small blue shovel. Over her skintite she wore a yellow dress, with formal high boots. She didn't try to build anything out of the indolent dust, but just let it sift down from her shovel until she had created a large area that was completely smooth.

She marked an abstract picture in it with her fingertips, then sifted it smooth again.

The recovery truck hooked onto the destroyed crawler and hauled it away. Breyten stood on top of it for a while, balanced precariously as it bounced along, ignoring the angry waves of the driver, until he lost interest and jumped off.

"They were doing something out here, weren't they?" Hektor asked his mother. "They weren't just racing."

"Lovers," she said, finally. "Their marriage was forbidden in their city. They thought they would have a better time of it in Scamander." She looked back in the direction from which they had come. "They would have, if they had made it."

And that was as much as Hektor ever learned. A dramatic story lay behind it all, no doubt—desperate passion, stern resolve, a grand double death. But the story never came out, and Hektor never learned the names of those two who had died in the name of love. After their crawler was hauled away and recycled, there was nothing left but a scrabble of marks on the wide Tharsis plain, which would vanish with the next storm.

Not too long after that, Sara Passman herself died on a rescue mission.

"No!" Sen Hargin goggled at Brenda Marr. "Rudolf Hounslow didn't say—"

"No." Brenda examined her onetime lover dispassionately. He tried to conceal the fact that the world had beaten him down. He'd been giving her a tour of his little corner of Scamander, and she'd put up with his swaggering all morning. But she still thought he would do. He now knew the consequences of compromise. "Rudolf Hounslow *didn't* say. But he wants action. This is action."

Sen was a slight man with a curling fringe of beard, and still gave the impression of an earnest student. She had been attracted to him at the Pure Land School, but not enough to violate Hounslow's austere rules by having sex with him on a pallet in some storeroom, as would ordinarily have been her solution. She wondered if he knew that.

"Action. We *have* action."

"You've got shit, Sen."

He turned away from her and rested his elbows on the railing. A train station cantilevered out far overhead, and its guy wires sang as the glowing lights of a train just in from the east crawled along the dark-sketched magtrack that emerged from a black tunnel mouth. The walkway Sen and Brenda stood on shot through a vast, irregular space called Rhenre. Other walkways passed above and below at unpredictable angles, some climbing up and down on steep stairs without obvious purpose. Magtracks split and rejoined. Just beyond the station, the train separated into its component cars, each getting routed to its individual destination in Scamander. A group of young men sat on a ledge above the walkway and took bets on the decisions of each individual car, cheering them on with idiotic enthusiasm.

"You've got shit." She spoke quietly in his ear. "You haven't done anything, not in the whole time you've been here."

"That's not true. We're ready, just like we're supposed to be. We've made the contacts. We have hold of our area. When the time comes—"

"The time is never going to come. Not unless we do something." She leaned toward him.

Sen called his local cell of Pure Land School alumni an Olympus Club. They lived their lives out here in Scamander, preparing hidey-holes in case of civil conflict, making friends with local citizens, counseling dying old people in low-rent chambers noisy with the rumble of pumped water, fighting with other organized groups for power and respect. The more they worked on these irrelevant things, the more important they seemed.

"I can't allow it," Sen said, feeling his authority slipping away. He ruled the other members of the Olympus Club almost by default. He didn't really have the personality for it, and he had no goals save keeping the little organization together so they would be ready when something happened. Well, Brenda was here. Something was happening.

"What would it take," Brenda said, "for you to make the decision? You want to make it, Sen. I see it. What would it take?"

"I don't need that decision."

"Come on, Sen." She was lightly taunting. "Do you want to fight for what you believe in?"

She was rewarded by a glimpse of a concealed knife-edge of rage in his eyes. Of course he wanted to do something. Of course he felt that his life was completely wasted. But he didn't want to hear that from Brenda, whom he had once so desired. He'd expected her to be impressed by the complex extent of his planning and organization. Instead, she found it all irrelevant.

A train car hissed by right underneath them, and Brenda caught a glimpse of honest citizens who had rearranged their magnetic-adhering chairs into a circle to discuss some important matter. Just above the walkway, piles of climbing equipment were jammed with joyously screaming children. And beyond, spotted with the lights of windows and observation decks, loomed the rough rocks of the cavern in which they hung.

One of the young men above whooped in triumph. "Told you, Pentock. Told you."

"Sure. And what about the last five?"

"Flukes. They didn't know where they were going."

The three men had the bald heads of restaurant workers, though they had vainly tried to conceal the badge of their employment with floppy hats. They were drunk, and the rows of lights from the passing train cars reflected in their glassy eyes. They had all worked long shifts, and had no idea of what to do between now and the next time they dragged themselves into their steaming kitchens. The sight of the small man and the heavy woman with the hair was starting to give each of them the same idea. They had known one another a long time.

"A duel, Sen," Brenda whispered. "Would that give you a way to decide?" She took his arm and swung him to face her.

"Damn it, I—"

"Five on the big woman," a voice said from above.

"Yeah, right, Pentock. I'll give you that."

Sen whirled and looked up at them. "You guys got anything better to do?"

The largest of the young men smirked. "Nope."

They were dressed in sagging garments slashed with bright color, an unsuccessful attempt to mimic the fashions of the down-corridor social crews.

"This is a private discussion," Sen said. "We have a right to talk without having you listen in." His voice was prissy, Brenda thought, just right for stimulating a fight. And he wanted one.

"Private discussion?" The big guy, Pentock, had the sort of round face, geniality crushed by frustration into sour anger, that would have played well as the corrupt uncle in an instructional play for children. "Unpucker, friend. I want to see you two mix it up. My money's on the big round butt."

"Sen—"

Too late. Sen swung up on some concealed handhold, taking a thrown beer right in his face. The three men had the advantage of altitude, the reason they had picked the fight in the first place, but he moved faster than they had expected, and was among them before they could react.

"My money's on the other guy, Pentock!" one shouted. He toppled off his perch and landed heavily on the walkway.

"Screw you!" Pentock managed to land a punch on Sen, who teetered at the edge of the ledge. The other bettor, a bald man, moved to add his weight against Sen.

"Get him down here—I'll finish him off," shouted the man on the walkway as he struggled to his feet. Before he could make it, Brenda kicked him in the temple. He rolled, threw up dramatically, and fell flat.

This was stupid. She should just leave, find some other ally for her plans. Instead, Brenda moved forward, toward the climbing set. A little girl with tightly braided hair hung from some overhanging mesh, then let herself drop toward the floor, five meters below. Her mother, if she had one, did not scream. No one paid any attention. She hit a low, wide trampoline and sailed into the air.

Brenda, surprised, caught her. The girl, ready to play with this stranger, looked up into Brenda's face and, instead, began to scream. Brenda dropped her and the girl ran down the walkway as fast as her little legs could carry her.

The voices of parents and guardians shouted after her as Brenda climbed up the children's play set. Children avalanched off, knowing a bad situation when they saw one. Its holds were meant for tiny hands, and its inside climbing spaces were too small to let Brenda through. She pulled herself up the outside supports, and managed to swing up onto the ledge just as Sen was going over, assisted by the drunkenly laughing Pentock.

Brenda waded into their rear. She smashed the bald man's head into Pentock's, delighting in the hollow thunk.

"Jump, Sen," Brenda said. "Damn it, go."

"We can take them," Sen gasped, blood dripping from the corner of his mouth.

"So what?" Pentock grabbed her from behind. She jabbed both elbows straight back and was rewarded by an oof. "Go!"

Sen rolled off the ledge and landed lightly on the walkway below. The bald man followed him, avoided Sen's wild swing, and fled down the walkway.

"Come on, honey. Now that the rest of them are out of the way . . ." Pentock, chuckling to himself, grabbed at her breasts. It was a useless move. He seemed to have completely forgotten that he was in a fight. He choked as Brenda jammed stiffened fingers into his throat, and lost his grip. She jumped down after Sen.

"Hey, sweetie, don't be a stranger!" Pentock's now-hoarse voice drifted over Brenda and Sen as they ran. Brenda spared an instant to admire his indefatigability.

"What the hell was that?" she asked furiously, once they had taken several random corners and were safely out of the area.

"It's all about instilling discipline," Sen said. "That's basic. We need discipline if anything's going to change."

"You call that discipline? Beating up punks in the corridors just because they've insulted you?"

Brenda didn't know about the rest of the Olympus Clubs, but this cell of Hounslow's Scamander organization was barely distinguishable from any other corridor crew. It maintained some of the rhetoric of the Pure Land School, and still inquired into Stoic and Neo-Confucian texts, but was otherwise little more than a surly social club. The outside world was stronger and more persistent than Hounslow had given it credit for.

Sen didn't answer, but just dabbed blood from his mouth, then looked at the spots on his handkerchief as if they contained some sort of message.

"This is serious, Sen. I want you with me. I *need* you."

He stood and stared at her. His eyes were big in his head, and his head was big on his body.

"All right," Sen said. "We'll talk to the others—"

"Not until we have a decision." Sen still wanted her. She could tell by the way he looked at her. She didn't want sex. Not now, and the liberation from that demand was one of the things that made her new mind so clean to be in. But she would use his desire, if it was necessary to get things done.

He knew what that meant. "In front of all of them."

"That would be best. Which of you keeps the weapons?"

"Tri. Do you remember her?"

Brenda nodded. Their time at the Pure Land School had overlapped. A good woman.

"She'll be my second," Brenda decided. "When do you want to fight?"

"Tomorrow morning. I know a good spot where the police don't come."

"Excellent." Brenda slung an arm around Sen's shoulder as they walked down the crowded corridor. "It will be a pleasure dueling with you after all these years, Sen Hargin."

Hektor perched on the edge of his seat. His view of the table was partially blocked by an abandoned service cart, its burden of steamed buns and fried noodles gone cold. With a glance at his fellow observer, a Delegate named Arenas from Hohen-Tinta, he nudged the cart over. Arenas was dead asleep, her head tilted over, so that she was almost resting on Hektor's shoulder. Another time he might have been interested. She had beautiful brown eyes. When they were open. She was the one who had gotten him into the empty observer slot. This wasn't a very important meeting.

Under Governor-Resident Sylvia Rodomar held the attention

of the Union Liaison Group without even speaking. She had her head turned to whisper something to Jay Carter, the most infamous of the three consorts she had brought with her from Earth. Carter stared forward as she spoke, the slight drift in his left eye giving him a look of holy ecstasy. Carter was from somewhere in North America, and had come to Mars only a few months before, but two chromed valves gleamed at his throat. His first act on arriving had been to visit a down-corridor surgery shop. He had a carbon dioxide indicator buzzing in his pinkie finger too, as the shining polish of that fingernail indicated. Hektor remembered him risking his neck on an ice cliff near Cuzco, purely to entertain his mistress.

Native Martians only displayed their tracheal attachments that way when on Earth, and modestly concealed them at home, a subtlety apparently lost on the ardently assimilationist Carter. On Palawan, Hektor understood, Carter had worn a sarong and had a kris made to his specifications. He wondered if the Filipinos had found the whole thing as amusing as Martians did.

Few enough Union administrators traveled with two official consorts, much less three, but Rodomar's very excesses gave her status, as if her appetites enlarged her abilities. All three were competent men, and trustworthy, lovers of long standing. In fact, since each of them had his own useful specialty, and was legitimately able to draw a full salary as a member of her private secretariat, three began to seem like simple prudence, rather than rampant sexual excess.

Rodomar brought her hand down, a pat on the massive ironwood table that clattered with her many rings. Her hair, brindled light and dark, was piled on top of her head. Her face was square, with wrinkled, sleepy eyelids. She had played lacrosse, hockey, and soccer in college, and her body still retained heavy muscle.

"If the Chamber of Delegates wants to allocate public funds for relief, the Governor-Resident's office certainly will not object. No workers should suffer for the crimes of their employers if they did not personally benefit."

"That's right," Governor-Resident Oswald DeCoven said in his reedy voice. He squinted down at his display. "Dortex-

Comm, Llando Style, Iqbal-in-Coprates . . . I must say, I admire the Chamber's quick action in this matter.''

Hektor took a glance around the table, but everyone—from Water Supervisor Michaela Techadomrongsin to Trevor al-Fiq, the Chamber Finance Chairman—looked perfectly serious. Nan Costra, Transport Chairman, doodled on a pad. Hektor had heard rumors that she was slated for investigation over irregular bidding on the new Hellas Planitia magtrack. If true, the prim, gray-haired Costra didn't show it: her doodles were various versions of the proposed concentric-shield logo of the Hellas project. Trep sat slumped in his seat, glowering around him as if kidnapped and held by enemies.

The Rodomar-led anticorruption drive had netted some high figures in recent months. Both Delegates and business leaders now sat in the preventive detention chambers set in the south cliff of Ius Chasma, telling time by shadows cast into the depths of the canyon. Their departure, and the sealing of their offices, had created economic chaos far beyond predictions—although part of that was due to deliberate play-dead tactics on the part of their subordinates and coconspirators.

The result was sudden unemployment among their workers, and resulting disaffection, calling the entire anticorruption drive into question. If corruption led to employment, then what was the problem with it? The question was rarely asked that bluntly, but the thought was there. Given the popularity of the drive against corruption just a few short months before, the turnabout was astounding. Hektor knew that Martians had a reputation for government by whim, and now he could see why Terrans felt that way.

The Governor-Resident could veto a Martian Chamber money bill, Hektor supposed. It was in the Treaty of Jakarta. But the result would be a serious crisis. At the very least, DeCoven and Rodomar would be recalled to Earth to testify before the Council of Nationalities. Thus: cheerful approval of a probably corrupt bill. Eating shit and calling it ice cream was the essential skill of colonial administrators.

Trep perked up. ''Is that it?''

''Just about.'' Oswald DeCoven put his long, dark hands on

the smooth surface of the ironwood table. His finger joints hurt at night and he suspected that fine Martian dust had somehow seeped through his skin and pooled between his bones. He'd be coughing it out of his abraded lungs for years after returning to Earth. If he ever made it back there.

"The Feast of Gabriel is in two weeks." He smiled tightly. DeCoven tried to make even ceremonial points seem like they concealed some subtle maneuvering. No one at the Liaison table was fooled. It was the only thing he had left. Rodomar had stolen away with all decisions of substance.

"I want to add to my appearance in Rahab Hex." He cleared his throat. "Pigeons. I want to add pigeons."

"Pigeons." Trep seemed to be noting the word.

"Of course." DeCoven was nettled. Everyone secretly made fun of his hobby. "It will make a lovely display. I can arrange it with the festival coordinators . . . Falu will help out. He's the only man for the job."

Trep frowned his heavy brows, but there was nothing overtly objectionable in the request. The Vigil was partially responsible for the Governor-Resident's safety during the Feast of Gabriel festivities, which meant he would have preferred that DeCoven stay in his rooms with his head under the covers, but if the Governor-Resident wanted to show himself to the people, that was part of the job.

Falu Kallender. Nice move, Hektor thought, though politically senseless. Kallender, as even Hektor had heard, was slated for investigation. But if Kallender was scheduled to make a personal appearance with the Governor-Resident of Mars at the planet's most significant public festival, it would look damn bad if Trep hauled him off and threw him in jail. A real arrest with actual, specific charges would have been different, but this was to be a simple investigative detention. DeCoven, with desperate generosity, might just have gotten his friend a few more weeks of freedom. Perhaps by that time enough records could end up missing for Kallender to stay free. It wasn't as if there weren't enough other people for the Vigil to arrest.

"Pigeons," Trep said again.

"Can you manage it, Colonel? I hope I've given you sufficient notice."

Trep examined him, carefully expressionless. "We can manage it. Just keep us informed about the . . . pigeon situation."

"Oh, rest assured, I shall."

Rodomar was already talking over her shoulder to another of her consorts, the slim Asian man named Askase. Probably planning dinner, DeCoven thought sourly. Askase was a cook of great repute, but the Governor-Resident had never been invited over for a meal. Sylvia Rodomar, most likely, did not want DeCoven to see her in a relaxed state. If she had a relaxed state. Her breasts were stainless steel. He was surprised her consorts did not have conical holes drilled in their chests.

"The meeting is adjourned," DeCoven said, keeping a sigh out of his voice.

Before leaving, he made a point of shaking Hektor Passman's hand. "I met your father once, years ago."

"Of course. He sends his greetings."

The young man was lying, of course. Lon Passman couldn't stand DeCoven. But it was a noble effort. "He was in the running for the Fossic Party chairmanship at the time, I think. I've always thought they made the wrong choice there."

Hektor shrugged. "My father has found, somewhat to his dismay, that he is an excellent Justice."

DeCoven managed a smile. So young, so eager . . . this Hektor Passman had just returned from Earth. DeCoven hoped he had learned something there. He wanted to ask what rumors Passman had heard around the Esopus Palace, where Rodomar had so much influence of late, but he couldn't bear to do it. Besides, who would have told this minor character anything?

DeCoven returned to his quarters down the narrow stone hallways. The walls had cracked and been resealed. Union House, the place was called, and it clung to the top of the canyon wall of Tithonium like a boil. It was one of the few surface structures on the planet, an actual honest-to-God *building*, and had stood for over a century and a half. Well, stood. It had been half blown up during the Time of Tumults, and lay long in ruins until being repaired thirty or forty years before, during the reign of Diomede II.

It was a stupid place, easy to attack and difficult to defend. Drop a rock on it and there would be nothing but eggshell shards and blood. Cut its connection to Scamander's systems and it would choke and dry up. It did have a nice sort of Byzantine-Palladian look, though, and, with the windows glowing, came out great in photographs. Only people from Earth cared what buildings looked like from the *outside*.

"There, there," he said. "I'm back. Here, Mannikin, let's see that spot." He reached into the cage that filled a corner of his bedroom, and Mannikin, a spectacular Queen Victoria-crowned pigeon, perched on his finger. One of the other birds had been pecking at it, causing it to lose some of the spectacular white-tipped blue feathers on its head.

Bird breeding was a popular hobby on Mars, where other animals were almost impossible to keep. Meetings with fellow fanciers were one of the few things DeCoven looked forward to. He'd made his closest friends there: Lars Song, Falu Kallender.

And now . . . he frowned to himself. Falu had been bitter lately. Some dubious investments in a new water mine, a deal with the local Delegate . . . Falu had been closemouthed about the whole thing, but it sounded serious. And Falu seemed to blame him! It was outrageous. As if Oswald DeCoven had anything to do with this goddam mess.

He flipped his finger and Mannikin flew into the air. She floated there, a spectacular show of fluttering feathers. Perhaps the honor of showing his birds off during the Feast of Gabriel would sweeten Falu Kallender's mood. And DeCoven would have a chance to explain how it was all Rodomar's doing, how he himself had no interest in causing trouble. He just wanted to fill out his tour of duty in peace.

Mars was a profitable place, DeCoven thought as he unpinned his sleeves and let them fall forward over his wrists. That was what the sighing court functionary had told him in that frigid winter room at the Esopus Palace when informing him of his appointment as Governor-Resident of Mars. So it had proved, almost true enough to make up for the melancholy savagery of the place. But that would be certain only when he finally put his butt on a soft cushion on a porch in Barbados and had a rum punch served him by a bosomy serving girl with flowers in her hair. As he stood there in that cold, still room, he could smell the perfume on her neck, taste the softness of her lips, and her weight would be gentle on his thighs. . . .

The thought of appearing in Rahab Hex suddenly turned his bowels to water. Trep had contempt for his pigeons, for him. Trep didn't know how much courage it took for DeCoven to confront those thousands of screaming Martians packed into the vast underground space, all of them outraged at the unexpected changes taking place in their lives. But he would show those rock worms a thing or two.

Besides, he risked his life every night, didn't he? Every night, by letting someone into his bed, no matter how much vetting the Vigil did. A silk camisole lay draped over the bed's footboard. He picked it up. Her scent still clung faintly to it. Selima, her name was. Tonight was probably her last night with him. She had a solid, negotiable savings account now, and could go home to live. She could keep the camisole. Its pale green suited her skin. DeCoven liked the idea of a piece of intimate clothing he'd given a woman exciting another man. The woman would never tell where it had come from, of course, or the circumstances of its first wearing. It was a small but guilty secret, and he shared in it.

"Here, sweetheart," he said. "Back in the cage. There." The pigeon floated spectacularly across the room, a shot of vibrant blue.

Oswald DeCoven sat down nervously on the edge of the bed to await the arrival of that evening's lover.

Sara Passman lost her air on a routine mission near the scarp that ran north of Hebes. Lost her air and fell off the outside of the flat, equipment-covered rescue crawler and vanished somewhere in the edges of Lunae Planum.

For days, that seemed like an illusion to her three children. With frenzied meticulousness they imagined her walking out of

Lunae Planum, and marked her route on a map. She could wash her air with a carbon dioxide filter, find oxygen in rocks, recycle her water. . . . At her brothers' instruction, Zoë drew little pictures of a struggling Sara. Zoë's draftsmanship was by far the best of the three children, and though she was a little frightened by the intensity of her brothers' imagination, she did their bidding as well as she could, and drew those images of what should have been. Breyten still had all those drawings stored away somewhere. Hektor had never been able to look at them again.

But of course Sara was dead. The funeral came and went, a sad affair with no body. They were silent in that house then, for a long time.

It was Zoë who conceived of the idea of finding their mother's body and bringing it back to Xui House for a proper burial. She'd had a dream. The details of it were hazy and contradictory, but Zoë suddenly decided that what most needed to be done was to find Sara and bring her back. Her desperate need persuaded her brothers of the same thing. They had all been waiting, silent, waiting for something to do.

Suddenly the three of them found themselves together on the North Rim Train, transferring to Hebes, their backpacks filled with survival equipment pilfered from Sara's personal stores. Breyten, the oldest, and used to such excursions up Valles Marineris, took charge, shepherded them through the transfer points, bought them food at the stands.

It was crazy, of course, and both Hektor and Breyten were old enough to know that. Neither of them had ever been young enough *not* to know it. But Zoë was so certain, as if she had seen a vision, and Breyten so excited by the chance to *do* something, that Hektor was taken away by the force of their enthusiasm. It was so seductively heedless of the existence of obstacles. It made no sense at all, this belief that a strong enough passion could throw a bridge over an impossible chasm, could make rain fall out of the dusty Martian sky, could bring forth the form of their mother from the endless chaotic terrain of Lunae Planum. It made no sense—and they pooled the money they had, all saved for other purposes, and bought their tickets for Hebes.

Zoë thought they would find Sara huddled just outside the westernmost air lock at Hebes. She flicked her eyes over the great dunes of spoil that surrounded all Martian cities—and it should have been at this point that despair overtook her, for the mounds were endless, the plowed road between them as tiny as a punctuation mark in a vast document. Instead, she pulled out the map, the fictional map they had drawn while hoping for their mother's survival. Now, still fictional, it would serve to find her after her death.

They were out a week. Bright sun, sharp shadows, a deluded sense of purpose. They had coordinates for the path of the crawler, and an estimate of where Sara Passman had been lost. The boulder-strewn wilderness had no relief, so there were a million different paths that were all equally reasonable. They walked along in a tight group, seeking minute variations in surface compression that might indicate the passage of a desperate woman on foot.

At night they erected their shelter, cooked their supper, and slept piled together like puppies. To Hektor, later, a large chunk of his memories of his siblings came from this one week. Zoë eating her soup, talking about her friends at school and speculating as to what they might be doing at that moment. And Breyten telling the story of how Fan Ruoushui failed his official examinations but then worked all alone, trailing silk strings in the water to understand the currents of the Yangzi, and figure out the way to build a dragon-boat bridge across the great river, enabling the Emperor Taizu of Song to reconquer southern China. The story of a bridge that floated on the swirling surface of an impossibly wide river, told in a tent pitched on the impossibly dry surface of Mars, while Zoë rested her sleepy head on his shoulder and Breyten stared straight ahead, seeing a task—Hektor wished his whole life could be both that story and the telling of it.

When they finally gave up and returned to the inner, real life of Mars, they were half mad. "Dust madness" was a recognized syndrome in Martian society, for it was known that the endless, pointless, landmark-less wastes of the surface were inimical to human reason. So perhaps they weren't to be blamed for their actions.

Near the air lock were a few sellers of trinkets and steamed buns. Hektor, Breyten, and Zoë were all starving. They had taken enough rations with them to survive for another week at least, but survival was not all their young bodies demanded. They fell eagerly on the bun seller and, to his delight, consumed the entire contents of his steamer without even sitting down.

There was fierce joy in that food, with the overwhelming power food has to a young mouth. And it may be that, finally sated, licking the last traces of oil from their fingers, they felt guilty, for in those moments they had completely forgotten their mother, who had kept them fed for so many years. Maybe that was the explanation.

Right next to the bun steamer was a seller of old jewelry. He had some ancient pieces: Orthodox crosses, silver raindrops from when terraforming had seemed possible, matrix-encased butterfly wings on beaded gold bodies. And, hanging up high, a heart-shaped locket. Very simple, nothing you would ordinarily pick out.

It was Breyten who concluded that the locket was the one Sara had been wearing when she left the house. She had a number of lockets, and at least one of them was shaped like a heart. The jewelry seller had clearly found Sara's body and taken the locket from it. The conclusion was obvious and instant. In later years, all Hektor remembered after that was jewelry flying, the jewelry seller shouting, running feet, Zoë's hair streaming, hands seizing him. . . .

Standing over the scene, hard and dominating, was Lon Passman. The jeweler stammered an explanation, interspersed with questions, while holding the side of his head, where Breyten had hit him. The three children were absolutely silent, feeling the yawning depths of their stupidity, but a surprisingly gentle question from Lon brought forth their justifications. He listened, shook his head, and cut them off. They'd been missing for a week, it suddenly occurred to both Breyten and Hektor. They hadn't said where they were going.

While they found the scattered jewelry on the floor and picked it up, Lon bought the heart-shaped locket. The seller protested— I acquired it fairly, not from any body. Lon cut him off, told him he knew, he understood, but he still wanted to purchase it. He snapped it open for a moment to look on the image inside, and Hektor caught a glimpse of a dark-skinned woman with two young children. Not Sara, not anyone he had ever seen. It was just a glimpse, but Hektor knew that for the rest of his life he would wonder who that woman was, and what had happened to her that her locket would be hanging there for sale in a corridor in Hebes.

They'll work for you, Lon told the jewelry seller. They will come here, clean up for you, take care of your booth. No, no, the man said. They lost their mother, it's a hard thing. I understand. They behaved badly, but it's so hard. It's all right. Take them home now. It looks like the children need a rest.

"Oh, good," Breyten said. "You're both here. That will save some explaining."

He pulled the door shut behind him, as if there were someone else in the house who could overhear them.

"Brandy, Breyten?" Lon asked. He had filled the decanter in the center of the table. Hektor had already had two snifters and was feeling pleasantly woozy.

"Sure, why not?" Breyten rarely drank. True to form, he took a snifterful, sloshed it around, sniffed at it as if suspecting poison, then set it down and ignored it. Hektor, who hated to see good liquor go to waste, put a mental timer on it. If he didn't pick it up in half an hour, Hektor would switch snifters and finish it.

"Hektor was just recounting today's Liaison Group meeting for me," Lon said. He sat back in the reading chair with the high, curved back and smiled, fingers intertwined over his belly. He enjoyed having both his sons with him. It didn't happen often.

"Oh, of course." Breyten was distracted. "Exciting?"

"I wouldn't say so," Hektor said. "Enlightening, maybe."

Breyten peered at his brother as if worried about being tricked.

Then he shook his head. "Father, why did you ever think I was the one suitable for a political career? It's clear that it's Hektor's forte."

"Because you would be, Breyten, if you were more patient."

"That's like saying I would be suitable for the priesthood if I believed in God."

Lon's laugh had a note of sadness in it. He had never gotten over Breyten's total lack of interest in any of the ambitious plans made for him.

"Enlightenment comes from watching Sylvia Rodomar lash us Martians on our way," Hektor said. "*She* has patience. Her whip hand must be getting tired by now."

"Did she acknowledge your earlier meeting?" Lon asked.

"No," Hektor said. Her eyes had flicked past him without a hint of recognition.

"Perhaps it was not politic at that point," Lon said.

"Perhaps it wasn't important." Hektor felt annoyed with himself for being so disappointed. It wasn't as if he'd pulled a thorn from her paw. He'd just chatted with her while watching Carter risk his neck on a cliff.

Breyten jumped out of his seat and paced around the room like a caged tiger. He stopped at a shelf and picked up a silver double-headed ax, an award from some juridical society. He turned, still holding it, and opened his mouth to speak. Then he closed it again. He set the award back in its place, then adjusted it so that it was exactly parallel to the edge of the shelf.

"Father, who was that woman?" It wasn't what he had originally planned to say. "Last night's woman, I mean. Not this morning's." He glared at the bewildered Hektor, who had no idea how much Pamaot had annoyed Breyten.

"It's not who she is that's important," Lon said. He started to lean forward in his chair and Hektor was there, adding brandy to his glass. Hektor tried not to notice the way Breyten's lips compressed. Breyten never saw the need to cater to Lon's needs, but then, he didn't have to.

"She was a messenger from an old . . . acquaintance of mine. Rudolf Hounslow."

"The Pure Land School," Hektor said quickly, to display his

knowledge. "In Nilosyrtis. At any rate, they were there when I left Mars."

"Oh, they're still there, all right," Lon said. "Rudolf's still building his Neo-Confucian structure on Martian soil. All financed by those novels he wrote."

This was a new one on Hektor. "What novels? I remember he ran for office once, but I didn't know . . ."

"He wrote under the name of Samantha Siirt."

Breyten was galvanized. "Really? He wrote *Young Cliffs* and *The Last Climb*?"

"The same," Lon said.

"And he's still legally allowed to run a school?" Hektor said. "Miss Samantha's books were . . . delightfully vile, I guess is the way to put it. The lean men, the fat, dripping prose, the last gauntlet handclasp as the moons rise in the sky. . . . I used to drive women into hysterics just by reading them at the right pace. I didn't have to use funny voices or anything."

"Miss Samantha earned Hounslow enough money that the Pure Land School occupies the interior of an entire mesa," Lon said. "I understand that the place is a city, all dug to Hounslow's obsessive specifications. He earned more money honestly than our current politicians seem able to steal with both hands."

"If you call that honest."

"Damn it, Hektor," Breyten said. "You're always sneering. And who gives a damn what you used to do with women?"

"I was just making a considered literary judgment." Hektor was startled by Breyten's sudden anger. In compensation, he confiscated Breyten's snifter ahead of schedule.

" 'Considered'!"

"What do you make of Hounslow, Hektor?" Lon's voice was serene.

"I . . ." He thought. Lon was always probing him, asking questions that required detailed analyses and then having no visible response to the answers. He couldn't tell whether his father thought he was intelligent or a fool. Hektor had no opinion whatsoever about Rudolf Hounslow, whom he thought of as an irrelevant dust-butt ranter, but if Father was asking, there was more to it.

"If he made his money without corruption, as you say, then he'll come out of this all right. After the corruption investigations are over, people might even take his school more seriously." Would Father have a response? How could he, to such a weasel-worded assessment? Hektor decided to go further. "He's biding his time out there in the wastelands. Reading Wang Yangming, doing tai chi, looking at his pupils' adoring eyes and trying to get them to dilate at the thought of duty. He's just waiting for someone to offer him an opportunity. He won't start anything himself, but if cracks open up in the system, he'll move in. It's happened before. He could be another . . . Joemon!" Hektor used the still-potent name of the old tyrant, and wondered if he had gone too far, wandered from analysis to hysteria. He resolved to find out more about Rudolf Hounslow and his damn school as soon as he could.

"Perhaps." As Hektor had predicted, Lon gave no indication of whether he agreed with the judgment or not. "You know, Hounslow and I—"

"Father, I want to leave Xui House." Breyten finally managed to spit out what he'd been holding on his tongue.

Lon wagged his tangled eyebrows. "You barely live here as it is, Breyten. Always coming and going, here and the corridors. . . ."

"I know, I know." Breyten drew himself up. The expression on his pale face was severe. "I didn't mean to be a problem to you. I'm sorry. But this is something more. I want formal permission from you to leave and not return to Xui House until I know . . . what I need to know." He faltered, not having thought out clearly what he wanted to say. Breyten knew that Hektor often carefully planned out even speeches that seemed completely spontaneous, and hated the self-regard that required.

Instead, Breyten reached into his jacket, pulled out a long piece of red silk, and held it out in front of him dramatically. Hektor stared at it in bewilderment, but Lon immediately recognized it as a strip of an old Xui House wall banner, one he had given to Breyten in a moment of pride and weakness when Breyten had won a long, dangerous foot race across the rocks on the edge of Tithonium. For years, Breyten had worn it as a belt. The younger Hektor had cried and wanted one too, but had had to be satisfied with a promise of some later reward, a promise he had long forgotten.

Breyten cut the banner strip in half with a pair of scissors. One half he handed ceremoniously to Lon; the other half he stuffed up his jacket sleeve like a handkerchief. Lon looked down at the cut edge of the ancient cloth. Breyten had always been given to these gestures, which usually meant much more to him than to whoever was the object of his communication. Lon still had a distorted ceramic pig with wide staring eyes, made by Breyten to commemorate some private revelation. Lon had never understood it, but still kept it in a drawer, wrapped in velvet. This fragment of banner would join it. Lon could not even manage anger at the wanton destruction of historical meaning. Breyten's relationship with the past was powerfully ambiguous.

"Please don't search me out or send messengers," Breyten said. "I'll come back when I'm ready."

Lon pushed himself to his feet. Breyten stepped forward and let his father hold him tightly. In his years in the Chamber of Delegates Lon Passman had argued, persuaded, made deals. In his years on the bench of Tharsis he had gotten used to inquiring, demanding, and rendering decisions. With this son he could do none of these things.

"All right," Lon whispered, knowing it was much more than a man's desire to experiment with freedom. Breyten was too old, and too dangerous, for that. Lon hoped that his son would decide to want the right thing, because he suspected that Breyten would get what he wanted.

Hektor stood to one side and looked off past them, through the doorway and into the dark-walled hallway. He swirled the last of the brandy in Breyten's snifter, watched it drain back down the side in long legs.

Breyten stood in front of Hektor and reached out his hand. Solemnly, they shook.

"Do you need—" Hektor began.

"No, little brother. I'm ready. Everything's packed."

"You're always ready."

Breyten shook his head. "I'm never ready. I just try to be prepared. If I'm lucky, it looks like I knew what was going to happen." He started to turn away, stopped. "When was the last time you were up in the Armory, Hektor?"

Hektor frowned. "Why?"

"Oh, never mind. Do you remember that old guy up on Salop Way? He had that little reptile zoo, they lived in the rocks and sometimes got away through the cracks?"

"Yes." The boys had loved the place, loved making the horned toad spurt blood through its eyes, making the lizard drop its tail. The old man had eventually died, and his lizards and snakes got distributed to various relatives or sold. His old shop was now the headquarters of a cleaning service.

"I once saw a snake shed its skin there. One of those big black ones—you remember. It rubbed its lips against a rock, then peeled the skin back, little by little. It seemed to get stuck a couple of times, but the snake kept working at it until it peeled completely off, all in one piece. The guy let me have it, though usually he sold them, for luck. I still have it somewhere. . . ."

Hektor remembered the snake skin too. He had coveted it, and sometimes when Breyten was away, he would sneak into his room and pull it out of its hiding place. It was a mysterious thing, that skin, like the ghost of a snake, hidden there in one of Breyten's wall drawers. Breyten had never caught him playing with it, otherwise there would have been a fight.

"Why don't you just tell me what you mean?" Hektor said, feeling truculent. Even now, if Breyten left Xui House, Hektor could not go up to his abandoned room and make that skin his own. It would never belong to him.

Breyten turned away. "I don't mean anything, Hektor. And don't you look for me either."

"Don't worry," Hektor said. "I won't."

"But, Hektor," Breyten said, "when you go up there, take some tea with you." Then he walked out of the room, followed by Lon, who would see him to the front door. As he walked past, Lon clapped Hektor's shoulder. Hektor smiled absently, but did not watch as they vanished down the hallway.

Hektor had watched hunters on Earth, in the great reserves around Mount Greylock, in the Berkshire Hills. He had watched, but not really understood, because his perceptions had not been attuned to what he was seeing. The hunters crouched feeling for something, but everything had been strange to Hektor: the bony trees soughing in the wind, the dark leaf-covered water, the infinite life in the decaying wood and wet leaves, from grumpy round-shouldered beetles to nervous red pointy-headed birds.

Suddenly the hunters' backs straightened and their hands tightened on their bows. One of them took Hektor's arm in an excited grip and pointed. A few moments' squinting and he had finally seen it, first the shivering flank, then the proud, combat-sharpened rack of the stag, its branching pattern different from the bare trees around it.

They hadn't managed to kill it. Someone's shift and indrawn breath and it had bolted through the underbrush and gone, leaving them standing stunned behind it.

But now Hektor knew what those hunters had felt in that quick moment of perception. He looked down the hallway at the light spilling out of the Armory. He heard someone move in there with the slap of foot on rock, a grunt, and the sharp clink of metal on metal. He should have been out already, trying to find Pamaot, though he knew he would still fail with her. Her mind was stubbornly fixed on the Feast of Gabriel, and he suspected that she had a lover she was faithful to, one she didn't care to lessen by discussing. Still, it would have been nice to see her, to smell her, and to listen to her laugh. And even women with lovers were known to weaken, at least momentarily.

The Armory had always been Breyten's territory. Hektor remembered a young Breyten standing at attention in the center of the table, like a chess piece, a shining bread knife in his hand. The light behind him had cast his shadow into the hall. Hektor had been looking for something in that hallway, but whatever it was would remain forever outside the stream of light coming from the Armory. *He* had never been allowed in that room, never dared to step over the rough threshold, and had caught glimpses of the gleaming weapons only in passing, through the winking circle of his mother's earring as she carried him to bed, her neck softly scented. The memory crackled like an old page turned to show the rest of the manuscript missing. He supposed he had thrown a tantrum. Only the insolent glint of the bread knife in Breyten's hand remained.

And their mother, Sara, had often sat in this alcove, the one with the alloy medallion of the falling Icarus above it. The Earth's Moon had gleamed just like that medallion, rising above more water than the Martian mind could possibly encompass. This alcove was where Sara had told Hektor and Breyten stories of heroes, here in this stone hall with its thick, intricate rug, not in the warmth of their beds.

Here the original Trojan Hektor's child had screamed at the shining of his father's armor; here Kusunoki Masashige, en route to his defeat at Minato River, had parted from his son at the posting station at Sakurai; here Bayard, *le chevalier sans peur et sans reproche*, had defended the bridge at Garigliano. Here, whenever he passed by, Hektor heard the dull clatter of their weapons and their muttered exclamations as they chafed, ready for war. And here, whenever he passed by, Hektor saw his mother, her long silk gown and her square face, as she held the attention of her sons, and tried to show no favor between the two. Much to Breyten's dismay, she had always sent them into the Armory together to get a weapon to illustrate a story. In their silent struggles to see who would carry it back to her, neither had ever been injured. Not quite.

Hektor held the copper tray in front of him, two tea glasses steaming on it, a brass pot with more between them, and walked forward on the soft rug, nimble as a servant.

Stepping into the Armory was like breaking out of layers of dust into sunlight. The room was narrow and high, with a row of lights that hung just below the peak of the vault. Rockmelt cabinets stacked themselves up a story and a half, their upper contents to be examined only by a balancing act on spinwire catwalks.

Miriam Kostal sat at the heavily grained ironwood table holding a long sword in front of her eyes, examining its edge. The blade was decorated with inlaid silver figures. She looked up, and they stared at each other for a long moment.

"I brought you some tea," he said.

"Thank you," she said.

She was flushed, and breathing quickly. She'd been sparring, he realized. He imagined her moving powerfully across the floor with the sword. A strong woman, big hands, big ears, strong features. She didn't want him to be there.

He shouldn't have wanted to be there.

"Does it tell you anything?" he asked.

"Does what tell me anything?"

"Using the sword."

She looked at the blade still balanced on her hands. "It's that damn rug out there. I couldn't hear you coming. It didn't give me enough time."

"Oh, no. No need. Father won't mind a bit. Nice to see the things getting used. But is the procedure . . . curatorial?"

Her lips twitched. Why was he trying to charm her? "Sometimes. You need to hold it to know it. Use it. You can tell a real sword from a decoration. How serious the maker was. How *good* the maker was. I think I got carried away."

"They need to be held, sometimes, so that they know they're real."

"I suppose."

He sat down next to her, close enough to feel her exercise-induced warmth. "My name is Hektor. I'm Breyten's brother."

"I . . . I know. I'm Miriam. Kostal. Miriam Kostal."

They touched fingertips briefly, more a brush than a handshake.

"Breyten's told me a lot about you," Hektor said.

"Has he?"

"No."

She slid the sword into its decorated wood scabbard and let it rest in her lap. The long sharkskin hilt got in the way and forced her to move slightly away from him. She picked up her tea glass.

"This collection is quite astonishing," she said.

"Is it?"

"Yes." She put the scabbarded sword on the table. "I've never seen one of these before. A Burmese dha. Beautiful work. A little fussy, maybe."

Hektor couldn't remember ever having seen it before. Why, he suddenly wondered, was she still here? Breyten had picked up his bags and left Xui House. By this time he was far away, lost somewhere in the corridors, on a magtrack train for the other side of the planet, moving, moving. "Probably belonged to the Xuis."

"That's what the record says." The sword was like a cave in a dust storm to her. She tried to curl up in it. "But then, the record says this is from . . . wait." She turned and peered up at the display card, high up the side of the room. Hektor could barely see it from where they sat. "Let's see . . . forged in Moulmein, used in the attempted conquest of Siam in 1767, abandoned in Lopburi . . . blah, blah, blah. Ended up in Hong Kong, moved to a museum in Fergana . . . oh, a whole bunch of nonsense."

"Why nonsense?" She was focusing her intensity on the sword, thought Hektor. And the sword didn't matter.

"Because the thing was made somewhere in all those mountains between Sichuan and northern Burma, and in the twenty-second century. A lot of refugees there specialized in historical reconstructions. Good work too. Want to look at the crystal structure?" She proffered a microscopic viewer. There was a slight tremor in her fingers.

"I'll take your word for it." He found himself trying to speak very carefully, as one would to the dying victim of a cave-in. He was beginning to understand what must have happened.

"The Xuis were always pleased with the Burmese line of their family." He sighed. "From kings, they said. They were descended from Burmese kings."

Miriam was unimpressed. "Maybe they were. Couldn't tell it from this sword, though. But it's nice work, as I said. Nothing to be ashamed of. As a sword." She held it up vertically, as if giving a salute before a duel. Her agate-dark eyes glittered at him.

"It's not hanging in that display case just as a sword."

"No, of course not. It was hanging there to show how important you all are, Passmans and Xuis."

"Well, yes." He smiled and put a finger to his lips. "Don't tell anyone."

"All right." His charm irritated her. "Let me hang it back up and make a notation. Or do you think your father would rather not know about it?" She rolled out of her seat and flew up the web-thin ladder to the upper level. She wore a practical but expensive-looking suit with trousers. The knees had dust ground into them.

"Oh, no. I'm sure that's why you're here. Truth. My father has an old-fashioned weakness for it." It had been stupid of Breyten to recommend her for this job, qualified though she was for it. Something had gone wrong between them, and his action had made sure the connection would remain painfully alive.

She slid dramatically down the ladder, landed lightly on the floor. Her movements were taut, constrained. She didn't want to be here, and, done with her sword, she was clearly about to go.

The only way to hold her was to open up the situation they had both been carefully ignoring.

"When my brother, Breyten, was—oh, I don't know, seven or so, he took to exploring the support air shafts of Xui House. Has he told you this story?"

She sat. "No. He's never been one for stories."

"Oh, but that's not true at all. Heroes, the acts of the ancient glorious ones—he used to tell them to me every night, just before bed. If he told them right, of course, I couldn't sleep."

"Perhaps I didn't know him very well."

Hektor saw they were sliding toward a precipice. "I don't think I know him very well either. And I have less excuse. I've known him all my life, after all. From my first moment of life he was there, somewhere."

"He was quite angry with you today, you know."

Hektor raised his eyebrows. "Really. That might explain something. Why?"

"Those jugglers and drummers in the dining room. And that beautiful young woman. He didn't expect them."

"Pamaot." Hektor turned slightly away and scratched his head. "A lovely woman. Why should she make him mad?"

"He was in a bad mood."

"Well, it's true I didn't warn him." He felt as if his sexual desire for Pamaot, vagrant though it was, was suddenly a visible object lying on the table in front of him. Why should that embarrass him?

"You were going to tell me a story." Miriam leaned back in her chair, challenging him. "One, I hope, with blood in it. I'm tired of dust."

She wore trailing earrings in her long earlobes. Her forehead was high, and the smooth skin was already creased with years of thought.

"Oh, there's plenty of blood at Xui House. Seventy years ago or so, there was murder in that dining room. Not political, oddly enough. It was right after the Veterans Uprising, when everyone was wound up tight, but it was a crime of passion. Right during a formal dinner party. Blood splashed into the dessert frosting. That led to a fashion in scarlet-dappled formal cakes for a while. You see them in old pictures."

"That's not the kind of blood I mean. That's all dried up. Dust. I want your blood, Hektor Passman. Yours and Breyten's. You were about to give me some."

He was shaken by her intensity, but managed to conceal it. She had a very long neck. "That's right, I was. It must have taken Breyten weeks of work to remove the denial baffles behind the formal conversation sofa in the Yellow Receiving Room. It was a boring room, adults just sat around and talked there, we never went in. So no one caught him doing it. And he didn't tell me."

"Did he usually?"

Hektor sighed. "No. I usually had to sneak around, figure out what he was doing. He had a lot of private projects. He didn't want his clumsy younger brother messing them up."

Breyten had been a secret even as a boy. He had slept silently, breathing so smoothly that Hektor had come up several times a night to make sure he wasn't dead.

"Once he got in he chimneyed up and down the shafts. Not much to see, of course, just a bunch of power and comm links, whatever connections needed to be dropped there. But one day Breyten slipped and fell to the bottom of the shaft, near the heat pump. Fortunately, he didn't land on the hot side. Those fins would have griddled him like a flapjack."

"You don't like your brother."

"Love my brother. Believe me. I can do nothing else. He fell on the cold side, the heat *suck* side. Still death, but slower. I heard him yelp. I was sitting in my room, reading, and I heard him up the shaft. No one else did. I suppose if he'd thought about it, or been older, he would have stoically died down there, I don't know. Fox-eaten livers are a Passman family tradition. But over a little air-shaft climbing? I don't guess even Breyten would have taken things that far."

"No," she said. "Probably not."

"Somehow I knew exactly what happened. I'd never thought it was possible to climb inside there, but as soon as I heard his ghostly voice, I knew he was trapped. I still remember my first reaction: jealousy. Once again he'd done something without me. It took me a while to figure out where he was. He didn't want to yell any louder because he was afraid our parents would hear, or one of the servants we had back then, when the house was busier."

"Was your father's discipline so harsh?"

"Oh, no discipline, not like that, not what you're thinking. No, my parents would just have been disappointed, particularly my father. He was in line for the Fossic Party Chairmanship, we thought then. A serious man. He stood above us like a Tharsis volcano. Breyten didn't want to disappoint him. Neither did I."

At this remove of time it was hard to explain, even to himself. Martian virtue was easy to discuss in theory, but difficult to live with in your own home. It was a constant affront, a goal visible yet impossible to reach.

"I finally figured out where he was. Underneath the kitchen, near the outside of the house. Just past there are some interesting buried statues, I don't know if—''

"I've seen them," she said crisply.

"Oh." He cleared his throat. "He wouldn't tell me, but he'd already lost feeling in his toes. I was very excited. It was a rescue mission, just like the kind our mother was in charge of. I went and took a length of climbing rope. Entirely without permission—it would have gone hard with me if anyone had found out. I would lower it to him . . . but there was no way for me to get to anywhere directly above him. I found the place he'd removed the baffles, climbed in, tried to follow his instructions. But there were places he had climbed across huge gaps, and I just couldn't do it. I remember crying, crying at some impossible traverse, and almost doing it anyway, which would have dropped me God knows where, leaving both of us in trouble.

"I finally got back to the kitchen. There was a vent there, a transverse link, coming out underneath the counters in the kitchen. It kinked a couple of times before getting to a little above him. His voice, already growing weak, sounded like it was coming from kilometers away, and it took a while for us to convince ourselves that he was actually quite close. You see, I couldn't fit into the shaft to get to him. It was narrow, and I was too big. So he couldn't get out that way either. But he could see, not too far above it, a wider one that would lead back to where he had come from. If I could get a rope in, pull him out, he could climb out himself. I tried casting the line down the vent, but even with a saucepan tied to its end as a weight, I couldn't get it around the kinks. We were stuck.''

Hektor paused and poured himself another glass of tea. Such adventures within these walls . . . for all its impositions, Xui House had been quite a place to grow up in. Miriam Kostal watched him steadily.

"Then I thought of something that, if it hadn't worked out, might have imposed suicide on me. Just because we were afraid to tell my father! I went upstairs, tiptoeing quietly, probably as suspicious-looking as one of those hooded criminals in the street plays, and got my sister, Zoë. She was asleep in her bed with a stuffed sand dragon that she insisted on bringing along with her in case it would help. She was three years younger than I was, could walk and could talk, though she didn't make any sense, except when she made too much. She didn't ask for explanations. She just came along. She was always one for conspiracy.

"I gave her the end of the rope and told her to walk to Breyten. Not too far, though. Breyten and I were terrified by the idea that she might fall in after him."

"Not so terrified that you finally called your parents," Miriam said.

Hektor shook his head. "No, no. We'd reached the state where we would have done anything to proceed with our plan. Chopped off Breyten's toes with a kitchen cleaver, had me go outside and try to drag him out through a maintenance access onto the surface, caused an explosive decompress somewhere so that Breyten's presence in the shaft might seem like a legitimate accident. There was no way we could back out, not in front of each other like that.

"In the event, Zoë was a perfect rescue-team member. She'd picked up something from our mother. She calmly crawled down the shaft, hauling the line in one hand and the stuffed sand dragon in the other, and dropped the end of the line down to Breyten. Then she sat, dangling her feet over the edge, and watched him haul himself out, with me belaying the line at the other end. She wasn't one of those children who always insisted on helping either, if she saw that it wouldn't actually help."

"She died," Miriam said.

"Yes, later. A climbing accident. She still wasn't that old. And it wasn't her fault." Hektor paused. "Breyten climbed back up the other shaft and out. He'd badly frostbitten his toes. We even stole medicine out of the cabinet: Breyten had somehow learned the combination. Peripheral circulatory system regenerators. That was probably more dangerous than the climbing around. He didn't lose any toes, though you might have noticed that a couple of them are a strange color. No one ever found out. I've never even told anyone about it."

"I've never noticed the color of his toes. I'll take your word for it.'' She stood and slipped on her jacket. ''Thank you for the story, Hektor.''

He wanted to stop her, talk to her some more. But he just sat at the table and smiled up at her. She was a Vigil officer: he knew her name. He should be able to find her again, if he had a mind to. But better she should leave and disappear.

''Let me show you out,'' he said. There were still the requirements of politeness.

''Fine,'' she said. ''Let's go.''

They left the Armory with its ranks of gleaming swords behind them.

3

From "A Personal Survey of Wood Mines in Capri and Ius Chasma," by Nate Khat, 2328, a private document for a potential investor:

To get there I had to wear eyecups and have my vestibular system disrupted so that I would be unable to tell where the cavern was in the wall of Ius. I suspect that my guides took this opportunity to stuff wood peelings into my pockets and shirt neck, probably as a childish joke. I can't imagine how so much came to be there otherwise.

It's obscene, how they do it down there. I don't know if you're aware of it. They jammed me into a narrow, airless passage and made me watch the workers flense great panels of wood from the swelling wall. I'm sure there were more convenient locations, but they couldn't be bothered to find them for me. The spinning blades were uncomfortably close, and the vibrating blades made my bones itch. I felt the tormented oak shudder behind me as it grew under pressure. They told me stories about human teeth found in the wood, from slow workers sucked up by the hungry growth. The thought seemed to please them.

These people have been in contact with wood for too long. Their manner is fibrous. Their joints are knotty. Their humor is intolerable. They pulled me farther, despite my protests that I had seen enough. I could see the whorls of old growth in their cheeks. They told me to be careful of quick atavistic sprouts that could grow through me and pin me to the wall and then left me in the dark while they attended to some irrelevant, probably fictional, task. Vast slabs of wood rolled past me like grumbling beasts. They were as big as construction crawlers. I could have lost a finger in a roller, or worse.

I've seen the ancestors of this wood on Earth. There they are flimsy vegetable stalks waving fragile leaves at the breeze, much more pleasant to look at than these giant, swelling bulges. That wood is light, and comes in pointless cylinders. Sometimes the cylinders fall over and crush passersby. The whole thing scarcely seems worth it.

Better to leave the wood here for these wood-boring bugs, who have been raised to it from birth. Better to avoid these dark, oily nightmare spaces with their fecund lignin. Better to invest in something less intestine, something that doesn't involve bleak superstition. When I was little, I was trying to build a fort out of my family's sirenwood table when it fell over on me. I still remember that live smoothness crushing my face. I was not found for hours. It wakes me up in terror sometimes. . . .

These men knew that. They know wood. They know the primitive terrors it represents to rational Martian citizens. And they glory in it, and in my degradation. When they finally pulled me out of the tunnel, they gave me noodles in a wooden bowl, to be eaten with a wooden spoon on a wooden table. I was calm. I am well trained. I wanted to throw it in their faces, but I ate it. I left my teeth marks in the edge of the turned bowl.

Someday I will start a fire. Do not worry, it will be after I have left your employ. Meanwhile, my advice is that you invest in an asteroid filibustering expedition.

"Hey, hey, hey, Fabian!" Fabian Xui awoke to a voice bellowing in his ears.

"What? What is it?" He couldn't see who it was, bastard had

shoved a bag over his head, something—these guys loved reminding him of how easy it would be to kill him. As if any Martian had a guaranteed life.

"Found two things you want, all in one neat little bundle. You want?"

Fabian could smell the rough anise on the man's breath.

"I want you to get this bag off my head."

A laugh, and sudden light. Marko, a member of the crew Fabian ran with, the Dust Beggars of Seven Knots. He had a solvent-tub face with hair that looked hacked by orbital laser. Fabian reached up with his wrist knife, cut his support lines, and rolled his sleeping bag down the wall to the floor. Camouflaged, insulated, he picked dark, high corners to hang in—and still these guys found him as if he was spotlit. He pretended to be doing it casually, and they pretended that they found him by accident.

Marko knelt over him. "We got the word out for you, Fabian, honey. Slip, slap, up and back, tones, groans, and knuckle bones."

"And?" There were various gestures, sounds, and postures that were used for secret communication in the Scamander corridors, but Fabian doubted his query had been made by means of them. His need had been very specific, and quite outside the usual round of insult and redundant crowd information that served as the bulk of the symbolism exchanged.

"And we got her. Your beauty, right out there. And a plus for you, like I said."

Fabian rolled out of his bag and stowed it. His beat for the *Moebius Daily* was the activities of those half criminal gangs/half corridor social clubs called crews. He'd searched around and decided on the Dust Beggars, based in the neighborhood called Seven Knots, as the most promising subject. They'd done some pounding on him when he started, just to let him know where he stood, but then had accepted him, partly because he gave them good write-ups and made them fashionable.

Too fashionable, he was starting to think. Marko, for example, always went on in this singsong jargon, hoping to get it into this week's feuilleton, though he had once talked perfectly normally.

"Okay," Fabian said. "I love pluses."

"A duel!" Marko was unable to stand the suspense any longer. "A clink-slice-bleed with swink nice speed like you like and you know you do."

"Swink?" Fabian did like cataloging duels. They were the main form of corridor entertainment, and he covered them well. It was all getting just too popular, though. Too many other journalists were encroaching on his turf. Pretty soon every other person in a corridor mob would be a wretched scribbler like him. Time for some other line of work. Maybe he'd cover politics, like Hektor did on the sly. With Rodomar and all those arrests, it was getting much more interesting, and potentially more bloody, than any feeble corridor altercations.

"Come on, come on. You'll miss it all if you don't hurry. So, go—shortcut, eh?"

"I hate your shortcuts, Marko," Fabian said, because it was expected of him. At least half his journalistic success was due to his constant reassurance of his sources that they were, indeed, desperate daredevils.

"Yeah, well. You got ten fingers, ten toes. Some of them lingers, some of them goes."

"Not bad, Marko."

"Go!"

Fabian slung his satchel and they trotted up the sloping corridor. Long ago, Fabian had enjoyed lying in bed in the mornings, piling up demitasses of Turkish coffee and reading other people's articles in the newssheets. He'd given those habits up, but still felt their loss almost physically. No one but Egypt knew what sacrifices he had to make for his art. . . .

This was an early area of Scamander, built during the scientific period of Martian settlement. Once a tedious array of sleeping quarters, dining halls, support areas—a warren for technohamsters—it had been re-formed and cut through in later eras. The style was oppressive to the modern Martian sensibility. The old technical zones, the original cities of Mars, were now almost all red-light districts, the bunks of the earnest explorers now cribs for dismal prostitutes.

An illegal tunnel had been cut through a wall and under the long-distance Coprates-Nissen magtrack and a temporary air lock, stolen from a repair facility, installed. Fabian shook his head and passed through. The air on the other side, while not quite Martian surface, was thin and cold. Through his feet he could feel the distant vibration of a train. Fabian popped an emergency rebreather bag over his head and stumbled after Marko, feeling the cold sucking at his extremities. Eventually, the authorities would find this illegal tunnel and seal it off with hardfoam. Meanwhile, it cut at least five minutes off their walk.

"The duel, Marko," Fabian said, once they were back in the air. "Brief me."

Marko shrugged. "They're a little club of their own, up near Rhenre. Know it?"

"Sure." Fabian made it his business to know every neighborhood of sprawling, inchoate Scamander. Rhenre was centered around an irregular carved space traversed by rail lines and walkways, like a contortionist's basket pierced by swords. It was always busy, and its social organization was too sophisticated to turn corridor-level enforcement over to crew members like Marko. "No duels there."

"No sir. So they comes down to *us*. Asks a favor, this Plimpus Club. We know how to rule a duel. They don't, they're some kind of debating society, for truth, not a crew at all." He sniffed in disapproval.

"Rudolf Hounslow. The Pure Land School." Fabian had seen the sigil on the note he'd carried up to Lon Passman that night, from the ominous woman in the anteroom. The entire transaction had piqued his curiosity, so he'd used his corridor-level sources to track her should she descend to the level they could perceive. If she chose to stay in a private suite at the Pasargadae or the Empress Wu, she would be invisible to him. But she had nothing of the scent of cinnamon bath salts about her, and sure enough, someone had managed to track her. He hoped she wouldn't get killed in this duel too soon for him to find more out.

"A good fight. Some blood. Get your damn priorities straight, Fabe."

"Let's get to this duel. We still in Squallo?"

"Yeah. Pain in the brain. But I'm getting to kind of like it."

Scamander Police had lately made a sweep of Kuster's Promenade, a decayed park that was the usual site for these duels. The authorities disliked unregistered dueling, which they pettifoggingly defined as murder. The joke in the corridors was that an unsuccessful duelist would always claim to have been murdered.

Kuster's Promenade being impossible for a while, duels were now held in a nameless place near Squallo where a floor had collapsed, combining two poorly dug corridors into one high rubble-filled expanse. The whole place was slated to be closed, sealed, and legally declared surface, and for now, no one gave much of a damn what went on there.

"Got him, Sildjin," Marko said. "Got him."

"All right, Mr. Xui." Sildjin was High Priest of the Dust Beggars. "We have obtained your target. You can watch her in action. And in return?"

"You want me to guarantee some specific number of column inches?" Sildjin scared him, he always did, but Fabian held on to his journalistic integrity as a defense. "You'll get what the story earns. You think I haven't been covering you enough?"

"Yes, well." Sildjin looked straight at him with pale blue eyes. "I've been *approached*, if you understand. Negotiations might proceed. Depends on what transpires."

Fabian really did need to find another journalistic subject. He should just tell Sildjin that, and urge him to make a deal with these competing journalists. Fabian could guess who they were. Instead, he found himself extemporizing. "Egypt's working on a play. *The Tongueless Singer*, she calls it. About corridor crews, based on some of my feuilletons. She's got a leader, a great character. Drax, she calls him. Aah!" He drew his breath in sudden pain.

Sildjin dropped Fabian's arm, point made. "What's wrong with 'Sildjin'? Too many syllables?"

"Yeah, and 'Marko,' don't forget 'Marko,' rhymes with . . . with . . ." Marko's voice trailed off under Sildjin's glare.

Sildjin was dry and dark of skin, with a forehead that leaned out like a toppling wall, implying a brain shaped like a soup tureen. Huge hands dangled from his thick arms. His body was crossed and recrossed by scars, earned, he said, as a mercenary noncom in brushfire wars on Earth. He really *had* served as a sergeant in a irregular group called Pranger's Scouts, Fabian had learned, somewhat to his surprise, since he had thought Sildjin was making the whole thing up. It was rumored that the scars marked powerful installed circuitry from his military service, stuff that could . . . well, everyone was vague about what it did, but they all agreed it was dangerous.

"Rhymes with get over to the other side and get to work," Sildjin said to Marko.

"Right, Sildjin."

The frowning Sildjin seemed to have forgotten his flare of public-relations pique, and was intently examining the dueling setup slowly appearing out of the tangle of people in the corridor, assisted by a nervous Marko.

"What is this business, Mr. Xui?" he said. "We aren't a public-service organization. Regardless of what you say about 'emergent social structures.' " Sildjin read copy about himself with an obsessed avidity. He sometimes got thrown by Fabian's convoluted prose, but would never admit it.

Fabian thought about pointing out that he had just wanted to find the woman, not manage a duel for her, but knew that such reasonable logic merely irritated Sildjin. He examined the two prospective duelists. The soft-fleshed woman with the long red-brown hair . . . yes, it was her for sure. Her opponent was a slight, thoughtful-looking man with a curling beard. Neither was the slightest bit impressive-looking. They spoke quietly to each other, set aside from the rest of the people milling about the corridor, but stood far apart, as if sparks would fly between them if they got closer.

Children dangled their feet overhead, on the leftover edges of the former ceiling, and threw tiny aircraft across to one another, shrieking and almost falling from their perches.

"It's not a grudge fight, from the look," Fabian said.

Sildjin looked amused. "I guess not." Fabian's urge to create taxonomies of dueling types perplexed the corridor crew members, who tended to judge by performance and not by motive.

"Do you know the story?" As Fabian observed everyone, things grew clearer. Most of the people were the usual sort of underemployed riffraff who made up the bulk of audiences at such impromptu bloodfests. But five or six men and women moved as tensely as the participants. They tried, by dress and hair, to blend in, and did so almost successfully. But they were bound by a net of exchanged glances. They were waiting. This duel was deciding something for them. Good. After a while you needed something more to pay attention to than anatomical damage.

"No story," Sildjin said with a snort. "They're pissed off at each other, think a little blood'll clear it up. Really, Mr. Xui, you think too much. Just watch, see if you can catch a few drops. Stick out your tongue and suck in."

A few weeks before, Fabian had watched Sildjin batter the face of a man believed to be a police informer. He'd done it with the loving earnestness of a boy chastising a younger brother, alternating hands and peering closely at the results. Sildjin's fists were as big and flat as bricks. The informer, as far as Fabian knew, had survived, but his face barely existed anymore. Since he was poor, the medical replacement would resemble a protective mask more than a face.

"Good advice, Sildjin."

"None better. So come on, let's get to work."

Fabian preferred being a witness. "What do you want me to do?"

"Assist. First: this is not supposed to be to the death. So watch the major vessels, help with the first-aid kit. Can you do it?"

"I can do it. I've got coagulator, nervegrow, the lot. Never go anywhere without it."

"Good. I like a man who's prepared." Sildjin nodded his approval and, despite himself, Fabian felt pleased.

The duelists drifted apart, their conversation over. One of their associates held their swords, standard rentals available at any bar. The red-haired woman stalked past Fabian, clearly not recognizing him outside his servile role at Xui House.

Amalie, another Dust Beggar, was snapping marker lines on the dusty floor, her blond head bent over intently. She checked distances with a little laser sensor. She flipped her hair back and gave Sildjin a sign.

The blood was pounding in Fabian's ears and he felt each breath sharp in his lungs. It was perfect because it was so precise. The thrill in a duel was the combination of punctiliousness and violence. Mere corridor murders didn't give that—the police should have used a more aesthetically based criterion for distinguishing between dueling and murder. Maybe he should become an advisor.

The duelists stood at opposite ends of the defined area and stared at each other. There was a definite charge to the air, something beyond the usual preduel tension. Erotic? It felt that way to Fabian. He'd heard of marriages being decided that way, by who drew first blood: women willing to slice their sweetheart's head open to make sure the love was there, men hoping it would never again come to this. Engagements were broken if the wrong one lost, and both fought as hard as they could to make sure the decision was a real one. The later wedding ceremony was an anticlimax.

Sildjin stood between the duelists and looked around at the crowded space. He was broad through the shoulders, and his cylindrical head sat massively between them. Fabian had convinced him to wear that robe of crimson ribbons. The color set off his face and the slits revealed those ominous scars that so frightened everyone. Some members of the crowd, either more peaceful or hungrier than the others, were already sneaking glances at the food table being hastily set up at the far end of the corridor by Marko and other Dust Beggars. Sildjin was what passed for a local headman in this area of Scamander, and like any other citizen greedy of prominence, he had to both put on a show and provide food.

"The Dust Beggars have organized this event," he said. "Let no one consider interfering."

The man seemed nervous, his prominent adam's apple bobbing up and down. The woman—Brenda Marr was her name, Fabian remembered—was self-possessed, confident, ready to impose her will on the situation. And that was what the duel was deciding, Fabian concluded: whose will would dominate. The result, as far as he could tell, was a foregone conclusion. Her opponent had already decided he had lost.

"All right," Sildjin said. "Remember, no mortal wounds. Well, you've given the rules yourself. Try to obey them." He stepped back. "Commence."

They were both good fighters, though there was little art to their struggle. They locked eyes and rang their metal. They moved their feet very little, save to draw closer together, so the carefully drawn boundary lines became irrelevant. They finally stood chin to chin, and cut away at each other's heads with the edges of the swords, being too close for the point to have any meaning. It looked like a deadly wound would be easy, but really, there was little space in which to put any decent force behind the blow. At most, a cheekbone would be laid open.

The man stepped back a few steps, pushed by her force. Instead of pushing in, she pulled back a little and flicked in a quick slice with the very tip of her sword. Without a sound, the man raised his sword in surrender, blood pouring down his neck from a neatly severed earlobe. The crowd murmured in disappointment and disgust. For this they had changed their plans for the morning? It was an outrage, a testimony to how far standards had fallen in these days of lead. Not pausing to cheer or applaud, they streamed from their places to the food table, and in a moment were cheerfully stuffing their faces.

Fabian felt relief that he was not called upon to block up an opened artery or search out a severed finger. He stanched the flow, foamed coagulator on the spot, and his job was done. If the man wanted to find his earlobe, he'd just have to look for it himself.

The woman stalked over, her eyes glowing, exalted. Fabian turned around and bent over, as if fussing with his medical kit, and eavesdropped.

"Do you agree now, Sen?" she said. "Are you with me? Will we all do it together?"

The man sighed. "I was always with you, Brenda. But such an act is just too severe . . . ah, but we'll do it."

"We will!"

"Whatever the consequences. Hounslow will—" He noticed how near Fabian's studiously inattentive back was, and fell silent.

Gaff blown, Fabian turned and smiled at them. "You should be all right now, sir."

Brenda Marr's eyes widened in immediate recognition. "You!"

Breyten leaned far out on his descent clip, letting the air current sweeping across the expanse of Slanted Slope ruffle his hair, and looked down at Fabian. "Are you sure it's all right? It's starting to turn purple."

"Yes—ow! Damn it, it's fine. Just don't talk about it. Every time you mention it, I'm tempted to touch it." He gave his swollen nose one last prod, and winced. Then he returned his attention to gaining purchase on the rocking surface toward which they were descending. Parts of it were already stripping off the underlying framework and the footing was uneven.

"She hit you just like that?"

"Not even any windup."

"Nice," Breyten said admiringly. "Quick decision. Pattern induction."

"If that's what you want to call it." Fabian found Breyten's fascination with that woman Brenda Marr discomforting. She was Fabian's target, Fabian's interest—and now Fabian's nemesis. He didn't want anyone else messing around with her. Particularly not his unpredictable cousin Breyten. "Sildjin and the rest of the Dust Beggars didn't care at all. They just stood around me and laughed."

Fabian removed his weight from the descent line and tried to flatten the sticky soles of his climbing shoes on the smooth surface. He didn't like being up here. It was unnatural to be surrounded by so much open space within the city of Scamander.

"But Sildjin still agreed to help you with this."

"Yes." Fabian still wasn't sure why, and it worried him. Usually Sildjin's motives were simple and clear.

Breyten unhooked his clip and jumped three meters down from his line. The surface was tilted where he landed, and he slipped perilously toward the edge, dancing to keep his balance. The lower face of the Slope was far, far below them, its lights still glowing in the dawn murk. He finally regained control and stood still. He grinned at Fabian, but Fabian could hear Breyten's harsh breathing.

"You know, I used to wait every year for this thing," Breyten said. "It was different every time, but beautiful."

Fabian looked up. His nose had swollen just enough to obtrude itself on the inner part of his vision. It was most annoying, like feeling an itch somewhere you hadn't even known *could* itch. The upper face of Slanted Slope loomed dominatingly over him. Vast structures hung down from it. Gossamer support lines gleamed in the early-morning light. There was native rock up there—Slanted Slope was an angled fault in the wall of Tithonium, a vast book-shaped space tilted at forty-five degrees from horizontal—but it was invisible under a riot of glittering crystals and boisterous pseudobiological structures that were the homes of people wealthy enough to have houses surrounded by breathable air. It was from the lowest level of one of the crystals that they had descended. The house was owned by a family friend of the Passmans. She was vacationing on Earth, so Breyten and Fabian had taken advantage of access.

Fabian waved, and the lines were immediately pulled up from overhead and disappeared. Sildjin had assigned Amalie to help them. What interest did he have in this operation?

"I remember it too," Fabian said. "The first year I was in Scamander. It filled up most of the space inside Slanted Slope, twisting in between the towers. . . ."

The Slanted Slope Dragon was one of the monuments of the Feast of Gabriel. A vast creature over a hundred meters long, with shining scales, dramatic claws, and glowing eyes, it hung

from invisible cables and seemed to fly over the expensive restaurants and clubs on the lower slope. Each scale seemed to glow
with its own iridescent light. Its claws were crystal. Its belly
looked like it was covered with jewels.

"So what happened this year?" Breyten said. "It's ridiculous." He kicked at a buckled plate like a cranky child.

"Talana Vopul usually finances the project," Fabian said.
"This year she seems to have had business reverses." Ms.
Talana Vopul was currently incarcerated in a detention chamber in the south wall of Ius, under suspicion of having bribed
legislators for a magtrack contract for the north edge of Hellas
Planitia. Her assets were frozen. The dragon had been lost in
the process.

"Where's the entrance?" Breyten asked.

"Behind the head. This way."

They made their way along the dragon's snaking back. The
project had been abandoned only a week or so before, but already most of the decorative scales were gone, with torn strips
marking where they had been. Pretty soon the skeleton itself
would become a target of cutting-torch–equipped vandals. The
ownership of the dragon, and responsibility for it, seemed to be
in legal limbo at the moment. No one was in charge of protecting
it, or arranging for its orderly removal.

"She was a fascinating woman," Breyten said.

"Who?"

"You know, the one at the house. Marr. She talked to me as
I walked her down. There was . . . I don't know, something clean
about her. She knew exactly what she wanted to do."

"People like that are dangerous." Fabian suddenly felt like a
prissy aunt.

"Maybe. But imagine it! This whole group she belongs to,
the Pure Land School. Hounslow. They seem to be the only
people who know what they're doing on this entire planet.
They're after something."

"What?" Fabian was curious about what Breyten had learned,
though he was reluctant to reveal his interest.

"I don't know! And I want to."

The dragon's head loomed in front of them. The light coming

through the skylight at the top of Slanted Slope, where it broke out of the wall of Tithonium, was growing stronger, which, paradoxically, made the dragon's structure look even less substantial than it had in the half dark. The ribs of the skeleton thrust out from beneath where they stood.

"But let's get on with this business first, shall we?" Breyten's eyes gleamed.

"Sure, sure." Fabian sensed some movement at the top edge of his vision. He looked up, narrowly examined the other structures on the upper face, but could see nothing.

Breyten had persuaded Fabian to use his contacts, and had found a group of would-be filibusters looking for recruits. More work than it was worth, in Fabian's opinion, but Breyten had been intent. The filibusters had at first refused contact, but had finally been persuaded by Fabian's connection with Sildjin.

Fabian climbed more sedately through the hole, and found himself inside the belly of the dragon, peering down between his feet at the lower face of Slanted Slope. The dragon was considerably less complete down below, and huge openings gaped everywhere. A few complex crew cartouches already glowed on the internal panels.

More interesting were the three people, a man, a woman, and a little girl, snoring away in sleeping sacks. The child's hand dangled over the edge of a panel opening out onto a dizzying drop and seemed to be gesturing at a restaurant balcony far below, where a waiter was busily dusting off tables before the morning's customers arrived. One bad dream and she would be landing in someone's breakfast. The family had a little stove and a yellow pet snake, which was coiled around the woman's neck, its head in her ear.

Since they were clearly long veterans of the corridor ecology, their bodily wastes were encased in bright red water-permeable membranes. Free-flowing water was far away, so the membrane-enclosed waste rested, like festive fruit, at the bottom of a transparent compartmented cylinder. Water would condense in the top compartment, leaving the waste to dry into powder in the bottom. One of the three would eventually pack a week's worth of dry feces into a satchel and hump them down to a real toilet somewhere, where he would get a disposal credit. Breyten and Fabian tiptoed by without waking them.

These squatters hadn't yet started building protective chambers and installing accelerated-composting dry toilets to produce fertilizer for their hanging gardens. If Scamander Police didn't intervene soon, there would be an entire wasp colony up here in the carcass of the stillborn dragon, dangling crying babies off the guy wires until they went to sleep and dropping whirligigs to watch them spin in the air. The neighborhood committees of both the upper and the lower faces of Slanted Slope would not be happy about that.

Breyten made a muffled sound, and Fabian turned, to find himself confronting a knife held by the little girl. Short as she was, she pointed it at his groin. He tried to smile at her. Her face remained grimly determined.

"We're here for the meeting," Fabian said to the man, who held a dagger to Breyten's throat.

"Ah, right." The man flipped his knife away, nodded to his daughter. She with a show of reluctance, put her own blade aside, and smiled knowingly at Fabian.

"This way," the man said. His wife sat down and began to prepare breakfast for their daughter, not acknowledging Breyten and Fabian's presence. The girl sat, a sleepily innocent child, and waited for her porridge. As they disappeared, she turned her head and winked at Fabian.

Screw the filibusters, he thought. This family was obviously a better story. But he kept following, down the narrow catwalk that led into the dragon's pelvis. This wasn't going to work out, he thought. It was absurd of him to have helped Breyten get this far. Still, if Breyten wanted to adventure in the Asteroid Belt, who was Fabian to impede him?

This bunch of filibusters had some famous members. Three of them had even participated in the ill-fated Hermione expedition—of three Martian ships attacking that asteroid, only one had ever made it back to Mars, and that one had disintegrated in the upper atmosphere after being attacked by Union spacecraft. Five survivors in the single survival capsule that had made it to the surface. Three of them were anxious to try again. After having discussed them at dinner, Fabian thought them a good choice.

The man's head jerked. "Quiet."

Thunder overhead as loud feet slapped down on the dragon's back.

He turned on Fabian. "You led them here!"

"Who?" he said.

"I don't know who, you son of a bitch!"

Fabian peered through a gap in the interior partitions. Light streamed in from overhead as the dragon's back parted in a dozen places, and men and women in dark green coveralls dropped through it.

"InSec!" Fabian said. "Son of a bitch!"

"That's what I said!" Their guide pulled out his knife, ready to stab Fabian for lack of an easier target. Breyten instantly grabbed an overhead stanchion, swung himself up, and clipped the man in the head with his heels. He rolled, came to his feet, and sprinted off to help his family.

"This way," Fabian said. He didn't envy the InSec officer who came in contact with that guy's daughter.

"What—?"

Fabian didn't have time for discussion. He ran down the cat-walk. An instant later Breyten was behind him. They were in the skinny part of the dragon's upper tail. Much of it was in-complete, mere framework, and Fabian found himself dizzy as he clambered over ever more exposed supports. The InSecs, dropping from somewhere in the upper face, were unlikely to risk themselves on something with such uneven footing. They landed where Hektor and Fabian had. They would work their way here from inside. He hoped.

Shouts, the blade-against-shield sounds of combat. The InSec force had met the filibusters, somewhere in the bowels of the dragon. If the two of them were lucky, Fabian thought, that would delay the InSecs for just long enough.

Fabian grabbed onto a projection and pulled himself up. It creaked perilously, and he hoped looters had not already taken off with all the connecting stays.

"What the hell are we doing back here?" Breyten said as he climbed up behind him. "The only way out—"

"Is here. Quiet; I have things to do."

Both faces of Slanted Slope were now in full morning light. Fabian had a moment of intense vertigo, feeling the tilted face above toppling down over him as he fell toward the distant slope below.

He held up his hand and blinked a light down at what he hoped was the right balcony. A moment later came the response flash.

The whole dragon shook as someone was slammed into an internal partition. Fabian wondered if the battle could get severe enough to take the entire thing to pieces.

He pulled the orientation loop out of his belt pack and held it up over his head. This meant he was holding on with one hand. Maybe the only story would be "Minor Journalist Falls to Death from Dragon. Restaurateur Sues Estate for Damage from Impact." He tried to remember if he liked the picture of him that the *Moebius Daily* had on file.

Breyten cursed. Fabian glanced down, to see an InSec climbing determinedly toward them. "Surrender!" he shouted. "You will be tried fairly in a Union court."

"I demand full political representation," Breyten shouted back. He managed to pry off a chunk of the dragon's back and flung it at the InSec, hitting him squarely in the forehead. The man almost lost his grip and swung precariously from the framework. Two of his fellows came up behind and tugged him back. He tumbled into shadow.

The line came whispering up from below, hauled by a compressed-air rocket. The rocket sensed the orientation of the target ring by its slight magnetic field, hissed a correction jet, and sprang through it. Fabian spun the loop to catch the line.

The two new InSecs, women with their hair tied under green bandanas, started climbing toward Breyten and Fabian. They did not try to negotiate. Their knuckles were cruelly spiked.

Fabian tied the line around the dragon's tail and clipped it tight with a timer box. A minute. He looked at the InSecs, lowered the time to thirty seconds. The box would blow the connection, making sure no one could follow Fabian down.

"Breyten! Never mind them, come on."

Breyten tossed another piece of dragon, this one much smaller, at the two InSecs, then grabbed the proffered descent clip.

"Got it," he said, grinning, as if this was all some sort of game.

Fabian attached his descent clip to the line and, leaving Breyten to his own devices, jumped.

Air rushed past him. The meaningless dots on the balconies gained definition, achieved personhood. The speed brake came on, to keep him from accelerating to a velocity high enough to injure him.

He glanced behind him. Breyten delayed his descent long enough to land a kick on one of the InSecs, then jumped down after Fabian. His hair streamed out and he laughed. Fabian looked back down toward the ground, rushing up at him at an uncomfortable speed.

There was Egypt. She was looking up at him from her table. As he watched, she poured tea into a cup and gestured up at him with it. Another glance, and she reached to pour another.

Fabian slammed into the balcony and grabbed at a table to keep himself upright. Flatware went flying.

"Oops," he said.

Egypt kissed him. "I'll take care of it. You looked great coming down, honey. I was worried. They just swarmed down from the upper face. . . ."

Fabian held her against him and looked back up the line. Breyten was approaching—the timer blew just as the pursuers were trying to grab onto the line and follow. With a whoop, Breyten dropped out of sight.

"Oh, my—" Egypt ran to the balustrade and peered over. She frowned. "I don't see—"

"His own damn fault." Fabian was shaking. He sucked hot tea and burned his tongue. "He had to land another kick before going. Fool."

"Fabian!" Egypt was horrified. "He fell. He might be hurt."

"Dead. He's probably dead."

Someone cursed in outrage below. Someone else made a quick apology. A moment later, a hand appeared on the balustrade. Then a second. Breyten Passman pulled himself up onto the balcony. The side of his head was bleeding.

"Sorry," he said. "Missed my mark."

Egypt rushed to minister to him. Fabian looked up at the dragon, which hung, still and silent, in the rock sky above. Why the hell were InSec officers coming up his ass like that? He didn't like it. He didn't like it one bit.

"Will it still be able to fly?" Brenda asked.

"No way," Kalina answered as she sprayed seal on a blood vessel. "To do this, I have to cut some of the flight muscles. I'll fold the wings in by hand, maybe put in a couple of spots of adhesive to keep them from flopping around."

She aspirated blood from the pigeon's exposed spine. The bird was held in the surgical stand with its wings spread, as if desperately trying to escape through the shining silver ring of the rotational mount. Its skin was pinned back from head to tail. Tubes perfused fluids to keep it alive. "The spine'll be completely rigid too. The poor thing'll look like a windup toy."

There was a spot of blood on the pure white breast feathers. Brenda dabbed delicately at it. She blinked, keeping back tears. The poor thing, indeed. It was unfair, the sacrifice it had to make.

"We'll need a couple of extras," Brenda said. "I'd like six altogether."

Kalina stepped back from the surgical stand. The blade of her vibrating scalpel glinted in the dangling overhead light Sprull had crudely attached to the low ceiling. "Six! Do you have any idea of how many I've already lost? I'm not used to working under these conditions!" Her scalpel sweep almost hit the wall of the modified survival pod that served as her operating room. She knew how to play the role of aggrieved technician, having seen many plays.

"Nine." Brenda was crisp, in charge of the number. This was better, to have everything neatly definable. It took her mind off the sad fate of the innocent bird. "We can get more. We have a source. We *need* six." There was a bin full of the dead pigeons from the unsuccessful surgeries. They had to be thoroughly destroyed so that no evidence was left of the modifications.

"It's not the number of birds I'm worried about. Though their quality has to be perfect if they're going to get anywhere near the Governor-Resident. A bent pinfeather, and he starts to twitch." Kalina had once dealt indirectly with the Governor-Resident, through the medium of Falu Kallender. At one time that had been a point of pride. "It's the *time*. Things are going so slowly. . . ."

"It's just what I expected," Brenda said, though this was a lie. She'd thought Kalina, an experienced veterinarian who had worked on the animals of high officials, would just slice the birds open and install the necessary gear, like putting a sausage in a bun. It disturbed Brenda that the clear image had been so wrong. It was those images, those visions of a realizable future, that drove Brenda forward, and allowed her to drive everyone else.

"We have plenty of time," she said. This wasn't true either. The Feast of Gabriel was in only two days.

"All right. I am getting better at it."

"You are."

"I'll get them done. This one's ready to be closed up."

Something thumped heavily on the roof of the pod.

Kalina looked up. "How did they get so far in?" The cheerful shriek of children was clearly audible. Someone danced a tarantella above them, then was gone. The three linked chambers that were the Olympus Club's secret place had been built into the depths of the climbing structures in the middle of Rhenre by Sen Hargin.

Brenda couldn't get used to the sound of laughing children. She had never realized how penetrating their voices were. She sometimes fantasized about heating up the struts of the climbing structures until they could no longer hold on and fell to the ground in an avalanche. In this fantasy, they did not scream but fell silently, as in a vacuum.

This let her know that it was not a real fantasy. In real fantasies, like the ones she had about Governor-Resident Oswald DeCoven, all the features were absolutely realistic, the timing, the decoy operations, everything. If they weren't, she would be unable to formulate her plans. There was no room for wishing, she thought, having already forgotten the problem with the pigeon surgery. Everything would work as she had planned.

4

From *Tale of the Three High Priests: Their Love and Revenge*, by Nathan Tso. Tso ran with the Mikado Khans, and died at the age of twenty-three in a melee. This novel was found complete in his database. Below are some of the footnotes from the Gowanus Translated Edition, used by new Union personnel at Government House to learn Martian mores:

6. Such snapping is not uncommon with rental weapons, such as the ones Hagopu and Miren are using to settle their dispute. To be "stub stabbed" is a discreditable way to die. It means that despite the weakness of the opponent's weapon, he has managed to kill you with what is left.

23. This hyperbolic description of the Chamber of Delegates is, of course, purely imaginary. There is no gold dome, no eagle with the moons as its eyes, and certainly no fainting couch for the Governor-Resident.

26. The Quicksilver Cascade is a recirculating fountain of liquid mercury. It drips from the teeth of carved cinnabar masks, swirls down the agonized curves of the paws of the great beasts, and at last settles in a concave spinning mirror in which, the story goes, you can see one, and only one, fragment of the future. Those who become obsessed with their future suffer progressive nerve damage, since there is an irreducible amount of mercury vapor in the air. It is that which has given Dr. Bren his shakes and his delusions of persecution.

38. The Officer of Gerberus is the Martian type of corrupt placeholder. No one lives in Gerberus, and no one ever has. But when territorial jurisdictions were being determined in the twenty-third century, it seemed a prime area. A scratch meeting at the Esopus Palace distributed Liaison Council seats more or less at random. While the Martian government does not recognize these jurisdictions, they still possess Council seats. The office is a pure sinecure.

40. These particular police detention cells are now a wine cellar for the San Gelani restaurant. The fashionably violent areas have recently migrated up past the Scamander River.

42. This mysterious ''Vizier'' is possibly a representation of an agent of the Academia Sapientiae. If so, it may be a piece of evidence for those who see Academia involvement in fragmenting Martian society.

57. Oddly, in Scamander corridor mores, being a police agent is not as desperate a crime as it is in other criminal cultures. This probably dates back to the Veterans Uprising of seventy years ago, when demobbed veterans of the Seven Planets War took to the corridors in an attempt to seize Scamander. They added a simultaneously disciplined and compromised style to the corridor crews, since their devotion was political, not criminal. Crews often serve as vigilante auxiliaries. So Dertouzos's crime is not automatically a mortal one.

Hektor scribbled quick notes on his pad. It had been a sharp debate—thundering denunciations, claims of peculation, a Minister of the North weeping in theatrical despair—about a minor allocation bill, and he wanted to write it down before he forgot the details. Audiovisual recording devices of any sort were prohibited in the Chamber. Delegates had been impeached, reporters arrested and imprisoned, for violating that law.

"Say, Hektor," Fabian said, peering down the wide flight of stairs on which they sat, "what the hell are they doing down there with The Seamstress?"

"A second, a second. Please, Fabian." This would make a good article, Hektor thought. He wrote for a city news source under the name "Kennedy." No one on the Chamber floor suspected him yet, though that would come, and be a problem when it did. But he needed the money. Low Chamber salaries encouraged either systematic corruption or moonlighting. If one did not violate one law to get by, one must violate another.

Fabian climbed up into the wall niche and tried to get a better view of what was going on below by dangling from the lip of the enormous porphyry jar displayed there. He optimistically assumed it was too heavy to tip over.

The vast stairway called Roman Steps started as a twisting set of steep steps no wider than a man's shoulders. As it descended, it grew wider, and the risers grew shallower, until it lost all sense of vertical drive and ended as the top of the West Gate of Rahab Hex. A statue stood in the center of the platform that made up the top of the Gate, now silhouetted against the angled sunlight shining across the vast space beyond. A group of people in severe Vigil uniforms were gathered at its base.

Now, the puzzle was how to reveal how closely the Uranius Delegates were tied to their industrial suppliers—unusual even by Martian standards—without serving as some sort of shill for Sylvia Rodomar. The Uranian Haustrae, someone had once called them. An ancient tribe. Hektor had looked it up, expecting some classical reference, Tacitus or something: haustrae turned out to be the rows of saclike structures that made up the large intestine. Funny, if abstruse. Hell, everything was falling apart. If he didn't use it now, he might never get a chance.

"Leave him alone, Fabian. Can't you see he's trying to get something done?" Egypt sat a few steps above, her own writing pad folded into the odd origami she claimed helped her manage her scenes. Her huge skirt had ballooned out around her until she was almost lost in the patterned fabric.

"If he wants to get something done, why is he trying to do it here?" Fabian asked reasonably. He shaded his eyes and again peered at the statue. "The Seamstress, an illusion. What *are* they doing under her skirts?"

The five-meter-high statue was an odd artistic hybrid of Julius Caesar and St. Sebastian. It stood with its head thrown back in ecstasy or despair, its eyes staring up at the apex of Rahab Hex's dome. Dozens of bronze dagger hafts stuck out of its formally draped toga in an even, hedgehog arrangement. It was Mars's own Ozaki, and the prickly artist had even come all the way to Scamander for the dedication. Ozaki was now on the Moon, Hektor had heard, working for one of the Judicial Lords there. The statue's name was "Julius Caesar," but the popular name had instantly become "The Seamstress." Ozaki had heard this, and thrown a tantrum dramatic even by Martian standards. Hektor hoped Ozaki's new boss was having an endurable time with him.

"Not an illusion," Hektor said. "Just another reality." He folded up his pad and stood. He wore a formal jacket with long, trailing sleeves, and a small cap tilted back on his head. It was an outfit suitable for strolling, and that was just what he intended to do. "We should be meeting Dek and Mini."

"Wait a second!" Fabian said. "I want to know what gives." He was almost dancing with the anxiety to investigate.

Hektor had, of course, brought Fabian here precisely to pique his curiosity, and perhaps to punish him as well, by withholding satisfaction of it. He hadn't heard from his brother since Breyten had left Xui House, and suspected that if anyone knew anything about him, it was cousin Fabian, who remained conspicuously silent on the subject.

The flare of a cutting torch working on the statue's base outlined the standing Vigils, who now wore reflective eye bands to avoid being blinded by the glare.

"Where are the ceremonial priests in their golden vestments?" Egypt asked. "The gowned acolytes? The procession of virgins?" She started slowly down the stairs. Hektor and Fabian followed. "Where the sacred oil? The pyx? The sickening smell of incense? Are these the last days, then, when the sacred becomes a procedure, and salvation a mere administrative detail?"

"Don't get out of control, Egypt, love," Fabian said.

"There's enough formal business on the Feast of Gabriel," Hektor said. "It was decided to handle this one simply. Administratively."

As they approached the statue, Hektor flashed a crystalline key at the Vigil in charge, an identification and authorization.

"Well," Egypt said. "There it is, my necessary *symbol*. What are you doing, Hektor? Is this your way of ringing in the Feast of Gabriel?"

Fabian's crinkled face suddenly cleared. "Of course!" He grinned at Hektor. "The Gates! You, good cousin, are in charge of opening the Gates."

"It's not much of an honor," Hektor said. "But it's all my own." He held the key up to the light and looked at it glint.

"There was a time when it was a grave responsibility," Fabian said to Egypt. "During the Gold Band Revolt, Joemon chopped Scamander up into tiny little pieces by closing every air lock, every gate, every checkpoint." He shook his head. "And still it took five long years to dig through all of Scamander, with its secret tunnels, its hiding places, its bolt-holes, and rip the revolutionaries out, squirming like worms, and hack their heads off. The last time anyone tried any political shenanigans like that. No one has used the Gate control for almost a century, save for Gabriel."

The Vigil workers had finally gotten the hatch at the statue's base unsealed. The surrounding metal still glowed red, and the radiated heat could be felt where Hektor, Fabian, and Egypt stood, looking out over the balustrade at the base of the stairs at the looming space of Rahab Hex. The hillocked surface was full of people, all intent on their own business. Pavilions, scaffolds, platforms were rising up and the air was filled with the clank of work, the shout of workers, all confused by endless echoes.

Egypt held tight onto the balustrade to avoid being sucked

into the great void of space that pressed into the densely tunneled rock of Scamander. It was so *big*, there was so much *space*, it seemed that you could see the air swirling around up there, trying to be as free and untrammeled as the air of Earth. It could be sucked out into the cold, dry atmosphere that surrounded everything, leaving the three of them heaving on the stone floor of the balcony.

Martian space alternated between the claustrophobic and the agoraphobic. Corridors dug their way through the walls and floor of Tithonium Chasma, one of the several parallel canyons that made up the vast Valles Marineris. Earlier settlements had hunkered just beneath the surface of the canyon wall, like beetles digging under the bark of a tree, but the city had slowly penetrated farther and farther into the rock face, until there were miles of passage with no connection to the surface.

Immense chambers swelled amid the tangle of corridors: the great public spaces—Rahab Hex, Pyramid and Jakarta squares, Hrost Dome—buried like the helmets of lost legionaries. The larger ones rose up through the more easily excavated compressed rubble of the canyon floor, only their transcendent oculi thrusting up into the unforgiving Martian air to stare at the stars. Rahab Hex was the product of a thermonuclear explosion in the wall of Tithonium early in Mars's settlement: many of the cracks that later served as the basis of Scamander's city pattern were the product of that detonation. It was the hollow suffering of these vast captive spaces that most aroused Egypt's agoraclaustrophobia.

"So you let people move freely," Egypt said, "for just one day. Is that freedom, then? To keep the Gates *shut* all the time?" She looked up at the transcendent political sacrifice of The Seamstress. "I've gone up those passages, the ones that run under us here. Once they were wide thoroughfares, probably filled with market stalls, traffic. Now they're blocked by monoliths, like something you'd find in a Pharaoh's tomb, and people throw trash there, and abandon babies. We did a little performance there once, remember, Fabian? The woman weeping at the stone that had slid into place, concealing her lover as he sought to rob the tomb. Hey." She was suddenly energized. "We should recast it, play it again, just as the stone slides back into place, at the end of Gabriel.''

"Bad luck for a slow actor," Fabian observed.

"We don't use Scamander enough. We don't need to build stage sets. We just have to use the right places. I'm making a change in my thinking.'' She adopted an expression of stern resolve.

"Everyone's too busy showing off during the Feast to watch someone else's theatrical performance," Hektor said with dry practicality.

"Unless you *guaranteed* that the actor would be too slow," Fabian said. He pushed his hands together and made a squishing noise. "Keep your mind on the aesthetic issues."

"No one's even going to be watching *my* performance," Hektor added. It was a purely ritualistic event, the opening of the Gates, and was usually under control of one of the junior Delegates in the Chamber, like Passover questions in a Jewish family. For some reason, he had wanted it badly, even angled for it. In the cold light of morning tomorrow he would turn his key, and the Gates that blocked the three old tunnels out of Rahab in this direction would slide silently open for the duration of the Feast of Gabriel.

"Poor boy," Fabian said. "I'll come see, if I can."

"They won't let you out here. The Vigil guards the whole thing."

"Then don't complain. A performance guarded by police is bound to be ill attended." Fabian craned his neck to see what was inside the base of The Seamstress, but the Vigils had already put up a tent of concealing fabric, and met his gaze with an impassive glower, a specialty taught at police academies since time immemorial.

"Let me look at that key so I can see something, at least."

"You can look," Hektor said teasingly. "But don't touch it." He held it in front of Fabian's eyes.

"Hey, don't mess with me. I'm not Breyten."

He knew as soon as he had said it that it was a mistake. He didn't even look closely at the key before his eyes, with the worn insigne of the tyrant Joemon, though under other circumstances he would have been fascinated.

"Where is he, Fabian?"

"I don't know."

"Don't screw with me!" The Vigils carefully did not turn to watch the argument, but continued with their operations.

"I'm not screwing with you, Hektor. I don't know where he is."

Hektor took Fabian's elbow, the first time he had laid angry hands on his cousin since childhood. "People lie on the floor of the Chamber. They prevaricate, they conceal, they deliberately misinterpret. They hide behind legalistic ambiguities in phrasing. That's the Chamber. My *God*, Fabian, why the hell are you doing it to me here?"

Fabian was sensitive to pain, but had learned to endure it from his encounters with Sildjin and the Dust Beggars. Hektor was unlikely to separate any of his joints or break any small bones. But it still hurt. Hektor had never hurt him before.

"Hektor!" Egypt said sharply.

Hektor let go, then, as if nothing had happened, raised his eyebrows at her.

"It's unfair to expect Fabian to be any more honest with you than Breyten would be," she said.

Hektor looked at them both, his friends, his cousins, and tried hard not to feel betrayed, as if they had made a choice between him and Breyten, and he had come up short.

"Another legalistic piece of logic chopping. I think the wrong man is serving in the Chamber. Either of you could—"

"Last I saw of Breyten," Fabian said, "we had just escaped an InSec raid on the dragon in Slanted Slope." He made it sound like he and Breyten were dancing on the dragon as a dare.

Hektor sighed. "The dragon. I would have liked to climb on there. It was the sort of thing we used to do."

Now Hektor was hurt because he thought he'd been left out of something, thought Fabian. "I'm sorry, Hektor," was all he could say.

"All right, all right," Hektor said, and hugged his cousin close.

"The worst place to be is in between you two," Fabian said, over Hektor's shoulder.

"Don't worry, Fabian. I'm sure the time will come when you won't be the only one."

High above the three of them, Gustavus Trep was climbing yet higher, into the narrow upper reaches of the Roman Steps, where they twisted like a snake with indigestion between bosses of gleaming tourmaline. Laughter came from behind Trep as he climbed. He stepped to one side and let a group of children run past him, though the steps here were taller than their knees, forcing them to ascend like manic mountain climbers. They would be tired soon enough, he thought. They disappeared ahead.

He remembered when he'd been able to run these stairs himself. He and his friends had raced from the edge of Rahab Hex, up through the tangle of caverns called the Sinuses, toward where the Roman Steps finally ended in the wide, low space of Cracked Lamina. The neighborhood grew worse as you climbed away from Rahab Hex and the stairs grew narrower. There were places it was easy to get jumped. That had made it more of a challenge.

Toward Cracked Lamina rather than to, because Trep had never known anyone who could run clear to the top. You always stopped and walked at some point, trying not to throw up, though Tony D'Souza claimed to have made it all the way once. No one believed him. Tony was dead now, killed trying to rob an old, bent-over woman who had turned out to be armed with a needle-tipped dagger, a family heirloom she carried with her because she feared someone else in the doss-house she had been reduced to would steal it from under her pillow while she was away. Tony's luck. He was just the sort who would finally make it to the Lamina, only to discover that his witnesses had fallen away, probably to relax themselves at bars farther down.

Trep slowed. Was he almost there? Of course he was. He did this every time. He peered up the stairs. They curved into a wider space with an irregular ceiling of torn rock. It had once been surfaced with subtle mother-of-pearl, like a sky of roiled cloud, but generations of decoration-minded looters had flensed the coating off, its replacement nothing but a tangle of dimly flickering gang cartouches on the roughly chiseled surface. Trep knew where his was, though he consciously tried not to look for it. He'd put it there when he ran the corridors around here and thought such memorials were important.

Ismee greeted him at the door. It was early yet, and the few customers at the tiny tables on their various levels huddled in earnest discussion.

"There's someone waiting for you," she said with a sort of gloomy satisfaction at ruining his relaxation.

He just looked at her.

"One of your people," she said without a trace of apology. "Take the private room in back. Just be out by eight—a marriage party wants it then."

"All right," he said. "Just send in double the usual—"

"She already gots it. Smooth as a skink, that one. Not like you were, roaring boy."

"Not like you either, Miss Razor Knuckles."

Ismee grinned. She'd dyed her teeth a delicate, pearly pink. She had a dished-in face, with deep-set eyes. When young, she'd been unusually beautiful. Now she was just unusual. She and Trep had known each other for years, and she'd run this restaurant for almost as long. One of Trep's first, almost-honest jobs had been as a bouncer in an early incarnation of the place. From there to police work hadn't been much of a step.

"You don't make business on smooth. Not up here. Go on now. Get her out, maybe you can put your feet up and take a rest."

"Not likely," Trep said, and stepped past her. "I've got too much to do."

"Bigger scams than we ever thought of," she said softly. "We worked hard, hit hard, fell hard. And got squat for it. What did we know?"

"Nothing," Trep said. "Not a goddam thing."

Miriam Kostal sat at the linen-covered table that filled the small rear dining room, making it look like a dining car on a long-distance magtrack. A small green bottle and a larger blue one stood on the table in front of her. Without speaking, she poured Trep his arrack, then added water from the larger, blue bottle until it turned opalescent.

"I thought it would be better if the hostess didn't know you were running Vigil business out of her restaurant."

"No need to be so nice. All sorts of business gets run out of here. Though you're right, little of it is as disreputable as ours."

Trep took a sip of the diluted arrack. The strong, sinuous flavor had its usual effect. He began to relax, despite the fact that he was going to ask Miriam to do something she would have every right disliking being asked. She slept with one of Lon Passman's sons, did whatever she damn well pleased, and was one of his best people. She irritated him, because he was afraid he would come to depend on her entirely too much.

"And you never feel like interfering in the local business transactions?" she said.

He snorted. "The delightful thing about being in the Vigil is that you never have to pay attention to real police work. A brawl, a theft, even a murder—call Scamander Police! Nothing to do with me. Never mind the hills, nothing less than Olympus for me. Give me insurrection, ethnic riot, criminals whose organizations require 3-D flowcharts to understand. Then I'm interested, I get on my happy face, my brass knucks. But here? Let people remove each other's intestines and throw them on the floor, I'll step over the mess, tell Ismee to get a mop over. It's all just personal incivility. I don't mind that—I grew up with it. So people talk to me, tell me things, sit down and vomit on my shoulder. Metaphorically, of course. You know how I despise literalism."

"I hadn't noticed. So this is where you relax."

"Ismee and I go back to the time when I was breaking heads myself. She used to hold them down for me. Yes. This is the *only* place I relax." Trep's corridor background was widely discussed in the Vigil, which was mostly made up of the children of middle-class families. They tended to be jealous of preferment, closemouthed, tailored-armor-vested. Both Trep and Miriam were rare within the Vigil for coming from outside that social stratum, but only Trep got respect for it.

"Quite a sacrifice, then, to invite me here."

"Damn right." Trep tried to smile, to take the sting out, but the effort proved merely dental. Somewhere out in the restaurant, voices were raised in anger. A shout from Ismee, and they calmed down.

"So why the little begging dance?" Miriam spoke with sudden heat, something he didn't permit any of his other subordinates. She was tense, he could see it, but it wasn't anything he could spare energy to think about. "It's something you know I won't want to hear, and you think inviting me into your clubhouse will calm me down. All right, I'm calm."

And with statuesque self-possession, she nibbled a bitter wafer, using only her prominent front teeth. She was a striking woman, if a trifle sinewy for Trep's personal taste. He preferred more padding. She was as formal as a society lady sending food back to the kitchen. Trep, at least, understood why she wasn't more popular among her colleagues.

"Filibusters," he said. It didn't do for a subordinate to be too perceptive. Some people liked that, secretaries who gave you your tea before you knew you wanted it, investigators who provided facts just when they were needed, informers who slipped you the kind of smoked meat you favored when you hadn't had it in a while. He didn't like it. It made him feel that his desires were too nakedly visible.

Miriam calmly took a sip of her arrack, then ran a finger through the hair above her right ear. It was clear she was furious.

"Fine. Take me off my duties, get me to chase after Lords of the Asteroids. Sure, they're a Vigil jurisdiction. But that's not why. There must be a good reason. What is it?"

"This morning a crew of InSecs tangled with a group of potential filibusters we've had our eye on, managed to arrest some of them. Blew our whole operation, right there. We'll have to start from scratch."

"Damn it," she said. "Who controls those guys?"

"No one. But that's not my concern right now. What I want is some information on how they found the filibusters. Last week they weren't anywhere close. There may be a leak—in the Vigil."

Her eyes grew wide. "Any suspects?"

"None I'm going to tell you about." He looked intently at her. "And stop running over possible suspects in your head. That'll only make things worse."

The Vigil, a Martian force, and Internal Security, the Union political police, had a long history of jurisdictional disputes. As far as InSec was concerned, the Vigil didn't even have any reason to exist. It also tended to operate with a wider, if more obscure, agenda, and most Martians suspected InSec of having designs on their independence.

"All right," Miriam said. "What's my investigation?"

"Confined to the facts in the matter at hand. How did InSec get its information?"

She frowned. "There's a reason you're asking me, and it doesn't have to do with my native talent."

God, he did hate perceptive subordinates. "Your point of contact is Fabian Xui, Hektor and Breyten Passman's cousin."

"*Moebius Daily.*" She managed to show no surprise. What a damn tar baby that family was turning out to be. . . . "He's good. I read him. But he's a journalist. He won't talk with me."

Trep grinned. "He'll talk. I got someone who—"

Voices bellowed in the dining room again, and frenzied pounding flexed the door. Trep and Miriam both stood, but there wasn't any space in the dining room to maneuver. The table filled almost all of it.

The door burst open and a heavy body came flying through it, to smash into the edge of the table and fall groaning on the floor. It was a large man with a huge flat face. A dense mass of sweaty, angry bodies jammed the doorway. "Asshole!" "Touched my woman—" "*Your* woman—" "That's right!"

A spin-off quarrel developed in the doorway. Ismee could be heard yelling ineffectually behind the angry wall of men.

"Lie down, Marko, and don't move!" Trep shouted. "Ms. Kostal, if you could assist . . ."

She instantly perceived what he wanted. Together, they picked up the heavy table, one on each side, and used it as a battering ram. They struck the men in the doorway without warning, knocking half of them over, and sending the other half reeling into the main room. They kicked heads as they went over them, Trep hoping they hadn't just concussed their informant.

The remaining drunkards rallied, but by this time Ismee had regained some control, and her bouncers quickly restored order. She grinned at Trep.

"Anytime you want your old job back, darling . . ."

"There isn't a week that goes by that I don't think about it."

Trep and Miriam grabbed groaning men by the legs and arms and flung them into the farther room, leaving, finally, only the recumbent figure of Marko in the small dining room.

He managed to grin up at Miriam. "I'm a man with a plan," he said. "Deadbeat, toilet seat, all that asks for introduction, get to meet. Let me take you on a trip, my sweet. Hey, hey!"

"Why'd you pick a fight out there, Marko?" Trep asked. "I asked you to wait."

"I got bored waiting."

"Fair enough." Trep looked at Miriam. "Your native guide. He can take you to Fabian Xui."

"Wonderful," she said. "Pleased to make your acquaintance, Mr. Marko."

"That's just Marko."

"I love men with one name."

Marko goggled up at her. "You do?"

"Sure. My dog has only one. What the hell makes you think any of you could rate two? Get up out of the vomit, and let's figure out what we're doing."

"I'll leave you two sweethearts alone, then." Trep tipped a finger to his temple and left.

Hektor, Fabian, and Egypt walked out on the quays of the Scamander. Living dust swirled at their feet.

"Hektor, Hektor." Dek Pargeter stood up from his cross-legged posture on the floor and took Hektor tightly by the elbows. "Good to see you." His blue eyes bulged in a narrow, almost-hairless skull, and he towered gantrylike above everyone else.

Hektor smiled. He had been nervous about meeting this human scalpel again, but now he focused on the fact that Dek's living was provided by a minor government sinecure that was held by the Chasmic Party: inspecting tourist hostels in west Scamander. Both the Fossic and Chasmic parties could have had honest reputations as patrons of the arts if they had wished. Most of the poets, critics, and columnists of Mars depended on one or another party-derived post for much of their income. Perhaps with the anticorruption drive, that would change. He wondered what Rodomar could do with the artists against her too.

Dek seemed genuinely glad to see him. Credit to Dek's soul, if not to his sense.

"Your dissection of Fatul's epic drama was discussed even at the Esopus Palace," Hektor said.

Dek half closed his eyes. "Not accidental, Hektor. I carefully put in plot summaries so the functionaries could fake familiarity with the deadly things. Now when people say Fatul, they mean Pargeter. The critic always wins the final victory."

"Really, Dek." Mini Pargeter kissed Hektor's cheek. "Didn't you have something for us to do? Hello, Hektor."

Mini and Hektor had been lovers shortly before she finally decided to marry Dek. She was almost as tall and thin as her husband, and they seemed a natural couple.

They all paused, indulgently, to let Egypt play with the dust. The Scamander began near the surface, just beneath a knoll otherwise indistinguishable from those around it. There was a story that the river's inspiration had indeed been a dust fall from the surface, swirling in through a collapsed passage, down over the contorted bodies of those caught in a catastrophic blowout, and that, in fact, the river was intended as a massive memorial to those now-unknown victims of inadequate engineering. Swirling dust is a poor medium for memory.

The river's fine dust, with its elaborate crystal structure, changed color with the light. Just now, at the onset of night, it glowed a dark, supernal blue, darker and more vivid even than the light of a glacier. The dust was magnetic, and cushioned with air, so that its passage was almost frictionless. Its movement was strange, unwaterlike, but Martians actually preferred it that way. A fine rill that ran down the edge of the Roman Steps finally scattered from a ledge overhead and fell into the main flow. All through Scamander, dust spilled from fountains, flowed like tears from the eyes of monumental rock-carved faces, crept from underneath the legs of public furniture, and all of it eventually made its way here to join the Scamander. And the Scamander ran through the center of the city until it reached the magnetic recirculators at the lowest levels of the city, its Ocean.

"Here, Hektor," Dek said, slinging him a satchel. "Make yourself useful."

It was heavy. "What is it?"

"The food." Dek smiled dreamily. "A feast tonight."

"Enough cilantro in the noodles this time, I trust," Fabian said.

"Coming from a man who uses sprouting garlic . . ."

"At least I don't burn it to the pan."

"A duel with noodles!" Egypt said. "Lasso each other and wrap them around each other's necks."

"Don't laugh, little one," Dek said. "I've witnessed such. Cooks are a serious business. The competing chefs at the Pasargadae once sliced each other up during a chopping competition. Blood all over, slippery floor. The one who lost passed out and banged his head on an oven. He resigned and pushed a noodle cart for expiation."

"That fight started a fashion," Fabian mused. "Those fingers delicately tangled in the noodles . . ."

"Re-formed meat paste," Hektor said, seeing that Egypt was growing queasy.

"Later on, of course." Dek was grand. "For those who were not privileged to be there at the original event, and get the real thing. They would make the crispy fingernails out of cuttlebone—"

"Please, Dek." Mini was exasperated. She looked to Hektor for support. "He eats in too many hotel kitchens. It's a life with too much broth and not enough noodles."

Hektor wasn't about to let her use him to bash her husband. He was too heavy a weapon. Though she had been quite pleasant to sleep with. . . .

"We'll never get a spot," he said, "if we stand here jawing."

"The voice of authority!" Dek exclaimed.

They distributed the rest of the gear—the sleeping pads, the silk privacy tent, the cookstove, the dry toilet—and started up the wide stairs that led from the Scamander to the main floor of Rahab Hex.

Hektor watched for Pamaot and her group from the Xui House neighborhood. It had been some time since he'd seen her, and found himself thinking about her.

Some of Rahab Hex's floor was flat, but much of the center was curved in sinuous humps, native rock carved into the semblance of windblown surface dunes. The five of them were supposed to meet other friends, people Hektor hadn't seen in years, on one specific barchan, the location of which Dek seemed unclear about. So they hiked along a dune crest, scouting out in all directions over the many encampments that already crowded the space. The dome loomed vast and high overhead, the air pressure within it being one of the things that kept it up.

"I'm helping carry a figure tomorrow," Egypt said. "Amme, I think."

"A good story, that one," Mini said.

"Fine, I've heard it. But what in the world does Gabriel have to do with anything?"

"Not hard," Fabian said. "You want the story?"

"*The* story?"

"Don't ask for too much." Fabian winked at Hektor. "Extremely important things like the Feast of Gabriel always have many more than one origin. That's what makes them so robust. So *true.*"

"*A* story, then."

They crossed down into a depression between two high carved dunes. The sounds of the crowd vanished. A group of people lay here in stern military rows, already asleep, save for a guard leaning on a spear, who watched the passersby warily. They were members of a tribe called Longing, a mixing of Tutsi and Sinhalese who had met on a settlement ship on the way from Earth over a century ago, their naturally tall builds amplified by low Martian gravity. They were migrating from east to west in Scamander, following some impulse known only to themselves. When they got to the western edge of the city, out past Xui House, they would turn around and come back, camping through the corridors. Westbound or eastbound, they always broke their eternal journey at Rahab Hex for the Feast of Gabriel.

"The explorer Hassan ibn Soldan got caught in a dust storm in the Vastitas Borealis. Half buried and dying slowly in the cold sands, he breathed shallow and saw visions: a great Ram standing on the ice cap, a spinning of the planets and the passing of time . . . there are differing versions as to the actual content."

"I don't need a variorum edition of the story, Fabian. Just pick one, for God's sake."

"Ram and spinning planets it is, then. After reaching down to clean the dust from ibn Soldan's air mask, a man climbed up and sat on the wreck of the explorer's overturned sandcart, and explained these visions to him: they were the news of the fall of the Orthodox Empire and the beginning of the Time of Tumults. This interpreter was the archangel Gabriel, he who came down to interpret the visions of the prophet Daniel. Some say that ibn Soldan saw the same visions as Daniel, only the interpretation being changed to suit the actual situation."

"Ibn Soldan said this?"

Fabian looked surprised. "Ibn Soldan froze to death there in the Vastitas Borealis. As far as I know, he never told the story to anyone."

"Oh!" Egypt said, exasperated.

"Here we are!" Mini said, and dropped her pack. It was a spot no different from a hundred others, but it was empty, and she wished to prevent an escalation of the discussion. Working in automatic cooperation, they hung their sleeping hammocks from the side of the steep dune and set up the dry toilet with its screen of patterned fabric. Barking suddenly authoritarian orders, Dek commenced the cooking operation, assisted by the grumpy Fabian, who was unused to being a sous-chef.

A vast tangle of scaffolding rose not too far away, like the skeleton of an excavated city. Workers moved in coordination, hanging from invisible lines. All the organization visible around him pleased Hektor, gave him a sense of underlying human structure. It was a world where the tensions from an anticorruption drive would soon dissipate, and he could get to some serious work of his own. Some unidentifiable tool was tossed by one worker, spun high in the air, and was caught by another, who immediately turned it to the necessary purpose.

Was that a drum array going up over there, beyond the scaffolding? Pamaot's group was equipped with drums. It had been a while since Hektor had seen her. Not, in fact, since the morning of the day that Breyten had left Xui House. Too long. Uninterested in him though she seemed, she'd think he'd forgotten all about her. If she was going to be uninterested in him, it wasn't going to be because he was uninteresting.

No one wanted Hektor to assist in the cooking. He was known as a clumsy and indifferent cook. The entire Passman family was hopeless when it came to creating food, though none of them was backward about consuming it. Hektor worked his way up onto the crest of the barchan and maneuvered through the increasingly dense crowd toward the distant drums.

Sen Hargin had designed the collapsing joint himself. Given thousands of years of human creativity, it was likely that it had been invented before, for a pivoting seal-harpoon head by a Nunivak Eskimo, for the framework of a Sultan's tent by an Albanian Janissary, for the leg of a robot used to explore a bubbling fumarole by an Afro-Asian American technician. Still, he didn't know about any of those things, and it was all his own. He tried not to be proud of it. When it worked, he would be proud of what it had accomplished.

"Are we set up?" Brenda asked.

"We are here." Sen's regular workers had done their jobs and gone off to get some brief sleep before the next day. Sen and Brenda stood at the base of the scaffold, looking off toward the platform where Governor-Resident DeCoven would appear toward the end of the next day. They had substituted the trick joint themselves.

"Balagan and Tri already have their schedules set," Sen said. "They're asleep at the doss-house."

"Good. We should join them too."

Sen moved a little closer. "Will we do it?"

"We will."

Since the duel, they had all thrown themselves into the task as if they had been looking forward to it their entire lives. Even Sen, doubts forgotten, had performed prodigies.

Tomorrow evening. By tomorrow evening it would happen.

"Got 'em," the tea seller said to Fabian. "Got 'em frozen."

"Ah, good. Good. Give me some tea while you're telling me."

"Sure. My real job, you know. And I'm good at it."

"I have no doubt that you are. But I think information goes with tea better than sweet wafers do."

"Depends on the information. Depends on the wafers. My wafers are good."

"Are they? Bake them yourself?" Fabian was always on the lookout for good streetfood.

"You see an oven on my back? Got a deal with a shop in Barneveldt."

"Ceebee's?"

The tea seller looked disappointed at Fabian's excessive knowledge. "Mpenge's Bakarium, actually."

"Not as good, but still okay," Fabian said with a shrug. "Give me two. And the story, quick. Your own product, I hope."

"No one in Barneveldt serves information as sweet as mine."

The tea seller squirted tea into a glass from the machine he lugged around on his back. Rahab was part of this man's regular nocturnal beat. By day he slept in the lower side corridors with the rest of the night workers, jostled together like puppies. Tonight he had more business than he knew what to do with, but he still made time to talk to Fabian, who paid well for his other product. He was one of Fabian's many info sources.

"Tri Bahari," the tea seller said. "She works for Hurrian Catering."

"They do some good stuff," Fabian said. "They have a great sea-liver canapé. . . ."

"She's off from her group dwelling unit." The tea seller was clearly getting exasperated by Fabian's alimentary focus. He really should get back to the camp, Fabian reflected. Dek was probably getting finished with the food about now. He should never try collecting information hungry. It distorted his priorities.

"And?"

"She's snoring at a doss-house up Chalfonte. Why? She has a perfectly good place. Wouldn't mind living there myself."

"Maybe they'll have an opening soon."

The tea seller brightened. "Do you think so?"

Investigative work depended on probabilities and lucky breaks. The whole art was in amplifying the chances. Fabian had gone back to the Squallo dueling site and started tracking some of the people who had been there. Not the main actors, Brenda Marr and Sen Hargin, and not the casual drop-ins, but those overly intense watchers who had somehow been participating in the action.

There was a story here. Something deep, like hearing a rock tunneler rumbling somewhere under your corridor, connecting two incomprehensible points deep in Mars. Something that Brenda Marr, alumna of the Pure Land School in Nilosyrtis, was planning. It might be a surprise birthday party, it might be something savage. He was used to playing the odds.

"Packed her sleeping gear, kissed her dwellingmates goodbye, took off. More tea?"

"Yes. And more wafers."

"Better than you thought, eh?"

"Yes, sure. Just give them to me."

This easy trace was a bit of a disappointment. It implied the surprise-birthday-party option.

Fabian paid for the information with a clean round coin. He didn't haggle cost with his regular info suppliers. He enjoyed hearing what they had to say too much. If he ever gave up the news business, he'd have to pull the cost out of his own pocket, just for the joy of it.

"I have other customers."

"Go, then. Good business."

"See you."

The tea seller, weighed down by his tea apparatus like a turtle accidentally issued a too-large shell, wandered off down the crest of the barchan. Fabian, even though hungry, sat down, looked off across the crowded corrugated surface of Rahab Hex, and started to make plans.

"So where is Fabian?" Miriam Kostal's voice was crisp.

"Somewhere...." Marko looked around, suddenly vague. "He told me he'd be out here...."

"Somewhere. There are thousands of people in here." They stood on a rise, looking out over Rahab Hex.

"Yeah, I see them."

"All right, we'll have to back up one step. Do you know what he's working on?"

Marko grinned. "Me! I'm his best story."

"No, seriously."

"Oh!" Marko flopped down like a sulky child. "Words, words, words. Herds of words. He just makes 'em, fakes 'em, rakes 'em. No one knows why or what for."

"Come on. There must be something you know he's interested in." Silently, Miriam cursed Trep. This was an informer? It was like following a running child, hoping he'd head for his neighborhood school on his day off. All you got was exhausted.

"Duels." Marko was suddenly certain. "He loves those duels. Asks questions like there was something to answer."

"Great. Any duel in particular?"

"We had a one a couple days ago...."

Hektor watched Miriam and the strangely twitching pudgy man from a dune some meters away, wishing he could hear what they were talking about.

She was sharp. The tight gray Vigil uniform suited her lean curves and made her overly large hands and feet look efficient rather than gangly. The smoothness of her movement and the slight sway in her walk made her stand out from the crowds around her. She wore her wavy brown hair loose, barely restrained by jeweled pins. She gestured decisively at the man sitting at her feet. He stood up with a show of reluctance, and they set off to some destination of her choosing.

Hektor managed to avoid following her with his eyes until she disappeared. That turned him from his purpose. Instead, he turned and moved toward the high stack of metal drums. It was indeed Pamaot's group. He felt that he was moving like a panther. He'd finally seen a panther, on Earth, but it had been lying crouched on a tree limb and hadn't bothered to move, except to turn its head. Its head, and those intent eyes. Those eyes had moved like a panther.

They were just finishing up. He'd waited for that. She wouldn't pay attention to him while she was working, but once she was done, she would want to celebrate, get a jump on the Feast of Gabriel.

She saw him, grinned at him from the top of the drum stack. "Hey!"

"Hey yourself. Come with me. I have something to show you."

"What?"

"I can't tell you, otherwise I wouldn't have to show you."

She looked at her colleagues, who shrugged. They were probably irritated, Hektor thought. They wanted her themselves, which only made sense. But they had let her know them too well, given her too much time to be sensible. Hektor was not about to make that mistake.

When Brenda Marr awoke and stretched, the impulse of her movement flickered through the bodies of the sleeping Olympus Club members on the floor with a rasp of rough cloth and a joint-crack of bending limb. They had all been toppled together in the manner of doss-house patrons. Corridor and free-room dwellers learned from birth to tolerate contact with other bodies, and though no one in the room had grown up in the corridors, they knew enough to mimic the manner. Sprull, for one, claimed to be beginning to enjoy it.

Sen Hargin squeezed Brenda's wrist once and sat up to activate a glow lamp. The room's lights would not come up for a few minutes, not that the fifty-watt sources, illegally converted emergency lights, provided much even when on. Brenda leaned against Sen's bony shoulder as she undid the cloth around her hair and let it fall over her shoulders. It was getting ratty, she knew, and today she would have to spend some time brushing it out until it was gleaming. Events demanded that care.

All six people in the square, low-ceilinged room were quickly alert. Pads were rolled and stowed in their rack, personal possessions slid into their lacquer cases, gowns resealed into active daytime configurations. Kalina scraped her tongue with the bitter disk she insisted on for her health, Balagan did a long series of lazy fingertip push-ups, Tri pulled at her own long dark hair and winced at its condition.

Kalina turned to the birdcages against the wall. One by one, she sedated the birds inside. They wouldn't move or make a sound for two hours. Together, she and Brenda wrapped them tightly in colored cloth, making them look like ceremonial presents.

"He'll be coming up the long stairs," Sen said in Brenda's ear. "Not too long now. First light, he said."

"Time to eat, then," she decided. "Where is that doss-keeper?"

The room lights came up and they heard his loud ringing staff on the jamb of the door opposite, and the low rumble of voices as the inhabitants of that room reluctantly awoke. Brenda waited for a second, then jerked the curtain aside. Staff just raised to pound, the dosskeeper peered expressionlessly into the room, nodded, and turned away.

"Let's get set up," he said, still facing away. "So that you can get your breakfast."

The doss-house had once been a much grander space, perhaps the home of some corporate official. The ceiling was carved into a decorated vault. The composite walls were peeling away from the underlying rock, but the main room still had a balcony hanging out over the Chalfonte fault, a crack that led directly down to the Scamander River.

The stretched glass that roofed the top of the fault was still a black strip high up the sloping rock and would not provide light until the sun was much higher. There was little scattered light in the Martian atmosphere, and no mirrors were positioned to warm Chalfonte with reflection. Lights of various spectra were coming up on the walls. This fault was old, lived in for over a century, and generations of replacements, modifications, and malfunctions had given its lighting a dappled appearance. The fashionable areas of Scamander had moved down past the river, into the rubble floor of Tithonium Chasma itself.

They set up the low tables and heated up the griddles in the kitchen. Vanilla-scented porridge was already percolating in the tanks, providing the morning rumble familiar to Martians without fixed abode. The sliding doors were opened to the corridor, and a few shabby regulars drifted in for their breakfast. It was perfect, Brenda allowed herself to think. A Vigil could come, sit down here for breakfast, and not notice anything out of place.

"Here," Sen Hargin said. "Come here, Brenda."

She joined him at the balcony railing, standing close to him. He'd kept the wound on his earlobe crusted brownish red, as a sign of his agreement with her.

"I think I see him," Sen said, pointing down the fault. "Just starting up that flight of stairs."

Stairs climbed up and down the stone walls of the fault, many hanging from suspension cables. Narrow, precarious bridges crossed here and there, their original, no doubt well-planned purposes now obscure, since the invisible arrangement of structures behind the carved windows and balconies of the fault wall had shifted several times in the course of a century.

Brenda looked down past Sen's arm. Was that him, that bulky white dot forging slowly up the endless stairs? She remembered the bird seller as she had first seen him, glum and huddled by his filthy cages, as likely to slaughter his stock as sell it. Then she had returned from Xui House with the empty cage, and he had, unbidden, told her how she could achieve what she desired.

"Are you ready for this?" she asked.

"You don't have doubts," Sen said. "Why should I?" Unconsciously, he touched his ruined ear.

She moved closer to him, to feel the warmth of his body. She had once been a prostitute in the Moebius district of Scamander. After the Pure Land School at Iqbal-in-Coprates, she had had dozens of casual sexual contacts. But she and Sen had not become lovers. Though she sometimes sensed the unconscious response in his body as they lay next to each other in the dark, each of them felt some strange need for purity. Looking at him now, feeling him near her, she suddenly regretted that.

"It will work," Sen said. "The Master will be proud."

"And surprised."

"Yes, of course. But it is his action we are performing." Sen took her elbow. She paid such attention to this gesture that it loomed larger than anything else.

A mutter of indignation followed the man climbing the stairs toward them. He was bent under a huge load of mesh cages, and the cages were filled with ornamental pigeons. He grinned vaguely around him, as if unaware of the source of the anger.

"Pigeons?" he asked. "Beautiful. Well trained. A comfort to your home. As fine as any the Governor-Resident has . . ."

"Bugger your Governor-Resident, and your pigeons!"

The pigeon dealer smiled. "Some other time, perhaps."

No one quite dared touch him, though some clearly would have liked to. As day came up, the stairs became more crowded, but he moved in his own open circle. He was a character from a comedy: bandy-legged, white-bearded, his sagging chest bare under the multiplicity of straps that supported the birdcages. He wore a hat with feathers on it. Plucked from the birds he was trying to sell? It seemed a poor marketing ploy.

"Amazing," Sen said. "Those birds are the only thing anyone seems angry about. He rules Mars from his invisible rooms, and no one cares that DeCo—"

Brenda pressed her fingers to Sen's lips, then took them quickly away. She had forbidden any mention of the Governor-Resident's name.

He smiled at her. "Anyway. The birds."

"Hey!" she shouted down at the birdman. "Come up here. You may have some customers."

Grunting, the birdman swung in from the stairs. The doss-keeper looked at him sourly. "Watch those things! Put them in the corner and don't bother my customers."

"Thank you, thank you," the birdman muttered.

"Sit with us," Brenda said. They helped him unhook his cages and pile them in a corner, along with the cloth-sealed boxes they themselves had brought in the night before.

The porridge was served. It was the poorest nourishing food there was, grown in huge vats. Odd that it should taste so good.

Brenda glanced around the room and almost froze. She willed her eyes to continue their slow scan. What was *he* doing here? The Vigil was much smarter than she had thought. She leaned over and squeezed Balagan's wrist. He was the assigned protector for today. He immediately understood the pressure signal, and leaned casually to one side to keep the room in view.

Fabian Xui slouched at the long table and delicately ate porridge off his spoon. Had he ever taken Egypt just to eat breakfast in a Chalfonte doss-house? It seemed a serious cultural oversight. However did dear Egypt understand anything about Mars with him so neglectful? He tried to pretend to himself that the porridge reminded him of his childhood.

He'd left the group this morning before anyone was up, following the tea seller's lead. Hektor had not come back from his little stroll, an interesting development, but now was not the time to consider it.

He finished his porridge and refilled his teacup. The group tried to look casual as they ate their breakfast, but they were tight as suspension cables. Fabian had no clue to what they were waiting for or what they were after. People came in and out of the doss-house, never staying long. He was becoming increasingly obvious. In a few minutes, regardless of whether he had figured anything out, he would have to leave.

But that tall man sitting at the table behind that overly gabby bird seller: Falu Kallender? It was, it was, he'd seen his picture. With Governor-Resident DeCoven, examining some goddam pigeon or other. Kallender was an animal breeder, a rich man, popular in various circles low and high. He bred the tiny floating hummingbirds that were popular in ladies' private rooms, some of the more miniaturized versions even serving as a sort of living jewelry. He bred workhorse pets like the turtles with the air bubble in their shell, which could survive explosive decompression and slide their way through rubble pulling air hoses to possible survivors by sensing the moisture in their breath. And, it was rumored, he bred fighting cocks for sport and toxic miniature snakes for use in private quarrels among otherwise well-behaved ladies.

Fabian had once tried to get Lon to talk about a trial resulting from one such quarrel, where Kallender had testified, but the Justice of Tharsis had been obdurate about the sanctity of the witness box. So Fabian had been unable to turn in his article to the school paper, in which he had promised to reveal the whole sordid story from ''inside sources.'' It had all come out badly.

That damn Kallender. What was he doing here, rubbing noses with pipe menders and foodsellers? And look, he was talking to that miserable-looking bird seller, examining a bird in a cage, fluffing out its wing feathers with delicate fingers. Always on the lookout for unusual breeding stock, that Kallender. And the tea was sour. Fabian felt that he had wasted his entire morning.

Kallender languidly chose three cages of birds. Two of the women wrapped them up like presents. For whom? The Governor-Resident? A peace offering, then. Fabian understood that Kallender blamed DeCoven for his business difficulties.

There was a bustle of movement. The porridge cooker functioned badly, and steam swirled in the air. A large group gathered around the bird seller, eagerly assisting him in reattaching his birdcages. Though the cages had been open on his way up, this time he insisted on having them all wrapped in a dark cloth. His irritable birds grew silent. Kallender picked up the three cages he had just purchased. The birdman swung back out onto the balcony, and Kallender strolled out into the corridor with peaceful sedateness, carrying his newly purchased birds. The corner was now empty. The doss-house was emptying too. It was time for Fabian to cut his losses and leave.

But wait. As he passed through the door, he looked back into the breakfast room. When the birdman had come in, there had been three covered boxes lying in the corner. Covered boxes . . . they might just have been wrapped birdcages. At any rate, through some sleight of hand, they were gone. And the birdman had covered up what he was carrying out of the doss-house so it couldn't be seen. He could have been carrying his own cages back out, and Kallender could be carrying those mysterious boxes from the corner. So, what the hell . . . ? Fabian hurried down the corridor after Kallender.

If there was something odd or mysterious about the cages he carried, Kallender certainly didn't show it. He strode down the

long straight corridor toward the Scamander River with them
slung over his shoulder like a householder returning with dinner,
the back of his elegant suit protected by a waterproof cloth he
had brought with him. It was bright morning, and the corridor
was full of people. Fabian did not have to hang back too far to
be invisible in the crowd.

The corridor broadened and deepened as it approached the
huge fault of the Scamander, until the floor dropped away into
a narrow gorge and they found themselves walking on a mesh
catwalk. The shops on the right had their backs out on Chalfonte,
and odd bits of sunlight now streamed into the corridor through
their wide-open doors. The left wall of the gorge was cut deeply
into high, pilastered facades, some of them flowing oddly to
conform to the twisted layers of the rock, as if they had been
cut before the rock had quite become solid. The gorge below
narrowed into a meandering crack, then opened out into a trans-
Tithonium tramline. Fabian could hear the rumbling of the train,
and just barely see the flickering of its lights as it passed far
below.

The catwalk split into a tangle of ramps and stairs. Kallender
climbed steeply. The number of people decreased, and Fabian
had to fall back. Above, the roof of the gorge climbed until it
broke through the rock wall to the canyon of the Scamander
itself. The edges of the arched opening were curved and ridged,
as if it was the orbit of some vast eye socket, the tangle of
dryland vines hanging down over it the desiccated remains of
some once-coquettish eyelashes. A single vast beam of light
streamed through the opening, silhouetting the tangled catwalks.
Far below, the tramway dove into a tunnel beneath the Scamander, and arched doorways on a platform above the tunnel opened
out onto the riverside promenade. Fabian could just see the tiny
forms of people as they strolled back and forth to the peaceful
river beyond, casting long shadows in the light coming through
the doorways.

A man and a woman stood on a bridge just beyond, their arms
resting on the guardrail, looking down at those same people. The
male wore a too-short jacket, the female's hair was ragged, and
Fabian recognized them instantly. They were both members of

the little group he had been observing only moments before. Were they gasping a bit from the run it must have required to get ahead of him like that? Their casualness had a quality so forced that Fabian found himself doubting that they were ever casual, even in their most relaxed moments.

He should have turned and run immediately. But Kallender was climbing toward a choice. If he took the lower passage, eventually he would come out onto the balcony overlooking the Scamander. But if he took the higher passage, he would be heading for the high-speed elevator that would bring him up to the corridors in the narrow space above Rahab Hex, where the offices of the junior Delegates were, or even higher . . . to Government House, squatting on the rim of Tithonium. Was Kallender taking a delivery directly from this odd bunch, agents of Rudolf Hounslow, to Governor-Resident Oswald DeCoven?

Kallender stopped and exchanged a few words with a turbaned woman holding a small child. The child was excited by the sound of the pigeons in their covered cages and reached a small hand out to them. Kallender laughed and swung the cages away, murmuring a warning to the mother. The child, not at all disturbed, switched its attention to the edges of its mother's coat. Kallender waved, then turned to the right and disappeared. He was heading for the elevator. That was as much as Fabian had time to figure out. He had to—

A foot sliding on the catwalk grating alerted him, and he had time to swing aside before the knife caught him. The blade rang on the guardrail, and Fabian ran.

There were many people far below. Fabian could see them clearly as they went about their daily business. But there was no one here on the high catwalks, he saw now. No one but his pursuers.

The knife had cut his jacket open and he could feel the cold air sliding across his rib cage. Over three goddam pigeon cages? If they hadn't wanted anyone to notice, they shouldn't have come up with such a complicated scheme. Those two unconvincing loungers were moving to cut off his escape ahead, and two more were leaping steps up from lower levels to get him from the sides. Fabian paused for a moment, looking out over the high, silent space, but saw nothing that could save him. There would be no negotiating with these people, he knew. A bunch of pigeons, and they wanted him dead. . . .

They came at him on the narrow catwalk, jostling for position, each wanting to be the one who finally spilled his blood to drip down through the grating onto the heads of unsuspecting citizens below.

At the last possible instant, Fabian swung himself over the railing and dropped. The world blurred around him. He'd calculated his trajectory correctly. He dropped onto the catwalk below. His feet slipped and he fell heavily to his hands and knees. His pursuers' feet clattered on the stairs as they sped quickly down toward him. But now he was far ahead of them. He chortled to himself. What a story this would make!

He got up and ran. Tried to run. Searing agony in his knee. He'd twisted it in his desperate drop and he now lumbered along, holding on to the guardrail for support. His vast lead had now shrunk to nothing. Still he ran, piercing flames rising up his thigh into his hip. Maybe he'd shattered the patella, or torn the ligaments on the inside of the knee joint. Unfortunately, he'd never know exactly: he wasn't going to be attending the autopsy.

They swept up behind him, sliding like a breath. One blade went in above his kidney, another quickly sliced the side of his neck, cutting the carotid. There was no question of another dramatic dive over the guardrail. They held him tight as he died. The last thing Fabian Xui ever saw was his own hands, massive and distant, stretched out toward the light.

5

From a review of Egypt Watrous's *Har Soon and the Moons of Mars*, in the May 2332 issue of *Useless and Dismal: The State of the Arts*, by Dek Pargeter:

   ... It is, perhaps, otiose to attempt to add my meager aesthetic and philosophical excrescences to *vox populi*: this ardent piece of philosophical corridor theater is already sold out for weeks. Your humble voice himself had to presume on a personal acquaintance to obtain a seat, and even that had sight lines seemingly willfully obstructed by a pleonasmic column left over from the era in which the theater was either a bordello or a police interrogation center, something even intensive documentary research has not clarified. Perhaps, characteristic of the shrewdness of the Vigil, it was both, with suspected perpetrators gasping out confessions in the last extremities of passion . . . but I digress. . . .

   ... must be familiar with some aspect or another of the story of Bertilla Li Prakrit. But the auditor is guaranteed to be startled by Watrous's handling of Har Soon, the eternal squire, for this is his story. One sees Har Soon staggering under the weight of her armored gauntlets, the brilliant edge of her silk robe as she romances the doomed Hugo, her furious shadow on the wall as she confronts Joemon, but the magnificent Bertilla is never actually visible on stage. . . .

... not to give away the conclusion. But this Har Soon is not the big, hairy warrior of popular song, but a humble man with a life in the Scamander corridors. Dare we say that he is likely closer to historical reality? Like a mammal scampering from the clash of Tyrannosaur and Stegosaur, his goal is to finally squat down for a decent bowl of noodles. Don't order the noodles on sale in the lobby, incidentally. The seller has some contract with Eleanor Blank of Gangis Water, who has sponsored the play as a way of demonstrating her resistance to arrest, and the noodles are indictably inedible. . . .

Hektor Passman descended the stairway through a massive, howling-face-topped gate into the Feast of Gabriel, where he was immediately buffeted by the loud, unruly mob that now ruled the corridors.

Behind him was the quiet lacquered dining room, where his father sat. Its vivid peacock decorations were polished to a high gloss, its gleaming wineglasses were never allowed to be empty, its specially bred flowers would open slowly as the evening wore on and fill the air with thickening scent. Wine-soaked cakes rested in porcelain bowls, surrounded by the hum of conversation. Lon held social court at a high cloth-shrouded table, the Ax of Judgment embroidered before him. With Hektor's departure, he was now abandoned by both his sons.

They had waited for Breyten to at least poke his head in, wish his family luck on the Feast. Melisande had come to cheer him, with a half promise from Trep to show up later. But the one Lon was waiting for did not show up. The only encouraging information they had about Breyten was negative: no cleanup crew had reported finding his body. Somehow that was not enough to base a celebration on.

Hektor was pushed against the wall by some informal parade: a succession of vast masks, each three meters high. The canyon was packed solid with humanity, and the masks made their slow, dramatic way toward Rahab Hex. One dark blue face had feathered silver eyebrows that fluttered gently in the breeze that blew down the canyon. No one could see even a hundredth part of the Feast of Gabriel, and each person's experience was completely separate. Yet it unified all.

Hektor was looking for Fabian and Egypt. He had not returned to them the previous night. He had, instead, taken Pamaot over to examine the mysteries of The Seamstress and impress her with his awesome responsibilities of the next morning. Pamaot had allowed herself to be impressed.

Giant mythic figures were carried on the backs of willing acolytes. One of them, arms outspread, head thrown back in ecstasy, Hektor recognized as the Terran saint, Aya Ngomo. A blue-green glow came from her forehead, the color of the ngomite she had discovered.

Egypt was going to help carry a giant figure of Amme, she had said. By waiting with his father for Breyten, though he had known it would be in vain, Hektor had missed their first time-place rendezvous point. He would have to find Egypt somewhere in this crowd of symbolic figures.

He had not thought about Miriam Kostal while making love to Pamaot. That, at least, Hektor was glad about. Once they had climbed into the tangle of silken sheets Pamaot had cheerfully looted from the privacy tents of her still-working colleagues and felt the smoothness of each other's skins, the ancient rhythms had reasserted their mastery, and Hektor hadn't thought at all. Poor Pamaot. Beautiful and charming as she was, she had become just a necessary distraction. On some level she had recognized this and, once morning had come, had refused to come see him do his one formal duty of opening the Gates. She said she had too much to do. Hektor knew that from now on their talk would be coolly formal. He was sorry, because it was his own fault.

The canyon grew wider as side passages entered and it neared Rahab Hex. He looked for some indication of Amme, the romantic figure who had murdered the father of her lover, Brakner, completely in error, thinking he had killed his own son. What would she look like here in this celebrating canyon? This wasn't the place for her. Hektor remembered a painting of Amme: her odd, large-wheeled bouncer flying over the lip of a dune as if trying for the stars overhead, the cliffs of the Chasma Boreale gaunt in the background, Amme's grim face just visible in the bouncer's front window, the center of the composition. You wouldn't be able to see someone's face through polarized glass like that, but it was art.

Other figures rose above the crowd, like dreams of their secret identities. Images from myth, from history, from imagination: the Gabriel figures, due to be destroyed at the end of the evening, the culmination of the Feast.

There, crouched protectively, was the tragic hero Brakner, Amme's lover. It had been his secret imprisonment by Perdure, Tyrant of the Canyons, that had led to Amme's violent and mistaken murder of Brakner's guiltless father. A poet had once said that Brakner was every young girl's first love. Amme and Brakner were an old and romantic story, and even somewhat true. Just like Egypt to deliberately confuse them.

Hektor paused and watched the heavily muscled figure lumber by. He examined the people beneath the bulging calves, but detected none of Egypt's quick energy there. Still, he followed, having no other target. Brakner swept around a curve. The crowd had thinned and Brakner's acolytes moved more quickly. Hektor pushed himself into a lope.

Gowned students ran past with unsheathed swords gleaming in the insanely bright overhead lights. The Feast of Gabriel was a security nightmare, as had been pointed out to De-Coven. Hektor could feel the pulse of excitement and the undercurrent of violence. The destruction of the Gabriel figures was more than symbolic, and the infirmaries would be full in the morning.

But the figure of Brakner had paused near the tiny rill of a dust fountain and was tilting as his figure was transferred from one group of acolytes to another. Was that her? He touched her elbow.

It wasn't her. A lovely woman, high thick eyebrows, lashes like ferns, skin fine and thin as a glowing nebula, curling brown hair pulled back and flowing down her shoulders—but not Egypt Watrous.

"Excuse me," he said. "I thought—"

"Don't," she said. "Not today." Her lips passed like a whisper across his, so light he wondered if he'd dreamed the kiss.

"Today, I'm afraid, I must. Do you know where Egypt Watrous is?"

Her face grew serious. "She was supposed to be with us. She was called away."

"For what?"

She shook her head. "I wasn't there. But it was serious." She smiled again. "So if you would—"

"I'm sorry." He didn't like the feeling her news gave him.

"All right." She shrugged. "Enjoy the Feast."

"I'll try to."

Egypt Watrous pushed herself back against the side of the spiraling corridor to let the cart pass. It was loaded with personal possessions—cooking gear, embroidered cushions, a pet lizard with a feathered headpiece—and squeaked as it rolled slowly down to the lower levels. Three small children sat on top, trying to touch the ceiling. They seemed unaffected by whatever change in the family's fortunes had necessitated this humiliating public journey.

They would probably descend to the Scamander River and cross it via the Bridge of Regret, a bridge that hung low over a deep defile. Dust poured down the sides of the defile, as if the rock itself was disintegrating, and the Bridge of Regret held on by shining wires. There was no need to cross it, of course, if you didn't want to. But rented carts full of belongings rattled across it all day long, even if they had to take a substantial detour. Regret had to be more than felt on Mars. It had to be seen and shared.

Fabian had explained it all to her once—ascent in life by stair, descent by ramp—but she could no longer remember any of the details of these social symbols, just the sound of his voice. Yesterday he had promised that he would show her all the sights of the Feast of Gabriel. She was climbing this passage in the wrong direction.

Fabian was dead. They had come to tell her as she was laughing and getting under the elaborate figure of the Martian hero Brakner, while feeling stupid for having told Hektor the wrong thing. A Scamander police officer with a black band over his eyes had called her name. The Feast of Gabriel went on through the canyons, domes, and corridors of Scamander, but her husband, Fabian, was dead.

She crossed the spiral—the wrong way to ascend—and found a stairway. It climbed at a dizzying angle. The combination of human physiology and Martian gravity created stairways that were something out of nightmares. Just below her was a crack like that in a cave where water flowed below. Since this was Mars, there was no water, but she could feel cool air being pushed ahead of some distant train.

Ahead, she could see her stairway climbing to join others. They were all outlined against bright lights hung from the walls of the swelling space above: police lights, with the police dark, insectoidal forms swarming over the maze of catwalks and stairways. And in the middle of their movement, an unmoving black dot, like a single drop of paint spattered on an otherwise crisp and linear composition.

Egypt pushed herself, flying up the stairs, feeling the breath in her chest like a live thing, something separate from herself. As, indeed, her heart had to be. She wore a flowing dress of many layers, and it floated around her as she rose, quite as if it would float the same way should she choose to jump over the rail and drift down to the distant tramway. Martian gravity was nothing. She ran only for the exercise.

Her throat burned. If her breath was something separate, it was suffering. She took a deep breath to open up a path of coolness for it. The catwalks cast gridiron shadows on the distant walls in a hundred intersecting patterns. Great fans of light reached out into the darkness as people walked in front of the lamps. Shadows flew out like bats. Fabian lay on his face, arms stretched out in front of him, as if reaching for something.

"Egypt Watrous?" A tall Vigil reached out and took Egypt's arm, a gesture half of direction, half of support. She had a long nose, a big jaw, and curling brown hair cut in a helmet. Her brown-green eyes were full of concern. "My name is Miriam Kostal. I'm sorry that we have to—"

"Let's go."

He was soaked in blood. It had dripped down many levels, through the catwalk gratings. Scamander police knelt near spatters of it, making it fluoresce and checking for any other blood disguised by it. Two officers knelt and turned Fabian over on the network of lines that marked his orientation for the police cameras. Egypt stared long into his bruised face and tried to tell herself he looked peaceful.

"Yes," she said. "Fabian. My husband." Her eyes were dry and hot.

"Oh! . . . Here, please, please, let me—" Miriam caught Egypt's weight as her knees buckled and held her. "Can you walk? Here, let's go over . . ."

Her knees wouldn't work, but every line around her was clear, as if inscribed with ink on paper. Egypt could see the police watching without appearing to, their eyes staring just past, until she couldn't tell who was invisible, her or them. Two of them were having an animated discussion, their faces close to each other. In Martian fashion, their gestures were confined like leashed animals: a fist pulled into the speaker's abdomen, a twist of the shoulders.

Fabian's leg was twisted at an odd angle, his own last gesture. Egypt wanted to observe it, to catch exactly what it looked like and what it said, but Miriam was in the way.

"Sit down here." Her grip was velvety firm.

"There will have to be a notice in the *Moebius Daily*. Bordered in black. Maybe they'll let me write it. I know a lot about him. . . ."

"I'm sure they will. Now, I'm afraid I'm going to have to ask you—"

"Ms. Kostal, could I talk to you for a moment?" It was the senior of the two arguing officers. He introduced himself as Suhashi. His pink face was flushed from the effort of the previous discussion, and it was clear he wasn't looking forward to this one.

They stood aside. It was a jurisdictional dispute, Egypt gathered, Vigil versus Scamander Police. Jurisdiction was based on motive. If Fabian had been murdered by whatever group Miriam Kostal had been trying to find—Fabian's filibusters, it sounded like, and here he'd thought they were so secret, all his own—it was a Vigil investigation. If it had been by someone else, Scamander Police took charge. Fabian would have been interested in this discussion. He'd always maintained that context was everything. But he was dead, and the context didn't matter. She was glad he wasn't around to see the wreck of his own argument.

"Maybe I can clarify," Egypt said. Her voice was steady, which surprised and disappointed her. "Fabian wasn't working on the filibuster story this morning."

The police officer gave Miriam an unearned look of triumph. "Very well," he said. "Let's get the story." He called over a few other officers and graciously permitted the Vigil to stay.

The Scamander police officer who leaned against the railing and took notes as casually as if they were for a personal letter had confetti on his shoulders, in his hair, in the folds of his sleeves. While they talked and determined here, Egypt thought, the Feast of Gabriel was continuing. That was where they should all have been, dancing with children and drinking rose wine.

"There was some group he was after," Egypt said. "He was very excited by it. I think, he never said, but I think it was because of that woman we saw. . . ." Egypt remembered her, striding furiously up the stairs after them at Xui House. Had she killed Fabian? She had certainly wanted to. She had wanted to kill both of them. Egypt had watched her movements, trying to catch them for a character. Little exaggeration would have been necessary for that chilling movement to play on stage.

"She was one of Rudolf Hounslow's people," Egypt finished. "Her name is Brenda Marr."

The Scamander police officer raised his eyebrows. "Perhaps it *is* a Vigil job. Hounslow's a political, isn't he?"

"Maybe," Miriam said. "But not an important one."

"Doesn't take an important one to commit murder."

"True enough." Miriam felt nettled by Suhashi's unexpected quickness. She redirected her attention to Egypt. "Would anyone else know where Breyten was going?"

Egypt shrugged. "Hektor, most likely. Hektor Passman. Today he'll be at The Seamstress, but otherwise at Xui House or the Chamber offices."

"Thank you for your assistance, Ms. Watrous." The police officer was gentle. "I must ask you to remain available for further questions."

"Of course."

The police were suddenly swarming, some of them heading up Chalfonte to where Fabian had apparently spent the morning. And they were now wrapping the body for transport, using thick white sealcloth with the black Good Fortune ideograms some long-ago Buddhist bureaucrat had mandated. Egypt watched carefully, noting their manner of tightening the winding sheet, and the tender yet impersonal way they handled the body.

"Are you a writer as well, Ms. Watrous?" Miriam asked.

Despite herself, Egypt smiled. "Do you find it heartless? My husband is dead, and I—"

"No more heartless than my own profession."

"But no less."

The two women's eyes finally met at an angle not purely professional. "Certainly not. Anything that involves cutting something open while it's still alive must be considered heartless. But I must go, Ms. Watrous."

Egypt felt a tingle of pleasure. "You're learning something. You're figuring something out."

Miriam shook her head slightly, less in denial than in confusion. "I don't know. But . . . I'll have someone escort you home."

"No. Please. I'll just sit here for a while. It was the last place he saw anything from. I think I should see it too."

"All right." Miriam was brisk. "I'll leave a guard up there, where she won't distract you. No, please. I must insist."

So she left Egypt there, sitting on the catwalk and dangling her feet over the edge. The glowing outline of Fabian's body would fade slowly over the next hour.

It was a bloody mess, thought Miriam. She had only been chasing Fabian Xui as a source of information on a possible

Vigil security compromise. Now Xui had apparently uncovered some other deep plot and been murdered for his journalistic pains. So Miriam had no choice but to be sucked after it.

Scamander Police were up Chalfonte now, checking out the doss-house where Fabian had been spotted earlier in the morning. Strictly speaking, it was out of her hands. Though Suhashi, the Scamander Police officer in charge, would permit her courtesy participation in the investigation, it was no longer a Vigil concern, since the filibusters seemed no way involved. Still, some form of organization clearly existed, and organizations were always a Vigil focus. She found herself walking the catwalks away from the Scamander, up to the doss-house.

"Please hold this straight out in front of you." The Internal Security officer handed Brenda a small weight shaped like a sleeping cat.

Brenda, her foodseller's tunic pulled partway off and hanging down from her waist, did as she was told. The InSec, a slight woman with violet eyes, narrowly examined the muscles of Brenda's shoulder and upper arm.

"Do you cook a lot?" the InSec asked.

"No. I only serve."

"Build a lot of muscle, hauling pots of soup."

Brenda didn't answer. Outside the security tent, the crowds in Rahab Hex were shouting, mostly at nothing. Drums pounded, music played.

"Did you just cut your hair? The ends are sharp."

Brenda ran her fingers through her odd, short hair. "Boss's orders. I keep it trimmed, or it gets in the food."

The guard hadn't really been interested in the answer. She was just proving her attentiveness to herself. "All right, get dressed." InSec provided close-in security for the Governor-Resident.

Brenda could just barely hear Sen's own examination just beyond the curtain. They had been searched. No weapons or toxins were in the meat pies they were delivering for Hurrian Catering, where Tri Bahari had gotten them temporary holiday jobs. And the InSec had just checked for evidence of martial arts training: unusual body-hair wear patterns, idiosyncratic muscular development, shock-induced bone growth, abnormal calluses.

Brenda stepped out into the light and noise. After a moment Sen joined her. His nostrils were flared with rage, as if fear of assassination was something unreasonable. The food carts appeared behind him.

The searches before entering Oswald DeCoven's private chambers had been much worse. His bodyguards had searched every orifice without trimming their fingernails. For the first time, though it should have been on her mind since the first moment she had conceived the plan, she wondered if he would recognize her. She had been his assigned lover for two months. An odd thing, choosing her, she gathered. He favored smaller, more feminine women. But he had actually turned out to be her most cordial client. As well as the most profitable. He'd seen her only in the half-light of his room, wearing the clothing that he chose for her. By the time he figured out who she was, it would be too late.

The crowd was just a disjointed mass of faces and limbs. She couldn't recognize them as human beings. She and Sen pushed their cart toward the clot of notables that stood in the middle of the platform. She recognized Falu Kallender, whose eyes scanned across them, carefully blank. Kallender had managed to delude himself into thinking that the modified pigeons were intended merely to humiliate his old friend in front of the Martian mob. Deliberate anagnosia, the disease of dupes.

The poor pigeons, Brenda Marr had time to think. It wasn't their fault. They had not chosen to make the sacrifice. It seemed utterly unfair.

A huge balloon floated, spinning, in the center of the dome, kept in place by calculated air currents. Very old, it had once blown free in the winds of Mars's atmosphere. It was the planet Mars, this one covered with cheerful oceans and forests, a premature celebration of the benefits of terraforming.

Specks flickered up along the vast buttresses, circling the balloon. Hektor squinted, trying to make them out. It took him a few moments to recognize flocks of fancy pigeons with multi-colored feathers. DeCoven was somewhere around with his fellow bird fanciers.

Disturbed by the absence of Egypt and Fabian, Hektor had retreated to one place they would be able to find him: the foot of The Seamstress. He paced nervously there, looking out over the crowd, no longer enjoying himself. He could see the drums of Pamaot's group and the gold-horned goat that was their mascot. Their repaired bird stalked next to them on its stilts. The tunnels through the Gate passed to either side, dipping down, and right ahead of him was the formal presentation platform.

Oswald DeCoven stood on the platform. He had garlands of flowers around his neck, given him by some schoolgirls in a staged ceremony. Though there were lots of people on the platform, there was a subtle gap around him, as if he secreted some sort of toxin. Huge, empty frameworks loomed over him like unfinished construction projects. There was no way to tell what they were supposed to be.

DeCoven looked confident, his oddly firm fat seeming to give him extra strength. He chatted with one of his fellow bird fanciers, Gar Song. Was this a time to discuss fine points of plumage? DeCoven's blitheness was a good move, Hektor thought, even though he knew it concealed terror. Martians would never respect a ruler who could not move freely among them. Though Rahab Hex wasn't as crowded as Hektor would have expected. There were a million interesting things going on throughout Scamander, and it seemed that the Gensek's representative on Mars was one of the lesser attractions.

"Mr. Passman?"

He turned, ready to bristle. There was a cordon around where he stood, no one should have been . . . it was Miriam Kostal, solemn in her Vigil uniform.

It was a complete surprise, and though he was doing nothing more than standing and waiting, he felt as if he had been caught doing something embarrassing. He was afraid that he blushed. Her mouth was parted, revealing clean white teeth, canines particularly prominent. Her eyes were strangely wide, and she was as motionless as The Seamstress looming above them.

"I . . . I have some bad news for you. Fabian Xui is dead."

"How?"

She told him. The crowd noise seemed to come in waves, sometimes silent, sometimes intolerably loud, almost blotting out her words.

"That wasn't what Fabian was made for," he said. "He wasn't made to die that way."

Tears streamed down his cheeks. He barely knew anymore where he was standing, but he had the presence of mind to take a finger and flick tears in four directions: behind, left, right, and to the front. His mother had taught him that. It brought safety to the ghost, a safety the living person had clearly lacked.

"Egypt?" he said. God, poor Egypt.

"She's been told. She gave us information . . . and I must ask you to—"

"Of course you must. Fabian never told me much—here, let's move away, not stand in front here on display." They stepped away from in front of the murdered Caesar, and he found them a seat on the steps to the side. They sat together like old friends watching people walk by.

"He never gave me much information about what he was working on." If he was to help find his cousin's killers, Hektor realized, he couldn't be coy. "Partly that was because he didn't want to tell me about Breyten, and what Breyten might be up to."

Now it was her turn to show color. They were just the right people to be speaking of this crime, Hektor thought. Only they could fully comprehend the emotional resonances. By some standards, that made them just the wrong people to be discussing it, but those standards were not Martian.

"Breyten has left Xui House," Hektor said. "Did he tell you that?"

"We have not spoken."

She was investigating the death of his friend and cousin, dressed in a gray uniform with glints of gold, but she was brittle, and Hektor found himself hoping he wouldn't hurt her by what he said.

"I suspected Fabian of helping Breyten contact . . . the sort of people Fabian wrote about. I didn't know who. Some group . . ."

"Filibusters?"

"Sounds right. Sounds like Breyten's kind of thing." He looked at her. They were too close together. He should move away. "Is that who killed Fabian?"

"No. Filibusters had nothing to do with it. It was a group of people, most of them students from a place called the Pure Land School."

"Hounslow's people!" After his discussion with his father the day Breyten left Xui House, Hektor had devoted some thought and study to that man and his movement. "One of them came to Xui House. A woman with long red hair."

"Was her name Brenda Marr?"

"Might have been. I only saw her briefly. I was worried that she was going to do some harm to my father. Breyten seemed to think that was foolish. He escorted her out. But Fabian . . . Fabian brought her up. From the front room."

"That's what Egypt told me," Miriam said. "But another thing . . ." Hektor half stood, looked out across Rahab Hex. "She brought a pigeon with her."

"What?"

"A pigeon. It was an insulting gift for Father."

Miriam stood with him. The pigeons that had been circling the high spaces under the dome fluttered down and covered the open frameworks that stood above DeCoven. They had been carefully trained, and their variously colored feathers turned the frameworks into yet new ceremonial figures. They were common and easily recognized: the Buddha, The General, and The President, a goggle-eyed figure with a bristling mustache made of fluttering pigeon tails. At the far end of the platform, Falu Kallender busied himself with some detail of the frameworks.

DeCoven stood, lonely in the crowd, a trained pigeon on his finger. It seemed the only living thing on Mars willing to deal with him. Hektor felt sorry for the man. The pigeon cocked its head and examined the Governor-Resident.

Miriam was seeing something else. She was seeing a single

fluttering blue feather. It had been found stuck in a crack in the empty sleeping room at the doss-house. There was nothing else there, not a single trace of the group they were looking for, latest of hundreds to sleep in that room.

There was no sudden flash of realization. Miriam still didn't understand what was going on, but had a sense of intolerable wrongness, as if, deep in one of the puzzle pictures she had enjoyed as a girl, there was a man with hands where his feet should be, or a woman unscrewing her child's head. Sometimes she had been unable to find the wrong thing, and those pictures had made her so anxious she had torn them out and hidden them behind the hall clock, where, as far as she knew, they still were.

A fight suddenly broke out in the crowd just below the Governor-Resident's platform. Miriam could see the flash of sword blades, though the fight was inaudible. Guards from the base of the platform forged forward, impeded by the crowd, who always liked seeing swordplay.

The crowd noise grew louder as the fighting seemed to become general. Blower-powered powder torches sent three-meter colored flames into the air. The strident metal-drum band frantically pounded out a counterpoint to the rising sound of the riot.

"Don't look at it!" Miriam shouted at the world. "It's just a distraction." She ran down toward the Vigil guards at Hektor's access into the statue's base. Hektor, having no idea of what to do, followed.

The platform seemed closer, as if his eyes had telephoto ability. A man and a woman standing near the Governor-Resident suddenly grabbed pigeons off the looming frameworks. With the gesture of a man pulling the top off a wine bottle, they ripped the birds' heads off with their bare hands. Blood spurted out of the necks. Suddenly they held knives, knives that had been concealed in the birds' spines. Hektor was momentarily awed by the bizarre pointlessness of the technique.

DeCoven jerked back, raising his arms to fend them off, but it was far too late. The assassins ignored the distracting forearms and dove in to slice open his belly. He wailed and fell backward, blood flooding out of his guts. Without waiting for anything else, the two assassins leaped from the platform's edge and ran through the cleared area at the base of the Gate, right below where Hektor and Miriam were standing.

Suddenly a long, scaffolded grandstand lost cohesion deep inside itself and slid to the ground in a tangle of pipes and flying bodies like a sand-and-dust avalanche. The shouts of those injured and trapped in the wreckage competed with the roar of the rest of the crowd. The guards at the base of the Governor-Resident's platform jerked, and some of them moved forward to assist the wounded.

"Move!" Miriam shouted at the guards, and sprinted down the access stairs that descended one side of West Gate, down to the surface of Rahab Hex.

"I'll—" She was gone. Without another thought, Hektor dove through the tent coyly hiding the access to The Seamstress's base and insides. He felt helpless, a mere witness, but there was one thing he could do. Of course, if the assassins had another path in mind, all his actions would do was confuse things, perhaps allow them to escape. But it was the only thing he could do.

The Seamstress was hollow. Decades ago, someone had strung lights inside so that its contents could be seen. Hektor had an instant of regret. He should have shown Fabian this sight. It was something he would have appreciated.

Hektor pulled the key from around his neck and jammed it into the ornate gold-trimmed box that had once been the tyrant Joemon's personal control center for impeding intra-Scamander travel. Only the controls for the passages through West Gate were still operable. Hektor slapped them closed with the back of his hand and, with the intolerable feeling that his chest was about to explode, turned the key.

He could feel the rumble of the heavy Gates closing. Warning lights and klaxons were sounding through the long, wide tunnels, sending festival-excited revelers scurrying. He hoped no one was passed out in the deepest levels.

For a moment he gazed up at the inhabitant of the darkness inside the ceremonial statue of Julius Caesar. The deformed and vandalized form of Joemon stared grimly out at his metal prison. It had once been a monument at the edge of Rahab Hex. Joemon had kept the instruments of his control in the base of his own statue so that he could look up at a many-times-multiplied image of his own face as he imposed his rule. The statue had been blasted and dented after his fall, but after the excitement had died down, it had simply been encased inside another statue and forgotten.

He pulled the key out and ran back outside. Miriam and the Vigil guards were gone, in pursuit of the assassins. And down below . . .

It was a Martian crowd. They didn't scream, stampede, rush forward to gaze greedily on the mangled body that lay on the ground. A ring of silence expanded slowly around them, preceded by a low hum of explanation—Martians had a gift for the efficient description of violent death. Within a few minutes, silence filled the vast rotunda of Rahab Hex, broken only by the flaring hiss of the powder torches.

Oswald DeCoven lay on his back, dead, the lower half of his body soaked with blood. His pigeon stood on the ground by his head, pecking desultorily at nothing. Falu Kallender, weeping melodramatically, was being hauled away from the body. The guards on the platform now regarded the fluttering pigeons with tense paranoia, and argued about what to do with them.

The crowd regained its life. Within five minutes, the roar was as loud as it had been before the assassination. But the mood had changed. It was not mere incomprehension or callousness, or even, yet, support or approval of the assassination. It was automatically understood by everyone that DeCoven's death marked the end of the Feast of Gabriel, which normally did not happen until just before dawn. Ceremonial figures toppled, shattered, went up in flames. They lived only here, in this festival, and the fall of the Governor-Resident marked their fall as well. Prolonging their existence any longer would have been pointless.

Hektor himself felt like leaping down at that giant slope-shouldered arhat holding a dragon and smashing it into flinders.

But he had things to do, calls to make. The political ramifications of the Governor-Resident's assassination would be far-reaching.

But before he could even get to a comm point, three Vigils had come to arrest him.

6

From *Tale of the Three High Priests, Their Love and Revenge*, the Gowanus footnotes:

58. The historical knowledge Hagopu casually displays here is not unusual. The corridors have risen en masse several times in Scamander history, most notably during the system-wide Time of Tumults (2197-2225), the Gold Band Revolt (2235-2240) against Joemon, and the Veterans Uprising (2260-2262). Songs and stories of all these conflicts are continually popular in the corridors, and crews have elaborate genealogies, based on adoption.

63. These ideograms hang on the dome pendentives in Pyramid Square. This passage is an indication of Nathan Tso's education. He came of good family. Your average corridor runner would not be concerned with them, save to pickpocket the Terran tourist who comes to stare up at them. The ideograms are made up of Latin, Cyrillic, and Arabic characters inlaid in elegant mosaic calligraphy, their meanings dependent on a delicate multilingual punning allusiveness that Scamander schoolchildren have to study for an entire semester before understanding. After that, the clues to their knowledge of a dozen national literatures can be found hanging above their heads when-

ever they go for a stroll. This, incidentally, is why Martian visitors to Earth sometimes seem bewildered and ignorant. They have left the abacus of their cultural calculations on the wall at home, and have never gotten used to simply working it out in their heads.

65. Bertilla Li Prakrit is a popular figure in Martian legend, and no tale of struggle and honor would be complete without mention of her name. She fought first for Joemon (2201-2241), then against him when he reached agreement with the Union to support his rule, and her death is popularly supposed to be the result of betrayal.

70. "Reach" is an indispensable Martian public attribute. It refers to the ability to dominate the space around you with the movement of your body. The exaggerated shoulder movement and sleeve sweep will mark any dominant Martian, from Delegate to High Priest.

77. Protector's Gate, with its countless busts, statues, and allegorical sculptures, is the repository of Martian political memory (see note 63).

85. That Hagopu's blood spurts so far is an indication of his high status.

89. It is not unusual for a crew High Priest like Anders to wear such elaborate makeup. Though the funeral is of a rival, the white powder and lashes are a sign of severe respect. That Anders is dressed as a "bride of the dead" is a charming but unsubstantiated theory.

Once, in school, Hektor had been taken on a tour of the Crystal. "Prisons and Discipline," the course had been called, a requirement for graduation. They had gone around the periphery of the confinement area, Hektor realized now, never penetrating into its glittering, refractive heart. Those being questioned—witnesses, criminals, relatives of victims—had been nothing but vague, distorted shapes, beyond human understanding or caring. And that had been the salutary schoolchild lesson: the actions of the Law are a mystery. You would be wisest to do your best to avoid them.

He remembered a narrow staircase pushed against one of the outer facets. Frost had formed on the cold crystal face and flaked off, to lie in piles at the base of the stairs. Hektor had looked down at the hand-sized translucent ice plates, lying like discarded playing cards, and concluded that the Crystal was profoundly frozen ice, kept scraped and polished by the tireless efforts of the Law's minions.

The minion of the law facing him now had what looked like fine linen cloth clinging to a face with a bulbous nose and a receding chin. The Vigil resembled a figure out of stock corridor comedy: he would have made a perfect cuckolded husband. Or rather, the mummy of one. High-arched eyebrows had been drawn above the invisible eyes, giving the face a look of supercilious disbelief, as if any answer was the wrong one. He had introduced himself as Lemper and had been questioning Hektor for most of the morning.

That damn face cloth! It was stuck on with some sort of dermal glue. Hektor wanted to lean across that absurd bean-shaped silkwood desk—what could they possibly keep in those tiny drawers with the triangular handles?—and rip the mask off his face, yanking every hair out of his skin.

"You were to turn the key at midnight," Lemper said for the tenth time.

"Correct."

"In no way were you authorized to turn it before that time."

"Correct." Hektor had resolved not to argue, not to try to justify himself. There was no point to it here. This was not the forum.

"And the key was in your possession for the entirety of the Feast of Gabriel."

"Correct."

The faceless Lemper would answer no questions, and Hektor had been unable to get any information since his arrest. He had no idea whether the assassins had been caught or what had happened to Miriam Kostal. All he knew was that he was in deep trouble.

"You used that key to close the Gates."

"I had to," Hektor said, forgetting his own resolution. "The assassins of the Governor-Resident were escaping by using the Gate tunnels as a route."

"You used that key to close the Gates."

"Were they captured? Did it work? If it did, the act is its own justification."

"You used that key to close the Gates."

"Yes! Correct."

The entire Crystal thrummed with eyewitness testimony, Hektor knew, though all he could see was distorted shapes through the transparent refractive walls. The Vigils sat like human microphones and noted it. There had been few still cameras at the Feast of Gabriel, and no video at all. The Feast was something to be experienced, not seen. Or, if seen secondhand, to be reproduced in some other medium than simple, direct visual representation. One might hear a song about it or see a puppet show, perhaps a bully bunraku where the puppets were moved around by being precisely smacked with bats. Smacked until the puppet Governor-Resident's powder-dry head flew off in fragments.

Hektor knew the trouble he was in, though no one had bothered to explain it to him. He had, by his own hand and by his own authority, closed the Gates. It didn't matter that they spent most of the year closed, it didn't matter that they were scheduled to be closed in a few hours, it didn't matter if closing them had trapped the assassins. He had closed them, and that was tyranny, and not to be borne. He should have understood the message in Joemon's shattered visage.

"Thank you for your time, Mr. Passman," Lemper said. "You may leave now." He put his gloved hands in front of him on the desk and sat motionlessly, exactly as if turned off.

"Am I being charged?" Hektor asked. Lemper did not respond, but a door slid silently open. After a moment's hesitation, Hektor stepped through it.

A pulsing red line guided his path through the refractive passages of the Crystal. He didn't know what would happen if he strayed from the line, and had no interest in finding out. He ascended a smooth ramp and found himself at the top of the

Crystal, leaving it through a circular hole in its top.

Above, he found himself at the bottom of an inverted conical space dozens of meters high, as if he stood at the base of a dust devil made of huge chunks of stone. Stone stairs, devoid of guardrail, ascended in a widening spiral. The roof overhead was monolithic stone, and the stairs exited through a small hole hacked in it. He shivered and felt suddenly foolish in his colorful festival dress. It was utterly inappropriate for this black, uncaring space. The cone was a trap. Anything falling into it would inevitably roll to the bottom, to fall through the hole into the Crystal. But the only light in the space came from that same Crystal, illuminating everything from below.

Some form of judgment had already been made, else Hektor would have been permitted to leave via another exit. There were many ways out of the Crystal. He tried to console himself with the thought that at least he hadn't been forced to leave through the one that led directly to the confinement chambers that were actually sealed cars on an Ascraeus-bound train.

He climbed the jutting stone steps in a widening gyre. They were just too high and too far apart to be ascended comfortably. His footsteps echoed and were lost in the wide space above. His shadow played on the shallow stone dome. He was above the Crystal, but this place had the psychological valence of the deepest hole possible. The stone blocks were marked with shattered holes where iron bolts had been gouged out.

The stairs climbed through the square hole in the dome. Above was a stone hatch. Holding his breath, he pushed it open. Light streamed down on him. He climbed through.

As a boy he had come to this place, Raeder's Flat, to see the suspected criminals climb, like wearily resurrected corpses, through the narrow opening in the floor. Once Breyten had, through some excess of judicial zeal, winged a pebble at a particularly fat suspect pulling himself into the light. The man had only winced and bent his head over further, his fleshy arms straining to pull him through the too-small hole. Breyten had been soundly whacked by a police officer's white baton, and been punished even more severely upon returning home.

Hektor heard the murmur of crowds as he pulled his way up

into the light. It was too bright to see. His eyes teared. But he knew not to pause and give people a chance to think. He randomly picked a direction and walked, head back and arms swinging, as he would always move in a public space. He heard a mutter of discussion as he appeared. The hatch sucked itself shut behind him.

Things swam into focus. Raeder's Flat was low and wide, the roof supported by irregularly spaced columns. There were no walls visible, and it vanished into a hazily glowing distance in all directions. The exit from the Crystal was only one spot within it, but it was here that the crowd had gathered, held back by the taut cords of police barriers. Hektor looked around at them, but no one would meet his gaze.

Without pausing, he ducked under the barrier and pushed his way into the crowd. They parted before him, each flicking him a look before affecting an interest in the now-featureless hatch in the floor. Clothing was dark and restrained, hangover cloth, the figured silks put away until the next public festival. Hektor was left like one of DeCoven's ornamental pigeons, vivid and bedraggled, trailing his tail feathers between them.

The crowd was dense near the barrier, but within a few meters there was no one. Hektor finally slowed, looked around, tried to figure out where he was going, but Raeder's Flat gave him no way to orient himself. It was like the mined-out seam of some no-longer-useful mineral. The sensible thing would have been to knock out the support columns and let the place gracefully collapse until it vanished.

He was in a dust storm. It was thrown up by DeCoven's assassination and would soon settle, but meanwhile, he had to protect himself and keep from being stripped down to the bone. He looked back at the crowd, which stood, barely speaking, and stared at the circle of floor, waiting for the hatch to open again. He wished he could go up and ask one of them what was going on.

The knot of people shrank behind him. It was going to be easy to walk in a circle, since the randomly placed columns did not allow for orientation. But there might be another crowd gathered around another hatch, though it would look like exactly the same one. . . .

"Hektor!" Egypt came running up behind him, her skirts and jacket flopping loose. She grabbed and held him as tightly as a found child. He gathered her up and looked down at the mass of curling dark hair that was all he could see of her head.

"Were—" His tongue was dull as a shovel. "Did they catch them? The assassins?"

She looked up at him. He often forgot how small she was. The top of her head was well below his chin. "Didn't you hear? Didn't they tell you in there?"

"No. They didn't tell me anything. They just made statements, had me agree with them. All clean, all procedural. I'm in deep trouble. I closed the Gates. . . ."

"He's dead!" Until this moment her eyes had been dry, but now she had found someone who would understand her tears. She jammed her face back against his chest and wet his shirt. "Fabian's dead."

"Fabian is dead." And he felt a sense of overwhelming shame.

"Yes, yes. They stabbed him. The same ones. The assassins." She babbled the story, and he listened, too shamed to tell her that he knew it, that he had forgotten about Fabian in favor of his own problems, his own questions.

"Oh, Fabian," he said. "He was going to stop, he said. Find another line of work. . . ."

She shrugged, a gentle, tremulous movement, like the wing flutter of one of those damn pigeons. "You and Fabian told me not to worry so much. It's Mars, you said. Mars isn't safe. Lock your doors, get into bed, keep the oxygen close by, it still isn't safe. You like it that way. He liked it too. Liked that edge between life and death. Childish. Like you."

"Like me? Not like *me*, Egypt. Not at all like me." He rubbed fingers in his dirty, disheveled hair. "Like Breyten, maybe. I can get through life without needing to taste death's tongue. Do you know where he is now?"

"I don't know, Hektor. I don't even know how to ask. I identified his body when it lay on the stairs. He didn't enjoy dying, Hektor, not at all, no matter what you read—''

"No matter how hard you try, there's still a distinction between life and literature.''

She managed a smile. "Oh, Hektor. He'll miss you, wherever he is.''

"I'll miss him too.''

He was too conscious of her body as she held him. She was small and quick, her body gently round. There was always a guilty way to comfort a widow....

The distant crowd murmured again. They turned and looked back at it.

"It's frightening,'' Egypt said.

"It's meant to be.''

They didn't move. Both were now curious as to who would be the next person out of the hatch, the next person to brave that crowd of curious, intent Martians. Just as curious as the rest of the crowd.

It was no surprise to Hektor when he recognized the swaying walk, utterly inappropriate to the hostile, buzzing crowd. Miriam Kostal paused for a moment, then put both hands behind her head to fluff her hair, as if she had just stepped off a train and was waiting to meet someone.

Hektor waved, and the distant movement caught her attention. He waved again, and gestured her over. She took a deep breath and came over in their direction.

It occurred to Hektor that if she was being questioned in the Crystal, she might face the same thing he did. Perhaps conspiracy was suspected, and she was now entangled in the closing of the Gates.

Miriam came up to them. Her posture was confident, but her face was tired and drawn. She tugged at the braid on her collar with her large hands. It slid off, and she put it in her pockets. A few other adjustments, and her Vigil tunic was nothing more than a plain jacket.

"It's rough,'' she said. "I'm no longer on duty.''

"Did you get them?'' Hektor asked, unable to stand it anymore.

"Yes," she said. "We got them. Trapped against that damn sliding rock you dropped. They didn't even fight. We just picked them up. They should have stayed on the platform, waved the bloody knives, *explained* what they were doing. But . . . nothing."

"And that," he said, "is why you're in trouble. I'm sorry."

"I suppose that's true. But don't apologize."

They were together now, he saw, associated because of that one flash of event. They looked at each other, her agate eyes against his dark blue ones.

"Excuse me." Egypt's voice, that of someone excluded. "Do you know where Fabian's body is?"

"Come with me," Miriam said, with the air of someone with nowhere else to go. "I'll take you."

"On Earth," Egypt said, "on the part of Earth I come from, we put them in drawers."

"Drawers." Miriam was musing. "At home?"

"No, no. In a morgue like this, but hidden. You slide them out when you need to look at them."

"Can anyone look?"

"No. Only doctors."

"That makes sense."

Egypt looked around the space they stood in. "You Martians are onstage too much. It's stressful."

"We're *all* onstage," Hektor said. "So we share the duty."

"Not everyone is an actor," Egypt said. "And the dead shouldn't be."

"Maybe you're right," Miriam said. "But you didn't grow up in a tunnel on Mars."

"No," Egypt said. "I didn't."

Egypt had her pad out. Her pen moved idly over it. Shamelessly, Hektor peeked over her shoulder, expecting to see some stern and futile note about the shoddy management of Scamander's North Morgue. Instead, there was a quick sketch of a seemingly infinite expanse of floor—she'd bootlegged Raeder's Flat into this cramped, almost-womblike space—and tiny, tiny bodies, each on its table with a lot of space around it, stretching out to the limits of vision. Other figures moved through the space, holding up heads to examine them, flopping dead arms over their own shoulders in a cruel parody of conviviality, pulling legs apart for an indecent peek.

That was unfair. No one was allowed to touch the bodies, at least not officially, and you could be punished if you were caught. Still, Hektor had seen one man run his fingers slowly through a dead woman's hair, though whether it had been a last, tender leave-taking or anonymous necrophilia was disturbingly ambiguous.

The space was a series of chambers with opalescent walls. The floor was softly padded. The bodies lay on their tables, each spotlit from the high white-coated ceiling, floating on a sea of darkness, sealed tight with preservative resin and already perfused by embalming fluid. Murder, household accident, old age, suffocation: the bodies were arranged indifferently, with no relation to the manner of their departure.

You could come in here. You could claim to be looking for someone and come in here whenever you wanted. And indeed, small, solemn groups made their way through, glancing from side to side but not looking with fearful intentness for a missing friend or relative. They wore cloaks, some with hoods. You look Death in the face when he arrives, but you don't go looking for him—that's impolite. These people were tempted, and ashamed. Their neighbors would think less of them if this came out, even if the neighbors came here themselves.

The bodies were naked. The dead are without decency or shame, and lie sprawled without attempting to cover themselves. Solid bands of color marked the sealed incision lines of autopsies. Organs not forensically significant floated in clear cylinders under each table, should a passerby wish to peer at a pancreas.

Something changed in the air. Hektor turned his head slightly, looking up, trying to see what it was. Something about the . . .

"Damn it," Miriam muttered. "Now this is just too much. Let me get some reinforcements in here—"

"Wait." Egypt took her arm. "I recognize them. Fabian's friends."

"Excuse me," Miriam said, raising her voice. The official

quality of her tone was obvious. "Are you next of kin?"

A half-dozen men and women in slashed clothes froze, holding Fabian Xui's body half off its table, looking like a satirical Deposition from the Cross. His knife wounds had been taped shut with vivid dark blue. His head sagged to one side, his mouth half open, as if he was a drunk being picked up off a floor. The light was dim here. It left the figures on the other side of the table as blue shadows. The change Hektor had half seen was a light-blocking tangler someone had tossed up to cover the overhead light.

"Are." The speaker was a pudgy man with hacked-up hair.

Miriam squinted at him. "Marko? What kind of games are you playing with me now?"

Startled, he blinked, thought about backing up, realized there was nowhere to go. He thrust his chest out in bravado. "He's our boy, Ms. Kostal. We take him."

"And you have authorization to withdraw the body?" She had no official standing anymore. She wasn't even armed. But she was pleased by how confident her voice sounded. It wasn't at all the voice of a woman who had just spent a sleepless night being interrogated in a crystalline hell.

"We got authorization." The speaker was a squat, powerful man with dark, dusty skin. "Want to see it?" The crew moved away from Fabian's body, letting it fall back to the table, and curved around to either side, threatening to flank Miriam, Hektor, and Egypt.

"Dammit." Now Miriam was mad. It was too late to call for reinforcements, even in this secure space, and she was about to get involved in something else she had no interest in getting involved in.

"Jesus," Egypt said. "Let them have the damn body."

Miriam shook her head. "It doesn't work that way. Doesn't work that way at all."

The gang's weapons were not too severe. A few clubs, short swords, brass knuckles. Stuff ill suited for open combat, better for jumping someone in a dark corridor and smashing him flat before he even knew what was going on. Still, they would do.

Hektor had no interest in mixing it up, even for his friend's now-cool corpse.

"Hey, now," he said. "What's the use of this if Fabian isn't even here to write it all down for us?" He stepped forward, quickly examining the faces that now looked, sullen and stubborn, at him. He tried to ignore the weapons they held in their hands.

"You're the Dust Beggars. I've read all about you. You, Marko. Still nursing a grudge against that guy from the Krimski Plague?"

Marko grinned slowly. "Took care, and he wasn't aware. Jumped him, bumped him, took him grunting, I was hunting. He'll be no trouble anywhere. One morning I was just running along, sneaking, seeking, when, no warning, I . . . I . . . well, I took care . . ." He trailed off in the face of the stocky man's glare.

"And you're Sildjin," Hektor said. "He liked you. At least that's what he wrote. But writers are liars, right? That right, Sildjin?"

"Get off," Sildjin said dangerously. "Right off." Sildjin liked breaking people's hands, Hektor remembered. "Giving them extra thumbs," he called it. He'd broken Fabian's little finger once, in an instructional mode. Fabian had described the dull, distant snap with such vividness that the reader learned to fear Sildjin too.

Hektor, trying to forget that particular feuilleton, looked at him. "He was my friend too. And my cousin."

Sildjin snorted contemptuously, but he didn't move forward. He just squinted, as if Hektor was getting hard to see. Hektor had picked the right one. As long as Sildjin didn't move, none of the others did either.

Hektor looked past them at where Fabian, their chronicler and celebrator, lay half on his side, one of his arms dangling down over the edge of the table. Fabian seemed irritated at the goings-on, but too tired to do anything about them.

The clothes the gang wore were stolen, or made to look stolen, in a piece of distinctive corridor-status coding. Deliberately the wrong size, they either were gathered up in flaccid bunches by riveted netting or were slashed through to fit over too-large body parts. The slashes were backed with other fabrics of contrasting colors. A little too deliberate, Hektor thought, but effective enough. One of the reasons the bodies around them were naked was to prevent the taking of corpse-cloth, a popular piece of style in the corridors.

"And Egypt is his wife," Hektor said. "She's in charge of his obituary. In the *Moebius Daily*." Egypt didn't say anything, but just nodded slowly. "So what are you planning to do with our poor friend?"

Sildjin smirked. "Cost you something to find out." He swung his club against his hand. "Not a lot. Cheap lesson. You wipe yourself right or left? I like to leave a man with his wiping hand, you know? A clean butt . . . well, it's something even a jellyboy like you should have. 'Course, you might hire someone else to do it . . . hell, either hand, right? Either hand. Hold them out, let's be a good boy. Teacher's choice."

Hektor shook his head and clucked his tongue. "You want Fabian or do you want to do some flailing?"

Next to him, Miriam sighed in theatrical exasperation. "Let's cut the fancy negotiation, Hektor. Save it for the Chamber." She had no visible weapons, but stood ready to produce violence. Hektor was startled by the change in her, the result of Vigil training. Perhaps Breyten had been right to suspect the effect of Miriam's profession on her personality. It seemed wrong that she should be able to pull on an invisible suit of armor with spiked fists at just a moment's notice.

"I'm busy," she said. "I don't have *time* for this sort of nonsense." She flicked the fingers of her hand dismissively at Sildjin. "Please vacate."

Sildjin and the Dust Beggars weren't going to vacate. They genuinely wanted to give their friend Fabian the proper send-off, Hektor realized. It wasn't just the desire to cause trouble— though that was there, of course. They would take trouble if they could get it.

For a moment Hektor was irritated at Miriam's raising of the emotional stakes. Violence had become not only possible but probable. Then he realized what she was doing. She was permitting him to take up the middle ground. Instead of being a threat to Sildjin, Hektor was turning into his only salvation, his only way of leaving the situation with any face.

"Sildjin," Hektor said, "Fabian's parents are dead. We are his only family. You"—he gestured at the crew—"me, and Egypt. Would you act without us?"

And Breyten, he thought, wondering where his brother was.

"I—" Sildjin eyed Miriam, who, still not manifesting any weapons, stood ready to fight. "What do you want?"

"Egypt has signatory responsibility over the deposition of the body. We can arrange for his funeral. All of us together." Hektor turned to Miriam. "Would that be agreeable?"

"If the body is here, the autopsy is over, and the forensic findings are on record. You can put your mark, take him out. After that, I don't care what you do."

Miriam looked at Fabian's body, felt a moment of sadness. She had never known him alive. To her, he would never be anything other than a blood-spattered corpse lying on a catwalk, for all that she had read and admired his work. And that, she could see from the eyes of all of these people, was a tragedy.

"All right then," Sildjin said with sudden decision. "We take him. Right on back to Seven Knots."

Martians did not dispose of bodies inside. No one was buried in Scamander. The laws were strict. Hektor looked at Sildjin, saw the air of frantic resolve, decided to go along. It might prove interesting.

"All right," Hektor said. They gathered together and lifted the loose-jointed body up.

"Would he have liked this, do you think?" Egypt said, holding Hektor's hand as they walked. With his other hand, Hektor pushed up on the back of Fabian's leg, though he felt no weight. There were so many pallbearers that the body floated along by itself and was touched only for comfort.

"He would have written about it," Hektor said. "And been accused of making it up."

"He never made anything up, you know. He *made* things

happen, so that he could write about them, that was part of the job, the art, but he never wrote a fiction.''

''He made this happen.''

''I guess he did.''

They waded in frictionless dust up to their knees, and slid on the eroded surfaces concealed underneath. They had more than once almost dropped Fabian's body into what was actually a small part of the Scamander River's complex dust-recycling system, but had thus far avoided this farcical conclusion.

The network of cracks that was Seven Knots had walls that rose up parallel to a height of fifty meters and were pocked by countless arched openings. The inhabitants of the district sat in their cave mouths and stared down at the procession that swirled the dust below.

High above the dark basalt of the walls, the vaulted ceiling glowed a riot of rich color: chryselephantine, chalcedony, lapis lazuli, malachite. It seemed that angels lived up there and sucked on perfect spheres of onyx to slake their thirst, like dust-storm–stranded travelers. Their radiance beat down on the dust as it swirled up over obscured obstacles, drawn by magnetism and contained air currents back to the source of the Scamander.

''It's a truce!'' Sildjin shouted in an ecstasy of excitement. ''We march together today. Just for Fabian. Just for him!''

Egypt watched Sildjin's display of excessive emotion with searing calm. He had not loved Fabian or even cared much about him. But for some reason, Fabian was now the arbitrarily chosen point where his passions could touch down. As they walked, Fabian's body had ceased to be the remains of her beloved husband and become something of a prop. She thought of the old Shakespearean actor who had willed his skull to his acting company, to represent that of Yorick, so that he could always be onstage. So went Fabian Xui, doing his best to make his obituary, written by his loving wife, his most entertaining feuilleton.

But after that . . . she didn't want to think about it. Others came out of colonnades and jostled their way into the procession, members of the crews that held randomly authoritarian sway through Seven Knots, Squallo, Frenesi's Corner, Moebius, and Darkup. Fabian, while concentrating on the Dust Beggars of

Seven Knots, had written on all of them, and now they came to pay their last respects. Due to ancient and honorable hostilities, they could never have thus celebrated the funeral of even the most heroic among them. But Fabian belonged to all of them.

Dear Fabian. He'd died and left her all alone on a windswept plain. He'd destroyed her entire life in an instant. Fabian, darling, couldn't you have paid attention to that?

High above: horns, whistles, and ululations, as elaborate crew messages were sent through the upper spaces of Seven Knots. Hektor could see brightly colored daredevils swooping at the tops of the high canyons, peering down at the procession like puzzled monkeys, then leaping ahead. They seemed to know where they were going. Hektor wished he did.

There was a figure up there whose motions looked familiar. Hektor tried to stop, but the crowd movement was too insistent.

"Breyten!" he shouted. His voice was tiny. He felt that he could barely hear it himself.

"Was it—?" Egypt said.

"Breyten!" He tore his throat with the name, and the figure was gone, ducked into a dwelling somewhere in the heights. "Damn you!"

"Why?" Egypt said. "He's come here, then, to see Fabian off. Just like us. What's wrong?"

"Not like us," Hektor said, though he knew that what she had said was true, as far as it went. Breyten was here, just as Hektor was, to see the funeral of their cousin and old friend, a man who had helped shape who they both were.

"Egypt, are they saying anything?" he asked.

She looked at him, frowning, already divining something of his meaning.

"I mean, would they have had this funeral if Oswald De-Coven had not died yesterday?"

Even as she thought, she saw the details of all that was around her. The lined face of a man wearing an elaborately knotted red turban floated up in her vision, stamped itself on her memory, and disappeared, as if recognizing that it had served its purpose and was no longer needed. A woman in dark mourning garb— it must have been her regular habit, there had been no time to prepare for this—pushed up on Fabian's shoulder while glancing suspiciously at the sober vigilante next to her. Sildjin's truce, if temporary, was obviously far-reaching. Egypt found herself gathering things in with both hands. A treasure chest had opened, and who knew when the top would slam shut again?

"No, they wouldn't have," she said. "But what does that mean?"

Hektor scanned the dark walls for the man who might be Breyten Passman, but saw no one who resembled him. There were times in history when things changed irrevocably, and no one could predict when they would happen. Yesterday, any crisis facing Mars had been destined to fade slowly until it disappeared. Today . . . today you had to choose sides. The crowd now packed densely into the high, narrow space was celebrating the end of equivocation.

"I don't know," Hektor said finally. "But I think we're all going to find out."

The canyon ahead debouched into a wider space. The dust crossed the floor and swirled up a concave cone expressing the complex curve of some mathematical function. The dust curved upward, moving faster and faster, until with an audible hiss it was sucked up into the dark opening in the center of the dome.

The procession, now huge, swirled slowly around the inverted dust devil: the God of the Israelites standing on his head. Hektor and Egypt, shouting and weeping with the rest of the voices, moved along with it.

7

From *The Red Gown of the Virgin: A Short Guide to Orthodox Sites on Mars*, by Agafia Mru, Pleroma Press, 2329:

 . . . which can be seen most clearly at the Monastery of St. Antony Abbot, in the rim of the crater Milankovic. In 2199, when the end of Imperial political authority became obvious, the monks fled St. Antony almost overnight. The uncompleted underground cathedral was abandoned by the stone cutters between one chisel cut and the next, and eventually found use as a crawler park. The mosaic artists dropped their gold tesserae at the feet of unfinished Virgins and Saints and disappeared into the fetid corridors of Martian cities. Little now remains save the gleaming halos in some of the high niches. . . .

 . . . St. Aya Ngomo, of course, is the one Orthodox saint still revered by Martians. Thus, her shrine here at Oudemans is scrupulously well maintained, in stark contrast, as we have seen, to the tragic state of most other vestiges of Orthodox culture on Mars. But even here, there are problems. Most obvious is the cult icon, a good likeness of the physically twisted saint, save for one thing: the glowing third eye in the middle of her forehead, made of a chunk of ngomite, the mineral she discovered in the Belt. This ill-advised interpolation of Buddhist iconography makes mock of what is otherwise a dignified image. The poorly repaired stone of the wall to her right marks where a statue of Joemon once knelt in prayer. His co-optation of the saint to his own purposes ended with his well-deserved death in 2241, and his statue was ripped out soon afterward. . . .

. . . this little structure in the Ascraeus caldera is a sad memorial to one of Mars's tragic heroes: Hugo Matuchin. Hugo's father, Rheinhart Matuchin, was the last legitimate Orthodox Exarch of Mars. In 2201, he committed suicide in the desperate prison into which he had been thrown by one of the ephemeral regimes that tore Mars apart before the rise to power of Joemon in 2226. Rheinhart's son was coerced into taking over the office of Exarch. He is not to be blamed for acceding, as he was only five years old. Strictly speaking, since the Patriarch of Moscow did not signal approval with a purifying cloud of frankincense from his censer, the appointment was invalid. Nevertheless, the unfortunate Hugo Matuchin was regarded, and finally came to regard himself, as the legitimate Orthodox Exarch of Mars until his brutal murder in 2226. What a desperate life the poor man lived! He spent most of it being traded from one group of bandits to another, occasionally even communicating with Earth, though never receiving any useful response. Earth itself was in chaos. Sometimes he could walk around; sometimes he was chained in small cells. He was just a counter in a power game, nothing more. He spent his last few years here, in these humble rooms, perhaps the only peaceful time in his life. He read, and worked on a biography of his father, whom he had barely known. It is to the credit of contemporary Martians that he is regarded by them as the tragic figure he truly was. It was from this seemingly secure spot that he was kidnapped, at Joemon's orders, by the adventuress Bertilla Li Prakrit. . . .

"Those damn court carvers they have at the Esopus Palace are just too good at their jobs," Sylvia Rodomar said, gesturing at the bust of Gensek Paramon in its niche just outside the Liaison Group meeting room. It showed a shifty-looking man with puffy cheeks. "He looks like a corrupt town alderman depressed by his own iniquity."

If the two Martians, Gustavus Trep and Lon Passman, were startled by this flirtation with lese majesty, they gave no sign of it, but merely gazed at the bust with morose intentness. If she had to choose, she would give Trep, the Vigil, an edge in lugubriousness.

"I'm afraid this is essential," Lon said. "We would not disturb you otherwise." The Justice's voice was as taut as a support cable.

"Everything's essential right now," Rodomar said. The two men were already walking ahead of her, down the hallway into Government House, as if it was their own home. Just as it seemed her first nonofficial act as Acting Governor-Resident of Mars would be to become angry with two of the planet's most prominent citizens, they stopped dead at the inner doorway, and she almost plowed into them. Private space, of course. Martians were fanatical on matters of definition. The hallway from the meeting room was obviously defined differently.

"Askase!" she called as she walked into the lower levels of her new private quarters, so summarily vacated by Oswald DeCoven.

"We cannot overemphasize the importance of—" Trep began.

"Please, won't you sit down?" They were trying to double-team her, get her to agree headlong before she knew what was going on. They should know better. "Askase!"

"Yes, mum?" Askase had been reorganizing the kitchen, certain that without his intervention the household would not run. A slender, gold-skinned man, he was her third consort, picked up in Sumatra during her unfortunate duty in that area.

"Some refreshments for my guests, please. After that, we will be talking and won't wish to be disturbed."

He rolled his eyes. "A disaster in there! I don't think the unfortunate DeCoven ever made anything more complex than a sandwich. The staff is—"

"Hot mineral water will suit," Trep said. "And a couple of

radishes, or something. No need for architecture.'' Lon nodded slowly in agreement.

Askase shuddered, bowed. To him, the Martian taste for fetid hot mineral water indicated a bizarre hostility to both water and comfort.

Tremouille, her second consort, had already hauled De-Coven's plush furniture out the private meeting room and replaced it with the proper stone and mined-wood chairs favored by Martians. Lon and Trep settled into their chairs, watching her narrowly.

Sylvia Rodomar was a big woman, had been all her life, always hulking above the other children like someone who had been left behind a grade or two to ripen and take out frustrations on the smaller kids now easy to hand. Instead, she had taken to protecting them—as long as they obeyed her, and they always did. The boys had been particularly afraid, she remembered, and the thought still pleased her at this remove of years. Her early boyfriends had been more in the nature of servants. She had always preferred the small, clever ones with neat, thin fingers and clean fingernails.

She still kept those tastes. By now Tremouille was safely ensconced in what he had already declared to be his chamber, a dark room off the main stairway, where he could meditate and draw pictures of nonexistent constellations on the age-blackened walls. And Carter was . . . wherever Carter was. Running the corridors, most likely. Carter, at least, was really getting to enjoy Mars.

''I don't think it's necessary to take too much of your time,'' Lon said. ''But the question will only get harder to answer as time goes on.''

''I know that,'' Rodomar said. ''And I don't relish it. What's the situation? *Your* view of the situation.''

''Brenda Marr and the other assassins of Oswald DeCoven are being held in a detention block just off Gnomon Passage,'' Trep said. ''Internal Security took possession of them shortly after the Vigil captured them. There's no good access, the passages in the area are narrow, it's a nightmare. It isn't even the closest lockup to Rahab Hex.''

"Please don't talk around the situation, Commander," she said. "There are a thousand narrow passages in Scamander. All the place lacks is a Minotaur."

"All right. The Feast of Gabriel hasn't ended down there in Gnomon Passage. The place is packed, has been since they were hauled into there. And it gets more and more packed, not less, as time goes by. The crowd is . . . let us say lively."

"You could clear it, couldn't you?"

Trep frowned. "Of course we could. With difficulty. With casualties. But this isn't just some sort of statistical crowd. They're there because of Brenda Marr. The entire area should have been cordoned off immediately after the assassination, but . . . InSec had control."

"We need to know the Union Government's intentions," Lon said, leaning forward.

Askase, with the sixth sense he had about such things, chose that moment to bustle in with a platter of artfully sliced bitter vegetables and a stoneware pitcher of steaming, stinking water, thus giving her an excuse not to answer the request immediately.

The Union Government had no intentions, not yet. InSec had possession of the assassins, and no one on Earth yet wanted to try to take them away. The right decisions here could create the right intentions there. And clearly these two were aware of that.

"Standard policy would be for Brenda Marr, Sen Hargin, Tri Bahari, Kalina Weng, Zeegee Balagan, Nance Sprull, and Falu Kallender to be removed to Scamander Spaceport at the first available opportunity for shipment back to Earth for trial. At InSec's request I have requisitioned a heavy transport vessel, the *Eloise Theisen*, for the purpose. Unfortunately, at the moment, the *Eloise Theisen* is not fully operational. Repairs are proceeding."

"We think that this would be an error," Lon said softly.

"Damn right it'll be an error," Rodomar snapped. "What can we do to avoid making it?"

"Marr and her coconspirators cannot leave Mars. They must be tried here."

"Fine." She poured a cup of hot water, drank, winced at the taste. "I don't want to start my administration with a corridor riot. But I don't think I need to remind you that Brenda Marr and the rest murdered a sitting Union Governor-Resident. Damn it, that's so stupid!'' The thought infuriated her. ''To kill Oswald! I had a cat once. It would hiss at a shoe that had stepped on its tail, once it was off and lying on the floor of the closet. These people—the Olympus Club, they're called?—must have nothing between their ears but dust filters.''

Lon was startled by her agreement, even though Hektor had assured him that she would be willing to go against InSec at the first available moment. Poor Hektor. Lon spared a thought for his son, his friend and cousin dead, his shiny new career in ruins. Xui House was in a sad state.

''So then—'' Lon began.

''But will that clear the corridors?'' Rodomar said. ''You're telling me we can't get them out to the spaceport. Can we get them out to Ascraeus?''

''An announcement that Martian justice will have its way should do the trick,'' Trep said, sliding over Rodomar's assertion that the trial would take place in Lon Passman's courtroom. They could argue that later. ''Most of them are waiting to fight a move to Earth. A little crowd control after that, and I can guarantee clear corridors.''

''We need other trials first,'' Marr said briskly. ''Or perhaps they're administrative procedures—I'm not sure of the details.'' She pushed a button, summoning Tremouille from his dark woolgathering. He would be grumpy, and it should take him a few minutes to get down.

''You mean Hektor Passman and Miriam Kostal,'' Lon said. ''Neither of those situations should be of concern to the Governor-Resident's office.''

''No,'' Rodomar said. ''But they are of concern to me. They both, as far as I understand it, are to be punished for assisting in capturing the assassins. That's fine; the charges are internal to Martian administration. Passman closed the Gates, is accused of making himself a second Joemon. Kostal took advantage of his action to pin the assassins against the rock. We all know that the anger is stupid. But I want—unofficially, of course—to ask you to make the punishments as severe as possible.''

"Why?" Trep said, coloring. "Hektor exceeded his authority, perhaps, but Miriam Kostal—"

"To give the appearance of objectivity," Lon said. "It pulls the crowd's anger away from InSec, gives them more freedom to negotiate."

She inclined her head. "Absolutely. There are times when a false perspective is necessary to show the truth. InSec was solely responsible for DeCoven's personal security. Does that matter? It does not. The head of the detail is being rotated back to Earth, by order of Marina Koep, Head of InSec for Mars. To investigate cases of lubricant theft at Union army bases in Kamchatka, if there's any justice, but don't hold your breath. So who gets the emotional burden? The people who actually captured the assassins. I must insist. Hektor Passman gets party discipline and is dismissed from the Chamber. Miriam Kostal loses her post, is reassigned. That covers me on one side."

"My son," Lon said, his voice heavy. "You've met him?"

Rodomar sighed. She had hoped he wouldn't make it so hard. "Yes, Justice Passman, I have. At one of the hardest times in my life, he took a chance to be kind to me. The fact that he was doing it for shrewd political reasons only increases my respect for him. The hour or so we spent watching Carter try to kill himself on an ice cliff was one bright spot in a miserable year. Is that what you wanted to hear?"

"No need to beat your breast," Trep said. "Let us get on with it."

"Ha!" Tremouille said from the doorway. "Good one." With his round, anxious face he resembled a confidential clerk, and his thin, slightly uneven mustache looked like something a clerk would grow so that he didn't look so much like a clerk.

"Don't be childish, Tremouille," Rodomar said, feeling tired. "I'm sorry I disturbed you. I need you."

"All right. What's so important?"

Tremouille always got this way when it was Askase's night with her. Such resentments were petty, but, being closer to her, affected her more than political crises. If they didn't settle it themselves, she'd have to intervene.

"Could you tell these gentlemen about Brenda Marr? I mean,

as far as it affects the Office of the Governor-Resident.''

Tremouille peered suspiciously at them. ''I don't know. . . . Who are they?''

''Tremouille!''

With easy cordiality, Trep and Passman introduced each other, falling naturally into the attitude that Tremouille was an obstreperous but talented child. Rodomar admired their perception.

''Oh! Of course. Forgive me, gentlemen.'' Tremouille bobbed in a nervous bow. ''I didn't mean . . . the documents don't have pictures attached. Anyway.'' He cleared his throat. ''Between April and June of 2327, Brenda Marr was the privately registered mistress of Oswald DeCoven. She was paid off on June 23, 2327, quite generously, as was DeCoven's habit, and replaced by—''

''Never mind by whom,'' Rodomar said.

Lon shook his head, awed. ''Even Fabian never found that out, and you know how the news diggers were always interested in DeCoven's mistresses.''

''The one successful part of Government House security,'' Trep said. ''But so what?''

''Justice Passman knows so what,'' Rodomar said, looking steadily at him.

''That's your legal pretext for pulling them away from Internal Security.''

''Exactly. Not that it would hold, ordinarily—but I can guarantee that the Colonial Sekretariat will be just as happy to have DeCoven's assassins out of their hands. We can get InSec to disgorge.''

Trep grinned, bleakly amused. ''So the assassination of Oswald DeCoven was actually a passion/revenge killing with no political implications? That is droll, Ms. Governor-Resident.''

''It isn't meant to be, Commander.''

''Fine.'' Trep was suddenly brisk. ''But we need another conduit for the data. Your own personal consort isn't a good source.''

''The data will officially come through a disaffected kitchen staffer,'' Rodomar said. ''Askase is about to fire him, says he can't even make a decent roux—the poor fellow's lucky Askase doesn't execute him. But he's been on DeCoven's staff a long time and has plausible access.''

''And he'll leave the planet on the *Eloise Theisen*? That is, when it gets, ah, repaired. We can go to documents—right, Lon? —once he gives us the hint.''

Trep wanted her to know that he understood the fictional nature of the *Eloise Theisen*'s repairs, and that he was willing to maintain the fiction. Passman knew too, she was sure, but he didn't need to prove his inner knowledge to her. That made him more interesting, and more dangerous.

''Yes,'' Rodomar said, and stood. ''The next few weeks will be unpleasant for both of you. My sympathies.''

''Thank you,'' said Lon.

''Save them for those that needs them,'' said Trep. ''And that's not us.''

Tremouille, no longer needed, was already gone, and Askase was out of the kitchen. She took the untouched food tray back to the cleaning area, then went upstairs. DeCoven had always told her how nervous Government House made him, and she was starting to feel why.

She heard the sobbing when she stepped into her room. It had been DeCoven's, and she had reluctantly concluded that it was the best one for her as well. He hadn't been assassinated in his bedroom, after all. There was nothing to be worried about.

This was her first look around DeCoven's private quarters. Decorations a bit too lush, but DeCoven had been on Mars for a while. It was a natural reaction to the environment. One end of the room was dominated by a huge . . . birdcage, was it? Askase knelt in front of it and cried. Part of his job had been the arrangement of this room so that she could sleep comfortably. It was late, she was tired, and it didn't look like he had finished his task. She didn't like that.

''What is it?'' she said, too sharply. ''What's wrong?''

He reached his hands through the open door of the cage. ''They just left them,'' he said. ''Went away and forgot them.''

She now saw that the bottom of the cage was piled with dead birds. They lay on top of one another, dust dimming but not concealing the brilliance of their elaborate plumage.

"They could have fed and watered them," he said. "Or let them free."

"No freedom on Mars for a bird," Rodomar said. "There's no air. Well, clean them up, Askase. Dispose of them whatever way you think best. It's time for bed and they're dead now, anyway."

"Yes," he said. "You are right."

She was brisk, but felt a chill herself. This one had a crown of white feathers, that one a vivid blue throat. They had been Oswald DeCoven's greatest joy. And they'd just died here, flapping their wings desperately against the decorated bars of their cage, while the Martian inhabitants of Government House walked back and forth in the hallway just outside the door. Only two days. It didn't take much to kill a bird.

Askase packed them up and disposed of them wherever you disposed of dead birds on Mars. He was usually meticulous, but this time he left a scattering of brilliant tail feathers on the floor. Also uncharacteristically, she didn't say anything about it to him. But later, after he was asleep, curled tiny on his side of the bed, she got up, gently so as not to wake him, and collected them, one by one, looking at the way they gleamed in the night light. She put them between the pages of a book she had brought from Earth, a leather-bound volume of *The Prince* and *The Discourses on the First Ten Books of Titus Livius*. She'd have need of old Niccolò's advice before long, she was sure.

"I did what I had to," Hektor muttered to himself. "I *had* to." The cushion had somehow slid out of the chair underneath him, and he found himself grabbing for the back, to pull himself out of the hole he'd fallen into.

"You'd think they'd understand that." It was easier to go all the way to the floor and just get up from there. Why had it taken him so long to figure that out? In addition, once there, he could use the table to support himself. And on the table . . . he'd moved the Armagnac bottle and the crystal snifter to the other side, far away, so that he would have trouble reaching them. Why the hell had he done that? They looked like they were a mile away, all the way past a pile of books and journals, which now resembled the Nereidum Montes as they loomed above Argyre. He'd climbed worse, though. Much worse.

Hektor had expected, at worst, the paper-skinned face of Marshe Kratak, Fossic Party General Secretary, gently informing him that he should resign his Delegate position for the good of the party. Kratak had been the purveyor of internal disciplinary messages for the Fossic Party for years. It had been a younger Marshe Kratak who had indicated to Lon Passman that perhaps a legal career was in order.

But the man whom he'd had to face was Lon Passman himself. It was his father who had sat him down and told him his career was over, told him why the decision was necessary, why it had been agreed to. Lon had always expected him to fail, Breyten to succeed. At least half of his prediction had come true.

Kicking his feet, Hektor managed to roll up onto the table. Too far to go around, too far, and he'd get lost, get stuck in a corner of the library, find himself at a shelf of brave stories about the opening of Mars, annotated by Breyten. He could see the bottle, the glass. Good stuff; he needed a little more, just to help him sleep, and to get this taste off his tongue.

Tyrant, was he? The denunciations were astounding. Who had given this unreliable psychotic access to the keys that could cut Scamander apart? Never mind that it was an old, traditional action, one performed at every Feast of Gabriel. But what they said about him . . . Like this article, here in this . . . he wrestled with the stiff sheets piled on the table, pinning them down with an elbow while trying to pull them out with the other hand. He'd circled the offending words, pen point tearing through the paper, it should be right here, he'd been wanting to check the phrasing of one particularly egregious . . . oh, who gave a damn anyway. His doom was clear even without that.

He'd been pulling books off the shelves all day, not looking for anything in particular, just for something to read. A library full of books and nothing to read. Just like the Passman family. They shifted under him, an unstable talus slope. With trained caution, he moved only one limb at a time, keeping the others down for stability. Rescue operation; he knew the drill. Right arm, left arm, left leg . . . leg . . . was it time for an arm again?

He was almost where he needed to be anyway. The bottle stood just beyond his fingertips. If he just . . . books slid out from under his body, and he coasted forward on his belly. His knuckles hit the bottle, the glass, and he watched them topple slowly off the edge of the table and shatter on the stone floor. The sound was far away. He closed his eyes and opened them. The glass shards gleamed up at him from the dark lake in which they floated. Quite a sight, like flying over the ice cap. It made him sick to his stomach.

He felt hands on his shoulders, lifting him up. Now, who the hell . . . He found himself looking into his father's face. Just the man he wanted to see.

"Thought I'd get plowed," Hektor slurred. "Just to see how the world looked."

"And how does it look?"

"Shitty. Funny, same as before."

"Does that surprise you?"

"Don't patronize me, Father."

"Then don't be maudlin, Hektor." Lon put his shoulder under Hektor's armpit and hauled him, leg-flailing, off the table. Hektor found himself standing unsteadily on the floor. Lon was taller than he was, and as the shoulder slipped out from under his arm, he grabbed for it.

"Did you feel this way?" Hektor said.

"I did. I was a wreck for weeks. With Sara's help I tried to hide it when abroad in the house."

"You did a good job. Too good, maybe."

Hektor remembered Lon sitting at the dining room table, sharply groomed, shaved, dressed as if for a private event of some formality. But the irises of his eyes had congealed, and his erect posture could not conceal the tremor in his hands. Hektor and Breyten had been terrified, feeling that their father had been seized in an incautious moment by some dust sprite anxious to taste water. They had performed an exorcism in Breyten's bedroom, one that Breyten had claimed to have found in an old book, though Hektor later discovered that he'd made most of it up.

Lon's failure to achieve the Chairmanship, the powerful opposition to him within the Fossic Party, and his final retreat from politics to the lonely peaks of the judiciary: none of this made any sense to the boys. It was too obscure and elaborately grown-up. A jealous dust sprite was much easier to grasp, so they huddled over a sputtering flame and muttered their chants. Eventually the dust sprite had left their father and climbed back into its lair in the regolith.

"Sometimes," Lon said, "there is no good solution to a problem. I did the best I could with all three of you."

"You must have been worried sick about us."

Lon snorted. "I didn't know what worry was then. You and Breyten taught me later."

Hektor felt like crying. "I'm sorry, Father." To have something to do, he started to kneel, to pick up the broken shards of glass with his bare hands. Lon jerked him back, not gently. "Damn it!" Hektor flared. "Let me handle this my own way."

"Handling, you call it." Neither tears nor anger disturbed Lon. He was long used to dust-storm tantrums from his sons.

"All right," Hektor said, looking down at the glass shards. "So my handling is not particularly adroit."

For the first time, Hektor managed to get both eyes around to focus on his father. Lon's long white hair was wild. He'd clearly been asleep before coming down here to check on his son. In the dim light of the library he looked ancient, like some ancestral ghost.

"Let's not discuss that. Let's, instead, discuss what you're going to do." He gave Hektor a sharp glance. "Maybe we should wait until you have a few more neurons operating."

"We can talk about it again, in the morning." Hektor felt his brain clarify, the skin on his face tighten. His father was focused on him absolutely. It was an exhilarating and frightening feeling. "See if we still agree."

For the past week, Lon had been presiding over the trial of Brenda Marr and her fellow conspirators. Tonight was the first time he was back at Xui House. Hektor hadn't really been following the trial, but the verdict was no way in doubt. He rather admired Acting Governor-Resident Rodomar's sublime self-confidence in turning the conspirators over to purely Martian justice.

"All right," Lon said. "I'll give it a try. Tell me: what do you think the situation is?"

"The situation?" Hektor tried to grab onto Lon's words, but everything seemed slippery.

"Yes." Lon was exasperated, already regretting having agreed to discuss a complex subject with a drunk. "The emotional situation, among the people of Mars."

"An explosion waiting to happen," Hektor said with sudden prescience. "Oh, I can't tell you about what people at, say, Hecates Tholus feel, but I know what I saw in Scamander. I was at Fabian's funeral."

"I know," Lon said. "I understand he was given an unforgettable send-off. I'm sorry I missed it."

"I didn't have time to notify you." Hektor realized how fond Lon had been of his difficult nephew. Had he tried hard enough to tell Lon about the funeral? He could no longer remember if he possibly could have, but felt his responsibility anyway. "But there's anger everywhere. Anger looking for the will to put it to work. Why? Because of a sensible anticorruption drive that benefits almost everyone? People have lost festivals, a Gabriel dragon, their jobs, and blame . . . they don't know who to blame, but they're looking, the way people do. DeCoven's assassination was like the first chink of light to a cave-in victim. Suddenly they saw their salvation. They'll start climbing toward it."

Hektor took a breath. His mouth was sour, and he had the smell in his nostrils that told him he might be sick soon.

"What do *you* think will happen?"

Another of those damn quizzes. "If they don't find a decent focus or a leader: nothing. Just a lot of fists pounded bloody against hard rock. But if they do: no telling. It won't even have to be a someone who has any idea of what he's doing. Stupid, Father. They're *stupid*."

"Completely true, but contempt for the voters is a poor attitude for a politician. Better you should stay a journalist. I need your help. I need your observation. Unfortunately, it's much too late for your writing, cogent though it is, to help. . . ."

"You knew?" Hektor had thought his identity as the political writer Kennedy was a close secret, known only to his friends.

Lon smiled tightly. "You've always had a style, Hektor, and—what's the tag? *Stilus virum arquit.* Our style betrays us. And it's not just me. Your secret would soon enough have been out in any event. And now that Kennedy is no longer privy to Chamber debates . . . people will note the timing, and draw their conclusions."

No longer privy to Chamber debates. Hektor, embarrassed, felt tears well in his eyes. It was all just too damn much. How could he be expected to stand it?

"Come on, Hektor," Lon said, holding him.

"I'm . . . I'm sorry, Father. I know that you always expected Breyten . . . that he was always the one you saw in the Chamber, following you."

"And if I did? I'm not perfect, Hektor. You told me that often enough yourself in your younger years. And though you may have overexpressed yourself, you were right. Yes, I expected Breyten to follow me. He didn't. He won't. You, in your own way, have."

Hektor wanted to ask his father if he loved Breyten more than him. But in the mood Lon was in now, he might just calmly admit it, and let Hektor deal with the consequences. Doubt is the parent of hope.

But the hell of it was, even in his absence Breyten was there. Hektor could feel him in the room. Neither of them knew where he was or what he was doing, but he still pulled on them both.

"Hektor."

"Yes, Father?"

"Don't throw up here. Go to the bathroom."

"Good idea." Hektor turned and walked slowly out of the library, bumping his shoulder against the doorjamb.

"I'll see you in the morning, son. We can see if we still agree."

Complete a vast circle around it, and perhaps the volcano, dead for millions of years, would erupt. Rudolf Hounslow raised his hand. This was a good spot to stop for the night: the declivity just ahead would be better crossed by light of morning. A laser caught the mirror on the back of his gauntlet and sent a narrow violet beam straight up into the darkening sky. He'd tried the hand gesture alone at first, but no one had been able to see it. Behind him, the procession stopped. Dust swirled around the crawlers for long moments, then settled reluctantly back to the ground.

Hounslow sat for a long moment on his throne—his control couch, rather, but some of his followers had styled it thus, and he hadn't the heart to correct them in their excessive enthusiasm. By his specification, his crawler had no cab. He sat outside, his throat valves linked into the crawler's lifesystem through the long insulating coat he wore outside his skintite. He could watch the sun as he rode, and the fast-rising moons. If he went fast enough, risking tipping, he swore he could feel a breeze.

Camp, by now a routine, was being set. The domes went up in close order, and cooking began immediately. Sleeping bags were unrolled, study groups set up, some fragment of Seneca or Oshio Heihachiro read aloud. On the move, the Pure Land School was a mighty organism striding through the sands and rocks of Mars.

The low shield of Ascraeus Mons rose in the distance. They were southeast of it now, between it and the beginnings of the Noctis Labyrinthus. The plain here, on the invisibly vast slope of Tharsis Bulge, was wide and featureless, like most of Mars. They had already almost circled the volcano where Brenda Marr's trial was proceeding, but it seemed to the eye that they had remained still. Ascraeus stood each day at their left shoulder, the rocks and sand spread out to either side, tireless to the horizon. Every day the sun climbed through the dust at the featureless horizon, hung overhead, then sank back through that same dust.

Stiffly, Hounslow unhooked his tracheal lines from the crawler's air supply and climbed down to the sand. His bodyguards had raised his tent, and waited inside for him. He could see their alert kneeling shapes through the translucent fabric. But instead of going in, he walked slowly to a rock outcrop barely higher than the surround and climbed up on it. The surrounding land looked no different from up here, but there was a little bit more of it visible. The blunt shield of Ascraeus looked exactly the same.

"We need to talk," a voice said companionably on his private channel.

"We have a procedure for new recruits," Hounslow said. They straggled across the wastes of Tharsis, seeing in him the inspiration for Brenda Marr's desperate act. There were too many of them, and they were rank with the stench of Scamander. They cluttered his operations, so he sent most of them away with a curt word and an injunction to study.

"I'm not a recruit." The voice came from nearby, but Hounslow could see no one. "I need to see you."

Hounslow skinned his lips back beneath his air mask in a grin. His bodyguards had warned him repeatedly of the risk of assassination. But no one since Brenda Marr had even given a hint of such a thing. Perhaps this was it at last. They could wrestle here, and both die.

"Intake is in the rear tent, the one with the red top," Hounslow said, feeling his patience erode. Dread popularity, which conceals all true opinions. He had always hoped for the sweeping inevitability of truth, beyond argument and opinion, when the inhabitants of Mars would gladly tear down their cities with bare hands and stand naked on the cold surface. Instead, he got fools drawn by a meaningless name. They trailed out behind, human litter.

"My name is Breyten Passman. Here." And, like the mystery before Belshazzar, a hand emerged from a crack in the rock bearing a sigil. It was Rudolf Hounslow's own. "Brenda Marr gave this to me."

Hounslow was as shaken as a prophet whose god had finally spoken. Shadows stroked across the wastes, and he sat here with a mystery.

"What does Lon Passman want to say to me?"

"He wants me to join you." And with those false words, Breyten finally clambered out of his hiding place and sat next to Hounslow.

This was the fourth time Breyten had tried this trick. On three previous nights he had estimated a day's journey for Hounslow's motley, ill-trained procession, and concealed himself at what seemed a natural stopping place for them at the end of the day. On the first and third tries they had stopped short or gone farther, while on the second they had swerved away so far that he still would have been coming into their camp from the outside.

But this try had repaid his efforts. He had not dared hope that Hounslow would come so close; he had braced himself for long explanations with guards, and even a possible term of imprisonment before winning through. Those were prices he would have paid, in addition to the cold nights alone in this flat, almost-featureless place, but fate had now taken a hand. It was too bad he had to lie to get next to Hounslow, but he wasn't prepared to wait around. He knew his father's name had potency with this man, without understanding why.

Hounslow looked at this eager young man. He could see Lon in him very clearly. He was so like Lon, in fact, that Hounslow felt choking in his lungs, as if his air had suddenly disappeared.

He felt a hand on his shoulder. "Are you all right?"

Hounslow punched him two-fisted in the stomach. Taken completely by surprise, Breyten doubled over, almost rolled off the rock. He scrabbled for grip, finally regained it. His eyes stared at Hounslow. He didn't try to attack. Good, thought Hounslow. He wasn't stupid.

"I want . . . to help you."

"You'll help. Believe me, you will." Lon's son. What a prize. A connection right into the heart of the corrupt system that ruled Mars. They would try to fight but would find themselves compromised, just like this. All Hounslow had to do was wait.

He jerked Breyten's arm and pulled him along behind him through the camp. He felt disoriented. It had been a spontaneous movement, this insane circumambulation of Ascraeus in honor of Brenda Marr. Now that they were here, Hounslow had persuaded himself that there was a purpose to it, that he had conceived of the idea as a way of building discipline and training for surface operations. But really, he had no idea what they were doing here.

Perhaps they would die here now. That was always a possibility on the surface. You could die without realizing it. That would be a clean solution. Just as what had almost happened to him and Lon Passman would have been a clean solution. The idea was clear for a moment: death spreading through this make-shift camp. It would be an image for Mars.

"We can do it," Breyten was saying, as if Hounslow's glazed stare was an expression of attentiveness. "We can take Mars."

"After you," was all Hounslow said as he gestured at the entrance to his personal shelter.

As Breyten climbed through the air lock into Hounslow's shelter, he was seized, and a knife-edge gleamed near his throat.

"Let him up," Hounslow said wearily, though he had done nothing to prevent this reaction. "He has news for me."

The six bodyguards stared at Breyten with suspicion and jealousy. One of them was Marder, the blond novice who had greeted Brenda Marr after her journey through Nilosyrtis. He took threats to the Master personally, and knew that those threats the Master welcomed to his breast were the most dangerous of all.

The soup was heavy with salt and thick with almost-invisible crystalline brine shrimp, as Hounslow liked it. He looked down at the water surrounded by the bowl. His own body had five and a half liters of blood in it, held in by his skin. He would always be a little water-filled bag on Earth. On Mars. Was it possible to make soup without water?—a bowl of roiled dust, like the Scamander River, a step in the right direction. Perhaps shrimp could even be bred to live in it. He could suck it erosively over his teeth and feel it abrade his throat.

"Your father has tried Brenda Marr as a common criminal," he said. "Her killing of the Governor-Resident is supposed to be a mere personal whim."

"Do you know different?" Breyten was cool. "Did you order it?"

"No!" Hounslow recoiled from the idea. "She was just supposed to carry a message to your father."

"But she expressed all the force of your philosophy in action."

"She did," Hounslow said. "That's why we are here. To

honor that.'' He looked at Breyten. ''To honor action.''

''What will we do next?'' Breyten asked eagerly.

Hounslow's face darkened. ''Do not question.''

''I won't.''

Despite the compromises of the situation, Breyten felt himself being swept away. He'd read the texts of the Pure Land School, studied the words and deeds of Rudolf Hounslow. He'd had the time, after his attempt to join the filibusters had failed. Going home to Xui House would have been bitter defeat, and he had no other goal. The flame in Brenda Marr's eyes was the only sign of life he could see, so he decided to move toward it.

But now he surprised himself. Before, it had been just an intellectual conclusion. It had suddenly become something more. He realized that this was what he had been looking for. He now had a reason to move forward.

He looked around at the grim faces of Hounslow's closest followers. It was here that he would find what he sought. Hounslow had provided them with the philosophy, but it was these men and women who would actually act. He wanted to be with them. That was what he had been meant for all along.

8

From *A Climber's Guide to Olympus Mons*, by Emily Mpenge-Yong, Terrane Press, Scamander, 2327:

. . . Thus, despite its impressive six-kilometer height (I've known Terrans who hyperventilated just on seeing it), the scarp around Olympus's base gives you mostly boring climbing. Strenuous climbing, no doubt, if you're out for a good sweat and have some oxygen to burn. I don't, and prefer the pitches in the caldera itself, as I've already mentioned (Chapters 7–12). If I'm going to sweat, I want some fun out of it. Rappelling down the scarp can be fun, though, if you pay a lot of attention to your lines, belays, and pulleys. And I mean a *lot* of attention. It helps if you get a Buddhist Perfect Master to give your belay points the Third Eye treatment. I've known rich guys who hauled entire monasteries out with them—high-risk sportsmen provide a lot of their annual operating budgets. Imagine all those orange saffron robes meditating on the rocks, waiting for some daredevil to go bouncing down the side! You don't have to go that far, though you should, if you can afford it. I'll give some hints on how to survive in Chapter 15, if you're still hot on the idea.

The one exception to the Olympus Scarp Is Boring rule is The Crater. Sure, it's dumb that, among all the craters on Mars, this one is The, but I guess since it's the only one human beings have made all on their own, it rates some notice. It's blown out of the northern part of the caldera, just south of that endless ridgeland called the Olympus Aureole, which is why it's so hard to get to. No maglev line, and only a couple of dug roads. But three of my favorite pitches on the whole damn mountain are there. It's worth the trip.

We have the Technics to thank for The Crater. During the Seven Planets War (or, as my grandad used to call it, the First Solar War—Grandad was not an optimist, and always waited for the Second), on October 11, 2252, a Titanian warship plowed through the Martian atmosphere and blew itself up on the edge of Olympus. That was during the asteroid battles, when the Technics finally convinced Earth that it couldn't hold on to them, but no one knows why the ship did that. It might have had a malfunctioning fusion-drive core. Instead of repairing it, the crew drove their ship into Mars, hoping to take a few Martians with them. They just missed what was at that time a big mining complex. Seems a drastic solution, but Technics are drastic people. St. Hilarion, a rigorous private school, is located right on the lip.

So the pitches are only eighty years old, and they look like they're still hot. Great climbing (details below). Maybe we should start another war, give Grandad his wish, and get some more great climbs on Olympus. You might as well get some good out of the failure of politics.

"We shouldn't have—"

Egypt cut Hektor off by pressing her fingers on his lips. "We did."

"Damn it!"

Egypt pulled the sheets around her, shook her head to feel the remaining clips in her hair bang around her ears, and let her profile be illuminated by the light from the high window.

"I assume this isn't your usual morning-after reaction," she said.

"No," he said. "It isn't." He slung his legs out of the bed, suddenly nervous at her touch.

She turned her oval face toward him. In the light from the

barred window, she looked more like a Madonna than ever. "You did a good deed, Hektor." And suddenly she was crying.

"See?" he said in agony. "See?" He slid up and put his arm around her, embarrassed by his floppy nakedness.

"No, it's all right." Her hand, searching blindly, found his face. "Thank you, Hektor."

"For what?" In all his years with women, somehow he'd managed to avoid this situation. He'd always found Egypt delightful, small and quick, with a body she insisted on concealing under layers of patterned cloth. But he'd never meant to . . .

"For comforting a poor widow." Despite her bravado, she didn't allow herself to be naked next to him. With unconscious artfulness, she arranged the sheets until she was wearing a loose kimono. "Rough sheets. Deliberate?"

"Yes. I didn't want them changed."

"Would they have changed them for you if you'd asked?"

The question hadn't occurred to him. "Maybe not. I'm not who I was."

"Still, you're not a state prisoner."

"No, not quite. No, no, not at all."

Hektor looked up at the rock wall next to his head. The ceiling was low, the light gloomy, the air still and only slowly replenished. He and Egypt sat on what was supposed to be a single cot for a state prisoner. Instead of a bathroom, it had a crude bowl and dermal scrubber in the wall. He'd come here to avoid being found, but Egypt had found him.

"It was my own choice, Hektor."

"Maybe that's what's bothering me."

"You don't like women making their own choices?" She shook her head. "You're not going to convince yourself it's some general man/woman thing that's bothering you, are you?"

"I can try."

"Don't bother. You just slept with your friend's widow on the eve of his murderer's execution and you feel guilty." He winced, and she hid her smile by leaning her head on his shoulder. "Have you ever been to an execution?"

"No," he said. "Father did not approve. Breyten once

sneaked into one, told me all about it, but I never quite dared. You?''

"On Earth they don't execute people in public. They perform them in dramatic places like mountaintops and old fortresses. No photographs, but artists are permitted to create whatever versions they choose.''

"A good idea.''

"I don't know. I want to see her dead.'' Egypt's voice was venomous. "Her and that whole gang. Hounslow and all his people to boot. I wouldn't want to wait for the statue.''

"They're not executing—''

"The whole gang,'' she finished. "Or Hounslow. I know. I'll take what I can get. For now.''

"Sen Hargin's going to be locked in a cell on Phobos so that null-g can dissolve his bones. He might live a century or more up there.'' Better to be beheaded, Hektor thought. Better immediate death than becoming one of those swollen, almost-spherical state prisoners, exiled forever from any planet's surface.

"I won't be able to see that. There's no drama in it.'' Egypt sounded petulant, like a child deprived of a sweet.

Hektor's suit hung on the opposite wall, sleeves stiffly out, like a mounted bat. It was black mourning, the silky cloth distressingly comfortable, something one could easily get used to wearing. Perhaps that explained the outfit's popularity among the older generation. It was in Fabian's memory, but the damn thing caused a lot of confusion in these times. No one knew quite what he was saying. Was he mourning the death of Governor-Resident DeCoven? Or the imminent death of DeCoven's assassin? Or was it, perhaps, his own now-moribund political career? He had stopped pretending, even to himself, that the confusion was anything but deliberate.

Egypt jumped out of her makeshift kimono. After a moment's disorientation, Hektor allowed himself to enjoy the roundness of her shape. The faint hint of a bruise marred the clear white skin just at the swell of her thigh, where his hip had pounded her. That visible memorial to their night together would be gone soon. A Martian might preserve it for months, the way they did all memorable wounds, but Egypt was unlikely to. They both knew they would not do this again.

She pulled on a shift, then stood, looking from one door to the one in the opposite wall as she tamed her hair with clips.

They were in a cell. On either side of a geometrically vertical canyon was a stack of detention chambers. One door opened out onto the canyon balcony, the other onto the corridor that ran behind. Depending on the number of prisoners in place, each chamber was either a cell or a hotel room. Families often stayed in them while awaiting judgment. It was convenient, and brought them closer to the emotions of their confined relative. As guests walked down the corridors, they could dimly see faces looking out at them. Two civilizations held each other here like the intertwined fingers of two hands, one free, one unfree. A room could leave one world and join the other with a flick of a switch, and a prisoner found innocent could enter his cell from the confined canyon and walk through it and out into the corridor, into the world of freedom, with never a look back at the dimly glowing rectangle of the other door.

"We should get going, Hektor. But not together. You have your business there, I have mine."

Reluctantly, he got up from the cot. "What's your business?" She had blown into his simple existence late last night, breathless, without explanation. Her luggage stood unopened in a corner.

"To see my husband's murderer lose her head. Then I'm going to meet Miriam Kostal. She's on her way north, transferred. You can come too, if you want." She turned luminous eyes on him. "I think you want."

Despite himself, Hektor nodded. "I do. But I don't know if I'll come."

"All right." She turned her back to him, began to dress. "Don't give them the satisfaction of seeing you afraid."

"You sound like a mother, Egypt."

"Well, we all do, eventually."

He kissed her on the top of her head, put his arms around her one last time, then fixed his attention on his own clothes.

*　　*　　*

Sparks sprayed from the grinding wheel and disappeared, bouncing, on the floor. Lon Passman readjusted his goggles and changed the angle of the ax blade. Sparks jumped farther.

"Lon," Gustavus Trep said, "is this necessary?" If Lon wanted some damn primitive ritual to emphasize his role, he should have performed it in some public place, where people could see it and be properly edified. Trep leaned against the wall, head bent over. Lon had set up his silently spinning grinding wheel—had he requisitioned it from some museum?—in an access vent barely taller than Trep was. They shouldn't have been in here.

"Not at all," Lon grunted. "You know that." A two-centimeter blade of micromachined surgical steel would be inserted into the end of the ax just before sentence was passed. No amount of grinding could get an edge fine enough to cut kindly between the cervical vertebrae. Microphotographs should show no tearing or bruising in the tissue of the spinal cord. Just a clean microtome cut, an earthly sign of the law in action.

"Then why—"

Lon held the blade up and examined it critically, as if what he was doing mattered.

"It relaxes me." The multilayered steel blade was finely textured, with a hideous little grinning face cut through it, after the fashion of bronze sacrificial axes of the Chinese Shang dynasty. The wood haft was inlaid with silver, now polished to a high gloss. Lon handled it only with a cloth, to avoid smearing.

"I think we should let that filibuster expedition take off," Lon said. "Now that InSec has released most of them."

"What?" Trep was caught by surprise. How had Lon found out about that one? "Why?"

"Scamander needs a distraction. Something to catch at the emotions. They're our best bet just now. What did poor Fabian call them? Our authentic Martian heroes. If you could arrange something dramatic, a chase through the corridors, perhaps a tampered nuke blowing out a section of the ice cap as their ship takes off—"

"Nukes are a Union asset," Trep said, grabbing onto a mere practical detail. "They don't let us play Gabriel with them."

Lon's frantic energy disturbed him. It seemed to come from nowhere, returning the Justice near retirement to his old political force.

"All right, no nukes. But Rodomar has agreed to let us handle it however we want. I think it would be a good idea. It will take some of the pressure off."

"Oh, you do? What the hell about Hounslow? He and his capering troupe of madmen are still hauling their weary asses around Ascraeus. Putting a curse on us, whatever they think they're doing. I'm tired of looking at the dust plume they throw up as they move."

"I know," Lon said. "If you peeked out of the window at the rear robing room yesterday, you could just see it. The God of the Israelites. . . ."

Lon touched the blade, then moved his finger to his tongue. He hadn't touched the blade for any real reason. Just to see if it was still hot. It was.

"I don't see why you're so damn cheerful about it. You're the one who got me worried about that nutcase in the first place."

"Gustavus." Lon settled the ax on its stand. "We're facing a crisis. No one seems to know about it yet. The Chamber fights over the order of corruption hearings while the chance that we'll soon be facing violent civil war grows daily. The newssheets report on crew battles and sexual scandals as if they were the real news. The Vigil chases filibusters and interconfessional murderers. . . . But you know, don't you?"

"I know," Trep said reluctantly. Through the Vigil, he'd been intensively examining the state of Mars after the Feast of Gabriel and the murder of Oswald DeCoven, and providing Lon, against regulations, with the information. Lon Passman was right. Something had changed in the mind of Mars. Somehow, the very anticorruption investigations that benefited them had undermined the legitimacy of the government in the eyes of the population. "But Hounslow . . ."

"Hounslow and his people will disperse after the execution. What else can they do? Keep circling Ascraeus? For all their efforts, they haven't made it around even once yet. Move through the Labyrinth toward Scamander? Even if that were physically possible, Hounslow doesn't give a damn about Scamander. That's his weakness. He wants to inaugurate the rule of virtue, but fears those who are not virtuous. Since that's most of Mars, he has a tough job ahead of him.''

''And you're giving him one in the eye by chopping off his minion's head.''

''She wasn't his minion.'' Lon blew on the blade to remove some invisible dust and stared at the macabre grinning face. It had evenly spaced teeth and staring eyes. Whoever had thought this an appropriate instrument for legal execution? It looked like something intended to threaten and terrify, not something to actually be used. The condemned prisoner was beyond any such artistically induced terror.

''That's exactly the problem,'' Lon continued. ''She acted on her own, but Hounslow's words were ringing in her ears as she did it. He's like a black hole. You can't see him. All you can see is the way he influences the movements of others. And he'll keep doing it after he goes back to Nilosyrtis. Even if he stays there, he'll be trouble.''

While listening to him, Trep was running through the rest of their conversation in his mind, comparing pieces of information. He had been there at that dinner at Xui House. He'd been tired, but he hadn't been dead. And the person who had made the observation about filibusters being authentic Martian heroes hadn't been the sardonic Fabian, but—

''Breyten!'' Trep said, breaking into Lon's words. ''You've been talking to Breyten.''

''Yes,'' Lon said, recovering instantly, though he had hoped to keep it a secret a while longer. He should have known better than to try to cover it with Trep, he thought. ''He's my eye into Hounslow's organization. It's an old family connection, you know.''

Trep had always been suspicious of Lon's relation with Hounslow. It had been a dramatic one, in their youth, and had almost led to their death. Lon had never forgotten it.

''I'd prefer that the Passman family did not practice amateur espionage.''

"Do you have a Vigil agent in place, then?"

"No. Of course I don't. They dig them out pretty quick. Along with a lot of their own people, I might add. No InSecs. InSec doesn't think he's important."

"All right, then. If this is what we have, this is what we'll work with."

"I'm uncomfortable with all your private acts," Trep said heatedly. "Not just this. The entire Olympus Club trial is a private act for you, isn't it? Hounslow sent that woman to your house—of course I know about it, Lon, don't look so surprised—and you want to get back at him for it. She didn't try to kill *you*, did she?"

"All we have now are private acts." Lon did not respond to Trep's emotional heat. "The Chamber is blocking Rodomar, and you yourself have to face a lot of resistance within the Vigil, correct? I thought so. You should discuss these matters with me. So you have to act outside normal channels to get anything done. We face serious times, Gustavus. You should be glad of private acts."

"Have you told Hektor?"

"Eh?" For the first time, Lon was taken aback. It had been such a joy to hear Breyten's voice again, to know that he was all right, and working for the right cause. For the moment, that was the only important thought.

"You heard me. Have you told Hektor that Breyten is your agent in Hounslow's camp? You've had that poor boy working his ass off for you, digging out information, having deniable conversations with politicos and businessmen. Your little ragged corridor boy. Don't you think you owe him full disclosure?"

Trep had watched the two brothers grow up. Breyten had come first and stayed first, at least in his father's eyes. For a long time, Trep had shared Lon's prejudice in the adventurous Breyten's favor. Now he was finding himself attracted to Hektor's own dry charm. It was a wonder to him that Lon wasn't.

"Breyten and I just talked . . . recently. There hasn't been a chance."

"I won't tell him when I see him, then. Just do it as soon as

possible." Trep had resolved never to interfere in Lon's raising
of his sons, but this was just too much.

There was a suppressed mutter in the corridor outside the vent,
a discreet signal from the others involved in the execution that
Trep and Passman should wind things up and get to work.

"You know, Gustavus . . ." Lon was meditative. "Your colleague, Ms. Kostal, told me that this blade's provenance was
incorrect. The collection was rather a mess, actually. . . ."

"Is that a fact?"

"She said it was made on Earth. Imagine that! Our old sanc-
tified blood blade from most ancient Tithonium was actually
made on Vancouver Island. That's just off the coast of—"

"Never mind where it is!" Trep moved from heat to rage.
"Keep your mind on things, Lon. Don't let your private con-
cerns destroy your public ones."

"I won't." Lon was already receding, surrounded by the dark-
cloaked officiants of the public ritual. Trep wanted to reach out
a hand and touch him, but it was too late. Events had Lon Passman in their grip.

On the other side of a few inches of fiber-reinforced rock from
Egypt and Hektor, Brenda Marr was looking forward to the execution as an escape from being lectured.

She tugged at her hair, wishing for the last time that she hadn't
been forced to cut it in order to achieve her goal. It would have
looked well, coming out into the place of execution.

Officials of the Tharsis Court had spent the past few days
explaining procedure to her. They had explicated the sight lines
of the space, where best to stand to be seen, where best to be
heard. They had tried to assist her with her final speech. Calm,
unctuous—she hated them all.

What speech? Hadn't her act spoken all? If only she had rejected their plans at that last moment and stood there on the
platform to die, or even killed herself. Instead, they had tried to
escape and been trapped by the Gate as it descended like a judgment.

She could have chosen her own final garb too, or gone naked
if she had wished. But she had suffered her advisors to dress

her. She now wore the traditional flowing, somewhat-too-elegant clothing appropriate to a criminal of her stature, the puffy sleeves and high boots of a regicide or an attainted traitor. Despite herself, she thought it looked beautiful. If only she had been able to keep the hair. . . .

They had even let her see Sen one last time. There hadn't been much they could do, standing in a featureless cell, everything done, everything said. She had almost decided that it would be useless, that it was better to never see him again. But she was glad she had been persuaded. His eyes, and one last embrace of that skinny, tired body. He was going to live, that poor man. It was too much. He should have been marching out with her today. They could have rested their heads on the block together. That they were not permitted to do it was the final injustice. It had not even been permitted that he watch, so no eyes watching her would matter. All the people there, and she would die entirely alone.

She felt the breath of air behind her. The door to the balcony had opened. Without another thought or moment of hesitation, she turned and stepped through it. An escort was obligatory, but they, knowing her sense of her own role, stood back and let her walk forward alone. Several other prisoners shouted greetings and encouragement into the deep canyon beneath her feet. It irritated her. She didn't know them. Their sins were completely separate from hers.

Alone, Brenda Marr made her way to the killing ground.

"Barely in time." Trep ran quickly down the hall, as if leading recruits in exercise.

"We're not late," Hektor puffed as he kept pace alongside.

"And we're not going to be."

Hektor saw no advantage in replying further and just concentrated on keeping up. The hallway was long and straight, carved through the compressed volcanic ejecta covering the shallow-sloping cone of Ascraeus Mons. There was no reason for it to be so far from the rest of the facilities at Ascraeus to the Judgment Chamber, Hektor thought irritably. It was just pointless processional, a sign that justice was not as easily accessible as it sometimes appeared.

"Here we are," Trep said. "They haven't started yet, thank God." They passed through the portal, beneath the massive-looking lintel. The stone was supposedly the first judgment bench of Mars, used by the first colonists and featured in the many paintings of the condemnation of Isaac Castor, famous as the first person executed on Mars. His crime, the killing of a sleeping friend in jealousy over a woman, was less remembered.

The Judgment Chamber beyond was huge, but clearly a room, not a public space. It was perhaps thirty meters high and at least a hundred long, carved out of volcanic rock. The interior partitions that normally divided it into separate court and hearing rooms had been removed, leaving the giant gold-glowing ovoid unencumbered, except for the high screen that blocked the front. The chamber was packed full of people.

And they were all staring at Hektor. A brief murmur went through the crowd, then silence. Trep forged forward grimly, Hektor after him. Their spot was a platform thrust out high up, where the floor of the chamber curved up too steeply for anyone to stand on it anymore.

Hektor looked out over the sea of heads. No political statements here, no matter what anyone secretly thought, no demonstrations of disaffection. Everyone wore the flat, dark hat that indicated participation in a solemn public event. Hektor's mourning stood out against the general chalky grays, light blues, faded greens that everyone, through some subconscious cooperation, had agreed to wear. There was something brazen about his black, as if he flaunted his political sins before them even here, at the death of the woman who had compromised him.

A woman stepped forward into his path, a self-appointed spokesman for the crowd. "Why are you here?"

He stared directly into her eyes and spoke deliberately. "To see justice done. Why are *you* here?"

"The same," she said, taken aback. "But you—"

"But I helped capture the assassins." Hektor strove for calm, though he desperately wanted to scream at them all, to denounce them for fools, to damn them to hell. "Is that what angers you?"

"You want to suffocate us!" Her voice suddenly rose to a shriek.

He looked at her with an expression of distracted puzzlement. "I'm sorry? I didn't quite hear that."

"You want to imprison us." She was more dangerous now, sad and despairing rather than hectically enraged.

"No, I—"

"Let's move." Trep took a frantic head gesture from a Vigil crowd-control guard and moved Hektor past the protestor, blocking her with his massive body. "We have an execution to watch." Softer: "Why the hell do you pay attention to them?"

"I have to face it sooner or later."

"Better later, then, when they've forgotten."

"They may forget why they're angry. They won't forget their anger. By then it will be impossible."

Reason didn't matter, Hektor thought. He was unlucky. The worst sin in politics.

There was a rustle and an indrawn breath from below, and the silence became absolute. A solemn figure proceeded up the aisle: the Justice of Tharsis, Lon Passman. His arms were tightly covered and elaborately knotted in ceremonial white, and in them he held the wide-bladed, razor-edged ax, its grin fiercely expectant. Hektor peered down, trying to see through his father's insignia of office. Every time Hektor blinked, his father looked older. At the moment, the harsh blade in his arms seemed to have more life than he did.

Behind Lon Passman came Brenda Marr, holding her head up proudly despite the obvious terror that had overcome her upon passing beneath Castor's Stone. She had not expected to be afraid. Two guards walked just behind her, ready to seize her should she struggle or collapse, their hands ostentatiously hidden. Like everyone else in the vast chamber, Hektor leaned forward just slightly to examine the woman about to die.

Hektor had heard of Brenda Marr's personal slovenliness, her aversion to theater, her resentment. Like everyone else, he was unprepared for this dramatic figure, with her long flowing sleeves and high boots, her red-brown hair cropped short. The style, though clearly not her own, suited this sullen fury in her last moments.

The Justice of Tharsis climbed a set of stone stairs and passed behind the screen. Marr paused at the foot of the stairs, the lowest point in the bowl of the floor, and looked at the silent mob that curved up around her.

Standing near her, half concealed from Hektor's view, was a thin, pale-haired man. Hektor thought that, even at this distance, he could see the high cheekbones, the skin stretched tightly over them, as if they were ready to burst through. Breyten, whom he hadn't seen since he had announced he was leaving Xui House. Months now. Fabian had still been alive. And that short person behind him, just her piled-up hair visible, must be Egypt, come to see her husband's murderer brought to justice. Who else, Hektor wondered sadly, saw Brenda Marr as Fabian Xui's killer rather than Oswald DeCoven's?

Hektor slipped his hands into the elbow holes of his sleeves and turned, thinking of pointing Breyten out to Trep, but Trep's attention was on the crowd, which he searched with scorch-eyed intensity.

Hektor barely breathed, waiting for a word from Marr. Anything she could say would help him by reducing her to human dimensions, any words of defiance, justification, explanation, anything at all. And if she reduced herself to the status of someone who had killed a time-serving official while he was feeding a pigeon, then the emotional power of Hektor's closing of the Gates would be reduced proportionately.

Marr closed her mouth, shaking her head slightly, as if in argument with herself. Hektor swallowed. Of course she wouldn't speak. The assassination had said everything she wanted to say. For a moment he hoped she would look up and catch his eye. He had a genuinely Martian envy for a gesture so pure. But she looked at no one. Marr climbed slowly up the stairs after Lon Passman. Her back vanished behind the screen. Her two guards followed. One of them would be the actual executioner, chosen by the flip of an ancient coin. Unlike the ambiguous ax, the coin was admitted to have come from old Earth—found in a tomb, was the story.

Hektor knew what to expect, but it still startled him. As if a mysterious underground sun had sprung above an invisible horizon, the shadows of the participants in the drama appeared, bulking and sharp-edged, on the rear wall of the chamber.

The figure of his father had been transformed into a looming black giant, who handed the ax to the executioner with a bland, uninflected gesture, all the more ominous for its lack of obvious theater. The shivering shadow of Marr was bent over the block. She moaned, a sound shockingly loud in the chamber's clear acoustics.

It was all over in an instant, the swing, the thunk of blade sliding between the cervical vertebrae into the solid block, the tumbling away into silence and invisibility of the suddenly detached head.

The crowd stood silent for a moment longer, spilling through the wide doorway, its job of witnessing finished. Hats came off and were folded carefully into pockets. A few glances at Hektor, but most already had their minds on other tasks.

Hektor thought about the situation and took a guess. "Did you see him?"

"Breyten? Of course. He was standing close enough to Marr to pick her teeth for her. You're a boiling-blood bunch, you Passmans, know that, Hektor?"

Hektor was not to be distracted. "You weren't looking for Breyten, or you'd have stopped looking when you found him. You were hoping Rudolf Hounslow was here."

"And why would I expect such a thing?" Trep was sardonic.

"I didn't say you expected it. I said you were hoping." Hounslow was the center of his father's obsession, though Lon tried to conceal it. Was Trep carrying out Lon's bidding? Hektor didn't think so. "But you didn't see him. He's still out there somewhere, circling Ascraeus. Why should he come here?"

"To see it. To establish his responsibility, to connect himself with it. He didn't order Marr to assassinate DeCoven, didn't even know about it. But despite the confusion of her motives, we know his thought was behind it. You have to know him the way I do."

"And how do you know him?" Trep looked hesitant, and

Hektor grinned. "Come on, Gustavus, you want to tell me, or you wouldn't have allowed yourself to talk about it at all."

"Smart boy, eh?" Trep felt the black material of Hektor's sleeve. "So what's this, then? 'Don't be mad at me, my friend is dead'? You think that calms anyone down? It's not smart, Hektor."

Hektor looked around the platform as if for help, but it was empty, the people standing nearest him having cleared out the fastest.

"You're screwed. Mummy meat." Trep's eyes gleamed at him in amusement. "What are you going to do now, eh? Just like that—isn't it stupid?"

"Why?" Hektor whispered.

"A brilliant career, right into the fractionating pool, eh?" Trep was relentless. The whole family bugged him at the moment, the entire Passman tribe, self-important and maddening. "Just a little slip, a valve left open, lungs sucked out. Just . . . like . . . that. Come on, come on." He tugged on Hektor's arm. "Let me tell you the story. Then maybe you can start on finding another life."

Hektor let Trep lead him out of the Judgment Chamber and up a hallway that curved to the surface of the volcanic cone. Eventually he found himself seated in a windowed alcove, far from any of the witnessing eyes from the execution.

"I knew Hounslow at school," Trep said.

"He was three years behind you at St. Hilarion." After that long-ago discussion when he had incautiously taken a position on Hounslow and his movement, Hektor had made it his task to know as much about him as possible.

St. Hilarion was a prominent school, located on the slope of Olympus Mons, significantly near the blast crater where, in 2252, a Technic ship blew itself up during the Seven Planets War. The Crater was the most visible marker of that conflict over the independence of the outer satellites left on the surface of Mars.

"Right. Since he was younger, I didn't see him much. Save for discipline, of course. Hounslow needed a lot of discipline, mostly because he liked to impose his own on the younger students.''

''A bully?''

Trep thought about that one, pulling at his lower lip. ''Nothing so simple. Just smacking younger children around is an easy practice to break, usually by making the bully responsible for the smaller kids' safety. Or by tearing his ear. But that was really the problem. Hounslow kept organizing the younger ones, before they were really ready for it. Solely for the purpose of causing riots, as far as anyone could see. Lots of banner waving, you know the thing. Disruptive of discipline. *Organized* discipline. Why else do we go to school?''

The students of St. Hilarion, boys and girls alike, were famous for their barracks-like organization. In later years they tended to become prominent military officers. Like Colonel Gustavus Trep.

''Was he expelled?'' Hektor asked.

''He was, but not just for that. He was an *articulate* son of a bitch, even then. He always had some historical backing for his actions, if you can believe that. Ancient Spartans, medieval Russian thugs, Japanese heroes who screwed up and had to perform abdominal surgery on themselves—all sorts of people. Nice, intellectual underpinnings, and they loved that at Hilarion. Hell, Hounslow even knew who St. Hilarion was, and I never did get that too straight.'' Trep looked wrathful, as if the saint's identity had been kept from him on purpose.

''But what did Hounslow do?'' Hektor said. ''Specifically.'' He was interested, not only in the story but also in why Trep was telling it to him. He'd always thought Trep simple and easy to read, a man of clear motives and goals. He had to learn that he, the world, and Trep all together were not what he had always thought.

''He mounted an expedition. Five of the younger ones went with him, three girls, two boys, all about twelve years old. You know kids that age, they'll do anything, particularly the girls. Wild things. It's what discipline was invented for. They were on a class trip out on the slope. He took them off from the main group—to climb the damn thing. They started at about fifteen kilometers in altitude. That leaves twelve kilometers to climb. Plus, I think Hounslow's real goal was *inside* the caldera. God knows what it was now. Acherusian remains, maybe. He always had a lot of theories about that.''

"He climbed Olympus Mons to perform amateur archae-ology?''

Trep bared his teeth. "You know, three of them actually made it. Hounslow and two of the girls. The others fell off along the way. Gave up their air, exhaled. One of them apparently crawled so far under a rock that we never found her body. Didn't want to leave evidence for the pursuers. The others were picked up . . . one of them dead, the other barely alive. Lost a lot of external tissue, that one. Frostbite, desiccation, oxygen loss. A little brain damage too. So they threw Hounslow the hell out. No parents to go back to, a state case. But you know, they still tell the story of that climb at that school. My daughter told me. Kind of dangerous, the school administration bans it, which just makes it that much more fun after lights-out, right?''

"Right,'' Hektor said, and thought of Breyten. That was ex-actly his thing, climbing a pointless volcano to die at the top for reasons known only to himself. The thought chilled him, and he wondered where Breyten was at that moment. Where would he have gone after leaving the Judgment Chamber?

"But you're not the only one who knows Hounslow from before,'' Hektor said. "So does my father.''

For a moment Trep did not answer, but stared off through the porthole window at the tumbled slopes of Ascraeus. To the Mar-tian eye, the horizon was weirdly distant here. Ascraeus, along with its fellow volcanoes Arsia and Pavonis, sat atop a vast bulge in Mars's crust, which lifted it kilometers above the general level of the surface, but with a slope too gentle to be perceived. In legend, heroes and explorers were forever standing on these slopes and looking out over the vast expanse of Mars.

"Hektor,'' he said, finally. "I wish I could tell you what you need to know. But that's not my place.'' And his eyes, when he looked back at Hektor, were wrathful. "I no longer know what my place is, but I know that isn't it.''

It took all of Hektor's acting skill to stay calmly in his seat and smile slowly. "That's all right. I'll talk to Father about it. He's just . . . a little touchy on the subject."

"On a lot of subjects." Trep shook his head. "You don't fool me for a second, young man. I don't envy you." Clumsily, he clapped Hektor on the shoulder.

"That's funny. No one does."

There had been no satisfaction in it. Egypt had braced herself for that result, but it still left her feeling hollow. They'd given her a place of honor, right up close, so that she could almost hear the gush of blood from severed carotids.

It wouldn't have meant anything even if she'd been able to hold the still-warm head in her hands. Not a damn thing. Still, she had gotten something from it. She'd seen the way people stared even when there was nothing to see. One woman, gray-haired, respectable, had bitten her lower lip with a sharpened canine until a single drop of blood welled out. And—was this satisfaction?—she'd seen an artery pulse in Brenda Marr's exposed target of a neck, an indication of fear. But it might have been just stage fright, or even a perverse excitement. No telling, the damning shortcoming of physiology: you could see the evidence of the heart's frantic beat, but you could never be sure what really caused it.

The crowd spilled from the Judgment Chamber. She clung to the wall of the corridor, trying to keep one hand on the rock at all times. Since the Feast of Gabriel, she hadn't been able to shake the feeling that she was going to be swept away amid the rolling population of Scamander and her feet would never touch ground again. These giant imprisoned spaces would suck her up, leave her hanging wrapped in silk like one of the mad blind worms of Charitum. No one on Mars called them mad, of course, but she was sure that they were.

But this wasn't Scamander. This was Ascraeus. She looked around herself, trying to see the difference. Miriam Kostal was passing through Ascraeus on her way to exile. That was the actual word she had used. Exile. From what little Egypt knew about Miriam, that was an excessively theatrical word for her. But what the hell, it was a theatrical situation. Miriam had done her duty and was being punished for it, just as Hektor was.

Like people trapped in a sudden disaster, Miriam Kostal and Egypt Watrous had grabbed onto each other for comfort. Egypt had seen the woman only twice before, but now felt like she was saying farewell to a childhood friend.

The corridor debouched into a wide, crowded space. The ceiling was much lower than was usual for Martian public spaces, and was held up by stocky, round-ridged columns covered with glazed tiles. This was Ascraeus Transfer, where long-distance trains from all directions exchanged passengers with the local cars.

The bright yellow Ascraeus Transport cars slid slowly among the cafes, restaurants, and waiting areas as if looking for a cup of coffee or a place to sit down. Ascraeus Transfer was crowded not just with travelers and their friends, but with random citizens who came here to watch the rest of Mars roll through on its way to somewhere else.

There she was. Egypt stopped, and apologized to the man who bumped into her. Miriam sat at a cafe table, her shiny beetle-green luggage piled neatly around her feet. It would have been held and transferred for her, but it was something she wanted everyone to see. She wore a simple dark blue dress, like a schoolgirl being taken to her first formal dinner, and leaned forward, scratching words on a transmission plate with a stylus. Occasionally, as she paused to think of the next thing to write, her face looked almost relaxed. She must be writing to someone she likes, Egypt thought.

Egypt finally reached out fingertips and touched Miriam's cheek. Miriam turned her head slowly and looked up at her with dark, glistening eyes.

''She's dead,'' Egypt said.

Miriam pulled the spoon out of the teacup before her and laid it precisely on the saucer. Then she stood up and put her arms around Egypt. Egypt leaned against her, almost serene. Miriam clearly thought Egypt was the one who needed emotional reassurance.

''Was Hektor—?''

''He had to face down a mob. Well, a small mob. And the

woman who nominated herself as spokesman was probably not
the best representative of it.'' Egypt kept her tone matter-of-fact,
as if she hadn't been terrified at the time. Her emotional reaction
didn't matter. The scene mattered. ''He looked like a drop of
ink in chalky blue-green paint. One that wouldn't mix in. And
he hadn't worn a hat. His hair was combed, but it still looked
wild against those little caps of theirs.''

Miriam frowned at the inappropriately visual description.
''Did he tell them to go to hell?''

''He wants them to understand why he did what he did. Once
they do, *then* he'll tell them to go to hell.''

''No large group of human beings will ever understand anything.'' Miriam said it with the certainty of a well-remembered
school lesson.

''But Hektor will never stop trying to explain.'' Egypt sat
down. ''So let's not tell him his efforts are doomed.''

''Agreed.''

Egypt was afraid for Miriam, for Hektor, for everyone, since
with Fabian's death she had ceased to need to be afraid for
herself. It hadn't been wise to sleep with Hektor last night, but
it had made perfect sense.

''Have you read him?'' Egypt asked.

''Hektor? I don't think so.''

''He writes political columns. Under the name Kennedy. He
always told me it was a Roman name. Anonymous political writers favor Roman names. But it isn't, it's Irish.''

Miriam smiled. ''Damn. I liked those columns. Just like Fabian's . . . all these people, and I never even knew they were real.
What will Hektor do now?''

''Whatever.'' Egypt was deliberately negligent. ''Maybe his
life is over. Maybe it doesn't matter.''

''I hope not. Mine isn't.'' She looked sharply at Egypt. ''Neither is yours.''

''Oh, don't worry about mine. I have plenty to do.'' Egypt
felt like pulling out her notebook and flashing her pages of notes
at Miriam to demonstrate the truth of that assertion. No one took
her, poor widow, seriously enough.

''Good.'' Miriam pulled her intent look away. ''That's good.''

Breyten lay between Miriam and Hektor like a pool of dust of unknown depth, Egypt thought. It was absurd that he should. He was truly so alien to both of them. But his history was not to be disentangled from theirs. Well, that was their business, not hers. Egypt had other theatrical matters to worry about.

"Hektor wanted to come here," Egypt said. She looked around the crowded space. "I don't know where he is."

"Busy, no doubt. And so am I. Wait, let me mail this letter." She scratched a few more words, signed it with a flourish, then connected with a data line.

Egypt couldn't stand it. "Who is it to?"

"Someone completely unconnected with this mess, thank God. A boy. I met his father a year or so. Lindgren, a security official from Earth. I liked him. His son's name is Anton. He's eleven, and my pen pal. He's wild to come to Mars."

"What did you tell him?"

"I told him that this was a bad season. Perhaps next year. He threatened to stow away to come. He knows things are rough here, he follows the news. He wants to protect me." Miriam shook her head at the thought of the boy who was desperate to attend a disaster. "Could you help me with my bags? We have a few minutes, but no sense in pushing it."

The Ascraeus–Boreale train was, at that moment, just a line of booths on the floor, like a string of noodle shops or dossing rooms. Its floor was level with the floor of Ascraeus Transfer, and its compartments were wide open on both sides. You could walk right through the train without stopping, and some people were doing that to avoid detouring around the long thing, though as passengers claimed their spots, more and more of the doors closed. Children particularly enjoyed mocking the petrified stillness of the usually frantic train.

"Something interesting," Miriam said as she led them to her compartment. "I requested it particularly."

Her compartment looked no different from the others: thick, gleaming panels of mined wood, tufted seats, a glass case in which a gleaming scarab beetle rolled an artificial dung ball as white as ivory across the sand, moving steadily toward the new day. It was an old car, an antique. Clearly the Vigil was not defraying the cost of this transportation. Miriam was paying for it herself.

They unloaded the cart and stowed the various pieces of luggage in their designated slots. By ancient custom, Martian luggage fit into specified spaces on transport carts, in train compartments, even in hotel rooms. Her luggage was completely out of the way, but Miriam could open any piece of it whenever she wanted.

"Here, watch." Egypt sat down in a too-richly padded seat and watched as Miriam felt down behind the seat opposite. "Ah." Miriam clicked something, and a circular opening suddenly appeared in the floor. Startled, Egypt moved her feet away from it, then leaned over to look down.

"These cars used to belong to the old Ius Chasma Rim Train. This is the notorious Compartment 7A."

"I don't . . ." Egypt couldn't take her eyes off that ominous dark hole.

"At the end of the Time of Tumults, Mars was ruled by the Joemon government. It was an independent government of survival—links with Earth were broken. Joemon eliminated political rivals by inviting them to take the Rim Train to his headquarters at the end of Gangis Chasma. They'd get on the train, usually in Scamander, settle into their compartment . . . and disappear somewhere between Scamander and Gangis."

Egypt pulled her feet away from the hole. "They'd go down here."

"Right. Usually dead already, killed by security guards. Then right off the train. They found a few dried bodies just below the Eos trestle a few years ago." Another click, and the hatch sealed again. "When the train got to Gangis, there was someone else in the compartment, and the passenger lists matched. No one found out about it until the Joemon government fell."

Egypt wondered at the relish with which Miriam told the story, though it was the sort of thing Martians liked: a secret death, one that remains forever a mystery.

Where Joemon and his bodyguards had been killed stood a monument, realistic bronze replicas of the skintites and air masks that had been hung up rods from a shattered rail trestle as markers immediately after the killing. Joemon had been set up by a close advisor who was enraged by a deal Joemon had cut with Governor-Resident Tolchko, allowing for decreased independence for Mars in return for increased personal power for Joemon.

Martians built their walls, layer after layer, then lay down on their hard beds and were killed by their closest intimates, walled up with them.

"Get another compartment," Egypt said suddenly. "Don't stay in this one."

"No one's going to try to kill me in here, Egypt."

"No . . . no, of course not." Egypt felt distracted, frightened, as if a foil executioner's ax had suddenly turned real on stage but none of the other actors saw it. "Besides, Hektor will pull you out if you fall into it."

Miriam turned her head away. "He won't know where I am."

"Oh," said Egypt, "I don't think that's true."

It would have to be here, Hektor thought as he contemplated the cliffs above him and the ledge thrusting out some hundred meters up. Breyten would never just take a hotel room, never just take the magtrack from Valles Marineris to Ascraeus, never just live at ease.

Night was falling over the rock-strewn plains to the west. Starting overhead, a huge V of red-glowing clouds drifted out toward the dusty horizon, an arrow pointing right at him and identifying him for viewers in orbit. The clouds were roiled and clenched, caused by the pressure-reducing climb of water-containing wind as it slid over the twenty-seven-kilometer-high bulk of Ascraeus.

The cliff was shattered lava columns, which left chimneys. Hektor slid his way up easily, grabbing onto flutes and strangely twisted plates, memories of long-ago liquid flows when Mars had been alive.

There was no Breyten Passman registered anywhere at Ascraeus. Hektor had used a few still-active journalistic contacts to find that out. But there was, as he had discovered after some thought, a Pierre Sanserif, registered as a camper on the volcanic shield itself. Pierre Sanserif was a playful childhood name of

Breyten's. Hektor could no longer remember how he had acquired it.

He hung halfway up and looked out over the high plains that sloped off toward the northwest. The ribbon of a magtrack gleamed on the rocky ground as it curved to the right, to head for the smooth gap of the Ceraunius Fossae and make its way to the north. The rushing caterpillar of a train slid along it, its lights already gleaming, and vanished to the north.

Hektor shook his head and turned his attention to his climbing. It was growing dark. He bounced easily up the last few meters and came out on the ledge. A tessellated pressure dome rested there, glowing with its own internal light. The sky was now black, the land around completely invisible save for the pinpoints of vehicles and dwelling places. Hektor clicked up the intensity of his earphones and listened to the rock-eroding hiss of the eternal thin wind.

Breyten sat, arms around his knees, staring off to the west. He glanced up at Hektor. "You know, I think I can just see the top of Olympus from here."

"You can't either. It's too far."

"It *was* too far. It's moved."

"Nothing moves on Mars. It's a dead planet." Grunting, he sat down next to Breyten. He'd strained his back while making love to Egypt. He was getting old.

When Breyten had been seven, they had come to the top of Ascraeus Mons with their mother and father. Breyten had insisted, to the point of red-faced rage, that he could see the top of Olympus Mons from where they stood, despite the fact that it was far over the horizon. Finally, their mother had been forced to carry him back inside as he kicked and screamed. It was one of Hektor's earliest memories.

"Human beings move," Breyten said softly. "That's why we came here to Mars. So that something would happen here."

"A lot is happening. Like my brother disappearing for three months, then reappearing, unannounced, at an execution."

Breyten shrugged. "Father did his usual fine job. I've always admired his sense of the dramatic."

"He was doing his duty." Hektor saw that this was going to

be as hard as Breyten could make it. "As I was. What's left of my duty, that is."

"I'd like to think I'm doing mine. Hektor, do you want some tea?"

"Yes," Hektor said instantly. "That's why I came to see you. No one else knows how to make it right. It's been years." It was Breyten's calming ritual. It would help him talk. And it would help Hektor listen.

Breyten rolled and stood. "Come on in."

They crawled through the air lock into the spare interior of the shelter: a sleeping pad, a travel case, an air plant, a water container, a heating element. It looked, Hektor realized, very much like Breyten's room at home, which was almost devoid of possessions or decoration. In his adolescence, Breyten had often cooked over a heater in his room, as if he was just temporarily passing through Xui House on a journey to somewhere else. Those rare occasions when Breyten had invited his younger brother to join him in a meal seemed to Hektor like an honor, despite the fact that the food was almost inedible, even to a Martian palate.

"Remember how we used to defend Xui House?" Hektor said. "Imperial cataphracts, Technic cyborg assassins, Gold Band marauders—we stood against all of them."

"They were imaginary, Hektor. Every last one of them."

This chilling bit of realism was completely unlike Breyten, who valued the things he had imagined in his childhood as much as he did the things he had experienced.

"Not all threats are imaginary. Our instincts were sound. We may have imagined the enemies, but we knew what was worth defending."

"Oh, really." Breyten gave his head an irritating, weary-older-brother shake. "What do you have left that's worth defending, Hektor? They're fools, corrupt fools. They threw you out of where you most wanted to be because you acted quickly. That was good work, by the way. I don't think anyone else could have made that decision so fast."

Despite himself, Hektor felt a glow of pride. It had always

been hard to impress Breyten, who respected most only those things he himself was best at.

"*You* could have," Hektor said. "That's why I need you. I feel like everything's falling apart around me and no one cares. Why is that? Martians, we hold ourselves to be so smart, so aware of the thousand threats that face us daily, and yet we can't see the thing that threatens us the most."

Hektor felt his heart beating as if he was doing something incredibly risky, like climbing a crumbling cliff without a rope. Persuading Breyten of the threat was suddenly searingly important. He needed Breyten, the man everyone loved because he could dance on the edge of a cliff and never, ever fall off. The need pounded against the inside of his skull.

The tea maker hissed and bubbled, and the smell of the tea suffused the thin, dry air of the shelter. Breyten had turned the interior light down to almost nothing, so that the darkness outside seeped in. His face was lit dimly from underneath.

"The threat's gone," Breyten said. "That woman is dead, her confederates decently jailed. Not much of a threat to begin with."

The dark speck of Deimos hung in the sky almost directly overhead, while Phobos crept up from the west toward it, moving almost visibly as it forged its way against the rotation of Mars.

Breyten was being deliberately obtuse.

"No," Hektor said. "That was nothing, just a little sand sifting down from overhead. The avalanche is still coming. Can't you feel it? Father does. With him I—"

"Oh, you and Father." Breyten's tone was airily contemptuous. "Don't get up in his strange obsessions, Hektor. They don't suit you. He doesn't just want things to stay the way they are, he wants them to be the way they *were*."

Breyten had always been disrespectful. Was that why Lon liked him so much? Hektor had tried it, but all it had ever gotten him was punishment. Breyten's words were not permitted to come out of Hektor's mouth.

He watched Breyten fuss with the tea maker and thought of him standing in the mob watching Brenda Marr die. For the first time, he thought, not of the emotional oddness of that, but of the practical problem: how had Breyten gotten a spot on the floor? Lon and Trep together had obtained Hektor's entry, for all the good that had done him. Breyten could not just have walked in from wherever he had been. He had made contact with someone. And who else but their father?

He opened his mouth to ask, then closed it. He didn't need to ask, to hear the confirmation from Breyten's lips with a subliminal jeer to give serrations to the edge of the news.

"Go back to Scamander," Breyten said. He busied himself with the tea maker, moving with the ease of old ritual. "It'll blow over. You know what Scamander is like. They'll be all excited for a while, then they won't be. You could still end up as the Voice of the Chamber, a Union Councillor, whatever you want, Hektor."

"I'd like to think that." Hektor kept his voice steady.

"So think it."

Breyten handed him a cup and Hektor took a sip of the harsh and bitter tea. He nodded his approval. Martian tea was a particular point of pride to Breyten, since no one from anywhere else in the Solar System could stand the stuff.

"Hey," Hektor said, examining the rough-textured stoneware cup. "This is mine!"

Breyten smiled at his brother. "Yes, it is. You made them in school, remember? You were proud of them, and we used them for a year or so for all occasions, even serious ones, and then you weren't proud of them anymore, and put them away. I rescued them. When I left Xui House, I took them with me."

Hektor held it up in what little light there was. "Huh. Not bad, not bad at all. Not like I remember them." It had been hard, hard work making them, he now remembered. Their instructor had been precise and demanding. Making a good form of something was an essential Martian tradition: everyone, sometime in his life, should make a precious, important object. These cups had been Hektor's almost self-mocking attempt. The green glaze gleamed at him from the cracks in the surface. He could no longer remember how he had managed that effect.

"Do you want them back?" The concern was clear in Breyten's voice.

"No, no. They go the best with your tea. I can't make it, not the way you can. They don't make any sense unless they're used right."

All of Mars was now like this tea, accustomed movements concealing incomprehensible motives. Things weren't going to calm down. That might have been true before DeCoven's death, but it certainly wasn't now, and Breyten knew it. Hektor wondered what his brother was concealing.

"Once you wanted to act, to have meaning," Hektor said, changing the direction of his attack. "Why'd you give it up?"

"I haven't given anything up."

"It doesn't look that way."

Silently, Breyten poured Hektor another cup of tea. "Look. If you want to find out what I'm doing, just ask me. Don't try to manipulate me into shouting out some sort of confession. Not my style, you know."

"All right. What are you doing?"

"None of your business." Breyten bared his teeth at the flash of anger in Hektor's eyes. "And it isn't. But you know what, little brother? I'm going to tell you anyway. I'm more concerned with things than you think. I've made contact with the man whose cooperation is necessary for the solution of Mars's problems."

Hektor waited a long moment before speaking. "Hounslow?"

"Exactly."

"Are you crazy? You are!"

"Not at all." Breyten was calm. "Or, if I am, Father is too. He knew Hounslow when they were both young. Did you know that?"

"I guessed it," Hektor said, feeling again the weight of Lon's unknown past. "They were involved in some movement . . ."

"The Third Moon Movement." Breyten grimaced. "Can you imagine Father being involved in something with such a foolish name? But both he and Hounslow were in it together. Thirty-five years ago. It wasn't really such a big thing, just an organized movement against some aspects of Martian government. There

were a few acts of terrorism, though neither Father nor Hounslow was involved in them . . . I think. Most of the members were
arrested. Those who had not committed actual crimes were issued pardons.''

''Among them, Lon Passman and Rudolf Hounslow.''

''Exactly.''

''So you are to be Father's contact in Hounslow's organization.''

''They drifted apart over the years. You know how those
things happen. That's why there's been so much trouble. But
together, they hold the solution to Mars's problems. And we can
help, Hektor, you and I.''

Breyten rubbed his hands together, as he did whenever he felt
he'd finally persuaded Hektor of something. For the first time,
Hektor realized how often he acquiesced just because he saw
that gesture and wanted peace.

''You're lying, Breyten—to me or to yourself. They didn't
'drift apart.' I don't know what happened between them, but it
was something powerful. Something that still resonates with both
of them. If you want to join Hounslow's movement, fine. But
don't take advantage of Father's emotions to make it seem like
his idea.''

''For God's sake.'' Breyten's smile of resolved conflict vanished. ''Don't get all jealous about Father again. I'm not responsible for your problems.''

''I'm not—''

''Oh, don't tell me that. It's always back there. Father has his
own life, with Hounslow, with me, with all sorts of people you
don't even know about. It makes you mad, but you can't manage
him, Hektor, much as you would like to.''

''None of that is the point,'' Hektor said, holding on to his
calm tone. ''You are joining Hounslow for your own reasons,
not Father's. I wish you'd stop pretending otherwise.''

''Dammit, aren't you ever happy? Everything's a struggle
with you. You have to challenge everything I do or say. Why?
After the way I slung Miriam your way, I figured you'd be
grateful.'' Hektor's face went blank, and Breyten chuckled.
''You didn't think that was just accidental, did you, there in the

Armory? No, things were over between us, and I thought you should have a chance to meet her.''

Hektor knew that Breyten had, in a self-destructive mood, sent him on a collision course with Miriam Kostal, and that Breyten was now deliberately misstating his own motives. But Miriam wasn't going to be the territory that the war between Hektor and Breyten was fought over.

"I knew you two would hit it off," Breyten babbled. "And working together to capture DeCoven's assassins . . . what a bond to have. . . ."

"Right now," Hektor said, "Miriam is the saddest person I know. She's not really like that, is she, Breyten?"

"N-no. She's serious, but . . ."

"Trep's been forced to transfer her back north, away from her work. It's not a defeat she was meant to have.''

"It's one she should have," Breyten said, hardening his face. "The Vigil isn't her place. It shouldn't be anyone's place."

"I think she truly loved you.'' Hektor was remorseless. He would not allow Breyten to pretend that it had all meant nothing. "She still hasn't gotten over it.''

"Well, I have.''

Hektor thought about Egypt, and the night they had spent together. Mourning was something each person did individually, even as each one wears the same dark clothes. After they made love, Egypt had cried and cried. Not from guilt, but from the certain knowledge that she would never put her hands on her husband's body again. Then she had apologized to Hektor. He had thought she was apologizing for crying and hastened to re-assure her, but now, looking at Breyten's stony face, he knew she had apologized for using him the way she had. She shouldn't have. It is a joy to be able to provide comfort. Hektor wished, despite his anger, that he could comfort Breyten, who slept on broken glass and pretended he was not in pain.

"Don't worry," Hektor said. "I'm sure she will forgive you that as well.''

"I don't give a damn what she does. Take her, Hektor. Take her and good riddance.''

There was a long silence, because Hektor could think of nothing else to say.

"More tea, please," Hektor said, and watched as Breyten poured. They would drink tea together. For now, he would have to be satisfied with that.

9

From *The Psychological Surface of Mars*, by Karen Hangbao, Grand Tour Press, Jakarta, 2330:

I write this in a ruin, a ruin on the surface of Mars. I sit under a weathered wooden lintel, in a place where there is no weather. The piled stone walls have lost their plaster. Rubble is scattered across the mosaic floor. The statue of a bearded man stands in a wall niche. In one hand it holds an ankh, the looped cross that symbolizes Life. In the other it holds the ax, cut through with a cruelly grinning face, that symbolizes Death. This building has never held air. No one has ever lived here.

Later on I will tell you about the sculpted head that emerged from the mining spoil of an excavation in the crater Brashear. It was of a smiling young woman, of local stone, in a vaguely Southeast Asian style. People argue about this. What no one argues about is the fact that in the sculpture's jaw was an actual human jawbone which could be radiographically dated to ten thousand years ago. A hoax, of course. It has to be a hoax.

Keep that head in mind, because this building is not a hoax. This is the palace of Ahab and Jezebel at Jezreel. The flat spot nearby is Naboth's vineyard.

If I stand up, I can look out over the Valley of Jezreel, the course of the Kishon River, Mount Hermon looming high over Israel. Elijah ran in front of Ahab's chariot to this palace all the way from Mount Carmel after defeating the priests of Baal. Jael pounded a tent peg through Sisera's head somewhere down in the valley, Josiah died at Megiddo in the attack of the Pharaoh Necho, and Gideon defeated the hosts of Midian by the hillock I must call Mount Tabor.

There are as many maps of the Martian surface as there are Martians. The one I am describing to you now belongs to Mars's Jews, and is the Land of Israel. Alba Patera—Mount Hermon—marks its northernmost reach. Ascraeus Mons—Mount Sinai—marks the south. To me, Jezreel looks like just another canyon here in Mareotis, north of Tharsis. I do not understand it properly.

"Your mother taught you well," Lon said. He stood on an outcrop looking down at Hektor. "You and Breyten—both of you could have worked rescue if you had wanted."

That seemed like an excessive compliment for having plotted their route across this broken country, particularly since Breyten could have done it more quickly, with much less effort.

"The coordinates you specified are over there, just at the edge of that graben," Hektor said.

He could hear his father's breathing over the narrowbeam channel. Lon had the gain turned up a little too high, so that Hektor could hear the noisy workings of his throat. Hektor worked hard not to feel annoyed. It wasn't his father's fault he was old.

"Yes," Lon said. "That looks like it."

Lon stared out at that old place, trying to match it against memory. He hadn't ever come back out here, not once, and had carefully mapped family expeditions to avoid it. Breyten and Hektor, excited at exploring the Labyrinth, had never noticed the deliberate omission, but Sara, he was sure, had. He had never really discussed it with her, and then suddenly she was dead, and he never would. It frightened him how easily he had evaded the resolutions he had made that would never happen again. It had been years, his sons were adults, and still he had never talked about it with them.

It was unusual for Hektor to have asked no questions, made no bright observations. In fact, this whole time, Hektor had said nothing not directly related to the physical means of their trip. He had even resisted going in the first place, and reduced Lon pretty close to begging.

It was Lon's own fault Hektor was angry at him. He knew it. What he didn't know was how to get out of it. Sara would have known what to do instantly, would have had some gentle way of releasing the tension, some joke, some non sequitur so foolish-sounding that it made Lon wonder about her intelligence even as she achieved her goal.

Lon considered just telling him the story. That would certainly distract Hektor from his anger. But that would also be unfair, and the anger would return once the distraction vanished.

"He called me, Hektor," he said. "Out of the dark, as if nothing had happened. Just his voice . . . it had been so long since I'd heard it. Children don't understand what that means. They try to, but they never can. It doesn't take a Prodigal Son, though, of course, that's what Breyten is. All it takes is silence."

"That's not the emotion that disturbs me," Hektor said, only partly lying. "It's . . . Hounslow." He shook his head. "I have no idea why—"

"I hope that by the end of today you will understand a little better. Hektor, you went to that little dismissal ceremony in Rhenre. What did you think of it?"

"A sham, of course. But an odd one."

Three days before, just as the tension of events seemed to be reaching an impossible maximum, Rudolf Hounslow had announced the dispersal of his exoteric organization, the Olympus Clubs, and his retreat to the solemnity of Pure Land Mesa. That the Scamander announcement was made in the spot which had been the headquarters of the most notorious of the Olympus Clubs, the one that had encompassed the assassination of Governor-Resident DeCoven, only made it that much more puzzling. Hektor had stood under the humming train tracks of Rhenre as a reporter for *The Tithonium Courier*, and tried to figure out what the hell he was hearing.

"Yes," Lon said. "A simple move, but an effective one. Everyone in the Chamber of Delegates, all the writers on the more responsible newssheets—your intemperate article was a notable exception, dear Hektor—all are so relieved that the immediate crisis is past that they do not care to inquire further."

"He's playing dead. He and his whole organization."

Lon frowned. "It's a little more complicated than that. That implies a degree of both control and guile that my old friend Rudolf simply does not possess. But yes. Everyone's now searching for something. Hounslow just wants to be found."

"Maybe it's not *his* control and guile that we're seeing." There, he had said it. He waited tensely for Lon's response.

"All right—Breyten. You haven't talked since Ascraeus, I suspect. You know, I've wondered how you found him. . . ."

"We've been brothers a long time. I have ways."

"Good. I want you to find him again."

Hektor felt betrayed. He had been sitting here alone with his father, seemingly being entrusted with a responsible task, something no one else could do. And what did it turn out to be? Finding Breyten, Lon's one true son.

"All . . . right," Hektor said. "Do you have any information?"

"Yes," Lon said reluctantly. "But wait on it a moment. Let's first see if we are searching for the same person."

"What person?" Hektor was in no mood to split hairs. "Breyten Passman. Your son. My older brother."

"That is not who we are looking for, Hektor. We are looking for the man who may or may not, by now, be one of Hounslow's chief lieutenants."

"But you sent him—"

"I sent him into Hounslow's camp as my agent. I should have known better. But who else to send? Even Trep hasn't been able to place an agent in that organization for very long. You must understand, Hektor, that these people are true believers. They are driven by a force beyond themselves, whether it is love of Hounslow, the Great Void, a zest for destruction, or something else. That's hard to fake. Breyten succeeded because he wasn't faking it. Rudolf Hounslow always had a hold on the Passmans. After all these years, it seems, that's still true.''

He stood and, without warning, started walking. Hektor scrambled to his feet and followed, not daring to speak. Lon crossed the broken land to the graben and walked slowly along the edge.

''Truths are dangerous,'' Lon said finally. ''Particularly now. There is a time to brandish truth and a time to sheathe it. But cautious wisdom always seems to prefer the scabbard. It's better that you and Breyten are not wise. Here—'' He pointed. ''Here I came upon Rudolf Hounslow. Thirty-five years ago. He'd put his shelter right out here on the edge of the cliff, a nice, dramatic location, though unsafe. Breyten favors this sort of place, right? Ruins the scenery, in my opinion.

''I didn't come upon him by accident, of course. We had agreed to meet here.'' He stared down at the spot, as if he was examining the shelter that stood there.

''We met at the Mount Fromkin School. He'd come there from St. Hilarion. . . .''

''Expelled for trying to climb Olympus Mons.''

''I see Gustavus has been trying to prepare you. He favors the best stories, though, not the ones that tell the most. It was a difficult time on Mars. They all are, it seems. Oligarchy, corruption, an ossified bureaucracy . . . thirty-five years ago. We joined something we called the Third Moon Movement. You've heard of it?''

Hektor shrugged. ''In some history lesson.''

''Ha. Don't be so hard. It was pretty foolish, in retrospect. We agitated, were arrested, were released. I guess it was that last that set Hounslow off. He'd been looking forward to some romantic imprisonment, and then found himself treated as if he hadn't done anything significant. I felt pretty much the same way. A ruined reputation and the inability to find a job aren't romantic, they just grind you down until there's nothing left.

''We had interpreted our joint devotion to dramatic reform as friendship. So we decided to commit suicide together, as the last adventure of dramatically doomed friends. It wasn't right, because we didn't have the personal bond that would have made that sacrifice have some meaning.

"While we were sitting out here staring at the bitter edge of the sword we'd brought with us—sharpening it had been our focus for days—and wishing we'd had the sense to call along some seconds to make our last moments less painful, we found ourselves suffocating. The shelter fogged up and our pinkies starting screaming excessive carbon dioxide messages at us.

"Hounslow's own fault, I've always thought. He'd screwed up a valve installation, it turned out. He always claimed, after that, that it had been sabotage, an attempt to kill him. Not kill *us*—I was clearly not the issue. He should have noticed the valve—it's poor sabotage that's so easily detected. Anyway, he lost consciousness. Moving entirely on instinct, I managed to get to the emergency air, keep myself from going under, and then feed him oxygen. By the time we were both fully conscious, it seemed foolish to try to kill ourselves. Ludicrous, even. We've never spoken since that time."

Hektor laughed. He tried not to, it was too cruel, but somehow he found himself howling with laughter. All the Martian pieties, crushed in one single, stupid event on the edge of a graben. And his father . . . to imagine Lon . . . and Hounslow . . . all these years he hadn't known.

"Shame on you," Lon said finally. "To so mock your aged father."

And, for an instant, Hektor felt an annihilating terror, as if one burst of laughter would destroy whatever bonds he had managed to build over all these years. . . .

"I'm sorry, Father," he gasped. "I—"

"Well," Lon said sourly, "maybe that's the best possible reaction to all of this. Are you quite finished?"

"Yes," Hektor managed. "It won't happen again."

"That I doubt." He didn't smile. It would have been a lot easier if he had smiled. "I told you the story so that you would understand. It's a paradoxical bond between Hounslow and me, even an absurd one—don't start again, Hektor—but it's real. Breyten took advantage of it. We need to communicate with him."

Hektor was finally serious. "So where is Breyten?"

"I have an address for him . . . it's down in Ringhoffer's Fossa."

"Ringhoffer's Fossa?" Hektor couldn't keep the surprise out of his voice. "*Breyten?*"

"Yes, Breyten. He's become a member of a social club down there, the Friends of St. Rabelais, I think it's called." Lon shook his head in disgust. "You have, I take it, heard of the place?"

"Well, of course I have. Who hasn't?"

Hektor certainly knew Ringhoffer's Fossa. He had spent many hours of his early manhood in that dark lubrication, the sweaty air that flowed there making almost-visible vortices.

"What better place for a virtuous man to hide," Lon said, "than in a bordello? Clearly your brother is looking forward to future plays and operas, with elaborately decorated bordello scenes to set off the virtuous hero. Singing and dancing—always breaks up the monotony of ethical drama."

"All right," Hektor said, feeling a return of the old chill, the sense that the only thing that really held him and Lon together was a mutual perplexed love for their dramatically erring Breyten. "What should I do when I find him?"

"Find out what's going on. He may talk to *you*. You've always been the only one he'll talk to. And look around, draw your conclusions." Lon turned the full force of his gaze on Hektor. "It's too soon to ask this of you, Hektor, but I want you to think about the necessary consequences, and understand them."

"What? I *don't* understand."

"That must be because you don't want to, because you're certainly smart enough. Why would the Olympus Clubs dissolve themselves into Scamander? Think about it."

"To prepare for urban revolt," Hektor said, reluctant because of the conclusion that grew out the premises. "Like the Gold Band Revolt or the Veterans Uprising."

The Gold Band Revolt, an anti-Joemon movement that had smoldered in the corridors for years, had a particular meaning for Hektor, since the Gates had been put in place in the process of stamping it out.

"Exactly," Lon said. "You know how dangerous that could

be. So you go to Breyten. It's your decision. But if it looks like Breyten and Hounslow are a serious threat, if it seems like a revolt could be imminent, I give you full sanction to do whatever is necessary.''

"Condign punishment." Hektor's voice was dull.

Lon blinked. Behind his air mask, Hektor could see the tears in his eyes. "You're right. I won't hide behind deniable phrasing. If it's necessary—and you'll know if it is—I want you to kill your brother." Lon almost smiled. "Breyten knows the situation. I'm sure he'll understand."

It was hot in the room. Not Martian hot, which could be comfortable for a Terran. *Hot.* And wet, as thick as the air Hektor remembered from the Amazon. He felt like he was sweating slithery gobs of semen. Jesus, why was he thinking that?

Probably because of the two naked women in the empty, gold-lined tub. They leaned their heads back, eyes closed, heads at opposite ends of the tub. One had fine skin and he could see the delicate vein in her throat. The other was darker and her huge breasts floated dreamlike in his vision.

"Sweat," the pale one said dreamily. "It all depends on how you feel it. I sweat quicksilver. I'll fill this tub, see if I don't. Here." She held a delicate pale blue flower out to Hektor. "Smell."

He'd been invited into the private headquarters of the Friends of St. Rabelais, not a hint of resistance, yet he'd been here an hour and not found anything out. Nevertheless, politely, he leaned forward and inhaled. A shy, fugitive scent, gone before he could really smell it.

"Breyten Passman," he said, not for the first time. "He's supposed to be up here."

"No one's *supposed* to be anywhere." The second one opened her eyes. "Don't you know that?"

The room's heat redoubled and Hektor's skin flushed. The itch of his clothing against him was almost intolerable. He shifted and—he had an erection. How had that happened without his noticing? And it *hurt*, goddammit, like a young man's raging morning hard-on. He felt like it was ready to explode.

The one with the flower raised a hand toward him, still without opening her eyes. It swelled in his vision.

"See?" she said. "What did I tell you?"

He squinted, trying to focus. Her hand was dripping like a squeezed sponge, and the liquid was gleaming silver. Hektor's clothing was hideously uncomfortable. He wanted to strip naked in the blessed hot air and slide into the tub with both of them. The silver sweat would heal him. He felt like he could have both of them, and a dozen other women besides.

He pushed himself back, gulping air that burned his throat. "Breyten," he managed. "Breyten Passman. He's my brother. I want to talk to him."

"It's a side effect," she explained. "The quicksilver sweat." She giggled. "Just a side effect of what I really want."

An upside-down head poked through a riser entrance just above them. Hektor focused muzzily. It was Breyten. He grabbed the bar at the entrance, swung himself around, and dropped to the floor. He grinned.

"Hektor! Good to see you. Glad you could come visit. I see you've met Belisanne and Plon."

"Yes," Belisanne drawled. "He's worried about sweating. Seems to be his main issue."

"Well, we all have those." And then Breyten leaned over and kissed her, a deep, tongue-lashing kiss. Hektor watched in stunned dismay. Hallucinations. He was having hallucinations. The second woman, Plon, climbed on Breyten's back, pressing her large breasts against him. Breyten reached a hand back and cupped a buttock.

"You can come back here later," Breyten said, standing. "I think they'd like that." There was silver clinging to his lips, great stains of it on his clothing. He smelled of some nostril-clogging, flowery perfume. "But right now we need to talk, right, little brother?"

"Let's leave here," Hektor said. "Out in the corridor—"

"No." Breyten was firm. "This is my place. You'll have to deal with me here."

They walked through several rooms before they got to where Breyten wanted to go. Two men copulated on a blower-powered air bed of the sort used in hospitals. They grunted noisily, competing with the roar of the misadjusted blower. A woman with long hair puked in a corner, not into a drain, just on the floor, getting her vomit in her hair and smearing it irritably with her fingers. A group of about six people lay on the floor in one room, clothing disarranged as if they had all just had sex without taking it off, snoring with desperate tenacity. Hektor recognized one of them, a delicate-looking boy with long eyelashes, Krlezha, formerly an austere wearer of functional coveralls who worked with a rescue team on Tharsis ridge. His fingernails were colored with rainbows. Hektor had seen a rainbow on Earth. They did not occur on Mars.

"Here, here." They sat down on some mossy stones underneath a waterfall. It was a statement of most un-Martian extravagance. Intellectually, Hektor knew that water was efficiently stored in almost any form. Given adequate energy generation, a waterfall made as much sense as any other. Emotionally, he found it a chilling statement, like letting your blood flow out over your skin in order to show off its color. Breyten contemplated the extravagantly splashing water, then ran his fingers under it and let the water drip onto the stone floor. Hektor stared down at the spattered wetness and shuddered.

Breyten handed him a bottle. It was Terran wine, Andean. Shipping it here must have been hideously expensive. Seeing his brother's confusion, Breyten took it back, gulped at the neck, and thrust it out again. Hektor sipped reluctantly. This was no way to drink fine wine, even to prove a point.

"This is the life, eh, Hektor?" Breyten's eyes gleamed at him.

"Father's worried about you," Hektor said.

"He's always worried about me." Breyten burped, then paused for a moment to contemplate how fine a thing he had just accomplished. "First it's because I don't have a good enough time and don't hang around with women, then it's because I'm having a too-good time and *am* hanging around with women."

"Breyten—" Hektor controlled himself. "Father wants to talk to you. He really is worried. And I'm worried about him.

He's getting old now. I think things are getting to be too much for him. . . . ''

"Oh, it's that old thing again? Hektor's trying to get into Daddy's good graces. Keep plugging, Hektor, keep at it. Just don't try to use *me* to do it, all right? Suck up on your own account.''

Hektor looked at his brother. Breyten's face was shiny with sweat. He looked desperately nauseated, keeping his guts down through sheer effort of will.

"So," Hektor said, "Hounslow didn't work out for you, did he?''

"No. It was all hollow. Just a lot of playacting . . . he's back at Pure Land Mesa now, meditating. I think he'll just stay there. And I'm going to have myself a good time instead. . . .''

Breyten really *did* think he was a fool, Hektor thought. Despite his resolutions to use that fact to his own advantage, the thought saddened him. After all those massive efforts he'd devoted to impressing Breyten, it was all worthless.

These people, if nothing else, were brave. Their membership in this most un-Martian social organization, the Friends of St. Rabelais, had destroyed their lives in the society outside, the world of Scamander. Many had been abandoned by parents, by children, by spouses, had lost their jobs and their habitual spots at dinner tables across Scamander. They were regarded with contempt and amusement, and their place in the world—built up of carefully considered gestures, of dramatic actions, of demeanor, will, and endless linkages to the lives of others—was destroyed, a hollow ruin filled with dust. It was courage of a pure and unusual sort, for Martian courage always demanded the recognition of others for its full expression.

Rabelais, as far as Hektor could remember, had never been formally canonized by anyone. But then, there were so many religions across the history of the Solar System that it was more than probable that some splinter sect somewhere had filed the necessary paperwork. The Society of the End of Days, some called it, the only proper response to the closing of the mental frontier that had once been Mars. It was all right here, in an open clubhouse on Ringhoffer's Fossa. And Hektor Passman could walk right into it.

What Hektor didn't see, and suspected was not there, was anyone who could actually start and manage any sort of corridor action. Before coming here, he'd gone through all of Fabian's files, a complete study of corridor crews, vigilantes, freelance criminals—dossiers, curriculum vitae, photographs, personal testimonies. Hektor realized that he himself had never taken Fabian seriously enough. The amount of work to put all that together was staggering. Not a single one of those people was a member of the Friends of St. Rabelais, or was even peripherally associated with it.

Hektor licked his lips. God, he never did that: a mark of lasciviousness from a street play that had entered real life through the behavioral virus of art. If Breyten and his fellow Olympus Club members could hide themselves under the frantic joy of the Friends of St. Rabelais, Hektor could too. Besides, it had been a while, and that woman with the silver sweat—Belisanne, it never did to forget their names—had a sweet rump. That silver sweat, whatever the hell it was, hung in tiny dots in her curly pubic hair. She must have followed them—there she was, earnestly addressing a comment to a slumped man who barely seemed conscious.

He needed another drink. He grabbed the bottle from Breyten and looked around for a proper glass.

"We never did this together, did we?" Hektor said. He caught Belisanne's eye and gestured with the bottle in invitation.

"No . . . no, we never did."

"Did you want to? To come with me, I mean, when I came out here." It would no more have occurred to him to have brought Breyten here than it would have been for him to eat sand.

"Sure! It's taken me too long as it is."

Belisanne—dedicated member of the Olympus Clubs or hired talent?—came over and slid onto Hektor's lap. He reached down and flicked away a sliver drop.

"Hey!" she said. "Don't yank. You guys never know how much that can hurt."

Hektor chuckled. "Sure, sure." She did feel good on his lap. Warm, soft . . . he ran his hand slowly up her back, felt the bristle of her close-cropped hair. She shifted her hips to shift back, wiggling her butt against his thighs. It was almost more than he could stand. There had to be privacy here somewhere. Or did they insist on doing their screwing out in the open, as some sort of statement?

Breyten, despite his bravado, was starting to look a little nervous. Good.

"Come on," Hektor whispered to Belisanne, and raised one of her legs so that the sole of her bare foot rested on Breyten's thigh. "It's all right. He's my brother."

He felt her muscles tighten. He kissed her, gently, just under her ear. Her blood pulsed there, in time with his own. She was excited and afraid, both. That was best. But it was not professional, or even experienced. She was probably just another damn Neo-Confucian. She still had a great butt.

"Come on, Breyten," he whispered. "Miriam left you . . . oh, don't look so angry, you know it's true. But she likes me, I can tell. So . . . well . . . maybe we should get her over here, you know? Together, the three of us, and settle it all. You'll see how foolish it is to be upset."

He could hear Breyten's breath, but it had nothing to do with sexual excitement. Belisanne twisted away, got to her feet. Excitement or no, she knew that she had no desire to be between two angry men.

"Let's practice on this one," Hektor said, slapping her rump as she tried to move away. "Good stuff, right? Then we can give Miriam a call. . . ."

"Goddamn you!" The punch knocked Hektor off his seat, down in the soaking water. Hektor rolled, feeling the obscene cold and wetness, and looked up at Breyten. The entire side of his head hurt, and his searing cheekbone might well be broken, but the one thought in his head was gratitude. For now, at least, he wouldn't have to kill Breyten. There was nothing to kill him for. Now all he had to do was persuade Breyten and his cronies that there was nothing, nothing at all, to kill Hektor for. He was just a drunken sex maniac, after all. . . .

"Jeez, buddy," Hektor muttered, managing to get up to his hands and knees. He pulled his legs under him, bracing his feet against the rock at the waterfall's base. "No need to get rough. . . ."

Breyten looked at him, trapped between rage and bewilderment. "Hektor—"

Hektor, pushing with everything he had, launched himself up from his crouch and hit Breyten in the solar plexus with the crown of his head.

At least that had been his intention. At the last instant, Breyten twisted and took the impact on his side—and his hipbone. Hektor's head snapped to one side, and stars flickered in his vision. But Hektor's momentum took them both forward into the waterfall.

It was like being smashed flat by the palm of a gigantic hand. Hektor lost his grip on Breyten and was slammed against the rock of the basin. He could no longer tell if the roaring was water or inside his own head. He fought the insistent grabbing weight of the water and made it to his feet.

Breyten was already there. Hektor's vision cleared just in time to see Breyten's fist heading for his jaw. Hektor ducked, bobbed, and took most of the blow on the part of his face that was already screaming with pain. He did have the satisfaction of landing one clean punch on his brother before Breyten pushed him back with a flurry of quick blows. Below him, Hektor caught a glimpse of his blood swirling in the water at his feet. His wet clothes seemed to pull him down by a thousand grasping hands. The gleaming waterfall fell around him.

Breyten stopped, looked past Hektor. Hektor stumbled toward him, but was grabbed from behind.

"Hey!" he said. "Wait. I—"

Someone smacked him efficiently in the side of the head and he went limp. Hands grabbed his arms and legs. Bleeding from lips and forehead, he was hauled out of the waterfall. The clubhouse of the Friends of St. Rabelais hung around him in a haze. Krlezha, Belisanne, Plon—everyone was suddenly cool and efficient.

They carried him a good distance and finally threw him to the ground in a urine-smelling alcove in a dark corridor. He managed to push himself up on his elbows before he threw up. Then he collapsed, barely conscious, into a pool of his own vomit. He tried to convince himself later that he had done that last as a piece of veristic detail, but in truth, drunk and beaten, he could not have moved away from that wretched stench if it had meant his life.

"We had a bunch of Health Department guys here the other day," Sildjin said. "They even had big equipment, wanted to take the thing apart." He chuckled raspily. "Showed them a little about health regulations. They're inspecting infirmaries now. Lucky they're not checking out body disposal themselves."

Again that chuckle. Egypt thought Sildjin was working too hard at the bleakly amused persona. Sildjin didn't really have much of a sense of humor. She leaned back against the footings of Fabian's coffin and stared out at the dust as it swirled up into the distant dome.

"Think that'll make a good scene?" Sildjin's voice, usually abrupt and demanding, took on a wheedling tone when talking to Egypt. She had his artistic immortality in her hands, to a much greater extent than Fabian had ever had. "A good *climax*? You should have seen those guys running around with their vibrating chisels and rubble cart, yelling about infection."

"How could it? I didn't see it." Egypt huddled in her gray-and-black cloak and ran her hands up inside her sleeves, along her upper arms, trying to convince herself she felt real flesh. Since Fabian died, she had never quite been warm. Occasional attacks of prickly heat, but no warmth. Her night with Hektor had been the closest she'd come.

"No time to notify. Sorry."

That had been the story of the past few months. Egypt had come out to Seven Knots to join the Dust Beggars. She wanted to see what Fabian had seen. But instead, she felt like she was wrapped in tight cloth—just as Fabian finally had been. She needed to witness, but saw nothing. It was as if Sildjin was deliberately keeping her from seeing anything.

Fabian's coffin loomed above their heads. Its basis was a rectangular block of extruded composite, but that was almost invisible under a riot of applied ornament. No master had guided the decoration, so that it looked as if it had been done by deranged, too-powerful children: mysteriously glowing dark blue spheres, heavy sheets of gold brocade blown up as if by some violent updraft and frozen there by quick-set, even the bust of some anonymous worthy, held by a tangle of wire.

It was against the law to dispose of bodies inside Scamander itself. All corpses were moved outside, to give their water up to the endless dry Martian atmosphere, the only kind of terraforming now practiced. Over the millennia, if enough people died on Mars, the atmosphere would become saturated with water, and rain, after millions of years, would finally fall. Meanwhile, health officials looked with disfavor on decaying bodies in Scamander's closed spaces. However, thus far they had not mounted a well-enough-armed assault on Fabian's coffin to dispose of him properly. Next time, no doubt, they would be back with Vigil reinforcements, but by then the crews might well have found something else to occupy their time and mental energy.

"But when are you going to finish *The Tongueless Singer*?" Sildjin's voice had that calm tone he used before breaking someone's fingers.

"When I see something worth finishing it with."

"All right. We'll give you a fight. I've got a score to settle with those guys in Moebius—"

"I've *got* corridor fights, Sildjin. Got them until I'm sick of them. Sillier when you stage them so I'll write about them."

"So who would you have us fight, dear lady?" Sildjin's voice was silky. "Is there anyone *you* want to settle a score with?" Any of his people—Marko, Amalie, the rest—would have been edging away, preparing to run. Egypt sat calmly under Fabian's tomb. If she had to die, what better place?

She'd thought long and hard about it, and reached a decision that really made no sense.

"Have you received the call?" she said.

"The—" He looked irritated. "From Hounslow's people? To join their great movement? Nothing to that, Ms. Watrous. No scenes for you."

"There might be, if you act. It'll take everyone by surprise. They'll be glad to follow."

Only at this moment did Egypt realize that she'd been aiming for this moment for weeks. She had been playing on Sildjin's vanity, his foolish ambition, his desire to be seen as a big man. Lately, in the disturbed state that ruled everywhere, even in the deeper corridors, his status, like everything else, had been thrown into question. His proposed incursion into Moebius was just another way of trying to retain control of the Dust Beggars.

Sildjin hunched in on himself, an uncharacteristic posture, and thought. After a long silence, he looked at Egypt. "We'll just have to see, won't we?" He brought his fingers to his mouth and whistled piercingly.

Marko had been waiting for this. Sildjin wanted Egypt to do something, Marko had no idea what, but he needed Marko's help in getting her to do it. It was good to be trusted with a responsible task. Marko was pleased. And more pleased that he had an extra fillip to add to the act.

"Hey, hey!" Marko scampered into view, kicking the dust like a child. "A rump, a bump, a big fat lump! Covered with crud, all that should be in it is on it, piss, shit, and blood, lymph, tears, and vomit!"

Sildjin regarded him with raised eyebrows. Marko signaled the troop following him to approach. They carried a recumbent body. It took Egypt a moment to recognize the blood-and-vomit–covered shape as Hektor Passman.

"We saved him!" Marko said. "They were ready to kick him. They were going to beat him. They wanted to kill him. And him just lying there. Easy to kick. Easy to beat. Easy to kill! Lazy people love that kind. Safe, relaxing, just a way to unwind."

The Dust Beggars dropped Hektor on the steps of Fabian's tomb. He started to groan, then drew in a breath and opened his eyes. The first thing he fixed them on was Sildjin. They stayed on him as Hektor desperately tried to gain a fix on an ever-more-rapidly vanishing reality.

Sildjin shook his head in acknowledgment of Marko's theatrical extra, though he knew it was mostly a matter of luck.

"Egypt has a proposal," Sildjin said. "She wants us to move." He repeated what Egypt had requested.

"Sounds good to me, Sildjin," Marko said. "Gotta go, gotta steer our way out of here. And finish the play! Good, eh?"

If Egypt had been less pleased with the unfolding of her plan, she would have been suspicious of Marko's easy taking of a concrete position without scoping out Sildjin's feelings first. Marko never did that. In this case he didn't have to, because he knew Sildjin's position beforehand. Sildjin wanted to break out of Scamander, head out into the wilderness. That scared Marko, but he would do it if he had to.

Later, Hektor and Egypt sat beneath Fabian's tomb, watching two Dust Beggars attach huge crystal spikes to the foot end. A vagrant static charge attracted the swirling River dust, causing it to crawl up the tomb's footings, covering both the spikes and the hopeful artists. They swept hands across themselves and threw dust back down, but eventually gave up with the spikes only half attached.

"Why are you doing this?" Hektor asked. His clothes were stiff with dried blood and vomit, so he lay back on the steps, moving as little as possible. He was still trying to get his mind around the fact that the Dust Beggars were going to leave Scamander and offer Rudolf Hounslow their unneeded help. The decision had seemed bizarrely easy for them, since most of them had never left the confines of Scamander.

"For Fabian!" she blazed. "No other reason." She thought a moment. "No, Hektor, that's not true. I also want to see it, to be there for what happens. And something big will happen. It has to. Don't you want to be there?"

"I do."

"Then you know where to go."

For the first time in his life, Hektor felt shy about going to see a woman. "Do you think Miriam will talk to me?"

"I can't think of anyone else she *will* talk to."

Hektor looked at Egypt. Without much change in feature, her face had lost its charming softness. It looked hard, determined.

"And then?"

"You, Hektor Passman, at a loss? I think you know. It's theater. All of it. The assassination, Hounslow, the Pure Land School. A piece of historical theater. The question is, who is going to write the text?''

He stared at her. "You think you can stage-manage a civil war?''

"Who better? *Catharsis*. It's a Greek word.''

"I've read it.''

"Good. Then you know what I'm talking about.''

"I'm not sure I do," Hektor said slowly.

"Then let me explain it to you.''

10

From *The Psychological Surface of Mars*, by Karen Hangbao:

Abraham raised altars at Shechem and Bethel, and his bones, and the bones of his descendants, lay at Hebron. These things are claims on the land. I look out now, on the lifeless Martian landscape, and try to see it. The land is a book, and the Martian Jewish education involves reading it by traveling over it. They come south from Mesopotamia to Egypt. Scamander is in Egypt. It is the corrupt city of the Pharaohs. Then they come back up here to Mareotis to take their Promised Land. They travel through Joshua, Judges, David, Solomon, the divided Kingdom, the destruction of Israel, the conquest of Judah; the path crossing over and over itself, sometimes coming a dozen times to one location, each time making it a different place, since something different had happened there to change it.

Early teachers built these ruins. They are always ruins, to indicate the past, never the present, to avoid the inevitable playacting, the hateful adoption of the roles of Elijah and Ahab and Jezebel, who, whatever their sins and virtues, had never played but always *been*. There is no ruin at Jerusalem. There is only one Jerusalem, and the spot with that name on Mars is not it.

It is not a hoax. Still, some have fallen for it, even if it does not exist. The Hill of Megiddo is, after all, Armageddon, the place where the final battle between Good and Evil will take place. To some dissident Christian groups, northern Mars is thus the axis of moral conflict in the universe. Their camps toward Mount Carmel cause occasional conflicts. Arguments about the difference between symbol and reality do not seem persuasive to them. To them the mapping is Truth, and Earth is a lie.

I look at the bearded figure in the niche. He is Melkaart, the Baal Jezebel worshipped. She brought the cult from her native Tyre, causing no end of trouble. It's a bizarre completeness, to include a graven image of a pagan god in the sacred walkabout of the Land of Israel. I am told that this god has lost his power, as have Dagon and Astarte and Moloch, and that their shattered remains no longer affright the children of Israel.

I don't know. Melkaart's blade is sharp. The grinning face cut through the executioner's ax mocks me. Symbols are wrapped inside symbols here on Mars. Where you stand depends entirely too much on what myth compels your actions. Lacking myth, I stand on bare rock and watch the sunset light on the endless shallow slopes of a dead volcano. There is no life, no air. I am defenseless.

Not for the first time, Lon Passman wondered if the malfunctioning of Hounslow's valve had been an accident. Not that he thought Hounslow had deliberately planned it all and thus made sure that he wouldn't have to commit suicide. But both of them had known they had much better things to do than die. . . .

A plume of dust rose up out of a graben, marking the passage of a crawler. Going much too fast, Lon thought, calculating its motion past various landmarks. You never knew what was around the next turn. Some accidents make themselves.

Lon walked slowly along the trail, pretending that he was the only man on Mars. The rock shone rosy in the sun. Lon stopped, smiling at himself. Stupid. The only man on Mars would have no trail to follow. The packed-down dust was the product of the passage of countless feet before his.

He looked back across the rocks. The dust plume was dissipating. The vehicle had stopped, no doubt to investigate something down in the graben. A sudden last, roiled column of dust rose up. That hadn't been caused by a crawler. That was a rockfall.

Lon remembered Sara's training. Though he wanted to run, he moved deliberately toward the last location of the plume. It was too easy to get excited and kill yourself while trying to save someone else. That would be foolish. His route was twisted and complicated, moving around holes and grabens, finding the best way down to the wall to the vehicle. He knew this area, had run it for years. It was a joy to feel the arrangement float in his head, to *know* that he was plotting the optimum path. Rescue workers tended to stay rescue workers for too long, just for this reason. Regardless of the purpose, it was always a joy to use your skills to their utmost.

It took a few minutes for his eyes to adjust to the shadows at the bottom of the graben once he had dropped to its floor.

He skimmed along through the sand. It was safe to move here, so he ran, throwing up his own tiny plume of dust. The walls rose vastly overhead.

Just at a sharp jog around a rockfall, the crawler had hit a spot where fine sand covered a smooth sheet of rock. Skid marks braided across the rock, ending where the crawler had smashed into the base of a vertically fissured bastion. The impact had snapped several of the fine columns into which the bastion was split, and they had broken and toppled down on top of the crawler. The crawler was vividly identification-striped: a tourist rental. Only someone from Earth could have managed to crash something as inherently safe as a crawler. The balloon tires could get a grip on a plate smeared with joint lubricant.

Lon bounded over a fallen column and ran up to the crawler. As he did so, he plugged his skintite radio into a long-distance satellite relay and reported the accident into the rescue net.

A voice came on. "Rented this morning, one person, male,

age forty-eight. Treated heart condition, no painkiller allergies, physical condition—'' The dispatcher paused, hummed under her breath. "Entry says 'unfortunate.' That's an irregulationary entry.''

"I hope it's not correct," Lon grunted as he flipped up the cover and thumbed the emergency hatch-release. It buzzed, but nothing happened. Falling rock had creased the hatch, jamming it shut. As he stared at it, another rock fell from overhead and bounced off the crawler's roof, leaving a dent. Those shattered columns had stood for millions of years, but now, suddenly, they had to make a lot of decisions.

"Correct? It's criminally vague. What the hell is it supposed to mean? The specs are written for a good reason. . . .''

Lon ducked under the front wheel. It was half deflated, and the escaping gas boiled through the sand, filling the undercarriage with dust. He was blinded.

"Well, I'll make a note," the dispatcher said. "It will be at least two hours before anyone can reach you, Mr. Passman. Do you need supervision?''

"I'm okay," he said, feeling up above the wheel. There was the rounded bump of the suspension control, so it should be just a little farther back. . . . "I'll call if I need assistance.''

"Excellent." Just as she clicked off, Lon heard one more exasperated " 'unfortunate'!''

Sara had always drilled him in rescue operations. She was expected to understand the laws of evidence and the principles of law, so she reasoned that Lon should understand the fundamental nature of her work as well. It was due to her that he could . . . there it was, by God. He grabbed the sharp end of the emergency lever and pulled it out of its secure clips.

He rolled back out past the wheel into the light. His faceplate's antistatic surface was clear of dust, though a lot clung in the folds of his outdoor coat. He wasn't dressed for a rescue operation. That took a certain slick style, and the right kind of boots. He climbed up onto the crawler and jammed the lever's sharp tip at the breakthrough point at the edge of the door.

Sara was never far from his thoughts. He'd met her shortly

after his aborted double suicide with Rudolf Hounslow, and it was only at that point that he had realized, in the depths of his heart, how misguided that action would have been. Her memory was always with him, but never more than at this moment. It was as if she guided the vibrating tension of the lever, and caught its sudden crack-drop as the hatch popped open. Lon felt that he would surely have fallen off if someone hadn't gently steadied him by grabbing his shoulder. . . . They had always been a team, and she was right there as he dropped through the hatch and unhooked the safety harness holding the bloody, plump-faced man in his control couch. A sharp spear of rock had punched through the thin roof of the crawler. Rubble had come down after it and split the cabin in half, as well as shattering the man's right arm.

The man, for a wonder, had been wearing his rental-issue skintite. His head whipped from side to side as Lon hauled him free of the ruined crawler. Just in time too. A few more rocks fell from the unstable columns that loomed overhead, a frozen avalanche suddenly thawed. One of them rolled right past Lon's foot, leaving an irregular track in the dust.

Lon could see the man moaning in pain as his arm dragged limply behind him. No allergies. . . . When Lon was far enough away from the crawler to be safe, he jabbed an emergency pain-killer hypo through the man's suit. Lon carried an emergency rescue kit at all times he was on the surface, a memorial to Sara's training. He even had a couple of quick-set splints in there. It wasn't strictly necessary, but he could set this guy's arm, give the eventual rescue crew that much less to do. He should prepare an emergency shelter and get the man into it. That would ensure against any unexpected suit failure.

The man was trying to say something. Lon tongued his radio control. A quick scan, and it found the narrowcast frequency of the victim's suit radio. The next agonized moan was loud in Lon's ears. He bent over to listen, as if they were using the air to carry their words.

"Did you . . ." The man's voice was a harsh rasp. "D'you get . . . her?"

"Who?" Lon demanded with a sinking feeling. The man had

been registered alone, and he hadn't been able to see the other half of the cabin.

"... daughter ... I brought ... last minute. ..."

"You idiot!" Lon shouted. "You should have changed the registration. Damn it!" The word "unfortunate" was right.

Unless this guy was hallucinating, there was someone still in the crawler. Lon slapped his emergency kit shut and ran back to it. As he did so, more rocks fell from overhead, and he dodged, pointlessly, as they hit to either side of him, as if he was playing some sort of dodge-ball game from his childhood.

He dove through the hatch, crawled across the driver's-side couch. There, sticking out from the rubble—a leg. Was she still alive? Lon desperately hauled rocks off and threw them over his shoulder, out of the hatch. He slowly revealed her body, examining each portion as it became visible. She was badly injured, left arm, left side, her rib cage crushed. But the tourist skintite had done its job, fusing onto the skin with impact and keeping an airtight seal.

Underneath the sand and rubble she had a serene face, as if thinking very deeply about something. For an instant Lon was frozen by it. "You poor thing," he said.

The harness release wouldn't work. The rock spear had crushed the mechanism. Lon fumbled with his emergency kit. Was she alive? Was that a flutter of her eyelids? Damn it, he'd have to worry about that later. He wasn't up to making medical determinations.

The harness webbing was tough and resilient, just the way it was designed to be. Lon sawed desperately at it with his knife. Each strand parted with languid slowness. Could he pull her out now? No. A few more strands. One, two ... the entire crawler shook as a massive boulder smashed into its roof and crushed down on the driver's side. Lon's eyes were focused on the sharp knife-edge as it whipped wildly around in his hand.

The shaking stopped. He hadn't sliced open her suit or jammed the knife into her chest. That would have been bad rescue technique. He kept cutting, not looking behind him to see if he could still get out. That would come later. Right now he had a job to do.

There. She was loose now. He pulled her free of the remaining webbing.

The roof was pushed in, but there was still room to pass. But not room to maneuver or turn around. With painful slowness, crawling backward, Lon pulled the woman out of her couch and through. His knees told him his progress. The shattered couch arm . . . the smoothness of the couch seat . . . the other couch arm. His waving feet contacted the edge of the hatch.

The young woman was floppy, and her limbs got stuck on every possible obstacle. Lon was beyond caring or kindness, and just yanked savagely at each obstruction. She was as limp as a rag doll . . . or a corpse. That didn't seem to matter anymore.

Finally his hips were over the hatch. One last, powerful pull and he had her weight up on his shoulder. She wasn't heavy. He climbed down from the hatch and pulled her completely free of the crawler. God, that had taken forever. His whole life. He slung her more conveniently and walked toward where her father had half sat up, supporting his weight on his one good arm. He was looking up past Lon, at something behind him. Lon found himself smiling. Sara would have been proud.

It was the vibration in his feet that warned him. Instead of running, he turned and looked up. He was just in time to see the shattered face of the bastion, no longer balanced on the broken column bases, come right into his face.

"You know," Miriam said in an entirely conversational tone, "some of the guys were talking about throwing you out of the air lock and letting you last exhale. Here, move—get in the way, and they'll stop just talking about it." She gestured to Hektor and they moved out of the path of two running Vigils laying a secure comm line.

"Did you explain that I'm on their side?" Hektor raised his voice to be heard above the din in the rapidly swelling shelter.

"They don't know what your side is. You don't know what

their side is either, though you may think you do.'' She held up a hand and turned away, to speak into a sonic focus. "Cool down those IR signatures a bit, Torson. You look like you're barbecuing out there. We're supposed to look like we're *trying* to conceal them, at least.''

Hektor peered at the infrared map image that floated above their heads, but couldn't make out any comprehensible details. Colored dots flickered on a map of Mareotis, indicating the locations of Vigil surface forces as they moved in a large-scale exercise.

"Astounding,'' he said.

"You haven't had this beat long, have you? Routine. Just drill.''

He shook his head, still staring at the map. "No.'' He finally dropped his eyes to her. "Don't screw around, Miriam. Trep sent me here for a reason, not just to get a good story for *The Tithonium Courier*.''

There was a trace of mockery in her smile. "The *Courier*? Is that the best you could do? You who were Kennedy?''

"God, what a secret that turned out to be.'' Hektor shook his head. "Yes, it was the best I could do. My byline didn't turn out to be much of a circulation booster.''

"I'm sorry,'' she said, suddenly contrite.

"Don't be. After all, weren't you exiled to some regional Vigil post to end your career arresting people who run floating crap games? A pathetic dead end. Right.''

He looked around himself. The command post had transparent walls, and was set up on a ledge just below the rim of one of the Mareotis fossae. The opposite wall of the huge crack loomed a few hundred meters away. Troops rappelled down it like sliding beads. Beyond it, the flat thumb that was the eroded shield of Alba Patera pushed its way insolently into the dark sky's dusty pink skirts.

"Don't play around. You're here to talk, aren't you? So talk.''

"All right. You and Trep are preparing for civil war. General, planetwide civil war. Training, setting up positions, preparing to blow transport lines. Just as if it was routine.''

"And meanwhile, in Scamander?''

"Lon and I are trying to *prevent* civil war."

She didn't flare up at him, as he half expected. "I'm impressed that you find it so easy to draw the line between those two activities."

Despite himself, Hektor smiled. "All right. Trep did send me up here for a reason. But I have my own reasons too."

Miriam shot him a sharp look, then examined a real-time processed satellite image of the Mareotis Fossae to see what of the Vigil emplacement was detectable from orbit. At subliminal gestures from her, the image swelled and shrank dizzyingly.

"Aranjuez," she snapped. "The edge detectors are giving us a length of unerased tread. Map coordinates—" She reeled off a string of numbers. "The sun falls a few more degrees, gives us some shadow, that'll be clear enough to eyeball from five klicks. Blow it off, and make sure it doesn't happen again."

She turned back to Hektor. "Are you going to stay a politician, then?"

"What do you mean?"

"What do I mean? 'I have my own reasons too.' Nice and clear, just the way regular people talk to each other. All right, I have reasons." He found himself staring into her agate eyes. "I loved your brother. You remember him, we spend a lot of time not talking about him. We'll have to talk about him—but just to get him out of the way. Then we can get to the fact that you've wanted me ever since you saw me in the Xui House Armory."

Hektor opened his mouth to speak, but the air was no longer in his lungs, and there was a sharp pain in his eardrums. He fell back from her and pulled his hood down over his head, feeling it slurp onto the skintite he wore under his clothes.

It took all his self-control to let the air slide slowly through his lips, avoiding rupture as the lungs reexpanded. Miriam, more quickly adjusted, yanked at his arm.

The shelter collapsed, falling in great folds of transparent fabric. Struts cracked and sprang open. Hektor stared off across the rocky flat, looking for attacking troops. Hounslow had tricked him, moved more quickly than was possible. It was Breyten, of course. Breyten had given that damn talky Pure Land movement something it had never had before, the ability to dispassionately draw blood. . . .

Disciplined troops sliced through the now-encumbering material with hot knives and tossed it into stacks. Everything was quickly back in order, there were no casualties, and Hektor realized that this was part of the military exercise, a reminder to the troops of the consequences of trying to fight a war on the surface of Mars.

"Nice, Miriam," Hektor said once he had enough air in his lungs. "Take my breath away."

"Coincidence," she said. "You don't think I'd plan my military exercise to make a point about my sex life, do you?"

"I don't know. . . ."

"You should. I'll leave that kind of theater up to Egypt." Egypt, who had, in some weird moment of intense perception, given Hektor the plan under which he was now operating.

"But if we're going to talk about Breyten . . . I have my father's permission to use him." Lon had been oddly energized when Hektor left, as if keeping the world from collapsing was tremendous entertainment.

"Use him how?"

"To start this civil war you and Trep are so anxious for."

He followed her as she stepped through the organized chaos. This entire operation, he thought, was in direct violation of the Vigil's charter. A much bigger violation, in other words, than his simple closing of the Gates, though it was being made in pursuit of the same goal. Was every law to be violated in pursuit of Law?

The edge of the cliff was shattered into platforms at different levels. A trail descended through the rubble between them: an old trail, sifted with dust, but solid and packed down so that it would reappear between storms. It was odd how the piled rocks hereabouts seemed regularly arranged, as if they were ruins. Stone along a fracture sometimes cracked in a pattern, giving that illusion. Hektor and Breyten had often been distracted by it, seeing traces of a purposive past where there was none.

It *was* a ruin. Hektor paused and looked at the wood lintel above a doorway. This building, square and impractical, had never been sealed, so no one had ever lived here.

"The palace of Ahab and Jezebel at Jezreel," Miriam said in response to his questioning look. "We're doing our best not to interfere with that past."

"Good," he said. "Having these also be the memorials of a real war would be much too confusing."

Her shelter was just beyond, squeezed against a rock face. They entered the lock. Half the shelter was set up as a conference area, with a small table, displays, maps, and a huge tea maker. The other half, screened by no more than a stretched fabric partition, was her personal quarters. Though her shelter was the largest, the space she could truly call her own was as small as that of the most junior recruit. She pulled him into it, her hand insistent on his arm.

"So you think you can trigger it," she said. "Using your brother."

"If I have to. My father agrees. You and I will have to do it. Together."

"Great," she said. "That's a hell of a bond to build on."

"Not our fault. It's the times."

"The times are our fault."

"All right," Hektor said. "Let's take responsibility for them."

"People are ready to negotiate with Hounslow, Commander Trep says. Ready to make a deal."

"Trep hates deals."

"That he does."

"My father likes them. If anyone can negotiate a way out of this, he can. But he wants a backup." And Egypt's theatrical proposal had met with his approval. Was he really so willing to kill Breyten to prove to Hektor his change of heart? Hektor was no closer to understanding his father than he ever had been.

Though they were alone in the shelter, she pulled the screen, hiding the calmly rational table, where one would, compelled by the surroundings, necessarily have a rational discussion.

They sat together on the narrow cot. The shelter had been set up only that morning, but Miriam had taken a few moments to turn this screened sleeping area into an intensely private space. A vivid print of a red-haired woman holding a pomegranate, an image Hektor recognized as being hundreds of years old; a bunch of silver trinkets, things like elephants and leaping dancers, dangling on colored ribbons; a fine red-chalk sketch of herself as a younger woman, lying on a couch, a mysterious smile on her face, her arm thrown up over her head onto hair that was, at that time, long—Hektor realized that all he knew was a crisp woman in a gray Vigil tunic, and that he knew nothing at all.

"Were all of these gifts?" he asked, running his fingers along the silk of the ribbons.

She looked around. She had never thought about it before. "Yes," she said after careful consideration. "They are. Why?"

He shrugged. "Oh, I don't know. It lets me know that I'm not just seeing *you*—I'm seeing everyone who means something to you."

"And you're wondering if any of them are from Breyten."

"No, actually, I'm not. None of them are. His taste is more . . . severe. But that one"—he pointed at the chalk sketch—"must be from an old lover."

"Yes. It was expected that I would marry him."

"But not by you."

"No." She tucked one of her legs under her bottom and stretched the other out until it touched the curtain. "If I had known you were so perceptive, I might not have invited you in here."

"If I wasn't, you'd have had to find some other way to tell me."

She was completely covered by her uniform, her legs were invisible, yet something in the languidness of the movement caught him, like hearing an old song through a wall. The words were inaudible, but the tune brought them back to mind.

She tossed her head. "Tell you what?"

He put one hand on the back of her head and leaned her back.

Her head was hot, and he could feel the dampness in her hair. She'd been working hard.

"Ow," she said. "You should be more careful. I've still got my leg under me."

"Sorry."

She untangled herself.

"Now, where were we?"

Her lips were salty, and for a moment were still and cool beneath his, making him fear that he had just made a gigantic and irremediable mistake. Then, suddenly, she responded, pulling him down to her.

They were both still wearing skintites under their outdoor clothes. It was going to be a ticklish operation.

A bell rang. Miriam sat up. "Yes?"

"Is Hektor Passman there?"

She glanced at him. "Yes, Setsurei, he is."

"Sorry to disturb. I'm afraid I have an important message for him."

"What the hell was he doing out there?" Hektor stepped into the black-shrouded front hall.

It took Trep, huddled in his mourning cloak, a moment to reply. "He was trying to save Mars. Instead, he ended up saving one stupid good-for-nothing Terran."

Hektor glanced up the stairs, half expecting to see his father at the top, ready to speak and explain. Had his father ever really trusted him? Or had Lon, to the last, suspected that Hektor would inevitably break? Hektor tried to shake off the delusion that one last conversation would have settled the issue, for good and all.

"Breyten is already here. You should go up. Here." Trep handed Hektor a package.

"I—" Trep looked at him, but Hektor knew he had no interest in anything Hektor might say to him at this moment. "Thank you, Colonel."

Hektor climbed the stairs to where his father's body lay. He passed through the green-silk-walled front room with its piles of awards and mementos, but paused at the black-garlanded door to the bedroom beyond. In all the years of his life, he had never been permitted to step through that portal. Breyten had sneaked in a couple of times and brought back excited and contradictory reports, but Hektor had never dared, always freezing right at the edge. His father's private chamber was a secret forever closed to him. He reached out and, holding his breath, pushed. The door swung open.

Lon Passman had been killed by a mass of falling rock. Much of his body was wrapped in shining black silk trimmed with red ribbon, to symbolize the shattered and torn flesh beneath. Most of his head had been destroyed by the impact, and was now a silk ovoid. His right arm and leg were missing, and lay in a case at the foot of the bed.

Hektor walked up to the bed and kissed what was left of his father's cold forehead. It was rough under his lips, contorted in a puzzled frown, as if Lon himself was wondering how it was he had come to die. Hektor turned his head and found himself looking up at what Lon must have seen every night when he went to bed and every morning when he awoke.

''She looks so young,'' Breyten said from where he sat at the desk.

''She *was* young. When she died, she was my age. Younger than you.''

The painting of their mother was sharp and hard-edged, her form clearly defined against the red rocks behind her. The paint was translucent, making the painting seem to recede into the wall. Her face was strong, almost blunt. She wasn't pretty.

''She was a brave woman.'' Breyten sat slumped with sadness, an emotion which sat poorly with his extravagant clothing and eye makeup. He had not changed his style for the death visit, and the deliberation of this lack of duty set Hektor's teeth on edge.

''I—'' Hektor looked at the painting. It swam in his vision; the edges got hazy. Sara had died so long ago that he had long thought of the two of them, Lon and Sara, as entirely separate. Now it was as if he had just lost the two of them together. ''I remember her. Her and Zoë. And now Father. I remember them all.'' Only Breyten was left.

"You should have come back," Hektor said. "At least once. Lon would have liked that."

"No!" Breyten stood and, dissipated look forgotten, paced tensely around the small room. "He knew what—"

"He knew what had become of you. He sent me to check, to see you. You never came back here, did you? He asked you, but you wouldn't. He never saw his son again." As he spoke, and saw the look on his brother's face, Hektor felt a hot point in the center of his chest. Did anything justify this? "It's just as well you never succeeded in joining the Olympus Clubs, I guess."

Breyten looked down at his father's body and said nothing.

"So, after our mourning is done, go back to your little club-house and relax. In a few days, Hounslow and his organization will have ceased to exist." He spoke casually, as if it was something everyone knew.

"What do you mean?" Breyten's tone had regained the hostility it had held in the Friends of St. Rabelais, and it was clear that the two brothers were enemies again.

Hektor and Miriam had, as the cementing of their bond, planned this betrayal. With Lon Passman's death, all Rudolf Hounslow would have to do to achieve victory was what his natural impulses would lead him to: absolutely nothing. If he just sat out in Nilosyrtis, the entire planet could drop right into his hands. Lon Passman had been the last organized opposition. Rodomar's Liaison Group was almost deserted, as prominent politicians and businessmen took the trek out to Pure Land Mesa to pay their respects to Hounslow.

To be defeated, Hounslow would have to be forced out into action.

Hektor shrugged and placed his shot. "Oh, I'm not privy to any military plans. Trep keeps those behind his forehead. But I have my sources. A special secret session of the Chamber has released the Vigil to do its tasks under emergency procedures."

If Breyten checked, he would find out, with some effort, that there had indeed been a secret session of the Chamber. A new, reorganized relationship with the Union of States and Nationalities had been discussed, as had the removal of the office of Governor-Resident. A military solution to the problem of Hounslow had not been mentioned.

"So, finally, there's going to be action." Hektor infused his voice with an enthusiasm he did not feel. This was a desperate, nasty expedient. And its results were unpredictable, which should have invalidated it immediately. But it was the only plan he and Miriam had been able to come up with.

"The Vigil knows where Hounslow's forces are: Nereidum, Focas, the Rim of Hellas." He named places the Vigil had found operational traces, tossing away intelligence data with abandon. Data he wasn't even supposed to be privy to. "I don't know what the Vigil will do. Actually, I don't *care* what they'll do. As long as they take care of the problem. Miriam's on it, so things are probably well in hand. You know her."

Breyten was speechless, and Hektor felt a great sorrow. He and Miriam had agreed. It was clear that Hounslow's organization was divided, with a substantial part of it calling for decisive action, while Hounslow himself, apostle of action, held back. Without their leader's authorization, Olympus Clubs, or rather, the Friends of St. Rabelais, were preparing for that action, just as Brenda Marr had. The Vigil, divided, properly suspicious of Internal Security, might be able to resist a concerted military effort, but the result would be widespread destruction.

All Hektor and Miriam had been able to do was to try to set off the explosion before those setting it were ready. And Breyten Passman was to be their fuse.

Hektor turned away from him so that Breyten could not see his face. "I think Father's sacrifice will not have been in vain," he said. "It achieved what it needed to. Put on your mourning."

Hektor opened the package Trep had handed him. It contained a swoop-sleeved mourning cloak covered with many buttons.

Breyten stood. Tiny sparkling balls flickered on his jacket. After a moment's hesitation, he pulled on his own cloak. When he was done, he looked normal, for the first time in a long time the Breyten Hektor remembered, pale, severe face above dark clothing.

"Let's go," Breyten said.

11

From "A Hollow Festival," by George Andrassi, in the 2 March 2333 *Moebius Daily*:

"Fabian could have covered this better than you," the old man tells me.

"Covered what?" I ask. The corridor is empty. Festival streamers and buns lie smashed underfoot.

"This. Everything!" Tears appear in his eyes. "He was with us in the beginning . . . and now, nothing."

The celebration of their return was frenetic. They went out to the asteroid Bolmok. They attacked it and got repulsed, the same way some of them had been repulsed at Hermione. They suffered heavy casualties. This old man, who refused to give his name, lost an arm. But when they came back, the corridors had a party, a wonderful party that lasted three days. Another Feast of Gabriel. The filibusters were chaired all over Scamander. Afraid of the mobs, the Vigil did not intervene. The corridors need entertainment. No one wants to think about what Hounslow might do. But now it is over.

"Fabian could have made it make sense."

Maybe it's true. Maybe my old friend could have written it so it made sense. I lack his skill, and Fabian is gone. An era, I think, dies with him.

*   *   *

Three days later, Internal Security took all decisions out of everyone's hands, through the final operation of a simple administrative order made months before. A spacecraft, the *Norilsk*, landed at Hecates Tholus on 27 April 2333. It was full of weapons.

InSec handled the arms shipment as a purely internal administrative procedure, on a par with uniforms and commissary coffee. A copy of the order was eventually found in the files of the Governor-Resident's office. Three hundred anticrowd wide-angle pellet rifles, five light armored surface vehicles—and a thousand surface-to-surface, high-penetrance, satellite-guided missiles were listed under the head Miscellaneous Security Gear, a category usually reserved for handcuffs and incapacitating short-range gas. The missiles would hold the balance of power in any planetwide conflict. There were no other such weapons on Mars.

The Hecates Tholus Security Chief had become uncomfortable with his exposed position east of Elysium Planitia and, suspecting that his colleagues felt the same, authorized shipping of combat weaponry from Union Army stores on Luna. The Union Army's complicity in the shipment was later investigated, and while no indictments were handed down, three officers at Tycho subsequently prayed, and received, early retirement.

It was after the touchdown of the *Norilsk* that the Hecates Tholus Security Chief made his real mistake. If he had continued his imposture of Miscellaneous Security Gear and treated the shipment as he might have a transport car full of the required new office portraits of Gensek Paramon, all might have been well, and by the time anyone noticed the nature of the new armaments, it would have been a fait accompli, impossible to do anything about. InSec could have rained destruction down on anyone who opposed them, and the nature of the rule of Mars would have changed completely.

Instead, he activated every Internal Security officer under his jurisdiction and cordoned off every corridor and surface transport lane leading to the landing field. Swearing at the unexpected orders, hauling bulky antiriot armor, they spilled off the mag-track trains at the lower stations for half a day before the ship's landing. As they tramped up the stairs and to their posts, a line of massive armored railcars squatted on the track opposite. As soon as the *Norilsk* landed, the train pulled forward and the weapons were loaded, under the nervous eyes of guards armed with crowd-control gear.

Immediate protests were made by local officials at this high-handed behavior. The Internal Security office made no response. Called into existence by a line of nervous armed guards, a crowd gathered. It stood by with silent grimness more frightening than any angry shouts.

Internal Security's own information security being poor, information about the shipment's nature leaked out even as the containers were being loaded onto the armored magtrack train. Or rather, rumors, which spread with extraordinary rapidity over the planet, mutating as they went. Popular report included everything from planet-busting thermonuclear weapons to instantly fatal gas scheduled to be pumped through city ventilation systems.

Responding quickly, Governor-Resident Rodomar froze the shipment at the Hecates Tholus port. To her dismay, she discovered that she could not order the arrest of the Hecates Tholus Security Chief. At least she could not do so safely. The arrest would have to be handled either by other Internal Security personnel, who refused to respond, or by Vigils, which might lead to a violent confrontation between the two security forces that were supposed to preserve the peace of Mars. Rodomar found that she had to refer back to Earth for authority. No one on Earth found it at all urgent to respond.

Mindful of Gustavus Trep's advice to avoid any violence inside a city, she ordered the train moved out of the loading station. The five railcars filled with heavy weaponry floated slowly up the magtrack to a side spur twenty-five kilometers away from Hecates Tholus, completely outside any inhabited area. The short journey took five hours. Other trains were rerouted or canceled, and chaos traveled up the magtracks. Rodomar had no official authority over the surface transportation network. Protests piled up on her desk. By the time she could deal with them, rerouted trains would be the least of her problems.

Riots broke out in Scamander, Garmashtown, Ascraeus, and other cities up and down the Valles Marineris and the Tharsis volcanoes. An official order from the Chamber of Delegates forbade the Vigil to use violent means save for "self-defense." Negotiations between the Vigil and officials of the Fossic and Chasmic parties, which had been mediated by Lon Passman, froze up. In essence, Mars now had a handful of competing centers of power: the Chamber and the official Martian government, the Vigil, the Governor-Resident's office, Internal Security . . . and Rudolf Hounslow.

The area surrounding the spur over which the armored railcars floated was mercilessly spotlit. Rough country around it made it difficult of access. The spot was guarded by a mix of InSec and Vigil troops, none of them too happy about the job. Mobs could riot in the corridors, but it would take a major military operation to get at those weapons. Rodomar hoped no one was planning one.

"I think you should see him." Carter twiddled his sword thoughtfully, then, recognizing the gesture as one that no Martian would make, settled the sword formally on his knees.

"For God's sake, why now, Carter?" Rodomar lay buried deep in her bed, head under a pillow, and her voice was muffled.

It was the dead middle of the night and she had just managed to get to sleep, after a useless and infuriating meeting with Marina Koep, the Head of Internal Security for Mars. As far as Koep was concerned, if the Governor-Resident gave InSec a free hand, all Mars's political problems would be over in a week.

Askase lay on top of the covers, dark on white, like a patinaed statue excavated from a snowdrift. "Indeed, Carter, this is most inopportune."

"Indeed my butt." Carter stood. "All right. I'll tell Passman to go ahead with whatever his wild plan is. An exclusively Martian solution might be best. Afterward, you'll just have to claim it was you who said so.''

Instantly awake, Rodomar sat up, her eyes fearsomely bleak. ''Carter, don't you even think—''

Inwardly Carter quailed, but he stood his ground. ''He'll be in the receiving room.''

''He's lost it,'' Askase said. ''Too much dust in his tea. . . .''

Carter became a fierce advocate for whatever culture Rodomar was attempting to rule, but this was worse than ever.

''He'll lose something else if he's not careful.''

With a fluid motion, Askase was standing, still naked. Rodomar admired him, the squared curves of his small, muscular ass.

''I will tell him to think again—''

''No.'' Rodomar rose to her feet. Mato Grosso, Palawan . . . Mars. Her career was probably over. Perhaps Hektor Passman would offer her a way to go out with a bang. ''Young Passman's calling in his markers. And he's the only Passman I have left. Help me dress.''

''Very well.'' Askase had the ability to hiss words that didn't have any sibilants in them. He suspected, Rodomar knew, that she was interviewing young Passman for a possible spot in her stable. Untrue, though the thought had crossed her mind. But he was too big, too ungainly, and such men did not comfort her. Let Askase worry. It was pleasant to think that someone was focused on something more human-scale than planetwide revolt.

''I'm sorry about your father,'' she said as she entered the meeting room. ''A great loss.''

Hektor's head tilted toward her heavily. The man was a wreck. Above the mourning he'd had to resume so soon after putting it off, his eyelids were puffy, his face creased with new lines, the corners of his mouth drooping. He looked ten years older.

''For all of us,'' Hektor said. ''He could have negotiated a solution.''

While Lon Passman had certainly been Mars's best chance to avoid conflict, Rodomar wasn't sure that even he could have held off the inevitable. No sense in arguing that point with his son.

"Could you give me your understanding of the situation?" Hektor said.

Rodomar felt a flare of anger. "Mr. Passman, it is not *my* job to brief *you*."

"Of course," Hektor murmured. "Of course." His hands were a problem for him. He had no idea what to do with them, and they seemed to wander around of their own volition.

People had lost fathers before. She would have to ration her sympathy. "Why are you here?"

"The Chamber of Delegates would like to cut a deal with Hounslow, correct?" His voice gained strength. "Techadom-rongsin, Kratak—they're trying to negotiate, perhaps bring him into a unified government."

Rodomar hissed her breath out in involuntary contempt. What was the use of defending a planet whose government had no interest in defending itself? "Yes, they are. A settlement. 'To prevent violence' is the formula, I think."

"Hounslow is enough of a politician to lead them on, promise release of imprisoned Delegates, a system free of interference from Earth—"

"Free of interference from me." Passman was encouraging her sense of bitterness. Was that a deliberate manipulation, or just because he shared it?

"Then he can slit their throats at leisure. He hates corruption too. Probably more than you do. It's tempting, you know. To all of us. A fierce cleansing. Death in the corridors, corrupt politicians foaming blood on the cold sand, a new Mars free of . . . free of . . . well, no one knows what it will be free of, do they? Revolutionaries never do."

"Mr. Passman, you didn't wake me up to discuss general theories of revolutionary fervor, did you?"

"No, I didn't." His gaze had been sharpening while he talked. He visibly gained strength from stoking his own anger. "I came to offer you a way out."

"You? A political journalist. In disgrace."

He shook his head. "You know it's not just me. The Vigil. Trevor al-Fiq and others in the Chamber. Call it a political party with an interest in Martian peace."

She snorted. "So they sent you."

"I was the only one they thought could get you out of bed at this hour of the morning." Finally, Hektor smiled.

Despite herself, Rodomar smiled too. Perhaps Askase's suspicions were not so far off the mark after all. "All right. What's the proposal?"

"You have five railcars full of weapons sitting on a spur near Hecates Tholus."

"That is correct."

"We want to use them to start a war."

The five floodlit silver railcars looked like mysterious sarcophagi excavated and displayed in the shallow trench of the canyon. Aside from the pale white line of the magtrack and a couple of paraboloid-vaulted equipment sheds, there was nothing but tumbled rocks all around. The interior of the canyon was lit on every square inch, but the rocks above it were slashed with impenetrable shadows.

Squatting in one of those shadows, Breyten found his hands shaking as he contemplated the fact that in five minutes he might well be dead. He hadn't expected that. He'd thought the pure excitement would blow his mind clear. His body was soaked with sweat under the shielding that kept him invisible to IR sensors, and if the attack was delayed for any length of time, he would pass out from heat exhaustion. Someone should have considered that.

The guards, both InSec and Vigil, didn't even seem to be equipped with IR sensors, or with any real military equipment, so perhaps all the careful precautions were irrelevant. Despite the fact that the site itself had been selected to prevent rioting mobs from reaching it, they were armed only with crowd-control gear. As a result of the hostility between the two forces, they had clotted like two different blood types mixed together. Each had chosen one of the equipment sheds as its HQ. The InSec guards tended to spend more time in their shed than the Vigil did in theirs, Breyten had noticed.

The timer at the right edge of his visual field marked down the seconds. Not long now. A few of the InSecs were peering anxiously down the rail to where it joined the main Isidis-Elysium line. They were expecting a supply car with material to make their headquarters more comfortable. As far as they knew, they would be sitting here for weeks while the politicians argued things out.

He bit his lip, trying to consider all the possibilities. He had some military training but was not a soldier. Others, though, had served in the small wars on Earth—Belisanne had been an under-officer in Sichuan. She had planned this assault. It must have been Hektor's influence that caused Breyten to find himself thinking of her naked body as it had been at the clubhouse of the Friends of St. Rabelais. . . .

Half an hour ago, a group of Vigil had departed on a crawler after installing an elaborate fence around the five railcars. It wasn't much of a barrier—it looked like the sort of thing city police put up to direct pedestrian traffic around a work site—but it had taken them a strangely long time to put up. Breyten suspected booby traps, crouched armored soldiers, fusion bombs ticking down in time with his own clock. His forehead pressed against the ominous ambiguities of war. Every action was potentially dangerous, every change in the situation a possible disaster.

The InSec guards waved at the railcar that came sliding down the track toward them, a foolish gesture, since the thing was entirely automated. But it was tough, boring duty sitting out here in the middle of nowhere guarding a train, and they were looking forward to the food and supplies the thing had carried out from Hecates Tholus. Breyten turned his head away, then, after a moment's thought, curled up on the ground and covered his head. If things had gone as planned, somewhere after the supply car had left the side of Hecates Tholus and started its descent across the sloping Elysium plain, Marder and his team had caught up to it with a stolen maintenance cart and hung just behind it for the few seconds it must have taken—

The flash of the explosion barely flickered. He was feeling with his fingertips, but there was barely any vibration in the rock. For a moment he wondered if Marder had failed, if the flash had been merely his imagination, or a defect in his optic nerve. Then, as rehearsed, he rolled to his feet and ran down the rocks toward the weapons-containing railcars. He could see his teammates doing the same. Their shadows danced on the rocks behind them. Even as he moved at top speed, leaping from point to point, he caught his breath at the beauty of it.

The explosion had shattered the supply car, and it lay off the track, its superstructure destroyed, its cargo spilled in the dust. The InSec guards who had been moving forward to greet it lay twisted on the ground. A couple were trying to climb to their feet.

Breyten pushed himself off from the last rock, floating in an endless leap. Every crack and bump in the shadowed rocks was clear, the silver railcars seemed to flow like mercury, and his teammates, for whom he suddenly felt a deep and transforming love, came flying down like avenging angels. People on Earth, when they slept, dreamed of Mars. . . .

Alert soldiers would have refused to be distracted and been ready to pick off the troops leaping down the tumbled rocks toward them, outlined like targets in some game. But these were natural garrison types, and no one was used to war, no one had expected it. Many of them were already raising their arms in surrender before anyone reached them.

Breyten slowed and gestured brusquely for three of them to lie facedown on the ground. Even through their air masks he could see their wide, terrified eyes. Breyten felt like twisting around to see what was behind him. He hadn't really expected to survive the run down the rocks, and now that he had, he feared an attack from those same rocks, from some reserve force so cleverly concealed that the Pure Land assault had slid right past it. The muscles in his neck almost spasmed from the effort it took not to turn his head around to look.

He felt like smashing these guys with his gun. Why wouldn't they get down? What were they trying to do? He gestured more frantically for them to move. They had to be searched, disarmed, confined. They still outnumbered the people who had captured them.

The InSec guards, who were terrified that the ominous Martian terrorist would make them lie prone on the ground and then would shoot them each in the back of the head, began to get to their hands and knees. They sneaked glances at the torn bodies of their comrades that lay near the destroyed supply car.

Breyten snapped cable cuffs around their wrists and slit off their equipment belts. He examined their surface uniforms as well as he could, but could find no sign of other weapons. No one had prepared them for combat or surface survival. He jerked each of them back to his feet with a vicious pull on the cuffs, then marched them in file to their shelter headquarters.

Three bodies lay sprawled at the other end of the armored train: two Vigils and—Breyten looked hard—Balladares, who had a bloody, exploded hole in his chest. He had barely spoken to Balladares, a bulky man with impossibly black skin, but now felt his loss keenly, as if they had grown up together.

The Vigils had reacted more quickly than the InSec officers and had managed to fight back, inadequate though their weapons were. They had caught fire from three sides, but not before they had managed to hit Balladares.

Belisanne pumped her fist over her head in a victory salute. Breyten looked down at the motionless bodies. Martians killing Martians. He hoped there wouldn't be much more of it before it was all over.

"It's ridiculous," Miriam Kostal said, staring at the map display of the Isidis-Elysium hemisphere of North Mars. "You can't fight a surface war on Mars."

"Why not?" Nina Aranjuez flicked her upper lip with her tongue. "Isn't that what we've been training for?" She was excited. She wanted to use what she had learned.

"Because you can *see* it. This isn't Earth, after all, where they let people fight wars without satellite data or air support. Satellite data gives us every detail."

"But everyone's equal. Unless they've got the crypto situation figured out."

"No," Miriam said. "They haven't." The satellite data links were general-purpose. Backup plans for encrypting the data had always been blocked by one political interest or other, afraid of being cut off from the data stream by an opponent. As a result, any opposing forces could see as clearly as the Vigil. That returned the entire thing to the status of a video game.

The insurgent force that had hit the railcars near Hecates Tholus and taken off with the weapons, including the long-range surface-to-surface missiles, had moved partway across the descending plain of Elysium and was now waiting just east of the Elysium Fossae. She wondered if Breyten was with them. She hoped he was. He'd always wanted some dramatic action in his life. That poor, frantic soul had been pounding his forehead against rocks for too long.

Meanwhile, Miriam's force was supposed to be broken up. The Chamber feared sabotage somewhere along the magtracks, the water lines, the power cables. Mars was wide open. Human beings were not meant to live on the damn thing after all. A few carefully placed explosives and Scamander could be as dry and dead as the rest of the Valles Marineris. Human occupation of Mars could prove to be just a temporary infection.

So the Vigil was being asked to pull back its surface operations to protect the heart of Mars. Elbow to elbow, Miriam figured, standing in a cordon around the frightened politicians of the Chamber, while everything else went to Hell. A good way to turn a difficult situation into an impossible one.

Fortunately, Trep had taken the precaution of moving her far across Mars. She and her force had shipped themselves west on the Arcadia magtrack, then moved out from the Garmashtown station, ignoring the civil rioting going on in the city. They were now in Utopia, some thousand kilometers northeast of Nilosyrtis—and the Pure Land School. It would take days to get them back to Scamander.

"We'll have to sweep northwest of them," Aranjuez said eagerly, "and descend Huo-Hsing Valis."

Miriam thought of the narrow, choked channels that made up Nilosyrtis. There was a reason that settlement had taken so long to reach that region. Transportation was almost impossible. Amateurs. They were all amateurs, learning about war. She hoped she and her people wouldn't have to learn about it by assaulting a fortified mesa in the middle of Nilosyrtis.

But war was what she and Hektor had planned, sitting side by side on her bed. A dramatic surface action, something that would partake of Martian pride. Sexual excitement had made them arrogant, she thought. Had Hektor ever thought that Hounslow's forces would seize control of long-range weapons of mass destruction?

Everyone waited tensely for a communiqué from Elysium. The missiles were capable of reaching almost anywhere on the Martian surface. While they were not nuclear-tipped—even Internal Security couldn't have gotten authorization for that—they could do severe damage to the cities. Politically, however, a threat like that would change Hounslow's status from romantic rebel to malign thug. Miriam thought that they would have been better off not having the weapons in the first place. Why had Hounslow ordered it?

"Goddammit!" Hounslow bellowed. "Who the hell allowed this? The fools! The self-destructive idiots!" He stormed around the room, his face red. His people tried desperately to get out of the way without appearing to do so. Despite the fear, despite the danger, more and more of them pressed into the room, until movement was impossible and even breathing difficult.

Hounslow froze, staring blankly at the mass of his followers who were pressed against the walls. Their eyes were on him. They expected a message. They expected the truth.

"More carefully," he said. "What happened?"

The student who had brought the news, who now wished that he had just fled Pure Land Mesa and opened up his lungs in the air outside, described the situation with tears streaming down his cheeks. The railcars successfully assaulted, the long-range weapons safely taken. . . .

"Where are they now?"

"They will communicate when they have reached their positions."

No one spoke. Hounslow looked around at his followers. They were alert, ready to move. He was surprised. They were not.

"Open revolt against the Union," Hounslow said. "All

choices have now been taken away. Ours and theirs. Only one narrow path leads ahead.''

And indeed, the dust was clearing. It had all been so complicated, and suddenly was so simple. All the delegates, all the negotiations, all the possibilities of compromise, modification in his position, agreements with various parties . . . that was all over. No more waiting, no more wondering which decision was correct and which one was a bitter compromise. No more watching the moment ripen and then rot.

Kirk Marder, Belisanne al-Bakhri, Breyten Passman—like Brenda Marr and Sen Hargin, they had acted, and changed the situation utterly. As he stood there now in front of all of his people, it seemed to Rudolf Hounslow that was all part of a larger plan, part of something that even he had only dimly perceived. Like the beating of the heart, like the inflation of the lungs, necessary actions took place without the operation of the will, took place because they *had* to happen.

''Be prepared to act. Stow your gear and present yourself at your emergency stations. Go!''

The room was clear in less than a minute. No one spoke, but all moved with intent eagerness.

''Khlestov,'' Hounslow said. ''What's the situation?''

Moritz Khlestov was a close associate of Marder's, and maintained Pure Land Mesa's situational database.

''There is a group of crawlers heading southwest from Utopia,'' he said. ''They aren't close, and their goal isn't obvious. Our people are out in Elysium, near the fossae.''

''Prepare to move out,'' Hounslow said.

''Leave Pure Land Mesa?'' Khlestov couldn't keep the surprise out of his voice. A lot of work had been done over the past months to make it defensible.

''Of course. We can do nothing here. No one can join us, no one can be inspired by us. We need to move. Then the cities can rise with us together.''

Hounslow had had no interest at all in the situation of the cities. Scamander, Garmashtown: he had regarded them as the sinkholes of Martian corruption, places to be swept clean when the change finally came. But now he saw them as his salvation.

He would move out, the weapons would be raised up in Elysium, the cities would rise in the enemy's rear, and Mars would be his, as it should always have been.

"You have the contingency plans?" Hounslow asked.

"Of course!"

"Then move."

12

Lines of communication girded the globe of Mars. The display lay on a flat stone, like just another chunk of the red planet itself, and the satellite links covered the thicker and brighter optic fiber connections like a dusty haze.

"It's all there," Belisanne said, peering at the display as if it contained actual usable information, rather than being an image talisman. "The satellites look down at us. We're like bugs on a plate."

"That's what we want," Breyten said. "They need to see us."

"I'd rather they didn't," she said. She'd taken a laser burn on her upper arm. Her outer sleeve was trimmed and pinned back, displaying the spot. A transparent patch on her skintite revealed puckered dark flesh. She'd added color to the wound, a jagged line of yellow-green setting off the bloody damage. She stroked it now, the dull pain serving as sweet reminder of damage survived and obstacles overcome. "The damn things are old, poorly maintained. I don't think they have the resolution to track anything smaller than an armored crawler."

She peered out beyond the confusion netting and was satisfied to see nothing. Their four crawlers and dozen soldiers were invisible, concealed under overhangs here where the plain of Elysium was broken by the narrow channels of Elysium Fossae. The dark sky hung heavy above them, and the world beyond could easily not exist.

"They have to see us," Breyten said stubbornly, "for our threat to use the missiles to be credible."

"It'll be credible," Belisanne said. "Believe me, it will be."

Breyten felt a chill at her tone. No one could seriously intend to *use* those weapons . . . he found his thoughts confused. No one had thought through the whole picture, the plan, what should happen. They simply had to act.

"Let's move Krlezha's crawler out through the fossa when it gets dark," Breyten said. "We can display that set of launchers at dawn tomorrow. By that time we should have coordinated with the Pure Land School. The others you can keep safe here."

Belisanne considered the proposal, nodded. "All right. Tomorrow at dawn." She grinned to herself, imagining the screaming horror in the densely packed mobs of Scamander. It was all worth it, imagining that.

The train stopped, then sank slowly down onto its track with its emergency power. The interior lights flickered, then came back on steadily.

The common car was packed with people fleeing one place for another they considered safer. Egypt was sure that trains proceeding in the opposite direction were just as full. Panic scenes in plays were exactly the same, where members of the crowd ran completely across to the other side of the stage to make their exits.

The windows to the right showed the clean wastes of Isidis, those to the left the beginnings of the rough, heavily cratered country that ran south for thousands of kilometers.

"There has been a malfunction in the magtrack." The announcement was icily calm, exactly as if that was all it was. "The delay may be extensive. We will do our best to keep you informed."

Calm up to now, the crowd picked up the undertones of the announcement and began to graduate to a grim panic, fearing the worst. The more practical members immediately pushed their way out, heading to the dining car to stock up on food. Others began to stake out territory for comfort during the wait.

"Goddammit." Sildjin stood, began to move. "Can't wait

here. Let's *go*.'' The Dust Beggars stood as a group. Egypt was startled. She would have expected Sildjin, reluctant recruit, to take this opportunity to delay joining Hounslow's force. Instead, he seemed obsessed, driven. Not for the first time, she wondered what really drove him.

They had to push through three crowded cars, each one seemingly more densely packed than the last, until they were actually climbing over people, pushing knees into shoulders, not bothering to apologize. Murmurs turned to shouts. Moving with quick efficiency, Marko smacked one protestor in the temple with his club, then, as a sort of bonus, took his food pack away from him. The car grew quieter.

''I'm sorry, there is no passage through here. This is the last passenger car.'' A train official had materialized from somewhere and stood blocking the emergency door that led out to the crawler transport cars. He was nattily turned out, with epaulets and collar bars indicating high rank. That he was here doing this menial duty testified to the chaos enveloping the entire planet-girdling magtrack network.

Sildjin, having finally agreed to Egypt's plan, now saw it as the most important thing in the world. He didn't argue with the official or stick his face right up close to him to scream. Without a word, he pulled out a stiletto and pushed it efficiently through the dark green uniform and between the poor man's ribs.

Egypt caught him as he fell, and saw the light go out of his bewildered eyes. He died not knowing what had happened to him, or why. She lowered him gently to the floor, though there was no longer any need for gentleness.

She looked up, frightened, to meet Sildjin's glower. ''Let's get on with it,'' he said. ''Right?''

''Right,'' she managed, through a suddenly dry throat. Her hand was bloody. Absently, she wiped it on the dead man's uniform jacket. There was plenty of room around them now. The rest of the passengers had pushed themselves into the other end of the car, but watched the scene without protest.

The Dust Beggars put on their external hoods, connected their air supplies, and pushed through the air lock into the storage car. Most of them were unused to being outside Scamander's corridors, and wore skintites and exterior gear with no more grace than a Terran would have. But Sildjin had bullied them into some semblance of efficiency, and they knew what to do.

Overhead emergency lights revealed a long double line of crawlers and other vehicles, their undercarriages clipped into the two tracks that ran from one end of the car to the other, curving out to the double access doors at either end.

"Move, move, move!" The Dust Beggars split into two groups and ran down along the vehicle line, searching for the crawler they had stolen from the vehicle yard at Scamander. Some of them, still unused to surface operations, had their direct-voice radios tuned to the wrong channels. These Sildjin hit violently on the shoulder, and they, figuring out his need, ran with the others.

They found the crawler, undid the hatches, turned it on. With the assistance of Egypt's Terran muscles, Sildjin tugged on an emergency release lever. The front loading door of the transport car slid slowly open, revealing the end of the guide slot and a drop of at least two meters to the ground.

"Damn!" Sildjin said feelingly.

For a moment Egypt thought he was upset about the distance to the ground, which was large but not impossible, in her opinion. Then Sildjin dropped to his knees to inspect the door edge more carefully, and she saw what he was angry at. An automatic interlock had sealed up the track. And each vehicle's undercarriage clip held it in the track. Unless the door was pushed against a loading dock at the same level, the vehicles could not be moved out of the car.

"Harlabee," he said quietly. "Up here, on the double." This was operational. This was what made him happy. He wasn't equipped for making elaborate policy decisions. He ruled his group in the corridors, and that was all he had ever aspired to. Events had pushed him into a situation he could not grasp. But this, a solid problem like the ones he had faced as an NCO on Earth, was something he could understand.

Harlabee dropped her pack. Without even looking, his attention focused on the end of the track, Sildjin reached in and withdrew a packet of soft explosive. Humming to himself, he pulled it into small lumps and stuck them along the inside edge of the door. Then he pushed detonator buttons into them, connected the wires, and stood. Where the hell had he gotten that stuff? Surely he hadn't just had it left over from his time in military service on Earth.

"Let's get into the crawler," he said.

"No farther away?" Egypt asked.

His gaze was flat and hostile. "I know what I'm doing."

With frantic eagerness, they all piled into the crawler. A light blinked at the end of the car, and Egypt could see the air-lock hatch starting to open. Train security, no doubt, come to see what the hell was going on in the crawler transport car. They were here just a little too late.

The explosion flashed bright and the car shook.

"Engage," Sildjin said.

Marko, sitting in the control couch, inched the crawler forward. The three crawlers in front of them shuddered, then slid slowly down the track. Only a few centimeters of the door edge had been destroyed by the explosion. Sildjin had cut it with professional fineness. The interlock was gone, but everything else was still in perfect working order.

The first crawler reached the edge of the door, then rolled over it and disappeared. The Dust Beggars cheered. The next two followed it, the third one bumping over the ones below and rolling over on its back before falling to the ground.

"Harnesses on?" Sildjin asked.

"No!" voices called. "Wait!"

Sildjin slapped Marko's shoulder. Marko jammed the crawler into maximum acceleration. The clip pulling it to the floor gave the large balloon tires excellent traction. They whizzed around the turn, hit the torn edge of the door.

And then they were flying. Instead of looking down, Egypt Watrous looked out, at the dusty horizon. As they hit the ground, bounced, and then dug their wheels into the dusty soil, it seemed to pull them forward.

"He must really think it is Armageddon," Hektor murmured. "A set-piece battle right in the open." The screen showed unit positions all across Isidis, Syrtis Major, Nilosyrtis.

"God knows what he thinks," Trep said. He drummed his fingers on the many-times-folded sword-blade metal of the crawler desk and stared at the dense concentration of points that marked Hounslow's people.

Hektor knew the old soldier was unhappy with his presence. Hektor was not a military person. From an operational standpoint, he could do nothing but get in the way, and there was no reason for him to *be* here.

Save for the inescapable fact that the Governor-Resident had ordered it.

"Is it some kind of feint? An ambush, maybe."

"Hektor." Trep's voice was calm, a knife so sharp you barely felt its tug going in. "I almost told Rodomar to go to hell, you know that. Close. It was close."

Hektor opened his mouth to argue, then closed it again. No reason to discuss things. He was here, where he wanted to be, and Trep wasn't going to kick him out of the rear air lock. Wasn't going to, that was, if Hektor just had the sense to shut up.

But it was all his doing, after all. His theater, based on Egypt's advice. An armored train. Hadn't Internal Security wondered about that? No magtrack had armored trains as standard rolling stock. They were all old, museum pieces. But one in particular, which had belonged to Joemon, had fallen into the hands of the organization that became the Vigil. It was maintained and updated every couple of decades, whenever some Delegate stuck in a few lines about backup security into an appropriations bill in the Chamber, and some pet contracting company got some extra work. They sat in a tunnel spur deep in the side of Pavonis Mons. When InSec had requested railcars, those were the ones they got, by Trep's order. Perfect for defense and security, as Internal Security well appreciated.

Except for one thing. Each of the cars had a secret access port just behind the front magnetic driver, unlocking to a security code kept by the Vigil, changed annually, not used for over a century. Joemon had never liked anything that didn't contain a secret. A sabotage team had pulled right up to those trains in the guise of maintenance engineers, climbed inside, and deactivated every single weapon aboard.

Hounslow's people had attacked, and the Vigil and InSec guards had defended, five railcars full of useless junk. Six people had died in that fight. And Hektor had arranged for it, as a way of starting a war. Well, he had it. And Trep was the one who had to deal with it.

Hektor closed up his skintite and hooked his valves into the crawler air supply to save his own. The rear of the crawler was packed with assault troops, most of them asleep with heads on knees, and there was no room for him. He hid as far as he could in a corner and watched Trep examine the mysterious firefly cloud of Hounslow, somewhere out in the expanse of Syrtis Major.

"Of course!" Breyten felt like reaching up and tearing off his own head in frustration. The missiles stood above him on their launch stands, which had unfurled themselves automatically, completely disdainful of the presence of human beings. The missile hung in its cradle, awaiting instructions. Overhead, it was still covered with the insulating netting that made it look like cold rock from orbit. They had planned to whip that off like a conjuror to reveal the deadly device.

"That's why it was so easy to hit the railcars. It's obvious!" Breyten stalked around the base of the launch framework. It had drilled itself into the rock, and stood ready to direct the missile in whatever direction was programmed.

But the missile itself had a guidance and fusing system that was dead as a blood clot. They could fire it off, and it would even land pretty near their target, but it would do absolutely nothing but crash. Someone had pulsed a powerful EM field through a critical part of the circuitry. Neatly, on each missile, going down the row. *That* was what had been going on behind those screens. And Breyten had watched it happen without understanding.

"We'll have to bluff," Belisanne said, slapping the framework. "The missile's visible from orbit, right? Just the way it's supposed to be. *They* don't know it doesn't work. The cities of Mars still sit under our hand.''

"Don't you understand?" Breyten shrieked. He took a breath, closed his eyes, spoke more quietly. "Don't you understand? They *do* know, because they deactivated them.''

"Who?"

"Maybe someone opposed to Internal Security, someone who didn't want them to have functional weapons. It might have been on Rodomar's orders. Does it matter who?''

But it did matter who. The question was not so much how the weapons had been deactivated as why they were set out so neatly as a trap. It had lured them in, and war had broken out. He didn't think the Governor-Resident had decided to start a civil war. That was the sort of thing that got Governors-Resident relieved of duty, even arrested. It had to be someone with a different stake in the situation. A Martian was used to sawing a stress slot to prevent crack propagation. Most of Martian society was a stress slot, from down-corridor duels to worship of surface death, a way of living with a situation that would otherwise break the culture clean open. As Hektor had more than once told him. . . .

"They know by now," Breyten said. "The Governor-Resident, the Vigil. They know these missiles are just so much junk.''

"But the cities don't know," Belisanne said. "And who's going to believe the Governor-Resident's announcement that there's nothing to be afraid of?" She climbed up the framework and dangled just under the missile's thruster. "As far as they know, they could all be about to turn black, cook, burst their lungs out over their chins . . .''

Breyten wasn't distracted by Belisanne's apocalyptic fantasies. He saw the real threat. The cities would explode from inside. Riots would spread through the corridors. It wasn't even necessary to fire the missile to cause destruction.

That wasn't the kind of action he wanted.

"Fine," he said. "But we have no defense. Any forces operating against us will know the missiles are useless, so our threat to use them will be meaningless. They'll run right over us. They must be heading for us now. And once we're wiped out, Scamander won't be afraid of us.''

Belisanne squatted down, activated her map display. ''All right,'' she said. ''We dump the useless shit in the fossa and move. All of it—we don't need the scatterguns. We won't be putting down any riots. Go tell them. Meanwhile, let me see what's out there.''

It had been a lot of pointless work, and Balladares had died because of it. Breyten expected anger and despair when he gave the news.

Instead, there was joy in throwing off the heavy weight. Krlezha backed the crawler next to a deep fossa and the rest, disdaining the use of mechanical assistance, bent and rolled the slender missiles off and down into the ravine with a childish abandon.

''Aim for that rock! Maybe we can snap it right in half.''

''That one? Too far—it'll get stuck before it gets there.''

''Want to bet?''

''Come on, come on, put your back into it.''

The rest of the InSec equipment followed them in. The relief was not only a practical one based on the uselessness of the weight. All the way along, it had seemed like there was no need for these clever, useless, Terran things. It was a foolishly practical thing, a sad necessity, one they were more than glad to shuck.

''Okay.'' Belisanne reappeared. She seemed more cheerful too. In a moment she revealed why.

''There's someone coming—much closer than the Vigil force. Just a couple of crawlers, putting up a huge plume, nice IR signature—must be InSecs.'' The display appeared on the ground. ''Don't think they're sure where we are. But they're hungry for us. What do you think?''

''I think we should give them a taste,'' Krlezha said.

Hektor had always mocked the self-conscious heroic dialogue of Breyten's favorite adventure plays and books. Would that he could hear it for real! Sometimes your blood got so hot you just had to sound like an idiot.

The two crawlers belonged to an Internal Security force operating autonomously in defiance of Rodomar's most recent directive. She had ordered that they refrain from conflict with armed Martian units and pull back at the slightest sign of resistance, as part of her pursuit of a Martian solution. But Lieutenant Khinchuk and her troops had had a better idea, recognizing that the Governor-Resident had no direct authority over the operations of Internal Security units. Though unused to surface action, she had requisitioned two crawlers from the vehicle yard at Podgriben, on Elysium Mons, and moved out to meet the enemy.

She knew that the bandit force had escaped Hecates Tholus and gone to ground somewhere at the northern end of the canyons that broke the plain of Elysium. When the InSec troops set out, mist still filled the shallow canyons, and swirled as the crawlers made their way through, pushing up to the northwest.

Three InSec officers had met their deaths during the attack at Hecates Tholus. A psych-up meeting by Khinchuk had persuaded her team that it thirsted for vengeance. Now, sitting in their crawlers and staring out at the unforgiving Martian landscape, they were not so sure. Some of them played cards desultorily. Khinchuk had military experience, but most of them did not. They were interrogators, investigators, prison guards, and office silicon shufflers. Most of them had already checked their employment contracts to see if they forbade "Military Operations on the Martian Surface." Through some legal oversight, the language completely neglected the issue.

The bandits, Khinchuk knew, were handicapped by the weight of their stolen weapons. They were constrained to move slowly, maneuver ponderously. It was possible they were even frozen in place, their launch gantries already erected and drilled into the rock. And they had to worry about preserving their deterrent. They had gone through a lot of trouble to acquire those weapons. They would be forced to defend them.

Just a few hours before, Khinchuk's analysis would have been absolutely correct.

A fossa is as constricting as a bowling alley. Khinchuk should have circled completely around, to come at the broken land at Elysium Fossae's northwestern end from some other direction. But there was no time. A vast wheeling movement like that would have taken days. The direct route took too long as it was. If it had been possible, she would have requisitioned magtrack transport to the nearest point on the Isidis-Elysium line and been to her destination in two hours. But the goddam Governor-Resident now controlled the magtracks. Any attempt by Khinchuk to use them contrary to orders, and she would have ended up sitting out the rest of the conflict in some security cell at Ascraeus.

The lead crawler came around a turn to find that an avalanche blocked the road. Khinchuk stared out at the strewn boulders. The road was used frequently, so it must have happened just a few hours before. But while the dust and sand around a new avalanche were smooth and clean, this showed the marks of feet and vehicle treads. . . .

"Pull back," she said. "Under the rocks. This is an—"

One huge rock slammed onto the roof of the crawler and bounced to the ground. Then small-bore projectiles banged against the windows, which darkened suddenly in response to the flare of a cutting laser. Both InSec crawlers pulled back to a partially sheltered overhang. There, at least, they would be enduring fire from only one side.

Rocks. Khinchuk looked along the cliff edge, searching for visual confirmation of her attackers. If she wanted, she could get a satellite image of rocks being dropped on her crawlers. But her attackers, at least, clearly had no weapons larger than small arms with which to hit her, any more than she did to hit them. Artillery, assault rockets, heavy explosives—none of those existed on Mars. But what should she do now?

The fire continued, rattling on the side of the crawlers. These two crawlers were old, but well built. It would take an armor-piercing projectile to do any serious damage. But the balloon tires, while self-repairing to a certain extent, would eventually get punctured too often to hold their gas. Then the crawlers could either be left, or attacked at leisure. Even if that didn't happen, too long a wait and rocks could be used to block their retreat back up the fossa.

Khinchuk scanned up the near wall. The fossa was not deep at this end, and the walls sloped back. The bandits should have blocked her in farther up, she thought. There she would have been completely stuck. Thank heaven for small favors.

"Higri," she said, speaking to the rear crawler, "get your squad out and up the crack next to you. Clear the top of the fossa so that we can get going."

Nor Higri, who until the day before had been Head of Investigation for the Gerberus District, held his gun tightly to his chest and hoped that the oily sweat he felt pouring out under his hair wasn't clearly visible to his squad.

"All right," he said. "Out the hatch and up."

They moved pretty quickly, considering the situation. In a few minutes they were all out on the surface, breathing their air, crouched down behind the crawler to avoid the sporadic fire still coming from the opposite side of the fossa.

The crack was steep and rubble-choked, but it didn't look too bad, particularly for Martian gravity. Only the first few meters were exposed to the opposite canyon rim. After that, a shoulder of rock served as protection. Feeling more confident, the squad scrambled its way up.

Breyten stood at the rim and tried to see the crawlers, but they had pulled out of view. What now? He thought they should just go and leave the InSecs to try to move rocks, but Belisanne wanted to do some serious damage. Crawlers, while not armored tanks, were built to resist damage. It could be a long standoff.

Could they climb down to the crawlers, assault them at close range in some way? He searched the area and saw the descending crack. If the angle stayed the same all the way down, it probably debouched very near to where the crawlers were concealed.

"Breyten," said Belisanne from the opposite side of the fossa. "They're coming up at you. Get ready."

They were coming up? What the hell for?

Breyten switched to his own short-range channel. "All right. Tso, Horst, drop and get ready. No, Horst, move to the left fifteen meters. That's it, that's a better angle. We'll cover them from all sides. Wait until I give the order."

They lowered themselves down behind rocks and peered into

the declivity. Time stretched taut. Mars was as dead and motionless as ever.

A head appeared, peering around a rock. Breyten almost fired, then, with a surge of panic, pulled his finger back. That would have been incredibly stupid. He consciously slowed his breathing.

The head's owner pulled himself around the rock, signaled behind him. Within a minute three others had appeared. Was that everyone? Breyten waited, praying that his teammates would not give in to the same urge that he almost had.

While rocks were piled everywhere, there was a stretch almost devoid of cover. Right at the near end of it was a crack, barely visible. When his foot touches the crack, Breyten thought. When he steps past it, that's when I'll shoot.

It was unbearable. His weapon shook visibly from the shuddering of his hands. God, they'd see the movement, dive back into the ground. . . . Breyten closed his eyes, took a breath, opened them again. His target was already past the crack. He was getting too close. In a few seconds he'd have to see what was waiting for him.

"Now!" Breyten shouted, and started firing.

Higri, who had decided that it would be unfair to ask anyone else to go first, died instantly, at least fifteen bullets shredding through him in the first seconds.

But Breyten had neglected to define fields of fire, so everyone fired at Higri first, and only then traversed down to the other targets. Vartunian, right behind Higri, died next, but by then the others had managed, by throwing themselves back and rolling like boulders, to evade death.

They ran, in blind panic, down the crack, smashing into rocks, rolling. One broke his leg and had to be carried the rest of the way down. They did not attempt to halt and spread out into a defensive ambush against possible pursuit. They did not stop until they had reached their crawler and collapsed on its floor, sobbing in fear and relief.

Breyten cursed himself. Only two! All that preparation, the perfection of the targets, and most of the squad had managed to escape. Damn it, damn those fools he was trying to command. No one showed any initiative.

Less than a quarter of an hour later, the InSec crawlers pulled out and retreated down the fossa. No one on the rim raised a cheer. They slumped back to their own vehicles and set course westward, toward Syrtis Major.

Miriam Kostal saluted, her face angry.

Trep looked up from his planning table. "What seems to be the problem, Ms. Kostal?"

It took her a minute to speak calmly. "We've been training for weeks. We're as trained as any surface combat units on Mars. We've come, as fast as we could, across Syrtis Major."

"That's a nice rundown of the situation," Trep said, wrinkling his brow. "What's the problem?"

"The *problem*—" She stopped, cleared her throat. He was needling her, enjoying seeing her lose control. It didn't happen often. "The problem is that we were in a perfect position, right at Hounslow's flank. Now what? Did you know that a crawler moved right past us, on its way to join Hounslow, and we couldn't do a damn thing about it? We might as well not have bothered to come."

"Oh, I don't think so. Your company is welcome—now, don't give me that look, Ms. Kostal." His voice sharpened. "You should know better than to think that I ordered you here capriciously, or without good reason."

She stood stock-still for a long moment, then let her muscles slump from weariness. "Oh, damn. You're right, of course. That was unforgivable. I should—"

"That's enough. Quite forgivable. I would have been furious too. How often do you get to fight a war?"

She stared at him. The only light in the shelter was shining on Trep's table. In the half dark, her eyes were dark, and the reflected light accentuated the drawn lines of her face.

"You don't want to fight a war," she said.

"So the Colonel tells me." Rodomar stepped through from her private quarters. "Ms. Kostal, I don't believe we've met." She extended her hand.

Miriam almost kissed it. Had Rodomar been trained to that regal manner, or was it natural? DeCoven certainly hadn't had it.

Tremouille appeared from behind, carrying a carved wood chair brought along from Government House. At a nod from Rodomar he set it up, rubbed his forehead, disappeared back into the private area. Miriam heard a wheedling, complaining voice before the door sealed—Askase's. Rodomar heard it too, and winced.

"Much pressure among my staff, I'm afraid." She sat in the chair. It looked odd on the grippy black floor of the inflated tent, amid the electronic and lifesystem gear. "It's been a difficult journey."

"No reason for you to be here in the first place," Trep said, unsympathetic.

"Oh, isn't there? I have to be here to watch you refuse to attack the forces currently in revolt against the Union."

"Oh, we'll do more than that, Ms. Rodomar. If we have to, we'll retreat, let them pursue us. Halfway around Mars. If necessary."

"I wish you weren't quite so gleeful at the prospect. Could you attack if you needed to? The Union, you may remember, requires swift and immediate punishment for insurrection. Regardless of casualties. That's doctrine."

"That's bullshit."

"True enough. But *could* you attack?"

"Ms. Kostal?" Trep turned to her.

"We're in an overwhelming position." Hounslow's people had stopped moving, pulled up in defensive array in the middle of the plain of Syrtis Major. Reluctantly obeying orders, Miriam's force had swept far out to Hounslow's east and finally joined the main Vigil force where it waited.

"More overwhelming a few hours ago, I understand."

Miriam looked at Trep. She didn't want to wander into their high-level argument, whose issues were subtle and obscure. Trep irritably gestured at her to continue. "Just give us the situation. We can take it."

"From a *military* point of view, yes," Miriam said. "My units would have been better off planning a flank attack. Additionally, some of Hounslow's units are straggling in from the east. Among them are probably the people who hit the railcars at Hecates Tholus.'' She wondered if Breyten was among them.

"And casualties?" Rodomar was focused. "If you had to attack?"

"Hard to say. Could be heavy. We don't know what Hounslow has. The ground is difficult, though there's no easy ground on Mars. I've trained my people, but still, we've never fought a war on the surface. We don't know what we're up against, not really.''

"Why are you on this?" Trep asked Rodomar.

"Because I need to know." Rodomar leaned back, played with her pearl necklace. She was a big, strapping woman and Trep suddenly thought that a daughter of his, if he'd ever had one, would have looked just like that. The thought was disquieting.

"InSec will push me. *Earth* will push me. I'm not just spouting doctrine to reassure myself. If I could have crushed this insurrection quickly, and instead sat out here in Syrtis Major while things fell apart around me, I would be—"

"You would be out of a job. Again."

Two red spots of anger on her cheeks. She *could* have been his daughter.

"You think Mars is safe."

"No, I don't. All the problems that were there are still there. But at least this lunatic is no longer a threat."

"He's an armed force, still in being."

Trep snorted. "Armed force. My command isn't even an armed force, as Miriam hinted. You people from Earth, you think things happen on the surface. You build buildings, you take walks. You fight wars. All out in the open, like it was nothing. Not here. Human beings have been on this planet for three hundred years, and we still can't live out here." He turned, looked out of the side of the shelter at the endless plain of Syrtis Major. "The total surface military capability of Mars couldn't defeat an InSec provincial platoon from Earth."

"So we're just going to wait," Miriam said.

"That's right," Trep said. "Day after day, week after week, month after . . . however long it takes. Hounslow is the apostle of action. His movement has no interest in the petty day-to-day compromises it takes to run Mars. How long do you think they'll enjoy sitting out there in the middle of Syrtis Major twiddling their thumbs? He'll get desertions, I don't care how dedicated his people are."

"As the pressure rises he'll try to attack," Rodomar said. "He'll be forced to act—just as InSec will try to force me to act."

"I appreciate your position," Trep said.

"I don't know if you do. This plan might have to change. I'll hold Earth off as long as possible. But they'll want action. And InSec will insist on acting—as it seems they already have."

"So hold. Meanwhile, we'll pull back, inflict as few casualties as possible, let them expend their energy for no reason."

"And you say you don't have experience in military operations?" Rodomar said. "That's got to be more difficult than actually fighting. You'll lose people."

"If we have to, we will. But every casualty we inflict will give Hounslow a charge. Blood sacrifice. Martyrdom. It's just his sort of thing, and what keeps him a romantic hero for the weak-minded. If everything goes perfectly, he won't suffer a single solitary casualty."

"It will drive him insane," Rodomar said admiringly.

"Oh, ma'am, I think it's much too late for that."

The pain drilled into Egypt's skull. The shaven-headed woman, insertion marks clearly visible in the skin over her own parietal bone, held Egypt close, as if she was protecting a child. The shaven-headed woman's colleague, a scholarly looking man with ridged, reptilian lips, brought the tiny device in to the other side of Egypt's head. It hummed, and she thought she could feel the substance of her cranial bones crumbling. This was worse than the first time.

She grabbed onto the bald woman's shoulder and dug her fingers in, but noticed that, soft as she was, the tendons did not stand out on the back of her hand. The woman's shoulder, by contrast, felt like ceramic and steel wires. Egypt found herself looking into her spatulate teeth, which were bared in pleasure at Egypt's agony-taut grip.

The pain stopped like a light being switched off. Egypt started to reach for the side of her head, but the woman grabbed her arm.

"Give it a second." Her voice sounded surprisingly concerned. "You won't like the way the skin feels."

"Here's your gear, your location." The man pushed a small bundle toward Egypt. An ID card clipped to the top had rows of alphanumeric data on it. Egypt couldn't focus.

She turned back to the woman. There was no stubble on her head; she must have shaved every morning. "Why—"

"Postmortem identification, why do you think?" She seemed surprised anyone should ask. "A line of numbers on the parietal bone. When they dig us up, they'll know who we are. Here." She reached into a battered snap-up cabinet, dug around.

Maybe she was surprised, at that. Egypt looked around at the huge Intake shelter Hounslow's people had set up in the middle of their encampment. It was a marvel of organization, considering the short notice. Its many chambers could have processed a thousand people an hour, given them new identities, assigned them dossing locations and food service, put them in study groups to learn the philosophy by which their lives would now be regulated.

As far as Egypt could tell, the stolen crawler with Dust Beggars dangling off it was the only thing that had come into the Syrtis Major encampment since it was formed. This woman had not answered many confused questions from new inductees.

With a grunt of satisfaction, the woman pulled a skull out of the cabinet. "See?" Indeed, a small row of gold numbers was incised into the skull. Now, unable to resist, Egypt did feel the side of her own head. The skin felt soft and dead, as if it was about to rot away from her skull. She yanked back her hand, glancing aside to avoid an I-told-you-so expression, grabbed the skull instead.

It was clean, but the left side of it was staved in and blackened.

"Blew up the Isidis-Elysium magtrack," the woman said. "Sat on the detonation to make sure. The other bones were completely shattered." Her voice held an awed respect, as if killing yourself while performing routine sabotage was a great achievement.

"But, here." She handed Egypt a small locket, with a gesture like a girl swearing eternal fealty to her friend. Egypt opened it. Inside, suspended in transparent plastic like a saint's relic, was a blackened fragment of bone. "We each carry one."

With a completely dishonest feeling, Egypt put the chain around her neck. The woman's eyes glowed at her, in an expression that, Egypt recognized, could precede either a passionate hug or a stab with a concealed blade. The woman was wound tight, her coiled nerves pushing out against the skin of her face.

"Are they coming?" she whispered. "Are they on their way here?"

"Who?"

"Everyone. The recruits. Those who would be with us."

"Yes." Egypt said. "Thousands. Tens of thousands. They are on their way. I know—well, I have more information. I don't know who to tell."

"Anyone. You can tell anyone."

Egypt shook her head emphatically. "No. There is only one person to tell."

"C'mon, Egypt, let's go." Sildjin stood at the exit to the examination chamber, blood streaming down the side of his head. Apparently he had struggled against the pre-postmortem ID procedure. "Everyone else is waiting."

The shaven-headed woman turned away in dismissal, and faced the other end of the chamber as if expecting a fresh intake of skulls to be tattooed. Egypt joined the rest of the Dust Beggars, who, wearing ill-fitting exterior clothing and huddled together in apprehension of the grim-faced Hounslow guards, seemed more like prisoners than new recruits to the glorious movement.

Guards accompanied them. As they left, Egypt saw all of their possessions lying in a pile like the personal effects of those already dead. They had all been stripped, searched intensively, issued new clothing. The only thing they had been allowed to keep was their skintites. Egypt had even been forced to give up her notebook. She saw only a corner of its lacquer cover. She'd just have to look and remember.

They clicked on their newly issued air masks and marched outside. Lines of shelters stretched out in all directions, until they ended abruptly and the uninhabited gravel of Syrtis Major began. That meaningless waste stretched out to the uninformative horizon.

The sky was dark overhead, as it always was. Egypt wondered what Martians had given up by living here. Symbolizing events by the weather was definitely one of them. A day of triumph, a day of defeat—both took place under the same dust-rimmed hollow sky. No wonder events became more intense here. They had to bear that much more of a burden.

Sildjin gazed intently around as they marched in two silent rows through the encampment. She couldn't tell what he was looking at. Aside from the shelters, there was nothing. The place could have been a refugee camp, a concentration camp, an exploration base, a religious revival meeting. And Sildjin, while a Martian, had grown up entirely in the corridors of Scamander. This was as alien an environment to him as it was to her. But, of course, he had served on Earth. What had he done there?

"Aren't you going to try to talk me out of it?" Hektor asked, only half joking.

"It's a pointless negotiation," Miriam said. "Nothing will come of it—and if you see anything useful from an intelligence point of view, they won't let you come back. Is that convincing?"

Idly she reset the program on the tester. It had examined the circuits and filtration fibers in Hektor's emergency air repurifier twice already, but there was more to be learned about the ions in the bilayer membranes. The thing had been in storage for years.

"I—" The argument was too good. "Do you think so?"

"Oh, Hektor." The readout flickered, all green, but she didn't look at it. "Do you want me to make some false emotional

arguments against your risking your life so that you can decide
to still do it and feel satisfied that I care? Or do you want a real
argument that will make you feel vaguely foolish for going?''

''Hell of a choice.''

''So don't make it a choice. Don't go.'' She held tightly on
to him. She was a strong woman, severe in her Vigil uniform.
The shelter they squatted in was tiny, the roof barely a meter
high. The Vigil discovered itself poorly equipped for a major
surface operation, and had been forced to dig out less-than-
adequate equipment to enable its mission. This shelter, for example, had no independent oxygen-generating capacity, and
relied on an underground hose run from a central generator. In
case of real war, that would have been insanely dangerous.

He met her eyes. ''Don't you think one of us has to go?''

''You think this whole thing is our fault?''

Hektor sighed and sat back on his haunches. ''I thought I
would know. But I don't. Was it our thrown pebble that caused
the avalanche, or someone else's? I don't think we'll ever know.
But we threw the pebble with the *intent* of causing the avalanche.''

''All right. You want to act *as if* it's our fault.''

''Someone has to.'' He lay down, and pulled her down next
to him. Surprised, she didn't resist. Miriam had given up her
precious sleep time to be here with him. In a few minutes she
would be on duty again. He hoped he hadn't compromised her
efficiency.

What did he want from her? She'd sat for an hour with him
and gone over every blessed piece of gear two or three times,
even though that level of consciousness-mediated redundancy
probably raised the risks of human error higher than the risk of
equipment failure. He'd have done the same for her, polished
her armor, set her helmet on her head as she set out for war.
There wasn't much else the one who stayed behind could do.

''But you didn't get what you wanted,'' she said. ''You
wanted something dramatic, didn't you? A dramatic, flashing
battle with minimal casualties.''

''Yes, of course,'' Hektor replied. ''That was exactly what I
wanted. Now all I want is to get us all home safely.''

She pushed her face in between his neck and shoulder. Hektor, just like Breyten, was obsessed with demonstrating his significance. "Hektor," she said softly, "why have we spent all this time on your stupid equipment?"

"I don't know," he said. "Because I'm a fool."

"We still have a while before I go on duty."

He kissed her. It was almost too late. He *was* a fool. The shelter's air supply hissed in the silence.

He undid the formal buttons of her stiff uniform, and his hands, surprised, slid over soft silk. She was warm underneath, her heart pounding almost audibly.

"Oh," he breathed. "Was this always under here?" The silk was coral, with lace on the tops of her breasts. She sat up a little and shrugged out of her jacket. Long neck, long arms, her strong-featured face as solemn as an ancient queen's—how could he have ever thought her plain?

Suddenly she smiled. "Yes, Hektor. Always. Standard Vigil issue. We all wear them. But you should see Trep's—"

"Get down here."

"Wait." With a single smooth movement, she tugged off the soft formal trousers he wore. The sudden blast of cold air softened him a little, to his embarrassment, but a single sharp flick of her tongue corrected that problem.

She leaned over and kissed him. He ran his fingers up the back of her neck. There was no time, no time. She would not forget her duty, as he would not neglect his.

She slid down next to him and pulled him on top of her. He lifted her camisole up just below her breasts but did not remove it, liking its smooth coolness under his chest. She stroked him gently, down below, and he felt like exploding.

"No," he gasped. "It's too much."

"It's all too much," she said, and, with the soft pressure of her hand, guided him in.

13

"We have to break," Krlezha said apologetically. "These crawlers were never meant to go these kinds of distances. Not in the design."

Breyten looked over Belisanne's shoulder at the readouts. Didn't the damn equipment know how important this all was? Humans were always harder than their gear, in the end. You could drive them beyond the edge of destruction.

"All right," Belisanne said. "We'll stop for maintenance."

They were in the middle of the featureless spaces of Isidis. The land spread out identically in all directions. Isidis was the remnant of a vast asteroid strike, and was relatively devoid of cratering. They had been making good time on some of the smaller plowed roads.

The troops, keyed and anxious to reach the Hounslow encampment in Syrtis Major, were not at all disturbed to be halting with distance yet to go.

Breyten understood why, because he felt the same way. Their triumph over the Internal Security troops at Elysium Fossae had had a paradoxically chilling effect. That battle, fast-moving and decisive, had seemed a reward for long struggles.

But a thousand kilometers or so to the west, Rudolf Hounslow and the rest of his forces sat in the middle of Syrtis Major, in pursuit of some moral victory beyond the reach of penetrating inertial bolts and cutting UV lasers. Belisanne and her troops were now the only native Martian veterans of military combat on the surface. Hounslow's passivity suddenly seemed an entirely inadequate and dishonest response to what confronted him.

Field maintenance on the crawlers was a necessary action that led to an even more psychologically necessary inaction. If Hounslow was going to wait and see what happened, so would they.

"Count yourself fortunate that we have allowed you air," Rudolf Hounslow said. "General sentiment was to just throw you out on the sand." He sat down on a military folding stool of the sort Gustavus Trep favored, put his hands on his knees.

"I'm grateful for the courtesy." Hektor was sure that Hounslow was right. "And for your resistance to 'general sentiment.'"

Hounslow was telling the truth. Hektor had seen it in the faces of the men and women who had hauled him in here. He could now see their shadows through the translucent interior partitions of Hounslow's shelter, ready to burst in at the first sign of trouble.

The Master of the Pure Land School had a stone head plunked massively down on his shoulders without the feeble intervention of a neck. Hektor could see why everyone found him so impressive, but not why anyone would listen to a thing he said.

"Ah, of course, I had forgotten. You are the *light-witted* brother." Hounslow's attempt at an ironic tone revealed that irony was alien to him.

"I am the loyal son. We missed you at the mourning." Hounslow's expression didn't change, but Hektor sensed he'd landed a blow. "You did know that Lon Passman was dead, didn't you?"

"Breyten told me."

"He died saving someone else's life. Just now it seems like a foolish way to go. Do you have a story about him?"

Hounslow was silent. In a moment he would order Hektor's removal, and he wouldn't have even gotten to the official purpose of his visit.

"You missed the mourning. Do you have a story for me about my dead father?"

Hounslow paused for a long time before he spoke. "If it will help you. I had camped out in the Noctis Labyrinthus. I was there to think. That was where some of my thoughts crystallized. I was betrayed. My air gave out. Something in the carbon dioxide filter had malfunctioned, and my blood alarm went off. I stumbled outside when I realized what my fate was, to die cleanly on the surface rather than suffocate in my shelter. I stood outside and felt the cold of Mars on me. I looked around at the cliffs. A figure stood on a far outcrop. It was Lon Passman. I turned away from him. I was no longer interested. I was ready. But he came. He recognized my situation and he came down. I was barely conscious by the time he did. He shared his air, though he had only enough for himself. He was willing to sacrifice himself for me, for Mars. With the new oxygen, I could think again, and I supervised the reconstruction of the carbon dioxide filter. That gave us enough usable air to get us to an emergency station."

"You bastard!" Hektor shouted, unable to stand it any longer. "Is that the only way you can live with yourself, to alter—"

Someone grabbed his arms, an elbow smashed into the side of his head, and a boot kicked him as he went down. Hounslow let them beat him for a few moments before calling a halt. They were in a frenzy, and it took a bit before they acknowledged the order. Hektor couldn't tell who they were. They wore concealing air masks inside, and billowing robes. He was getting tired of being beaten by hysterical Neo-Confucians.

"Enough, enough," Hounslow said. "Let him up. Leave us." The harsh fists and feet became shadows again. Hektor stood, refusing to feel for injuries, though he felt blood dribbling down the side of his mouth.

"You asked for a mourning story," Hounslow said. "You received it. Is there anything else, Mr. Passman?"

Rodomar had allowed this trip, over Trep's objections. She hoped . . . Hektor wasn't sure what she hoped. At this point she was throwing everything she could think of at the problem. His presence, at any rate, discomfited Hounslow. Half an hour after he had said a final good-bye to Miriam, a crawler had dropped him off at the Vigil perimeter. From there he had walked. It had taken him six hours on foot to get to Hounslow's forces. Desperate for evidence of mass support on Mars, they had hauled him in and almost inducted him as a new recruit before he could identify himself as a semiofficial envoy.

"I am here to offer you terms."

Hounslow's hands tightened on his knees.

"Nothing has happened," Hektor continued. "You have moved your forces out from Pure Land Mesa—and violated Union regulations about weaponry. But you have raised no revolt, given no sign of standing against the legitimate government of Mars." Hounslow's face grew darker. "If you allow the Vigil to disarm your forces and return to Pure Land Mesa, no charges will be brought, save against the specific forces that hit Hecates Tholus."

"No." Hounslow said. "We will fight. We will defeat you, and Mars will be ours."

Hektor managed an exasperated sigh, calculated to annoy. "They'll just sit out there and wait. They don't have to move against you. And you will sit here, sit until your air runs out and you feel dry choking in your lungs." Hounslow had almost suffocated once. Perhaps he could make him feel that fear again. "Other than that, nothing will happen."

"They won't wait. They can't wait. Mars will rise up behind them if they do. No, they have to act, and attack. And when they do, we will be ready."

Hektor tried to ignore the fact that Hounslow might, in the end, be right. Pressure from Earth, and from InSec, could still force Rodomar to order an attack. If she did, it would be bloody, just as Hounslow wanted. It was clear that Hounslow would never surrender, not to the compromising regime that ruled modern Mars. To that extent, Hektor sympathized with him.

"You goddam egotist," Hektor said. Though he addressed Hounslow, he pitched his words at the others beyond the partitions. Perhaps one of them might be convinced. "You can't win, so you want to make sure no one else does either. You've dragged your followers out into the middle of Syrtis Major to be slaughtered so that your opponents are covered with their blood and you can be a legend. They could have disbanded and surrendered. Most of them would not even have been prosecuted. Instead . . .'' He found himself becoming furious as he spoke. "Your own people aren't anything to you but Gabriel figures. You make me sick.'' He turned away from Hounslow's enraged face, dismissing him.

If Hektor had expected some sort of bravo from Hounslow for his courage, his forthrightness, he was disappointed.

"Take him out,'' Hounslow said, and that was all. His students, used to translating his cryptic pronouncements into concrete action, hustled Hektor out of the room.

". . . so we see the influence of Yomeigaku, of Wang Yangming philosophy, in the actions of Oshio Heihachiro during the year 1837 . . .''

The Pure Land School tutor assigned the Dust Beggars' education had a voice like a sandstorm. One could not listen to it, but only wait it out. The Dust Beggars slumped on the floor, with every expression of listening. Some of them scribbled in the notebooks they had been issued.

Egypt was fascinated by the scene. They were in an ancient shelter, exhumed from a storage dump on the edge of Syrtis Major by the advancing Pure Land force. It had once belonged to some magnate or high political official, but the old trim and braid had long ago fallen off, leaving only shadows and attachment marks to indicate where they had once been. It now served as their dormitory as well as their schoolroom and, in fact, they had yet to be permitted out of it.

Sildjin sat smiling blandly at the grimly intent man who was their teacher. Three other Pure Land students sat with the Dust Beggars, seemingly entranced with the lecture on subjects they must have known by heart. Like all of Hounslow's people, they were irregularly armed, short swords and the like, as if they were just some minor corridor crew without the organization for proper operations.

Egypt let the words wash over her and watched the faces. Sildjin and the Dust Beggars had spent all of last night working away at the old shelter. Deprived of their weapons and supplies, they had managed to devise some makeshift knives from support struts. She wondered that no one had noticed the effects. The shelter was visibly lopsided and would no doubt collapse soon. Perhaps that would be attributed to its vast age.

"... Oshio said that the main aspect is *sincerity*. Only through sincerity can one eliminate false thinking. ..."

Didn't the Pure Land guards see the faces? The Dust Beggars were aglow. Amalie, Crisk, and Parfali leaned into their assigned charges, almost resting their heads on the shoulders of the guards. Sildjin moved toward the teacher, as if overwhelmed by the significance of his words. But the teacher, more concerned with his words than with the reality around him, was not alerted.

A guard sighed loudly and fell over, as if overcome by the rhetoric. Sildjin, never losing his bland smile, launched himself at the lecturer, fulfilling the secret urge of generations of bored students.

But this lecturer, tedious droner that he was, was still a Pure Land student. He twisted and managed to pull his knife. He cut a bloody slit across Sildjin's chest. Sildjin smashed him savagely in the throat, tried to bash his head against the soft mat of the floor.

Egypt was buffeted as the Dust Beggars fell on their guards. They confiscated the knives and, with a casual air of cleaning up loose ends, used them, showing no more emotion than they would have if disposing of some unpleasant trash. For a moment Egypt almost felt sorry for Hounslow's revolutionary soldiers. In putting themselves against the darkest elements of Scamander's corridors, they had chosen a conflict impossible to win.

"Damn these guys," Sildjin gasped, dabbing at the blood streaming down his chest. "They aren't armed for shit. How are we supposed to fight with this stuff?" He kicked the recumbent body of the philosophy teacher. Some reflex made the man's arms jerk open wide, and Sildjin grinned. He reached down, searched through the man's gray cloak, came up with another knife, which he examined disdainfully.

"Wha—wha—" Marko was having trouble talking. "What we do now?" The other Dust Beggars looked around themselves. Their faces revealed their sudden apprehension. They were in the middle of an armed camp, an armed camp they had come thousands of kilometers to join. They had obeyed Sildjin as their leader, without questioning the ultimate motives for his orders. Now, for the first time, they wondered if his motives were the same as theirs.

"We go." Sildjin looked challengingly at Egypt. "Chronicler? You want a good final scene, I got one for you."

"Let me be the judge of that." She knew how these Pure Land maniacs felt. The breath seemed to glow in her chest, and her head to float free of her body. Death was close, sliding over her like silk, licking her earlobes, putting its arms around her chest. For an instant she closed her eyes and saw Fabian. He was a journalist. Of course he'd be here. She wondered if he had known who Sildjin actually was.

"Move it. Come *on*." The Dust Beggars didn't respond with their usual alacrity. "We'll be done soon. Then we can go home."

With that hollow promise echoing in their ears, they pulled up the hoods of their skintites and stepped through the air lock.

As they walked, Hektor made a few last, irrelevant observations, as if he would be reporting them to Trep. The encampment was dense, rather than spread out and camouflaged. It was a massive sacrifice, not a fortress.

His two guards stood close, but had let go of his arms. Why didn't they simply execute him here, right in the middle of everything? Were they actually ashamed of what they were doing? Perhaps they thought it was bad for morale.

Breyten. Where was that bastard? He was one of the reasons Hektor had come here in the first place, on this futile, doomed mission. To see his brother. Perhaps to save him. Perhaps to kill him. It didn't seem fair to Hektor that he should die without seeing Breyten again.

Hektor contemplated running. It had always seemed so stupid, the way victims in historical plays just knelt down and let their guards shoot them in the back of the head. Why not run, try for one last chance?

Now Hektor knew. Each second that went by brought the question: now? And it also brought the answer: not yet. In a moment one of his guards would be distracted, and there would be a better chance of dodging behind a shelter, surviving for at least a few desperate seconds. The next second was always a better time than this one. They might change their minds. They might forget about him.

They were ready, hands on their guns. He'd be brought down screaming before he'd gone two steps. He couldn't soil himself, at any rate. The waste recycler in his skintite was still operational. No one would be able to tell, postmortem, what had happened to his bowels and bladder.

Hektor thought about Miriam and calmed himself. She'd had bad luck with the Passman family. After this she should just move on. Now that he had thought of her, he couldn't stop thinking about her. Even as he and his guards passed the edge of the encampment and worked their way into the broken land surrounding it, he felt her lips on his. Maybe, at the last, they would let him record a message to her, write a note, let her know what he had felt and not had the time to say. . . .

"Here." The voice was cool in his ears.

They stood on the edge of a tangle of ravines cut by ancient water. Probably released from underground ice by the heat of that low shield volcano barely visible at the horizon, Hektor thought. A stupid thought to have in the final moments of his life. His shadow stretched out before him, thrown by the slanting evening light.

"Kneel down," the voice said. "This won't take long."

He could leap down the slope. He'd be a difficult target. There was just the slightest chance . . . every fiber of his being concentrated on relaxing his muscles, giving no sign whatsoever of his intentions. Not on his knees, though. On his knees he would be defenseless.

"Wait," he said. "Couldn't I leave one last—"

He met the man's eyes, and the other did not care in the slightest. Irritated at Hektor's minor resistance, the guard brought his gun around to shoot without any other preliminaries.

Hektor turned his head so that he couldn't see his killer's eyes, crouched slightly in preparation for his leap—

A bright flash broke the rough rock into an instant of brightness and shattered dark shadow. His two guards turned to glance back at what had just happened back in their camp and Hektor rolled forward, out of their grip, not stopping to question or understand.

A few meters below, a rock exploded next to his head as a guard recovered and fired. A burst fragment hit the side of his head, and his consciousness almost disappeared in a roar. His body, somehow, kept up the desperate run. Breyten, he thought. He had to catch Breyten. He'd always been faster than Hektor, cleverer on the rocks. But now, with new strength, Hektor felt himself gaining on him.

"Who are you?" Egypt shouted over the thunder of escaping air.

Sildjin, his hair blown by the breeze, just smiled at her and continued to remove his skintite as the air disappeared.

"Tell me." In a few moments there would be nothing to breathe. That didn't seem to bother Sildjin. He had no skintite, but stuffed an air hose through a hole in his throat, directly into his trachea. He shook his head. The smile had not left his face since before killing the lecturer.

He stood before her naked. His scars, which she now saw were all over his body, stood out livid against the paleness of his skin. His muscles were crisply defined. He didn't seem to notice the near vacuum that should have killed him in less than a minute.

The skintite had been the one piece of equipment they had been allowed to keep. Probably a convenience to the Pure Land School, so that their new recruits could be moved from one shelter to another.

Sildjin now shredded his in his bare hands, though that too should have been impossible. He gestured for Egypt to leave. The other Dust Beggars already had, those who had not died in combat with the three guards lying at the entrance to the air-supply shelter.

Two matte-finish teardrop shapes lay embedded in the shelter floor. She and Sildjin stood in the generator room for the encampment. While each shelter had its own emergency air, as did every individual student, it was this large power source that generated most of the oxygen that got used under regular circumstances. It was as powerful, Egypt reflected, as an entire rain forest back on Earth. And for an instant it seemed that she heard jungle birds twittering high overhead. But that was only the last shriek of air escaping through the holes Sildjin had cut in the shelter.

She had always known he was something other than what he seemed. Fabian probably had too. That was why he had been so fascinated by the figure of the crew High Priest. He was dark doom, and like doom, he was unclear and arbitrary. That was why she had helped him here, to the heart of those who had killed her husband. Alone, she could have done nothing against them. But it hadn't been until she had watched Sildjin blow the edge of the door on the stranded train that she had known she'd made the right choice.

She watched the culmination with awe. Sildjin stuffed the shreds of skintite around the base of the oxygen generator. Then he hunched over them like someone who had just built a fire on a cold day. His spine thrust through his translucent skin. His back shook convulsively, and he threw up. His retching was impressively violent, as if he was suffering electric shock.

Fascinated rather than disgusted, Egypt peered more closely. Amid the steaming gray matter that had been their tasteless porridge breakfast were two orange crescent shapes. As the pseudo-skintite material dissolved in the stomach acid, Sildjin pulled them loose and, yanking on the ends, drew them out into chains of small spheres.

Detonators. Concealed in the folds of his stomach lining for God only knew how long, physiologically inert, undetectable by anything short of exploratory surgery. InSec, Egypt thought. He had to be an InSec agent. The cleverest of them all. He slapped the detonators down on the gooey mass of dissolving skintite and half-digested porridge, pinched the ends, and, with a wink at Egypt, turned and ran.

After a moment's hesitation, cursing, she chased after him. The explosion caught her in mid-stride. She flew through the air, fragments of debris skimming past her, and smashed into the ground. She tried to push herself to her hands and knees, but her limbs, wherever they were, would not obey. There was no pain, none at all, so she lay back and went to sleep.

"The Vigil are attacking," Belisanne said crisply. "Into battle formation." The troops on the other crawlers scrambled to obey.

"No," Breyten said. "They haven't moved. Look. The Vigil force is still at least ten kilometers away."

She stared at the display. "Then what the hell—"

"I don't know."

The flash of the explosion had been clear, even at their distance. They had been sitting in defilade, hull down, for several hours, debating what to do.

All of them pretended to themselves that it wasn't odd at all that they had desperately plowed across a thousand miles of rough, open terrain to get to Hounslow and then stopped only a few kilometers short to examine and chew over the situation.

It was comforting, Breyten thought, to contemplate meeting his end with Rudolf Hounslow. Mars would be suffused with blood. He felt the clean, hot, red glory. His life was a mess, everyone's life was a mess, compromised, petty, intricate, demanding. It would be such a relief to scream your throat out and let the blood flow out over the skin, to feel your blade slicing cleanly through flesh.

But something had happened to Belisanne and her force in the rough times since Hecates Tholus. They had become real soldiers, and real soldiers do not commit mass suicide to make a philosophical point.

"Something's happening down there," Belisanne said. "Move forward. Be ready to turn back."

Indeed, there was some sort of activity down in Hounslow's encampment, though it was impossible to tell what it was from this distance.

"All right," Breyten said. "Let's see what it is."

*　　*　　*

As soon as he was around a projecting rock spur, Hektor clambered up the vertical wall, grabbing desperately at barely visible toe and finger holds. He willed himself to slow down. There was no way to just scramble up. He had to distribute the force of his weight in the right directions, at the right places. There a toe jam. And here he could hook two whole fingers at once over a projection.

His pursuers would by now be moving more carefully, expecting ambush. One of them was limping. Hektor thought with satisfaction of the impact of the thrown rock. Not much of a weapon against projectile weapons, but it had served.

A crack overhead, a wide one. He jammed his hand into it, tightened it into a fist. It held his weight. He swung forward and jammed the other hand in. Then he stopped as still as he could. It was a difficult angle. Pain grew in his shoulders.

One of his pursuers stepped into view. He moved with excruciating slowness. Hektor waited. At any moment he would look up above and, with one shot, bring Hektor down. Still Hektor waited. He had to get just underneath, a straight drop down. Three more steps would do it. Hektor willed him forward.

The man said something, communicating with the other guard on their private channel. His head turned slowly, and his eyes flicked at every shadow. Relaxing a little, he moved forward. One step, two. . . . He paused to look around again, then took another step. Hektor's painful fist loosened slightly in anticipation of the drop and a few grains of sand fell at his pursuer's feet.

Hektor let go just as the man whipped his gun up to fire. One of Hektor's feet hit his pursuer in the shoulder and the other knocked the gun fractionally to one side. The bullet blew flinders of rock from the overhang.

The use of the gun had thrown the man off balance. Hektor smashed down on him, trying to weigh a million tons, and kneed him savagely in the neck. The other twisted under him, but Hektor bore down and brought both his elbows down together on the man's jaw. The gun fell out of his hand. One more smash, with both his fists, and Hektor rolled and grabbed it.

His opponent was out, dead or unconscious. Hektor would

have to make sure of him later. He stood stock-still, elbow bent, gun raised to his shoulder, and looked across the tumbled rocks. The low sun cast long shadows. Hektor scanned, trying not to look for specific shapes, only for movement, any sort of movement. Aside from human beings, Mars was a dead planet. Human beings just did their best to join it.

There, way off, seemingly at the horizon, a flicker of shadow. The other would-be executioner was somewhere up on the ridgeline. So what did that shadow tell him? He couldn't tell which of the shadows was cast by the ridge directly above him. Hektor felt disgusted with himself. Breyten would have known right away. The shadow moved again.

Trying to move with the sinuousness of the snake whose skin Breyten had kept in his room, Hektor slid between a boulder and the rock wall. He himself was completely in shadow. No distant mark would reveal his movement.

But where—the other pursuer was standing almost directly over him, speaking frantically into the unresponding air. He saw Hektor at the same instant as Hektor saw him. He fired down as Hektor fired up.

A hot pain punched its way through Hektor's upper arm. Its force threw him half around and down on one knee. Desperately, Hektor brought the gun around to fire again, knowing it was too late, that this one quick shot had given the other enough time for a more accurate one.

Before he could get the gun to the point where he could fire again, the other man's body had toppled off the ridge to land almost at Hektor's feet. A bullet had taken off the lower half of his face, and the blood bubbled out into the thin air. Ice crystals quickly formed on its surface, concealing the white fragments of teeth and bone.

The heat of Hektor's wound was replaced by sucking cold. Stupid to die now, after all this work. He dropped down on both knees, searched the body desperately. Damn these Hounslow bastards. They sought death out here on the surface, not life or enlightenment. There was no first-aid kit, no way of patching his damaged skintite. And even with the knife at the man's waist, it would have taken much too long to cut anything from his skintite to do Hektor any good.

If he just reached his hand around his biceps, he found that he could block the holes with thumb and forefinger. The only place to get help was the Hounslow encampment, and that was certain death.

Well, Hektor said to himself. At least he hadn't just let them kill him. If he died now, he at least had that.

Holding one arm with the other, he stumbled up to the ridgeline. What he saw there made him freeze with astonishment.

"Dammit, something's wrong." Miriam stared at the display screen.

"You're right," Trep said, snapping out of a half doze. His eyes did a quick flick-scan of the displays. He straightened his uniform jacket, as if for a photograph, and leaned forward to talk into a sonic focus. "Hideo. Order lines forward. Array . . . make it Seven-*Shin*. Weapons tight—wait for an order to fire, even in close self-defense. Now. Yes, you heard me correctly. Seven-*Shin*. And be prepared to offer assistance. *Now*." He slammed back in his seat, irritated at the questioning of his orders.

Miriam stared at him. He had just ordered an attack on the Olympus Club encampment, only two hours after a desperate, sweaty argument with Sylvia Rodomar in which he had persuaded her to continue waiting. She had negotiated some post-conflict concessions from him as head of the Vigil, and Miriam knew that she was aware of the terrible consequences of a mass assault but was willing to use Martian fear of it as a negotiating tool.

But Trep had just ordered an assault, in a predetermined array that did not allow firing even in self-defense. Reminding Major Hideo of that would have been insulting, if it hadn't been such a bizarre command that Hideo would certainly have had to question it as a matter of duty. Every contingency had been planned for, but no one would ever have expected Array Seven-*Shin* to be the operational command.

"Good you saw that," he said. "It might have taken me a few more minutes."

"They're losing air in some of their shelters," Miriam said. "But I don't—"

"There's more than one possible explanation," he said somberly. "But it looks like the one thing I feared more than an attack. Suicide."

Egypt climbed back to consciousness through shards of broken glass. The explosion had broken her legs. She could tell by looking at them. Those angles looked strange. The mind rejected them. An optical illusion, it had to be.

And she didn't have her notebook. She cursed Hounslow with her last breaths. To see this, to feel it, and not be able to write it down! What was the point of it all, then?

By concentrating on pushing her elbows back, she managed to raise herself up far enough to see what was going on around her. It was getting dark. Not just loss of consciousness, she reasoned. The sun was pushing its way down below the horizon, and already a large part of its light had diffused into the horizon dust.

A flicker of movement at the periphery of her vision. What had it been? She breathed shallowly, ignoring the pain that was starting to creep up from her shattered legs. There was nothing to that; it didn't tell her anything.

This time she saw it. Two of the shelters collapsed with dramatic quickness. Was Hounslow breaking camp, getting ready to move to the attack? With his long-term air supply gone, that would have made sense. The two crawlers she could see from where she lay weren't moving, and no one was climbing into them.

Then a chain reaction. Shelters blew out in quick series. It was not normal deflation procedure, but emergency voiding. It had to have been planned in advance to be done so fast.

There were people in those shelters! She stared in astonishment at the figures struggling beneath the suddenly loose fabric. Several made it into the open, clutching at themselves and one another. Some had skintites and air supplies, but others did not. They were exposed, open, and then empty.

They were dying. Right in front of her, they were dying: tens, maybe hundreds, of people, on the surface, unprotected, exposed to Mars's casual rage. A few had breathers that they were sharing. Hadn't they, in an encampment surrounded by a hostile enemy force, slept in their skintites, air at their sides? She imagined Hounslow convincing them all that they could now breathe Mars's impossibly thin air. That wasn't it. It was that they hadn't cared whether they could breathe or not.

They continued dying. It was an almost negligent process. No need to exert yourself to kill anyone on Mars. The planet is always there, waiting, ready to destroy your interloping, unadapted life. Some dug themselves into the sand, as if for protection, and died there, already half buried. Others ran, as if to outrun the death that already sat on their shoulders, lips on theirs.

Egypt saw two figures sharing an air breather. One suddenly tore away and ran, sacrificing herself so that the other, at least, could live. But the still-living one threw the breather up into the sky and fell himself. Egypt watched for the long moment it took the breather, glittering in the last rays of sunset, to flip up, rolling in the dark sky, and then fall slowly back down to the dusty killing ground.

Egypt blinked furiously at the darkness that rose up behind her eyes. She had to *see* this. Every detail was important, every detail mattered. If she could write it nowhere else, she would write it on the inside of her forehead.

A woman wearing a skintite stopped, looked around herself, and opened her hood. As she collapsed, it almost looked as if she was smiling down at Egypt.

Egypt smiled back. Her elbows gave way and she fell. Only a few inches. It shouldn't have felt like such a deep pit. As she fell, Egypt concentrated desperately, trying to catch the sensation, the emotion. This was what it was like to die.

Rudolf Hounslow felt at his throat valves, then pulled his hands away. Not yet. The time for that was not yet.

Dead and dying human beings littered the ground at his feet.

His order. He had given the order, as if it had come from somewhere beyond him. If they could not purify Mars, at least they could purify themselves. They had all trained for that final necessity. Those who refused had been assisted. Many had required assistance, too many. Some held his teachings lightly, as he had always feared.

There was nothing but darkness and shadow. Where was the Vigil? They had attacked, suddenly and treacherously so that there was no way to resist, but now there was no sign of them.

Even among his closest lieutenants, not everyone had wanted to obey the order. Shizgal had paused, thinking, and been cut down by Kung. Kung, without a backward look at the body of the man who had been his friend, had stepped through the air lock. He had stood, looking off at the distant horizon. His head had tilted slowly back, as if tracking the approach of something in the sky. Then he had fallen in a heap on the ground, blood bubbling out of his mouth.

Hounslow, not knowing what he was doing, had run out of the shelter, but with his hood and air mask still on. Lon, he thought. Lon was dead. But he hadn't had to suffocate. Lon, always smarter, had managed to avoid that. As had Brenda Marr. She had killed the Governor-Resident and then run. Tried to escape! That was the incredible thing. That madwoman, who had brought them all to this point. At the last, she too had tried to survive.

Here. Here was a good place. Hounslow lowered himself slowly to his knees. Nothing was moving around him any longer. Wait. Maybe he should go through the camp, make sure everyone had done his duty, check every shelter . . . ah, to hell with it. He bent his head over, put his hands on his throat valves. . . .

Some rumble in the ground distracted him. The Vigil? Then he should . . . he looked up. A battered crawler stood in front of him. As he watched in bafflement, Breyten Passman climbed out of it.

Hektor stumbled toward the now-dead encampment, sobbing and choking. Those tiny, meaningless figures had been human beings, dying. But for a long moment all Hektor could think about was the fact that now, perhaps, he was safe. No one would kill him if he returned, because there was no one left.

For a few moments he left his wound open, almost in expiation of what he saw before him, but then grabbed it closed again. Damn, damn, damn. Who were they? Who had done this thing?

Now he was among them. He walked slowly, looking down at their faces. Some of the air masks were frosted on the inside and he couldn't see what the person behind it looked like. One he recognized, a woman who had been on duty in Hounslow's command shelter. Her face was frozen in a rictus—it couldn't have been a smile.

The body of a small woman lay just beyond.

"Egypt?" Hektor said. "What—?"

He dropped down next to her, picked her head up. Her legs were twisted and broken. Her head weighed almost nothing. Her whole body was like something dry and abandoned.

"Oh, Egypt. Why?"

Her head sagged to one side in his hands. He couldn't think of anything to do, anything to say. He sat for a long time while it grew darker.

Just as the last bits of light were leaving the sky, something caught his eye. He looked up.

A dust storm grew to the south. It had a shape, almost solid, a dozen thick, striated columns that merged together into an overhanging cloud. It looked nothing like the usual wind-borne dust storm.

Crawlers, big ones, their precipitators off. High above, the cloud caught the light that was now gone from the surface. The dust looked heavy, as if it was about to topple over onto Hektor. The Vigil, finally, had arrived.

"Was it just a feint to delay us?" Trep raged. "A distraction? All those people?"

If it had been that, Hektor thought, it hadn't worked. The Vigil force had checked quickly for survivors and found a few. Then they had moved on, swerving to avoid the bodies. They would go back later: military forensic teams, witnesses, agents of insurance companies. Now there was work to do. A still-functioning military force of uncertain size was retreating before them.

Hektor sat in a couch and concentrated on breathing. His arm was bandaged and splinted—it turned out that the bullet had cracked the humerus. Miriam sat next to him and, quite contrary to the military discipline she should have been maintaining, held his hand.

"That stupid son of a bitch!" Trep was suited in military gear, crouched tensely in his seat, ready to burst from the crawler to lead if a close-order assault proved necessary. "Brutal, okay, I can deal with that. But stupid! Killing . . . all those people. In revolt. Their lives were up for grabs anyway. But just like that. . . ." The expression on his face was almost one of fear, Hektor thought. Exactly the emotion Hounslow would have liked to see there.

"So they've made a break to the north, into the Nili Fossae," Miriam said. "Who are they?"

"Probably the ones who hit Hecates Tholus," Trep said. "They also encountered some sort of InSec unit operating without authorization at the north end of Elysium Fossae."

"What happened?" Hektor asked.

"God only knows." After Hounslow, this didn't make Trep angry. It would have been too self-indulgent an emotion. "There's a security screen over the incident. Even the Governor-Resident can't get through it. Oh, hell. It doesn't matter a bit anyway."

Breyten was up ahead, Hektor was sure of it. The force had arrived late, pulled close to the doomed encampment, and then moved as fast as possible. And Hounslow's body had not been identified, at least by the frenzied preliminary search.

Hektor looked at Miriam. "Is Hounslow broadcasting? Any versions of the massacre? He can still use the comm satellites as relays."

She shook her head. "They're buttoned down. Not a transmission from them in the past hour or so."

"Good. We can move first. This isn't a tragedy, Miriam. This is a crime. He'll claim it's mass suicide, loyalty, all that. I know it. We want news teams on the ground by tomorrow morning, dawn. Can you arrange that?''

''The investigatory teams won't even be completely assembled at that point,'' Miriam said.

''They have to be. The Massacre of Syrtis Major can mean any of a number of things. We know what we want it to mean.''

''The Massacre of Syrtis Major? Is that what we're calling it?''

''That's what it *is*. Someone made the decision that they should all die. Hounslow.'' He thought for a moment. ''What I don't know is who detonated that explosion. I shouldn't question it too much, I guess. It saved my life. The Vigil?''

''No!'' Trep barked. ''Not the Vigil. It had to have been those goddamn InSec bastards. We'll get to the bottom of this, find whoever did it, chop him into pieces . . . that was what started the whole thing off. Just as they were about to wither right where they were. . . .''

Miriam and Hektor went to work. As the crawler ground across northern Syrtis Major, they were in contact with every news service, with the Chamber of Delegates, with anyone who could witness what had occurred.

The pursuit took another six hours. The remnants of Hounslow's force moved up to the beginning of the Nili Fossae canyons, turned . . . and sent the signal for surrender.

Trep sent crawlers forward and watched tensely, alert for a trick.

But there was no trick. Everyone climbed out of the crawlers and stood, hands in the air. They were instantly surrounded, taken to the ground, searched. The crawlers were checked for booby traps.

There were seven prisoners. To Hektor's bemusement, the commander of this successful force proved to be Belisanne, the woman with the quicksilver sweat from the Friends of St. Rabelais. And to think he had once held her in his lap.

But of Breyten Passman and Rudolf Hounslow, there was no sign.

14

From a personal letter from Anton Lindgren to Miriam Kostal,
24 June 2359:

> ... of course, never realized the depths of your involve-
> ment. And you never told me! After all that we've been
> through together. You are indeed a sphinx. I understand why
> you might be offended by Prophuët-Merino's book—surely
> you did not support InSec's censorship of it?—but she at least
> gives you your due. Do you think her attempt to rehabilitate
> Hounslow will succeed? I think he is more of a romantic
> figure on Earth than he ever can be on Mars.
>
> So whatever did happen to Hounslow? They found his
> body, but ... well, you know it is all quite unsatisfactory.
> Please, Miriam, as an old friend. I'm sure you're aware of
> how it all happened. You did, after all, marry Hektor Passman.
> Say you'll tell me the story once before I die.

"Whatever was she doing there?" Miriam asked. "How did
she even get there?"

"I don't know," Hektor said. "I have no idea."

"Getting the story," Miriam decided. "*Seeing* it. She had to
do that."

"I don't know." Hektor thought about turning on a light so
that he could see her, then decided against it. They were all too

319

far away. "That wasn't all that was driving her."

Miriam touched him lightly on the shoulder, as if making sure something other than his voice was lying next to her. "You knew her better than I did."

"She was a loyal wife. Hounslow was at the root, at the *heart,* of what happened to Fabian. He squatted out in Nilosyrtis, just thinking and talking, while things happened. Always to his great surprise. He was guiltier than anyone. Egypt went out there to witness his punishment."

"With an InSec officer."

Morning was approaching, and the lights were coming on. The walls loomed vastly on all sides. Hektor and Miriam had chosen to make their bed this night in the middle of the dining room table at Xui House. It was like an encampment on a mountain ledge, preparatory to further climbing.

"She may have thought he was what he seemed." Hektor sighed. "A crew leader from Seven Knots. Though, of course, Egypt saw pretty clearly."

He thought of the quick, ominous Sildjin with his scars. An unlikelier InSec agent would have been difficult to find. Officers of Internal Security tended to the blandly bureaucratic. Someday InSec would claim credit for him, but not just yet.

Though they had reason to be pleased with the job he had done. Among collateral consequences was the recall of Sylvia Rodomar, to face yet another inquiry in the Council of Nationalities. She had, after all, permitted a revolt and a massacre. Hektor had gone to bid her farewell.

She had taken his hand when he came in. "Again you had no trouble getting an appointment. Cuzco—and Mars."

"Neither of us is lucky," Hektor said. "Perhaps we shouldn't be in the same room together."

"Perhaps colonial administration is not really my forte." She sat as proudly on a stone-and-wood chair as if she had been entirely victorious. "There's an old, out-of-fashion luxury hotel for sale near Ban Don, on the Isthmus of Kra. Askase told me about it. Perhaps . . ."

Hektor tried to imagine Sylvia Rodomar, iron hand of Mato

Grosso, purifier of Palawan, balancer of Mars, running a hotel. It would no doubt be run efficiently. He wasn't sure it would be a place he'd want to stay.

"You've lost your family, Hektor. The Passmans have suffered the most from this little incident in Martian history. I hope you find a way to live."

"I will," Hektor said. "I'm going back into politics."

That made Rodomar laugh. "If you, why not me? They're releasing everyone, aren't they? All those people we built such a careful case against."

"Not all of them, but . . . yes, they are." It was as if the anticorruption drive were being held responsible for all the events of the past year, as if Martians themselves had nothing to do with it. Corrupt legislators and businessmen were popularly regarded as political prisoners.

"But that's now." He leaned toward her, suddenly intent. "In a year or so, the pendulum will swing back. Hounslow's movement showed that things will crack, if not this time, then the next. Our efforts will be remembered. Perhaps we'll even build you a statue."

She had managed a smile. "Probably like that figure of Joemon in Rahab Hex—half melted and hidden inside another statue."

"Mars's greatest faith is in those things that are concealed."

Hektor climbed down off the dining table. The entire house was cold and silent. There was no one to live in it anymore. Amid the crowded corridors of Scamander, it stood empty. The cold floor was smooth beneath his feet.

Someday they would have a decent wedding, Hektor thought. The family would demand it—Miriam's family, at Kostalgrad. Hektor had little family left. For some reason, a ceremony performed by the Commander of the Vigil in a dark hall in Xui House seemed inadequate to them. But the bleak circumstances overhanging the nuptials had, for the moment, kept them quiet.

"You're going out again?" Miriam said. He leaned his bare buttocks back against the edge of the table and she curled herself around him, resting her head on his shoulder.

"Yes. He'll be there. Eventually, he'll be there."

"Will it be over then?"

"As much as anything like this can be over."

He felt her heart against the skin of his back. "Find him, then. So that we can go on."

Hektor made his way slowly up the rough trail that led to the rock called Camelback, in the approximate center of the Noctis Labyrinthus. He'd start there, at that old jumping-off place. He remembered running desperate races from there, orienteering competitions, daylong games of hide-and-seek. Those had once been the things by which life was measured.

Breyten and Hounslow had disappeared from their crawler somewhere between the killing field at Syrtis Major and the place of surrender at the southern opening of the Nili Fossae. Intensive interrogation of Belisanne al-Bakhri and her troops had not produced a coherent story. Some acknowledged their leader's presence; others denied it.

He knew Breyten. If he had not fought to the death at Syrtis, if his body had not been found, it was not because he had escaped to hide himself. It was because he had felt that the simple twisted form of his corpse was insufficient communication. As to what had happened to Hounslow . . . well, that was probably exactly what Breyten wanted to communicate.

It had been over a month. If Breyten was still alive, he would try to send a message. Hektor was sure of it. So, almost every day, he came up here, to their old haunts, to look for a sign. Sometimes he wondered if he would still be doing this when he was an old man, in an insanely repetitive obsession.

So Hektor climbed his long and weary way up from the magtrack station to Zoë's grave. In the narrow spots the trail was too scuffed up with many comings and goings for anything to be visible, but wherever the ground widened out, there was a single line of footprints forging on with determination. Hektor paused and looked at them. He was sure they belonged to Breyten.

This trail climbed high, then dove into a local depression way above the bottoms of the grabens. Whether it was a dramatically eroded crater or a miniature fault was a subject that had much exercised them when they were boys. For a while Breyten had insisted that it marked the remains of an Acherusian city. Hektor paused just at its lip. High to the right was a cairn perched on a precarious outcrop, put there not to mark a trail, but just for the sheer exuberance of it, the thought that others would say, "How the hell did they get up there?" Hektor remembered scampering up and down, each near fall a fresh exhilaration. A new rock now teetered at the very top of the stack, an immense flat slab that would topple with the winds of the first dust storm. Hektor continued up the trail.

Breyten was sitting on the great slab that was Zoë's tombstone. Hektor stopped. "Hello, Breyten."

"Hello, Hektor."

They embraced. Both were thinner than they once had been, and older. It was as if they had traveled a journey of many years to come back to this place.

"Oh, Hektor, those bastards. Those stupid *bastards*. To die like that. Whatever for?"

"Too much bravery. Not enough brains." Hektor wasn't going to play to Breyten's need for romance.

Breyten smiled at him. "Well, that's true enough, isn't it? They did . . . die . . . bravely." He reached down behind Zoë's slab and pulled up a satchel. "Did Father ever tell you the story of him and Rudolf Hounslow?"

"Yes. He told me *a* story, at any rate."

"About how they were friends, and how they tried to commit suicide together. And how almost suffocating accidentally made them both decide to live."

"Yes. Hounslow, when I talked to him, had a somewhat different version."

"He did. Whatever the version, one thing is constant: Rudolf Hounslow had an un-Martian fear of suffocation. Stupid, eh? If you don't want to suffocate, go live somewhere where there's air. Simple. Just buy a ticket."

"Breyten—"

Breyten held up a hand for silence. "That was what betrayed him in the end. That fear. And the inability to act. Hounslow had the ability to inspire action, but he never managed to act himself. Philosophers, I've noticed, often have that problem. When we arrived at the encampment, he wasn't dead. He was still alive, Hektor. His people were dead all around him, and he was still alive!'' Breyten shouted with rage. ''He'd almost suffocated that time, all those years ago, and was too afraid. Too *afraid*.''

He reached into the satchel and pulled something out. Hektor looked—and closed his eyes. Opened them again. Leering at him, eyes bulged out grotesquely, was the severed head of Rudolf Hounslow.

''Jesus, Breyten—''

''He wanted to survive,'' Breyten said with surprising calmness. ''He pointed out that Brenda Marr had fled the assassination of DeCoven, tried to save herself. She had become some sort of symbol to him.''

''It's true. She ran. I take comfort in that. Maybe there's more sense around than there seems at first glance.'' Despite himself, he stared at Hounslow's head. The mouth was open, the tongue exploded out of it. Tendrils of frozen gore hung from the severed neck.

''I take comfort in the fact that, at the end, Hounslow did kill himself. With encouragement. He could obliterate the corrupt globe of Mars just by closing his eyes.'' Breyten, holding the head by its hair, waggled it at Hektor.

''Will you put that thing away?''

That made Breyten grin. ''You think I'm crazy, don't you, little brother? You think I've gone around the bend.'' He flipped the head up in the air, caught it in the palm of his hand. ''Well, perhaps I have. Don't you think I deserve it? What should we make him, then? A hero? They died bravely, fighting for what they believed in, Rudolf Hounslow standing nobly—''

''No!'' Hektor knew it could be done: the Last Stand of Syrtis Major. And Mars would have another dramatic legend to whisper amid the stones. ''No. Leave it, Breyten.''

''It's a symbol, right? Syrtis Major is a symbol of . . . I guess you're going to have to decide what it means, eh, little brother?''

''I've already decided. A pointless and bloody tragedy.''

''There are a lot of those.'' Breyten shoved the head back into the satchel. "Shall I tell you another?" He patted the great stone slab. "I killed Zoë."

"What?"

"It was my fault, Hektor. You didn't see it. You thought you did, but you didn't. I was climbing above her—"

"We both were. It was just a random—"

"Will you let me speak?" Breyten's eyes were wild behind his air mask. Hektor fell silent. "We were unroped, remember? Bold boys. I slipped. A rock I thought was a firm foothold was just jammed in dust. It fell out under my weight, and I almost went after it. I ended up hanging by a couple of fingers at a bad angle, and I couldn't get my feet up. The face was too far away.

"Zoë came up. She was a rescuer, that one. She would have followed Mother in her profession if she'd lived. She climbed up after me, telling me, very calmly, that she would give me purchase for my feet. I don't know what she saw. For all I know, she was going to climb up under me and let me stand on her shoulders. Who knows. But at that moment I kicked out and managed to get my feet on the rock. I pushed—and the slab came down. Right on her, Hektor. She was coming up to help me, and I killed her. Right here."

Hektor was shaken. He'd never known. He thought he knew what he'd seen, but he'd never truly known. But the feeling of shock was quickly followed by anger.

"So that's it?" he raged. "Everything is your fault? *You* did it all? Bad and good? *That's* the story. Breyten Passman did it." He kicked the satchel. "Chopped off Hounslow's head, killed Zoë, everything."

"Don't be jealous, Hektor. It's nothing to be jealous of." Breyten's tone was so cold and bleak that it stopped Hektor's fury.

"I've done my job," Breyten said. "Everything that you needed me to do. Take the head. Make politics out of it, throw it in a graben, whatever you think will be most effective. I give the Hounslow legend over into your capable hands. And now I want you to help me with something."

Hektor felt ice on the back of his scalp. "You can face trial— like Belisanne, the others. After the first flush of vengeance, the court will be more lenient. You know how it will happen.''

"I know. I'm not interested in lenience. You should be glad I waited this long, Hektor.'' He looked at his brother. "I wanted to see you.''

"I'm glad you waited.'' That was going to be Breyten's way. He was going to leave, and Hektor would have to stay to pick up the pieces. That was the way it was destined from the very beginning.

They embraced. Then Breyten stepped aside, paused for a long moment to collect his thoughts, and opened up his throat valves. He choked, and fell slowly to his knees. It was the Martian way of suicide: let the planet itself kill you, as it so wants to do.

Death is always ugly, and death on the surface is the ugliest of all. Hektor did not turn away from his brother's agony. He held him and provided the ancient service of the assistant. He pushed hard on the carotid arteries, cutting off blood flow to the brain. Unconsciousness intervened quickly, and Breyten was dead in a few moments. His body huddled in Hektor's lap, arms around his waist.

It was a long time before Hektor stood, and laid his brother's body on top of the slab that marked the grave of their sister.